A VICIOUS GODS NOVEL

COURTING WAR

HAZEL ST. LEWIS

HIDDEN SIREN

A VICIOUS GODS NOVEL

COURTING WAR

HAZEL ST. LEWIS

For my Familiars: Bacardi, Bella, Loki, Tigger, and even you, Cinder.

Yes, I did just dedicate this book to my cats. And yes, there are five.

Copyright

Publisher's Note: This novel is a work of fiction. Names, characters, places, and incidents are either products of the author's imagination or used fictitiously. All characters are fictional, and any resemblance to actual persons, living or dead, events or locales, is entirely coincidental.

Courting War / Hazel St. Lewis - 1st ed.

Published by Hidden Siren LLC

Paperback ISBN (Ingram): 978-1-962023-00-9

Hardcover ISBN (Ingram): 978-1-962023-02-3

Audiobook ISBN: 978-1-962023-01-6

Hardcover ISBN (Amazon): 978-1-962023-04-7

Paperback ISBN (Amazon): 978-1-962023-06-1

Cover Design: © Leila at Opulent Swag & Designs

Formatting:© Leira Lewis

Under-Jacket Hardstamp Case: © Leira Lewis

Editing: Noah Sky https://noah-sky-editing.com

Line Edit & Proofreading: Jennifer Murgia https://www.jennifermurgiaedit-s.blogspot.com

Author Photo: Copyright © 2023 by Cynthia Smalley Photography https://smalleyphoto.com/

Character Art & Illustrations: Copyright © 2023 by Giulia F. Wille Art www.giuliafwillearts.com

Author's Note

Theo goes by Morrigan in her human form as an ode to the Celtic Goddess, The Morrigan, who I wanted to honor and deeply appreciate in this book. The Morrigan is one of my favorite gods, and I love her so much. Theo is also equally inspired by the Goddess Athena from Greek mythology, and while Theo has villainous moments in this book, I do not consider either The Morrigan or Athena to be villains. I consider them to be epic queens whom I have deeply admired from a very young age.

This book has characters with dyslexia and color blindness. All depictions of Kellyn's learning struggles are based on my experience living with dyslexia. All ablest terms used in the book, such as slow, dumb, idiot, stupid...etc., represent a realistic picture of what it was like for me growing up being neurodiverse. I consulted with people who live with color blindness to portray Cecile's disability in the book. I have tried to honor and depict these disabilities accurately and to the best of my abilities. The gods, however, are rotten assholes and will use anything to destroy and kill the champions during the Sacrifice.

This book also deals with sensitive topics such as suicidal ideation and severe depression. Although the character experiencing suicidal thoughts is a 10,000-year-old god, I based the depiction of her depression on my experiences in my early twenties. If you or a loved one is experiencing suicidal ideation, severe depression, or have a plan to complete suicide, **please call 988** to reach the Suicide and Crisis Lifeline.

There is hope. I thought I would never feel joy again—I didn't even know what it was—but I found happiness and meaning through therapy and strong social support. *You can too.*

Content Warnings:

This book contains graphic violence/death on the page, suicidal thoughts, graphic descriptions of bodily fluids (esp. blood and vomit), and sexual content (2.5 chili pepper level).

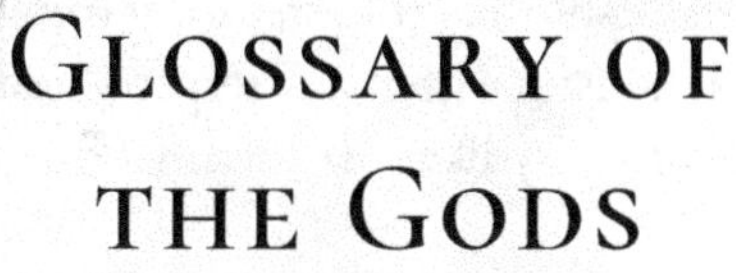

Glossary of the Gods

The Pantheon— The Major Gods

- Queen of the Gods—Nefeli
- Goddess of War—Theodra
- Goddess of Death—Havyn
- Goddess of Light—Andromache
- Goddess of Love—Rougoine
- Goddess of Health & Disease (aka Poison)—Maledy
- God of Fire—Silas
- God of Festival & Trickery—Heroki
- God of Harvest & Growth—Teirnan

Lessor Gods Mentioned

- Mistress of Fate—Erety—part of the Death Court
- Destruction—[name redacted]—part of the War Court
- Night—Marguerite—part of the Light Court
- Medusa—is a Gorgon who turns humans to stone with a look
- Sthenno and Euryale—Medusa's sisters; also Gorgons
- Nymphs—nature deities

Creatures Mentioned

- Vampire—long-lived mortals
- Witches—long-lived mortals
- Giant wolves—long-lived mortal shapeshifters
- Pooka—shapeshifting, trickster spirit (often a horse)
- Hydra—a monster with many serpent heads
- Spirits—small fairy-like creatures that feed on human emotion
- Banshee—female spirit who wails when death is near
- Centaurs—half human, half horse
- Harpies—half bird, half human
- Dullahan—headless horse riders

FACTS ABOUT THE MAJOR GODS

Nefeli—Queen of the Gods

- Patron Country: Nefesia
- Colors: Royal blue & robin's-egg blue
- Symbols: Peacock, lion, oak, scepter, & diadem
- Gemstone: Diamond
- Flower: Blue rose
- Torc: Peacock
- God Knots: Spiral knots
- Food: Lions are eaten as tribute once a year

Goddess of Death—Havyn

- **Leader of the Death Court**
- Patron Country: Ertomesia
- Colors: Charcoal, thistle, pomegranate
- Symbols: Black butterfly, pomegranate, white poplar tree & snake
- Gemstone: Blood ruby
- Flower: Black rose or thistle

- Torc: Black butterfly
- God Knots: Four trinity knots interlinked & forming a tree
- Food: Pomegranate is sacred & eaten as a tribute

Goddess of War—Theodra

- **Leader of the War Court**
- Patron Country: Theoden
- Colors: Blood red & raven black
- Symbols: Raven, shadow cats, spear, & snakes
- Gemstone: Garnet
- Flower: Red rose
- Torc: Raven
- God Knots: Shield knots
- Food: Birds are sacred & not eaten

Goddess of Light—Andromache

- **Leader of the Light Court**
- Patron Country: Andromada
- Colors: Gold, silver & purple
- Symbols: Sun, stag, fox, laurel, wolves, & snake
- Gemstone: Yellow diamond
- Flower: Purple rose
- Torc: Stag
- God Knots: Sun knots, looping like infinity knots
- Food: Deer are scared & forbidden from being eaten

Goddess of Love—Rougoine

- **Leader of the Love Court**
- Patron Country: Rougeland
- Colors: Rustic orange, red & pink
- Symbols: Dove, swan, pearls, & apples
- Gemstone: Rose quartz

- Flower: Tulip
- Torc: Swan
- God Knots: Love knot
- Food: Foods made with apples are a cherished

Goddess of Health & Disease (Poison)—Maledy

- **Leader of the Health Court**
- Patron Country: Maleden
- Colors: Green and yellow
- Symbols: White horse, Asclepius wand, & belladonna
- Gemstone: Amethyst
- Flower: Petunia & belladonna
- Torc: Aesculapian snakes
- God Knots: Healing knot
- Food:Ambrosia and nectar are eaten for strength and restoration

God of Fire—Silas

- **Leader of the Fire Court**
- Patron Country: Simark
- Colors: Orange, red & bronze
- Symbols: Fire, hammer, axe, & rope
- Gemstone: Red jasper
- Flower: Fire poppy
- Torc: Swan
- God Knots: Sailor's knot
- Food: Spicy foods are cherished

God of Festival & Trickery—Heroki

- **Leader of the Festival Court**
- Patron Country: Lokai
- Colors: Wine red and mint green

- Symbols: Wine chalice, grapes, tortoise, Fox, & masks
- Gemstone: Emerald
- Flower: Daffodil
- Torc: Fox
- God Knots: Duplex knot
- Food: Grapes are eaten daily

God of Harvest & Growth—Teirnan

- **Leader of the Harvest Court**
- Patron Country: Teirland
- Colors: White and gold and Forrest green
- Symbols: Wheat, vines, ivy, ox, sheep
- Gemstone: Emerald
- Flower: Daisy
- Torc: Ox
- God Knots: Dara knot
- Food: Wheat is sacred and sacrificed weekly

The Three Life & Death Balance Goddess

Light (of life), War (strife of life) & Death (end of life)

Symbols: Three interlinked snakes & the triquetra

***Special Note: all of the pantheon gods are balance gods. They represent both sides of a coin: life/death, health/disease, love/hate, etc. In this book, you typically see the darker side of that coin because it is The Sacrifice, and their goal is to kill.

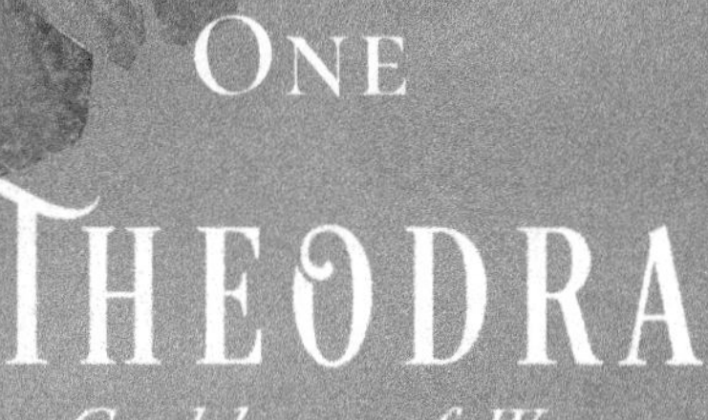

ONE
THEODRA
Goddess of War

Eleven Years Ago

LETUM CLIFFS, ERTOMESIA

Men were such loathsome creatures.

Theo stood on the cliff's edge, her eyes barely focusing on the crimson blaze far off in the distance. Seagulls croaked overhead, the aroma of salt permeating the air as sable waves crashed into the jagged cliffs—splintered like the sharp granite edges of her heart.

Shifting her eyes to the seaside below, Theo pondered jumping. Her life was a hollow echo, repeating through time and space. But even if she stepped off the cliff and crashed into a tangled mess below, she would barely feel it. For only another god could cause her true pain—a lesson she learned long ago.

Pleading voices split the wind as she half-listened. *Humans.*

Dying humans.

A steamboat burned to embers, licking the flesh from men's bones. Theodra, Goddess of War, didn't enjoy the show, but these men deserved their fate. They trafficked in evils far darker than the depths of the underworld. Their pleas would go unanswered. The steamboat would burn for their crimes, and if they managed not to drown, so be it.

"What are you doing?" A voice split the sky like lightning. Theo's lips lifted into a ruthless smirk as she turned to meet the God of Fire. He towered above her, an expression of pure loathing on his sculpted face. The once-vibrant flames of his hair, now a dim ash-grey, danced in the wind. His hair had never been the same since Theo tricked him into giving up his fire magic.

The God of Fire's eyes turned solid black, and his olive skin flaked like crumbling ash. Oh, he was angry. Theo's wicked grin widened. "Yes, Fire, what can I do for you?"

"Evil child of a nymph, you're murdering my men." He scowled as he delivered his insult. Nefeli, Theo's mother, and Queen of the Gods would take offense to being called a nymph. They were creatures of the earth and sea, and the lowest-ranked immortals.

"Am I?" The words twirled off her tongue to a mocking rhythm. "Oh, I hadn't noticed."

"You will pay for this." Fire lunged, power rippling in his veins. Was he going to use his magic . . . on her? Theo snapped her fingers, and he collapsed, clutching his stomach, and riving in pain.

Theo's heart thrummed to an unbreakable tempo, always playing a two-step dance in her chest. The rhythm steady and unchanging.

Like her.

"I thought you would've learned your lesson by now." Her raven mark branded on his wrist flared. It allowed her to control his powers. Mostly, she just held his evil in her hands and kept it from spilling onto innocent female lives. But in moments like this, she fought back. "I've never forgotten what you did and never will."

He knew what she meant. They both knew why she'd stolen his autonomy. They both remembered.

His mark was a punishment, for all men were the same . . . even gods.

"Perhaps next time you challenge me, I will give you a taste of your own flames." She snapped her fingers again, deepening his pain.

"You—will—" Fire sucked in a tortured breath. "—Pay for this," he muttered between spasms.

A tiny trickle of fear rolled down Theo's spine. Fire couldn't do anything to her anymore, but the memories remained.

He would never treat another that way; she wouldn't allow it.

Theo—War—stalked toward him as her midnight hair morphed with her magic. One strand at a time, it grew and changed into ravens. Once fully formed, they flew in circles, dancing around Fire—taunting him.

The leftover feathers painted the collar of her bustled gown, framing her feminine figure. She was the picture of terrifying elegance. Crimson streaks dripped from the bodice down the skirt, creating the effect of spilled blood. Theo looked like she'd marched through a deadly battlefield and collected carnage in her wake.

When she reached Fire, she clutched his chin tightly and forced him to meet her gaze. "Never threaten me again. Never question me again, or I will destroy you." Theo released him, disgust radiating through her bones. "Now, leave."

She waved a hand in the air, shooing the god away. He glared up at her. Defiant malevolence littered his cold, icy eyes before he disappeared into the setting sun.

"Tsk, tsk." A feminine voice clicked her tongue. "Hello, sister."

Theo's neck prickled, and bile rose in her throat at the arrival of the Goddess of Death, Havyn. She appeared from the shadows, her black cloak billowing in the crisp autumn wind as the raven feathers of her massive wings rippled with the breeze. Her hair dripped like spilled ink, and her moon-pale skin reflected the rays of the setting sun. Havyn was beautiful and terrifying, the angel of the afterlife coming to collect.

She made everyone's skin crawl. Dark, cold, and empty—Death personified.

Theo sucked in a breath.

Staring at Havyn was like looking into a mirror. The goddesses were nearly identical, apart from the beauty marks on Theo's left cheek and Havyn's wings. They had the same eyes, hair, and general demeanor. After all, they were two in a set of triplets.

"Hello, sister. Where's your wife?" Theo flashed a false smile and turned her eyes back to the blaze.

"She's already on the steamboat, taking the souls from your reckless temper." Havyn's voice was a velvet cravat, circling and strangling her.

Theo forced a shrug, a sign of how unimpressed she was. "Some men deserve to die."

Havyn sauntered to the cliff's edge and stood inches from her sister. The hair on Theo's arms rose with the closeness. "True, but you're getting sloppy. Your apathy has obscured vital information."

"Oh," Theo raised an eyebrow, "and what is that?"

"The girls. Erety is furious with you. But as you know, it isn't our job to save human lives."

Theo's heart surged, leaving its steady, unbreakable tempo for the first time in hundreds of years. Her heart never changed. It was constant, like her unending echo. Nothing affected its rhythm.

Nothing save for this.

Girls? No girls were on the ship, only the evil men . . . unless she'd slipped up and made a mistake. She sucked in a deep breath.

Theo didn't make mistakes.

Turning to meet Havyn's cold violet eyes, Theo asked, "Girls?"

"The girls trapped in the wooden boxes being shipped like cargo to Simark. The girls who have no chance at surviving your inferno."

Theo's body froze. Heart, blood—ichor, and breath. Everything was shattered granite.

She'd made a mistake.

A mistake.

Death didn't lie. Not about this.

Havyn winked and refracted, turning her matter into energy, and traveling at the speed of light to her destination. The process took less than a second. She disappeared, and a moment later reappeared on the ship.

Theo followed, dread solidifying in her stomach as she stepped onto creaking wood. The world smelled of smoke and tasted like rotten, decaying hopes, metal melting and crumbling around them.

Havyn strolled into the flames.

The fire didn't affect Havyn. It couldn't, for she traveled to the edges of life and pulled souls back with her. It wasn't a glamorous job, yet from the merciless smirk, it seemed she loved her purpose.

Theo pinched her eyes shut and listened. If the girls were on this ship, Theo would find them. Generally, she found female humans to be irritants—not vile like their male counterparts, but obnoxious inconveniences. But Theo never targeted them for her swift justice. It wasn't her way.

Hearts pattered like tapering music from the last cabin of the boat. Nine hearts.

Nine girls.

In an instant, Theo appeared in the rear cabin, smoke swelling around her, dancing to a somber melody of screams. The cries echoed, turning from piercing to croaking. Nine coffins littered the room, holes drilled into the sides to allow the girls to breathe.

Fury tore at Theo's heart.

War did not make mistakes.

Havyn was right. This was sloppy.

The heat made Theo's skin itch, but it was her inferno. It couldn't consume her.

Out of the fire stepped Erety, the Mistress of Fate, her fearsome expression cutting at Theo's composure. The blaze lit the god's tawny skin and golden eyes. Eretoime Devi, the once human goddess, was considered a legendary beauty. Songs and sonnets were spun in her honor, and humans worshiped at her feet.

"Are you here to watch your work up close?" Erety's voice was a hiss. "To witness these girls take their last smokey breath?"

"No," Theo whispered, her eyes stinging. "No." Her heart was unbearable now, its perfect rhythm interrupted. Her body was reacting in ways it hadn't in hundreds of years.

Theo was a villain.

A god all humans feared.

But she had a code. She was justice, killing only those who deserved it and never killing innocent girls. Theo swallowed and closed her eyes. She wouldn't let these girls die. Concentrating fiercely, War refracted each coffin, one by one, to safety on the shores of Ertomesia.

Time spilled like liquid wildfire, yet the task dripped like molasses. Every second represented a last breath. Every moment a fracture in the delicate balance of life. And Theo was moving far too slowly.

Finally, she finished the task and was surrounded by nine smoke-damaged coffins. Frantically, she tore off the lids and healed the girls. Some had burns, but all had smoke damage to their lungs.

The Death Goddesses watched silently, their wings billowing in the breeze.

When Theo reached the final coffin, her blood thickened as anxiety crept up her throat. There was no heartbeat. Theo tore off the top and stared at a pale, lifeless brunette girl. A girl who looked to be ten or eleven years old.

Dread swam in Theo's core as she checked for the pulse she knew she wouldn't find.

"No," Theo breathed. "No, no, no . . ."

The girl was dead.

Theo blinked, and her vision shifted to God's Sight—the ability to see the strings of life. All living things, from plants to reptiles, to aves, to mammals, had invisible—to the mortal eye—threads. Even the gods had them. The strings glowed a lilac purple color, with speckles of silver dewdrops interwoven, making them look like tears from the stars.

Humans had three fragile strings, while the gods had nine unbreakable ones—unable to be cut.

Unable to die.

A human's strings were mortal, and when they died, they frayed at the center and crumbled. This girl's many strings were fading quickly, and her translucent soul stood beside a comforting Erety. Theo's heart hammered in her skull, and her breaths grew stilted, like fire burning through her esophagus.

War did this—she was responsible.

Regret and shame trickled into her blood. It was dishonorable. And honor was currency among the immortals. Honor was praised above all else.

Theo was the devil that everyone had always expected her to be. She was the monster, not Fire, not Death. But perhaps there was something she could do. The girl's soul wasn't yet in the underworld—not yet crossed the River Orcus—her body wasn't cold enough to be uninhabitable. If Theo made the bargain with Havyn, this girl could still live.

"What do you want?" Theo pleaded, something entirely foreign to her. She'd only pleaded one other time in her life. Theo didn't show weakness. "Havyn, what do you want for her soul?"

Havyn crossed her arms while her wife narrowed her golden eyes.

"You'd trade for her life?" Havyn asked.

"Yes," Theo whispered, rolling her shoulders back, trying to regain her unbreakable calm. "What do you want? I have many things of value."

Erety stepped forward, leaving a very confused ghost behind. "Are you willing to trade Fire's ember whip for this human girl?"

Theo's palms grew clammy as she peered down at the lifeless body and then back up at the Goddesses of Death. Was Theo willing to trade the whip? A whip that was so hard to steal?

Yes.

The world believed Theodra to be the villain amongst the gods. Her name feared and whispered—a word of nightmares.

And she was terrible . . . but she had a code.

It was the only thing she had. The only thing that mattered, and she would not break it. Besides, Theo never wanted the whip. She wanted freedom. She wanted bad men punished. Theo squared her shoulders. "Yes."

Erety turned back to her wife, Havyn, who said, "How interesting." The goddesses shared an intrigued look. They were rhythmically aligned—perfectly fitting together. Perhaps it was why Havyn kidnapped Erety. She knew the girl would be the ideal partner—compliment her in every way.

A love that would defy a thousand lifetimes.

Havyn turned to the ghost, her violet eyes sparkling with wicked intent, but she spoke to Theo. "I won't take your hard-earned whip. Instead, I want a life."

Theo cocked her head, confusion lighting her insides. "A life?"

She didn't keep lives or resist their taking. She didn't even have faithful servants like all the other gods. Theodra hated inconvenience, and humans were *so inconvenient*. She wanted nothing to do with them.

"You are the second most powerful and most feared god in all the pantheon," Havyn said. Theo suppressed a chuckle. She'd spent lifetimes instilling that rumor. It was always more valuable to be feared than to be loved. But Havyn's statement wasn't entirely accurate. All the triplets were equally strong and shared the same power source, but many believed Theo to be the most skilled at using it. "If you wanted to protect a human and throw your will behind something, you'd be nearly unstoppable. So, I want an equivalent soul you love in exchange for her life." Havyn waved a hand at the spirit.

A human soul.

"Why would you ask for that? I'm not capable of loving a human."

Theodra was the only triplet who didn't love and the only one smart enough never to break the Immortal Law. True love was forbidden. A god could not fall in love with a mortal, nor the mortal fall in love with a god. The punishment for true love was death for the human and a hundred years of torture for the god. Havyn had been lucky and slithered out of the consequences, but the Goddess of Light—the third sister—lost her lover, Deveraux, to eternal damnation.

"You take nothing from me," Theo said. "I cannot love."

"That's where you're wrong, dear sister." Havyn's bearing was insidious. "Think of the prophecy."

The prophecy claimed that the triplets would each fall in love with a mortal, and it would end in death.

"Prophecies are the playthings of fools," Theo said, examining her fingernails.

Erety giggled. "Oh, you poor silly goddess, you can't even see your heart. If you care nothing for humans, you wouldn't trade Fire's whip for one. And if you can care for one, you will care for more. You will love one . . . eventually."

Theo shook her head and stepped away from the coffin. "You're wrong. I don't care for this girl. I care for justice."

"Of course you do." Erety ruffled the feathers of her wings, her face alight with amusement. "So, do you accept our bargain?"

"Yes." Theo's voice lingered in the air.

Havyn appeared beside her sister. Lightning lit the sky, and the ground trembled as Death and War shook hands, sealing their fateful deal.

Two
Theodra
Goddess of War

Eleven Years Ago

LETUM CLIFFS, ERTOMESIA

Wisps of a silver elixir looped through the air and settled into the girl's body. Her life force returning, one drop at a time—one string at a time. The girl's pallid face flushed with heat, and she gasped, clutching her throat as if she still felt the smoke burning inside her.

Her eyes were wild and coated with panic.

Theo stroked a feather along her skirt, needing something to do with her awkward hands. She opened her mouth to say something but closed it when she realized she had no idea what. Comforting humans wasn't among Theo's many talents.

She turned, searching for Death's help—knowing how to handle dead humans was her expertise—but both gods had vanished into the darkness, their laughs lingering and dancing on the wind.

Theo loosed a belabored sigh. Then she flashed her teeth to the girl, attempting a soft smile that looked far more like a grimacing twitch. Curling her fingers into the feathers of her skirt, she listened to the calming beat of her heart, which returned to its steady two-step dance.

Beat. Beat.

Beat. Beat.

Beat. Beat.

Having no idea what to say, Theo settled on, "Hello, Cecile Declaire of Andromeda. Welcome back to life."

When Theo wanted a name, it came into her mind. It was one of the perks of being divine. All pantheon gods could bend matter and energy. Energy, including neural pathways in the human brain. Theo couldn't read humans' thoughts per se, but she could influence them and read their patterns. Patterns like names and places often visited. From those patterns, gods could deduce information.

Cecile's eyes locked on the goddess. "Oh, *Valysia*," Cecile cursed as if she couldn't believe her eyes. "The Goddess Theodra. I'm not dreaming."

"No, dear child, you're not dreaming," Theo said in a poor attempt at a motherly voice.

Dear child? What was she, Nefeli—Queen of the Gods? Theodra certainly sounded like her mother. This wasn't entirely a bad thing. Nefeli loved mortals, especially females, but she was also a tiresome hypocrite. If she loved humans so much, she wouldn't interfere in their lives.

She wouldn't revel in the Sacrifice every four years. Of course, the gods needed the Sacrifice to fuel their power, but Nefeli didn't have to enjoy it so damned much.

"I was dead." Shock lit up Cecile's face as she sat up. She patted her chest and the coffin around her as if making sure she wasn't in a dream.

"Yes." Theo clutched the coffin so hard the wood cracked. Releasing it, she attempted another smile, unsuccessfully. She didn't know what to do with her hands, so she patted the girl on the back, barely placing any pressure. "There, there . . ."

Theo grimaced.

Everything about this moment was horrific.

There, there?

It was what she'd seen others do in situations like this. It was supposed to help, right?

She didn't even know why she bothered comforting the girl. It's not like Theo felt affection—at best, she was annoyed. But honor dictated that she at least made sure the girl was okay. After all, she'd accidentally killed her.

Theo sighed, defeat lingering on her lips. It was useless. She couldn't reassure human children when she was the personification of devastation.

As if feeling Theo's struggle, a tiny tuxedo kitten appeared out of the mist and curled around Cecile's feet. It was Bella, one of Theo's nine magical familiars that could change shape and color at will. Of all her cats, Bella was the most therapeutic and sensitive, always appearing in times of great need.

Instinctively, Cecile scooped up the kitten and cuddled it against her face for comfort. "But you're cruel," Cecile breathed, clutching her mouth as if she hadn't meant to say the words. Her fingers trembled—still clutching the kitten—and her heart raged in her chest. It was so loud Theo wanted to cover her ears.

"Worry not, dear child."

Dear child, again?

Theo rubbed her face, exhausted.

This day wasn't going the way she'd planned.

Sobs littered the air as the other six girls broke down. Many fell to their knees wailing, while others stood as still as a gorgon's stone statues.

Oh gods, not more of them.

Through it all, Cecile's eyes never left the goddess. They were cobalt-piercing daggers, eating away at Theo's resolve. Once the mortal regained her composure, the fear faded, and only courage remained—which was extraordinarily unsettling.

"Why don't you fear me?"

Cecile's sapphires twinkled as she sat up straight and met the goddess's gaze as an equal. The feathers surrounding Theo's collar ruffled. She wasn't used to a human who didn't cower at her immortal features and arrogance. "Because you saved my life and traded for my soul." Cecile's little voice was soft and full of hope.

"Do not mark that as a sign of caring." Theo made her eyes

turn a deep wine red and she called her ravens to circle nearer. She couldn't have a human so unafraid.

Fear was a useful emotion. If people feared Theo, they would leave her alone. All she ever wanted in this long, empty life was to be left alone, to live out her days in peace and tranquility.

Cecile flinched and averted her gaze. Instead, she petted the kitten, her chestnut locks dancing in the wind. "You saved me."

"Yes."

The ravens pulled back and began to dance above the cliffs, away from the girls.

"You saved my life."

"Yes, we've already established that." Theo swallowed, trying to bottle up her annoyance. There was no reason to let it spill out now. From the frantic beating of Cecile's heart, the girl was rightfully shaken . . . finally.

"Yes," Cecile's voice cracked. "But honor compels me to make it right. I owe you a life debt."

Theo almost jumped back at the words, and a shudder ran down her spine. This was the last thing she wanted to hear. No human had ever owed her anything.

It was the last thing she could possibly want.

Honor, Theo cursed under her breath. It was currency but also a curse. "No, no. no." The goddess raised her hands. "You owe me nothing. As I told Death, your life matters very little to me. I need nothing in return."

Cecile's face paled, soaked with despair, but the kitten headbutted her as a sign of deep affection and an effort to calm her down.

Theo sighed. *Cats and their vendetta to do whatever they pleased.*

Cecile's face was still moon white and coated with hurt, and it made War's brow furrow. Had the girl thought the goddess cared?

"Even so, I owe you. I will devote my life to serving you." The girl gulped and rolled her shoulders back.

Oh, gods, no. Not this. "Trust me. You *don't* want to do that."

Cecile pulled herself onto her knees and stepped out of the

coffin, standing to her fullest height. The top of her head met the goddess's core, and Theo wasn't distinctly tall. She was average among the gods, which made her only slightly tall for a mortal woman. Some mortal women were even taller than her.

Despite her tininess, the girl was undoubtedly feisty and brave. She'd have made a perfect Theoden warrior. Perhaps it was the near-death experience that gave her the courage. Still, Theo suspected it was more of a personality trait.

War enjoyed strong-willed females—they reminded her of herself.

"I want to do this." Cecile held her head high and tilted her chin to meet the goddess's violet eyes. "I'm your loyal servant now and forever."

Theo cringed. War kept zero Godmarked servants. She had priestesses and temples as obligatory power sources, of course, as all gods did because their strength relied on devotion, worship, and prayer. It was the way of the universe. But she'd have none of it if it were up to her.

"You know this means I can compel you to do whatever I want, and you cannot refuse me?" Theo asked.

Cecile didn't flinch. Instead, she held firm, unblinking. "Yes."

War sucked in a slow breath, not knowing how to respond. She didn't want a servant or the bond it created, but this girl wouldn't take no for an answer. Theo respected that strength and resilience, and if she were to have a servant, Cecile would be a good choice.

"Fine," Theo said, resigned.

Clutching Cecile's wrist, War held her thumb to its center. Ink spilled from the fingertip and formed into a raven tattoo encircled by silver filigree and Theodic knots—looped infinity designs with no end or beginning.

It was the Godmark, connecting Cecile to the divine and linking their hearts. From now on, Theo would know when the mortal was in peril, and, if she wanted, she could send mental messages and commands. But the bond also created a fierce need in the god to protect and defend. It wasn't something one did lightly.

"We are forever connected unless I decide to remove it." Theo nodded at the tattoo. "And now, my first command is that you never make a deal with a god ever again. You will never let them control you."

Cecile stared at her forearm—the kitten still perched on her shoulder—the feathers on the tattoo rippling and moving to its own volition. Godmarks were not stagnant. They shifted, changed, and sometimes communicated with the tattoo's recipient. It was a living thing, much like War's ravens. Theo commanded them, but they were separate from her and had their own personalities. That was the thing with god magic: it was always in flux, and sometimes it morphed in ways even the gods couldn't predict.

The tattoo would protect Cecile. That was its one command, and it was up to the marking on how to achieve that mission.

Theo cleared her throat as the Goddess of Light, Andromache's chariot left the sky, and the sun fell asleep. The country of Ertomesia was now under the rule of Night, who shot forth into the sky and danced among the evening stars.

"It is time that I see you all home. Line up and tell me where you'd like to be taken."

The girls followed suit, and Theo refracted them to their homes one by one. Cecile was last in line.

"Where do you want to go?" Theo asked.

"Theoden," Cecile said, storms in her little irises.

Theo creased her brow. "Why? Andromeda is your home."

"Not anymore." Cecile crossed her arms. "My parents don't want me, so why should I return to them—to those traitors?"

Theo nodded, not wanting to know any more details. If her parents didn't want her, that was their business, not Theo's.

"Alright." Theo clutched the girl's wrist too tightly and refracted to the palace in Theoden.

Using her abilities to bend matter, Theo conjured a letter that read, *Take care of the child. Give her everything she needs. If you don't, you will deal with War's wrath.*

Theodra attached the note to the girl's chest with magic and walked her up the palace steps. In her most terrifying voice, Theo said to the guards, "I trust you to get this child to the king and queen." She plastered a smile as fierce as fangs on her lips. "I will know if you don't."

The guards nodded, fear caking their features.

The kitten still rested on the girl's shoulder. Theo sighed. Bella would stay with the girl until she felt like leaving. After all, cats did as cats pleased. "Fine, stay with her then," Theo whispered so low only the cat's ears picked it up. It flicked its tail and nuzzled back into the girl's shoulder.

Theo rolled her eyes.

As the guards moved to take Cecile to the royals, Theo grasped her wrist. The goddess turned her gaze to the raven bristling there. "You can use it to call for me. I will come. Be safe; for now, you're a Servant of War."

Without another word, the goddess disappeared into a cloud of angry ravens.

Three

Kellyn

Prince of Theoden

Present

RYFEL PALACE, THEODEN

A conspiracy of ravens stalked the dawn.

Thousands of birds speckled the skies like a haze of locusts, their ink-black feathers glistening in the rays of the rising sun. A gust of icy wind ruffled the pleats on Kellyn's tartan vest, highlighting his dark olive skin as he watched the horde forming below. The fog mingled with the bodies cramming together, all eyes fixed on the palace balcony, awaiting the prince's speech. Camera shutters pounded with the frantic beats of Kellyn's heart, and gramophones played the Song of War, mixing with the somber croaking of the birds circling above.

Anticipation licked the air.

Kellyn towered above the crowd. Truthfully, he towered above all mortals. He wasn't a giant, but his height was said to be equal to a god, for on his natal day, he was blessed by both the gods of War and Trickery. One god publicly bestowed him with strength, agility, and wit, while the other secretly graced him with an affliction hindering the latter. He would be Theoden's perfect warrior, impossibly tall, sculpted, and nearly unbeatable in battle—except he would struggle to read, impeding his wit so much he'd convinced himself of his stupidity. So, despite his commanding looks and stern face, Kellyn's heart pounded, and a bead of sweat rolled down his temple. But he couldn't let anyone see it because he was known as the handsome prince who made girls and boys alike swoon with his perfection.

And he would cultivate that image until death, his motto being: *Never let the world see my weaknesses.*

"I cannot do this." Kellyn stepped off the balcony and ducked back into the safety of the palace walls. Trying to quell his nerves, he pulled a wooden carving block and knife from his pocket—etching calmed him, but it didn't help today. Nothing was more unsettling than reading aloud, let alone in front of thousands of people. At twenty-four, he should've gotten over this fear already.

But he hadn't.

"You don't have a choice," Cecile whispered. She was a girl with the looks of a goddess and the personality of a fox, and she was the only person outside his family who knew about his affliction.

"I can't," he said, sucking in a breath. Cecile's black shadow cat, given to her by the Goddess of War, rubbed its head against his leg in a comforting manner. "I'll forget the entire speech, and everyone will figure out my secret."

It was Decision Day, and as the prince, he had to announce his country's champion for the Sacrifice—a deadly game of tricks, fantasy, and deception that pitted nine human pairs against the gods. The Theoden champion was chosen by the three legislative branches—the Temple of Theodra, the Council of Warriors, and the Council of Scholars—but the Royal House held veto power and the final decision.

As the heir of Theoden, Kellyn confirmed the decision or vetoed it, choosing his own—which he would never do.

"Just breathe, Kel," Cecile whispered, her eyes darting around the room of gathering council members. "You don't want anyone to hear."

Kellyn clutched his wooden carving so hard that his knuckles lost all color, and his fingers turned red, causing three yellow wind sprites to burst out of the air and feed on his worry. Kellyn swatted the little creatures away with a hand, and he dropped his voice so low only a god or Cecile could hear, "Pronouncing an unfamiliar name is impossible."

Nearly impossible.

Kellyn's affliction made it hard to differentiate words and sounds. When he read, none of the characters made sense, and he often reversed sounds, confusing letters or words that looked alike. During his time at the Agoge Academy—the seven-year military and scholarly training mandated for all Theoden children at age sixteen—Kellyn was called *a big dumb brute* by his peers. The worst label to give a kid in a country that valued strategy and wit above all else.

Kellyn's reputation became so bad that his parents considered faking his death and stripping his inheritance.

They couldn't have an *unintelligent* son.

Cecile's shadow cat meowed and headbutted Kellyn's leg. The magic little thing did not like it when he degraded himself—even in his head.

"Kel, no one will find out about your . . . struggles." Cecile's voice had an Andromaden lilt, and her comforting smile was like midnight lightning. Brilliant and spellbinding. She was like a painting of the Goddess of Love coming to life. "We've spent the past seven days memorizing the speech. There's nothing that could go wrong."

He peered over the balcony ledge. "I have a terrible feeling about today."

"It's only a feeling," Cecile said as her ash brown curls bounced in the wind and sparkled in the morning sunlight streaming through the balcony, the blonde undertones peeking through.

"What are you two talking about?" Emmett Evans, the perennial rogue, and Kellyn's best mate, asked.

"Kellyn's nervous," Cecile said.

"Don't worry. All you have to do is say a name, and it doesn't even have to be the correct one." Emmett smirked, his russet-brown skin glowing with amusement as he slid his hands into his pockets. Bluntness was Emmett's currency. He said what he wanted when he wanted, and he didn't care about anyone's reactions.

"Emmett, that's horrible." Cecile punched him. *Hard.*

Unnaturally hard.

And Kellyn knew it hurt. He'd been on the receiving end of her punches far too often in the Agoge.

Emmett held his arms up in surrender. "I'm just saying it's an option. But we all know I should be this year's champion." He tilted his black top hat in a false salute, mocking Cecile. His style matched his flippant, extravagant nature. The double-breasted midnight suit had his house tartan stitched into the vest and was woven from the most expensive spider silk in the world.

Cecile balked. "A terrible option. We all know whatever name Kellyn calls is a death sentence." A Theoden champion hadn't won the Sacrifice—or survived—in over 500 years.

"It is a death knell, true, but it's also a chance to claim the highest honor imaginable and get a guaranteed ticket to the Valysian Fields," Emmett said.

"But you'll be dead. The Fields are for heroic and virtuous *dead* souls." Cecile crossed her arms.

It was a common argument between them. Cecile never fully embraced Theoden culture. Honor was everything. *Potius mori quam foedare.* Death before dishonor. To die an honorable death was more valuable than any worldly riches. But Cecile was Andromaden at heart, and honor, while still significant, was less critical.

"I'd rather die with honor than lead a meaningless life. Besides, it's only a death knell because our venerable goddess can't seem to show up," Emmett said, poison dripping from his tongue.

Kellyn sighed and turned back to his lovespoon carving, which he would sacrifice to Theodra at his altar later that night. "Careful, Theodra might hear you."

"She doesn't listen, and if she did, she would've come down to smite me long ago."

"Perhaps she doesn't smite you because I've asked her not to." Cecile clutched the balcony railing and leaned her head out as if basking in the crowd's excitement. A wind sprite landed on her shoulder and played with her hair—feeding off her emotions.

"I forgot I was talking to her Godmarked, and most loyal male devotee." Emmett rolled his eyes dramatically. He wasn't wrong, Kellyn and Cecile were among the Goddess of War's most dedicated followers.

Cecile loosed an exaggerated sigh and turned her attention to Kellyn. "You look like Death ripped out your heart."

Kellyn sucked in a breath, and nerves rattled his bones. The anticipation was the worst part. He just needed to start the speech, and it would be fine. It was the waiting that might end him.

"Anyway, have you seen Kellyn's royal fan club today?" Emmett said, nodding at a group made up of six girls and three boys—the prince was popular with all young people who found men attractive.

Kellyn's eyes tracked to them, and he swore one of them let out a soft feline sigh. He forced a smile and an awkward nod. How did one ever get used to that type of attention?

"Do you think it's your abs or your face they like more, huh, Kel?" Emmett asked, trying to distract Kellyn from his nerves.

"My face has scars."

"Oh, that just makes you look more rugged and handsome. It really works with the ladies . . . and gents."

"Right . . ."

Cecile shook her head. "What do you like better, Emmett, his face or his abs . . . or is it his ass I find you ogling the most?"

"I ogle your ass just as much as his. I can't help it; the two of you are so attractive. I do have eyes, even if I'd never fuck either of you." The sides of his mouth tilted up, and he oozed smooth charm like enchantment and wore it like his breathtaking smile. "Speaking of fucking, have you tumbled in the sheets with any of them?" He gestured once more to the "fan club".

Shame rippled up Kellyn's throat because he didn't know, and he really should have. He'd had so many lovers. After all, that's how everyone made it through the deadly Agoge—fucking like they might die the next day. It was *very possible* he'd slept with one of his admirers—if not many of them.

"Uh," Kellyn grunted.

"You can't remember, can you? No worries, brother, I've

fucked nearly all of them for you. They weren't that memorable, except for the blond at the end. Oh, and the beautiful redhead next to him was great too . . . and at the same time, you can't imagine their—"

"—Emmett, we get it, you're quite skilled, but can we—" Cecile was interrupted by a footman approaching and handing over a message. "Miss Declare, you have a telegram from Andromeda."

"A telegram?" Emmett asked.

Cecile unfolded the letter. "It's probably a notice telling me who Andromache picked as her champion for the Sacrifice."

Each country had a different way of choosing its champion. In Andromeda, Andromache, Goddess of Light, selected her champion and blessed them. Because of this, the Andromaden champion almost always survived the games.

Cecile's eyes traced the message, and her smile faltered, her fingers shaking. Visibly gulping, she folded the paper and slid it into a pocket in her dress.

"What is it?" Kellyn asked. Something was off. He knew her expressions better than his own.

She flashed a false smile. "It's nothing. We should focus on your task."

"That isn't nothing," Emmett said as he tried to snatch the paper from her pocket.

She was far too quick for him. Twirling out of his reach, she thrust her fist up and grazed him on the chin. Cecile was by far the fastest—and most vicious—of his friends. "Try it again, and I'll break your perfect little nose."

The royal retinue and council representatives in the ballroom flashed their eyes to the warriors but immediately lost interest. Sparring among the warrior class was so frequent no one batted an eye.

"Fine." Emmett let out an intentionally dramatic sigh. "What would I do if I weren't the *most* beautiful one among us?"

"Probably grow a pair of—"

"—Cecile," Kellyn chided. "There is no need to attack his masculinity. We all know he is our pretty princess."

"You two are merely jealous that I look better in a ballgown. It isn't my fault that I have far superior confidence, taste, and style than you two and far superior luck with the ladies . . . and gents." Emmett winked at them.

Kellyn turned to Cecile. "He's wearing your ballgowns again?"

"My periwinkle Vorthe gown was loose the last time I tried it." She narrowed her eyes at the boy in question. "Buy your own dresses already. I know mine are spectacular, but you aren't wanting for money."

Cecile flattened out a wrinkle in her glimmering scarlet Andromaden-styled dress. Like most Andromaden citizens, Cecile had ostentatious fashion choices like the diamond encrusted crimson flowers raining from her bodice like blood-red tears. It was the polar opposite of the simplistic and functional style of Theodenites.

Emmett opened his mouth to make a retort but was cut off by the commanding entrance of Gallagher Healy.

Oh gods, just what Kellyn needed.

Gallagher spoke with a soft, pixie-like voice, but she had the presence of a praying mantis seconds before killing its mate. She dominated every room she entered, despite her petite stature. She was like a termite, whittling her way into power and prominence. She wore a deep purple pinstriped dress, highlighting her tawny skin, and her silver-blonde hair was sculpted into an elaborate chignon.

Spotting the trio, a vicious smile danced across her ruby lips, and she nearly bounced across the room to reach them. "Are you ready for your big speech?"

"Yes, of course." Kellyn smiled through his teeth, with all the arrogance and dominance of a god.

Gallagher never had an ounce of concern for anyone other than herself, and she certainly didn't care now. She was up to something. Gallagher had unusual, often inappropriate, and sometimes vile tastes and tendencies. She adored tricks and watching things burn . . . sometimes literally. During the Agoge, she nearly killed Cecile and sabotaged her at every turn.

"Your speech is all prepared?" Gallagher asked.

"Yes, of course." A muscle in Kellyn's cheek twitched.

"Oh, good, I am glad to hear it. I must confess, I was worried you might soil yourself from all the pressure." Gallagher smiled like a tiger. "We all know how you get sometimes." She spat out the last word like hydra acid.

Did Gallagher know about his affliction? Kellyn felt the blood drain from his face, and his heart thudded, but he squared his shoulders in a battle stance.

Never let anyone see your weakness.

There was no way Gallagher could have found out. Kellyn has been so good at hiding it. He learned to pick locks and steal assignments to memorize them so he wouldn't stumble over the reading in classes. Moreover, he pretended to be an arrogant, dominant asshole to keep most people at bay and away from his secrets. He was excellent at hiding his shame. *Gallagher couldn't know.* Emmett didn't even know.

Kellyn rubbed his left pectoral muscle for comfort, where his three house sigils were etched into his bronze skin with black ink. He was an heir to three important family lines in Theoden and the greater world.

"Gallie, go prance off to somewhere you're wanted." Cecile used the nickname, knowing the girl hated it, and shooed her away with a careless gesture.

"I'm a council aid," Gallagher said, smugness pouring from her pores. "I'm more than wanted here."

"It's starting," Emmett said, stepping between the girls. "Go stand in your proper place, Gallie."

She glanced one final time at the crowd before rolling her shoulders back and walking to her assigned spot.

Cecile turned back to Kellyn and clutched his hand, squeezing it. "You're going to do great."

The three council heads, their aids, Kellyn's parents, and his two best friends gathered behind him on the balcony. As Kellyn walked up to the newly invented microphone, a tear of sweat rolled down his spine.

It was the moment.

Possibly the most significant moment of his life.

His valet handed him the altered speech with the final name of the champion typed in. Kellyn held it between his fingers momentarily and took a long deep breath. He could do this. He had practiced and studied the words over and over and over again.

He was prepared.

Kellyn started the speech from memory. "People of Theoden, a country devoted to our Goddess of War, I welcome you to the Day of Decision. Every four years, our great councils come together to choose our newest champion and the pride of our country. A champion representing our great courage, strategy, and strength. A champion for us to be proud of. So, I stand before you today to humbly declare the name . . ."

Kellyn unrolled his speech. His eyes scraped across the words, but none of them were familiar. The entire thing was completely and utterly changed from the original. His heart stumbled and dropped to his toes. Somebody switched out the proper speech with a handwritten document in cursive which was utterly impossible for his brain to translate under stress. Cursive was hardest to read because the letters danced and looped. He couldn't use his typical trick of memorizing the words' shapes because they were all different.

It was bad.

Kellyn's heart beat to a rhythm of war.

His chest tightened, and his cravat felt suddenly stifling like it was suffocating him. He stared at the paper, begging it to make sense. But the more he looked, the more desperate the situation became.

He closed his eyes and tried to breathe in deeply, but his breath was a fire burning his insides to embers.

"The new champ-cha-champion," he stuttered.

Kellyn's eyes scanned the paper again, searching for the name. He didn't need the rest of the words. All he truly needed was the champion's name. But the terms blended into a watercolor painting of dread.

His fingers tightened around the snow-white paper, earth sprites dancing around his head, licking at his fear. Cecile's shadow cat rubbed against his leg, trying to offer aid, but it didn't help.

Kellyn stared out into the crowd, wondering if they had all noticed the sudden pause in his speech.

They must have. How could they not? Everyone saw his stupidity on full display.

Everything stilled, freezing like a gorgon statue. But the birds mocked him overhead, as did the sprites.

They croaked a song of his failure.

Cawing, and cawing, and cawing.

Each call a nail in the coffin of his reputation.

Caw.

Croak.

Caw.

The song of his destruction.

Caw.

Croak.

The sound of his secret crumbling around him.

Caw.

Caw.

Caw.

Kellyn sucked in a poisonous breath and tried again to find the champion's name. He scanned the paper, his panic a visceral thing clawing at his chest. He needed to do something—fast.

If people learned of his affliction, his parents would disown him and name his younger brother the heir.

Kellyn needed a solution fast.

He could, like Emmett suggested, call out a random name. He could even call one of his cohorts he didn't quite like. Theoden schooling created enemies and unbreakable allies. It was its way. Gallagher's name came to mind—and it would be the perfect form of revenge. But Kellyn didn't have that type of vengeance in his blood. Instead, he'd take on the burden rather than condemn the wrong person to death. His eyes scanned the now crumpled paper again.

Nothing.

His heart stumbled in his chest, and he searched all his options.

He had to name a champion but would sentence them to a

gruesome death if he called the wrong name. But if he remained silent for much longer, the entire country would know his secret.

If he stayed silent, he'd lose everything. If he asked someone for help, he would lose everything. It was his father's motto: *Ellis's don't need help; asking for help is a form of weakness.* Under no circumstances could Kellyn ever seek help. And he couldn't find it within his soul to name someone else. Kellyn was many things, but he wasn't a murderer.

He wasn't cruel.

Honor burned in his blood, and he knew the only honorable thing left to do, but that didn't mean he liked it.

Kellyn's hands trembled as he crushed the paper between his fingers. His stomach turned to pure ice, and every part of his body resisted what he was about to say.

"I have decided . . ." His voice came out in a low rasp, almost like his vocal cords revolted against the following words. He cleared his throat and tried again. "I have decided as it is my right as the heir of Theoden to break the tie and name the person, I see most fit as the champion." He swallowed hard and rolled his fingers into a ball to keep them from trembling. "I shall be this year's champion in the Sacrifice."

A shattered silence descended among the crowd. People looked at their neighbors as if they hadn't heard the prince correctly.

Once the retinue on the stage stumbled out of their shock and began whispering in concerned tones to each other.

Kellyn gritted his teeth and inhaled sharply before repeating for another time. "I name myself, Crown Prince Kellyn Ellis, this year's champion in the Sacrifice."

Four

Kellyn

Prince of Theoden

RYFEL PALACE, THEODEN

Kellyn's foot jolted back as the weight of his words crashed down, burning, and suffocating him. It felt like Fire's ember whip was a noose circling Kellyn's neck. His throat stung so bad it clenched and spasmed from the strain.

Panic burst around him, many voices mingling together.

"What in all monsters was that?"

"That wasn't the name."

"He switched it."

"The idiot."

"Why?"

"That can't be undone. Once announced, it's final. The name is placed on the Scrolls of the Gods."

"Is he truly that arrogant to think he could win?"

"I've always said he's a big dumb brute."

Kellyn's mother shrieked, his father bellowed curses, the counselors debated roughly, and his best friends stared at him in shock.

The heir was never supposed to be chosen. It just didn't happen—not as an heir of Azraelle.

Kellyn stood tall, not letting any of his internal turmoil spill out. But the wind sprites, dancing cursed circles around Kellyn's head, gave it away. Or would have if anyone paid close enough attention, because he had no energy to wave them off.

Ravens croaked overhead, a song of battle clawing from their beaks.

A song of foreboding.

Did they know this would happen? Ravens were War's birds, and they predicted the future. If a raven touched a man's shoulder before a battle, he would die by the end of the day. They took no prisoners and showed no mercy—like the goddess herself.

Today, they were foretelling Kellyn's inevitable death.

A thick haze settled over him like the black veil obscuring a widow's tears. But instead of tears, it obscured his thoughts. Kellyn's heart thudded, and his fingers trembled, the speech lingering in his hand. He'd ruined his life—ended it.

It had been 500 years since a Theoden champion survived. The tournament was designed to kill humans. That was its purpose, and the Theoden champion had always been a true sacrifice—sent to the games to die and feed the gods' powers.

There was no hope of living through it.

Because Theodra never showed up, and no human could beat the Sacrifice without a god's help.

It just wasn't done.

A cacophony of noise bombarded Kellyn's senses and ripped him from his thoughts of death.

He needed to get away from everything. He couldn't gather himself with all the noise and pale faces, all the devastation, confusion, and anger coating the air. But Kellyn couldn't move or focus. His father shook his shoulders and spoke words he couldn't understand. It was most likely Theodic, but it didn't matter; Kellyn understood it about as much as he would've understood the language of the gods—not at all.

But none of that mattered. Only his reputation as an arrogant prince did. He cleared his throat and told everyone present, "I am the commander of the Raven Battalion. I am one of the best warriors in Theoden history, I do not trust anyone else to win."

Without listening to any response, Kellyn rolled his shoulders back and placed a mask of disinterest on his face. He pivoted on his heels and strode away with a falsely-calm bearing—making it look like he cared very little about the concerns of others. Fast footfalls rang behind him, and Kellyn didn't even need to turn around to recognize the gaits of his best friends. After seven years of school, he could recognize them blindfolded. They had distinctive movements.

"Let me see that." Emmett ripped the paper from Kellyn's hands, his eyes scanning the letter, his face paling as he dropped it to the floor.

Cecile bent down and scooped up the letter before flatting it with her skirt to get the crinkles out. Her shadow cat weaved around her feet as she began reading it. "Oh." Cecile gulped, turning her sapphire eyes on the gentleman. "This isn't good."

A thick and sticky silence filled the air between the friends. It was hot and burning and felt like Kellyn's soul was being tarred and feathered.

All three of their expressions were different versions of horrified. Emmett's face was red hot, and filled with fury, Cecile's was a dance of sorrow, and Kellyn's was an image of horror.

"I hope you have an explanation for that," Kellyn's father said, catching up with them, a horde of vultures flanking him.

One vulture was Gallagher, with a feral smile spread across her gleeful features. She bathed in disorder and pain. "How truly terrible. You're going to die, probably horrifically; you must feel so curse—sived." She said the word cursed like cursive, and Kellyn's mouth dropped open.

She did this.

She intentionally switched out the typed pages with cursive handwriting. The large loops and self-indulgent lettering could easily have been Gallagher.

"You did this?" Kellyn's voice crackled like embers.

"We can fix this." The queen approached with her head held high, holding the dignity of the gods on her shoulders.

Kellyn's proud mask slid across his face. "There's nothing you can do, Mother."

"The idiot announced it in front of the entire country." The king's words twisted off his tongue. "There is nothing we can do except watch our eldest—and heir—die before our eyes."

"I see you have such little faith in my abilities." Kellyn sucked in a breath and stilled his movements, glowering at his father. "I am the commander of your best forces. I'll be fine."

"Even if you were the most skilled Theoden Champion in the last 500 years—which you're not—you still couldn't win the Sacrifice without the aid of a god, and since Theodra hasn't bothered to show up—"

"There must be a divine reason for all of this," the queen interrupted.

"Divine reason?" The king scoffed. "The idiot couldn't read the correct name. It seems pretty simple to me." A muscle in his jaw feathered. "Perhaps this is for the best. How can we have an heir of Theoden, a country built on strategic intelligence, who can't even read?" he said, the last bit through his teeth and lower than a whisper.

The words hit like a spear to Kellyn's heart, but he lifted his chin and raised an eyebrow as if none of this small talk meant anything to him. He was forever the arrogant, unbothered prince.

"Iwan," the queen scolded, her eyes darting to everyone who didn't know Kellyn's secret.

"What's done is done. No one can change it. I'm the champion." Ice slid over Kellyn's countenance and under his breath so that only his parents and friends could hear what he said, "At least now you will get an heir you're not ashamed of." He said sternly, "If you would excuse me, there is much to prepare."

Without waiting for a response, Kellyn strolled out of the ballroom, heading to his room. His friends followed in silence. They knew better than to discuss any of this in the hallway—in the open. One never knew who was eavesdropping. The paintings had ears in the palace. As did the doors, walls, and sculptures. Not literally, although given the gods' unknowable abilities, no one truly knew the depths of their spying.

The gods knew far too much for their own good, but they weren't omniscient.

Once the chamber doors clicked shut behind them, Emmett

rounded on his friend and demanded, "Why did you do that?" The boy's face was the red of a firestorm. "I could have done it. You didn't have to be so damned proud and arrogant. I don't need your protection."

Kellyn glowered and flexed his feet like a feline preparing to strike. With such remarks, Emmett very much needed protection . . . from the prince.

"You stole my glory," Emmett continued. "This was my chance to prove myself. My chance to die honorably and join the heroes of old in the Valysian Fields."

"I—what?" Kellyn's frustration simmered as the strength of the words hit him, a bleak understanding settling into his bones. The name on the paper—the true champion—was supposed to be Emmett. It made sense. Emmett was first in their class of the Agoge, Cecile was second, but Kellyn was seventeenth. He would've been ranked far lower if not for his unmatched talent in physical challenges. But Emmett was intelligent, strong, honest, and clever. All traits valued beyond all others in Theoden.

"I'm not weak," Emmett said as the shadow cat butted her head against his legs—always trying to comfort, especially in times of high stress. "I'm a warrior like you, and I've earned my place among the aristocracy in Theoden."

The class system in the country worked on merit and inheritance. Either someone was born into the upper classes or earned their way in through works and talent.

"I didn't, you—" Kellyn began.

"Oh," Cecile interrupted, staring at the paper. "It's in cursive."

"What does that have to do with anything?" Emmett yelled.

"Nothing," Kellyn bit back, "nothing. That's enough protesting Emmett, I didn't believe you could do it. But I can." The lie slid off his tongue seamlessly; after all, he was an expert liar. Kellyn didn't want to lie to his best friend, but he'd do anything to protect his secret—including hurting Emmett. But under no circumstance could he find out.

"You arrogant, pompous asshole," Emmett growled, and Kellyn's insides caved in. "I shouldn't have to remind you that I was far superior in our classes."

Not *all* of them. Kellyn was the best student in their botany class, but now wasn't the best time to bring that up.

It was a horrible situation because he couldn't tell the truth and apologize, but without it, Emmett would despise him. Glory was currency among warriors. It was how society functioned. All Theoden champions entered the Sacrifice seeking glory. To die by being outwitted or outbattled was the highest honor a Theodenite could achieve.

That glory was all Kellyn could hope for now.

But it was supposed to be Emmett's glory—a fact Emmett wouldn't accept easily.

Kellyn couldn't think of anything to say, so he doubled down. "Yet I'm taller, stronger, and the better choice."

Emmett balled his fists. "You're a piece of shit—"

"Shit," a voice from the side of the room said with airy delight. Gallagher leaned against the wall. "I think I prefer being called a massively destructive bitc—" Before Gallagher could finish her sentence, Cecile was on her feet and flinging herself at the girl—a ball of fury and vengeance.

Like lightning, a crack echoed through the room as Cecile punched her nemesis in the nose. "You did this."

Gallagher wiped a streak of blood from her lip before shrugging nonchalantly. Not an answer but also not a refusal. "I don't think it matters at this point." She smiled like a snake and wiggled her eyebrows just as Bella jumped onto the wicked girl's shoulders, snuggling in. Cats could be such traitors, and Bella had always liked Gallagher, to Cecile's dismay. "The question I'm dying to know, little Kels, is now that you are champion, what will you do about it?"

Kellyn ignored the question, instead asking one of his own. "How did you get in here?"

The outburst derailed the boys' argument, but Emmett stood seething, his face cardinal red and his hands preparing for a punch.

"I opened the door," Gallagher winked, "Anyway . . . what is your plan?"

"He plans to die," Cecile spat back, "because you've sentenced him to death."

Kellyn swallowed past the lump in his throat. Not even Cecile believed he could live through this—and she was the optimist.

"So defeatist," Gallagher said mockingly. Cecile wound up her arm again for a second punch, but Gallagher held out her hand. "I have such a pretty face—I know you like it, Cealy." Gallagher smirked and stepped forward, catching Cecile, and pulling her into an awkward embrace, managing to hold her temper and especially her arms at bay, their faces inches apart. "There is no need for more violence." Gallagher placed her lips against Cecile's ear. "At least not today. If you wanted to be violent with me some other time, *alone*... I wouldn't mind."

"You killed him." Cecile's voice shook as she tilted her head and forced the other girl to meet her eyes.

"I didn't do anything," Gallagher said.

Cecile's nose flared, but she still didn't fight to escape the embrace. "Theodra won't show."

"Maybe," Gallagher said, her amber eyes twinkling like she knew a big secret. "Theo might show this year." She shrugged. "One never knows."

Cecile growled, "Just leave."

"I'd rather not. I'm having too much fun watching the three of you squirm. Besides, I'm dying to know, Emmett, will you be Cecile's priest or Kellyn's?"

Every champion in the Sacrifice received a priest or a priestess to help them through the games. Anyone could volunteer for the position, and the friends had all vowed that if they entered the Sacrifice, one of the other two would act as their priest.

"What?" Emmett's eyebrows pinched together, and Kellyn's heart sank to the floor as he remembered the telegram Cecile had received earlier. When she read it, she'd paled, and her fingers trembled. It was terrible news—perhaps the worst news.

"No, it can't be," Kellyn whispered. "Not both of us."

Cecile nodded, her face falling as they shared a look of horror. "Yes, me, too. She pulled out the telegram and handed it to Emmett, who hadn't quite caught on yet.

As he read it, his knuckles turned snow white as an ominous chill settled over the group.

Cecile gulped, and visible tremors ran through her body. "Andromache has named me as her champion."

Five

Theodra

Goddess of War

Present

ARS ATROX, SIMARK

Screams were Theodra's anthem. She was the villain of the gods—or at least one of them. A part she played admirably. However, this time, the screams weren't only from the pathetic humans but also from a banshee. The beautiful woman with snow-white skin and blood-streaked cheeks. The omen of impending death.

A creature forged in the courts of War and Death.

"Please, I have children." The wretched man begged at Theo's feet, his hands clawing at her legs. She shuddered. Men were utterly disgusting. "Please, I beg you, their mother is dead, and I'm all they have."

Men were clichéd creatures. Always begging, pleading, bargaining, and blaspheming. All crying useless speeches at the end.

Speeches that would never suffice.

The sky darkened and twisted behind Theo to the march of her wrath, her ravens and cat familiars on the prowl. The familiars were her nine enchanted cat spirits, and much like her ravens, they morphed with magic to sizes, colors, and ferocities of their choosing.

"Perhaps you should've thought about that before," Theo said, her voice as haunted as the shores of the underworld.

Instead of focusing on the man before her, she examined the carved wooden lovespoon between her fingers. It was an offering from one of the mortals of Theoden. The raven ones were her favorite. She received them every week from a loyal devotee. Lovespoons were decorative wooden carvings in the shape of a large spoon given as a romantic gift—symbolizing courtship. Theo never wanted to be courted, but there was just something about the spoons. Typically, she hated offerings, but she was drawn to these. So much so she had a pile of them on her nightstand in her bedroom. Gods didn't need to sleep, but having a bedroom made her feel . . . something.

Connected? Home?

She shrugged. It was always so unclear.

"Please, please, I beg you. I don't want to die."

Theo cocked her head in a birdlike manner . . . *Oh, the human was still here.* She'd fallen into thought again.

Theo slid her lovespoon down her bustled skirt as raven feathers cupped it, forming around it like a pocket—to hold it for safekeeping.

Right now, she had to deliver a punishment.

A vicious smile climbed to her lips, and she snapped her fingers, stealing the man's voice. She was over listening to him. What was there to say? He was a murderer, and his sentence was set in stone—already whispered on the wind and written in the clouds.

The banshee screamed once more and sealed the deal. This man would die for his crimes, and Theo wouldn't be swayed.

From the darkness, Theo braided a rope of shadow, forming it into a sword, and with a flick of her wrist, she sliced it across the man's throat, spilling out his life force.

This was justice.

Blood rained down, pooling in the dirt, and Theo felt nothing. She never did. Staring down at her justice, she wondered if she'd ever feel anything again. Was she forever empty, forever cursed to a life like this?

"Have you no mercy?" A reprimanding voice formed from pure power danced along the streets.

"Not for them," Theo answered her mother.

The darkness parted, and from the setting sunlight spilling over the country of Simark, the Queen of the Gods stepped out. Her presence foretold peace or horror and nothing in between. A goddess with no middle ground.

Nefeli's half-black, half-white hair framed a falsely soft expression. "Would you show mercy if I told you that man's death would cause a chain reaction leading to catastrophic events?"

"Not even you can predict the future, Mother," Theo said, bored and pretending to pick at her fingernails.

Nefeli shook her head. "Where did I go wrong with you?"

Theo bristled. What right did Nefeli—of all the divine—have to question her actions? Nefeli was just as wicked as her daughter, if not more. Nefeli bathed in the Sacrifice—in killing innocent humans for sport. At least Theo killed for justice.

"What do you get from your crusade against men?" Nefeli asked. "What's the goal?"

To feel something. Revenge. "I have no goals."

Nefeli's eyes raked over her daughter, and a frown littered her features, but as usual, her true feelings were buried deep beneath an impenetrable veil. "Are there any good men, in your esteemed opinion?"

"No."

Goodness and men couldn't peacefully coexist.

A silence soaked the air between the goddesses, leaving the aftertaste of traumatic family memories and untamed nightmares.

The women glowered.

The Queen's violet eyes were a tempest of sadness, and Theo's were an echo of brokenness. Yet still, neither shattered the quiet. Instead, they talked with their magic, with the manufactured twirling of the Queen's hair and the dance of Theo's ravens.

"Well, I didn't come here to reprimand you, darling," The Queen's face lit up, and she spoke with an unsettlingly cheery voice. "I wanted to talk to you about the Sacrifice."

"I'm not going."

"Oh, I know, darling, but hear me out." Nefeli snapped her fingers, and time and space lurched together, pulling the two goddesses to The City of the Gods and to the Palace of the Sacrifice—to Nefeli's quarters and office.

Theo stumbled a step as she got her feet underneath her. Whirling around, she glowered at her mother. She hated when any god did that to her—without permission. It was unconscionable. Fury bubbled from Theo's pores, and blades formed from the morphing feathers in her hair. She looked like Medusa, but instead of her hair being formed of snakes, it was composed of black-feathered daggers.

"Calm down," Nefeli said, noticing War's hostile bearing. "I wanted liquid courage for this conversation." She ran a hand through the white half of her hair, exasperated. "Please, sit. It will be fast, I promise."

Theo sucked in a breath and searched for patience. Plucking a blade from her hair, she caressed it as she sat down, appeasing her mother. It was better to get the conversation over with. The last thing she wanted was to get into a battle. It would take far too much energy, and Theo had no interest in wasting her precious fuel.

She ran the feather blade along her lip and froze as her mother said, "I would like you to play in the Sacrifice this year."

"No." Theo didn't bother saying anything else. She'd made her opinions about the Sacrifice abundantly clear. She may have helped her sisters broker the peace treaty, but she had no interest in playing along and killing innocents—especially not innocent women.

Theo only killed the guilty—*men*.

Two thousand years ago, during the Clash of Mortality, humans fought the gods and refused to worship them, causing their power to wane almost entirely. Realizing their dire straits, War, Death, and Light—the Divine Death Triplets—brokered a peace treaty. The gods agreed to reduce their acts of terror if and only if the Nine Great Countries worshiped them properly and sent a champion every four years to the Sacrifice Games.

Nefeli loosed a belabored sigh before crossing the room to her liquor cellarette and filling two glasses with absinthe. She took a sip from one glass and handed the other to Theo, who eyed it with suspicion.

"Do you think I'm going to poison you?" Nefeli asked, grasping the glass in question, and taking a swig from it, her eyes locked on her daughter. "See, it's fine."

Theo took it but still refused to sip, stroking it with her knife tip and causing a loud reverberation—a sound Nefeli loathed.

"It's absinthe," Nefeli said, "your favorite."

Theo had no urge to respond. Instead, she sat silently, waiting for this torture to end. Eventually, it would. It always ended. It was how all her conversations with the gods went.

"As I was saying," Nefeli continued, "I would greatly appreciate it if you joined us for the Sacrifice this year."

Theo sucked in a breath. Her mother was getting repetitive and exhausting, and she was sick of it. How often did she have to tell the other gods she'd never attend the games? Theo changed her mind about the alcohol. She needed it for this, so she took a massive gulp from the absinthe, feeling nothing as usual.

She never felt anything.

Except—

Theo clutched her throat, the glass falling through her fingers. A surge of heat stroked through her body, and the blade feathers of her hair evaporated—fading from existence—leaving only ink-black strands in their place.

"What have you done?" The world swam, and rippling colors invaded War's senses. Pain poured through her head as ichor dripped from her nose.

How could Theo be so foolish? Rule number one, never trust a god.

Never trust a god.

Her mother had poisoned her—her *own mother.*

Theo's blood burned with fury. "What—" she tried to speak but her lips wouldn't move. Her usually steady heart broke tempo and pounded a staccato rhythm in her chest. Terror clawed its way up her throat, and her limbs went completely limp.

The Queen of the Gods cupped her daughter's face and said,

"I'm sorry, but you must learn your lesson. You've broken the rules of the Sacrifice far too many times, and that can no longer go unanswered."

Six

Theodra

Goddess of War

TEMPLE OF THE SACRIFICE, CITY OF THE GODS

A soft stream of sunlight cut through the Temple of the Sacrifice and shined directly into Theo's aching eyes. Ensconced torches lined the walls, the flames dancing to a song of unease. Ivy and mildew snaked up the marble colonnades, shadows stalking the narrow corridors. On an altar burned a bushel of sage and a gnarled tree branch covered in disease and termite tracks.

A frisson of anxiety churned in Theo's stomach. Something was terribly off.

All 639 muscles and 206 bones in her body ached. And gods *didn't ache*. A flash of memory cut through her thoughts.

She'd only ached like this once before.

Theo sucked in a deep, miserable breath and forced the trauma back down into a locked box where it would never resurface again —where it would rot forever in the untouchable parts of her brain.

A blasting steamship horn caused a piercing, throbbing sensation behind her eye sockets. Instinctively, she clasped her ears, sending another jolt of pain through her weak muscles.

Dirty ambrosia. Something was horribly wrong.

Blinking her eyes, trying to adjust to the light, Theo let out a tortured moan.

"Ah, she wakes," a beautiful and enchanting voice floated softly through the room. A softness that caused gooseflesh to rise on Theo's arms.

Theo shuddered. That wasn't a voice she wanted to hear. She tried to lift her head to meet her mother's eyes, but her skull was too heavy, leaving her feeling like a marionette with all its strings cut off.

Theo inhaled sharply, and dread clawed at the nape of her neck.

She was mortal. She was *human.*

The thought sent a visceral tremble through her body. Theo hated this. To be stripped of divinity was the worst imaginable punishment.

Only an ichor spell could affect a god in this way. But Nefeli didn't have Theo's blood. Theo made sure of it. No god or mortal had the power to hurt her . . .

Except Andromache—Goddess of Light. But Andromache wouldn't do this.

Not to Theo.

Andromache wouldn't betray her sister like this. They were too close—inseparable. They were two sides of the same coin. Utterly different but bound by love and an unbreakable bond. Yet fear raged through Theo because if Andromache thought she'd get her human lover Devereaux back from the dead, she would do anything.

She'd become a villain.

"Your wicked ways must end." Nefeli clicked her tongue and swung her heels over the arm of the marble throne.

"My wicked ways?" Theo laughed as if her mother told an overplayed joke.

"You've spent the last 500 years wasting away your divinity." The Queen's violet eyes swirled with rotted spells. "You've broken the Sacrifice treaty by killing humans on a whim."

Theo raised a midnight eyebrow. "I never kill on a whim, Mother." *The men always deserved it.*

"I've had enough of your antics. The Sacrifice hangs by a thread, and you're threatening it," Nefeli said. "If humans stop worshiping us and sending their bravest souls to the games, our power will weaken."

Theo scoffed. "And to be weak is the worst fate imaginable?"

"Do not mock me, girl." Nefeli's voice shook with her tone, the spark that would ignite a wildfire. "You're human and vulnerable. Your pride will be your noose."

"And what is yours?" Theo threw the comment back. Both gods were proud creatures. Pride was in their very nature. "You've come here for a reason—to say something. Perhaps you should get on with it."

Theo shouldn't provoke her mother. Especially not as a mortal, but thunderstorms raged in her blood. *Being a human was vile.* Even the idea made her want to spit at Nefeli's feet.

"If you insist on speeding up our glorious meeting, so be it," Nefeli smirked. "My intentions are simple. You will remain mortal until you can learn to respect the Sacrifice."

"What do you want me to do? Prostrate myself for your sick pleasure?"

"Wouldn't that be a sight?" Nefeli's lips dripped poison. "But I don't want to see you in pain, Theodra. Your villainy needs to be stopped, and you must learn your lesson. So, prostrate yourself if you want, but it won't break your curse."

"Villainy," Theo scoffed.

"You will play the Sacrifice as Theoden's Priestess, and you will finally aid your champion as you should have done for the last 500 years."

Theo clenched her teeth. "I will not."

She wouldn't appease her mother. She wouldn't give in, which meant she absolutely wouldn't aid the Theoden Champion under any circumstances. Ever. Instead, she would spite Nefeli and find a way to break this wretched curse. Theo *would not* bend.

Nefeli chuckled and played with her fingernails. Each stroke a slow taunt. "You may try to undo my spell, but you will fail." Nefeli ran a finger along her throne, her magic twirling around her like a ballerina on pointe. "Learn to respect the Sacrifice, and you will get your divinity back."

With those final words, Nefeli vanished, leaving Theo alone in the cold, bleak temple, defiance coursing through her veins and a small trickle of fear biting her neck.

Mortality was a noose.

Theo smoothed her skirt for comfort and found a lovespoon offering within the pocket. She ran her fingers along the wood, comforting herself.

Theo had only one recourse available to her: no matter what happened next, she would resist her mother's machinations and regain her divinity.

Inhaling sharply, Theo examined her mortal body. Disgusted, she flexed her toes, legs, and arms and scoffed at her dexterity. It was nothing compared to her immortal reflexes. She was slow, weak, and stiff, her human bones brittle and her muscles not nearly as defined.

It was unimaginable.

Her heart sped up and slowed down to the rhythm of her emotions. And her emotions were bombarding her like cannonballs. Ripping and exploding, leaving carnage in their wake.

Theo flexed her fingers and tried to feel magic surging in her veins. But nothing came. Not even a tingle.

She clutched her hair—where her magic ravens hid and slept when not flying around. She frantically felt for her birds. Her friends. Her family. But nothing. Her *poor carrion birds.* They didn't deserve this. To be turned to nothingness.

The only magic she had left was a raven Warmark—on her left wrist. The sentient tattoo stared with one obsidian eye, blinking, and taking her measure. Then it danced, flapping its wings in a comforting pattern before rubbing its beak against her skin, trying to preen—showing affection.

It wasn't one of her usual ravens.

She had seventeen mates and one lone raven. But this one was new.

"Hello, pretty little one," Theo said, running a finger along one of its wings. "What is your name?"

The raven puffed out its feathers and rubbed her with its beak.

"How about Dahlia?" Theo asked, gently petting the bird

again. She got the sense that it was a girl. A precious and elegant one at that. Dahlia seemed a fitting name.

She puffed out its feathers again in agreement.

"Good." Theo smiled and returned her attention to her plight.

Theo touched her neck. Around it was a raven torc necklace with the intricate knots and spirals of the Temple of the Sacrifice interlaced.

A death snare.

It symbolized the priestesses of the Sacrifice—the poor souls forced to aid the champions during the seven days of games. Often, they volunteered for the role, but just as frequently, a poor young soul was forced into the games—as punishment—their prognosis far worse than that of a champion, dying at twice the rate.

Theo looped her fingers around the torc and pulled, trying to loosen it and get the cursed thing off, but instead the torc magically tightened—choking her.

It wasn't until she released her fingers and let go that the necklace stopped tightening. Theo coughed and clutched her throat, the phantom sensation of choking—dying—lingering.

A knot formed in her stomach. Could she die?

Theo didn't intend to find out. She had to get out of this place and off this treacherous island. The only chance of reversing the curse rested in Theoden at the Temple of Sereni. It was where Theo kept all her artifacts, spells, and potions. It was where Hecate's Grimoire was—a magical, sentient book that answered any question. At least if it were in the mood.

A steamship whistle blared as Theo sucked in a breath. She needed to get to the docks and on a ship set for Theoden.

Exiting the temple, Theo entered a cobblestone street, and two steps into her journey, she cursed loudly, a loose pebble digging into her big toe. Theo clutched her foot and let out another low curse. A tiny drop of red blood dripped onto a cobblestone.

Red blood. Not silver ichor.

She let out a string of impressively crafted curses—after all, she'd been working on them for 10,000 years.

The red was a visual symbol of her nightmares.

Her heart rumbled, and her palms grew clammy. She needed to find the docks quickly and escape this damned island. But to do that, she had to traverse the labyrinth of the City of the Gods.

The place radiated enchantment; the entire island a living, breathing trap. Buildings moved of their own accord, and streets twisted and hooked—built to ensnare. The city wasn't built for mortals. It was made for monsters and protected by the gods.

It was composed of nine quarters and designed like a clock. At its center rested a palace formed out of an enchanted volcano.

The docks were on the outskirts of the Queen's Quarter, which was laced with animated statues of monsters like chimeras, kelpies, merrows, and centaurs. Nefeli's favorites.

Wicked little spies.

Ducking behind a pillar, Theo hid from a gilded statue. Statues, mirrors, and paintings talked, stalked, and watched—reporting their findings to the pantheon.

Finally, after thirty minutes, Theo found the marina, and nine titanic steamships docked along the piers. It was the Day of Arrival when the Nine Great Countries brought their champions and spectators to the sacrificial games. It was their last moments of freedom—the last before fate was written in the stars and scorched into stone.

An unwelcome jitter burrowed into Theo's chest as her eyes searched the ships. At the third pier, a blood-red flag with a raven at its center danced in gusts of wind. The symbol of Theoden. Raising her chin, she sucked in a breath and tried to force power into this human body. Trying to awaken magic in her veins.

Nothing.

A raven feather floated in the wind, light glinting off the obsidian vane. It drifted as though it was the petal of a wilting rose. Lost and decaying. Each inch of its descent was a nail in its coffin. Each inch an inescapable distance from its home.

It felt like a metaphor for her life.

Theo ran her fingers through her midnight curls, lamenting the loss of her birds—losing thirty-five pieces of her soul.

Her mouth fell into a solid line. Theo was *not* her magic. She was radiant and terrifying without it. She was War. Destruction.

Sorrow. The devil that haunted peace. A mortal body wouldn't change that.

Nothing would change that.

Her footfalls sparked with a profound arrogance as she walked up the gangway to the ship—to her deliverance. She reached the top of the ramp and stepped onto the boat deck and was greeted by the wheelhouse and crew. A man clad in a tartan sailor uniform obstructed her. "Miss, may I help you?" His accent was a thick brogue.

Theo's lips curved into a jaguar-like grin. Dominance and entitlement oozed from her every nerve ending. "I demand passage to Theoden."

The captain tipped his chin as if amused. "Miss, we don't return to Theoden for another ten days—"

"I don't care." Theo didn't let him finish. His lack of immediate compliance grated at her nape. No one denied a goddess. "You will take me to Theoden *now*."

"Look, miss, I don't know who you think you are, but I don't work for you or answer to you."

Theo rubbed her face—a face nearly identical to the Goddess of Death. But the resemblance wouldn't matter now that she was mortal. Havyn could stand next to her, but a human wouldn't be able to tell. The concept of a god in mortal form was so inconceivable it couldn't translate into a mortal's mind. Nettled, Theo said through her teeth, "Who do you answer to?" Fire licked at the back of her irises. This man. This human was defying her. She lurched forward, unsure of what she was going to do. She wanted to hurt him—to show him what happened to men who got in her way.

But a second stranger stepped into her path before she could deliver on her silent promise. "He answers to me."

The young man towered—an inhuman height—over her, bathed in the morning light and casting a shadow of strength and authority. His long redwood hair was pulled into a messy low bun—almost as if he pulled it together in a rush as he worked. Or perhaps he did it just before a sparring match. One thing was abundantly clear: this young man was a warrior. It was written in how he moved, in the sculpting of muscles, and in the scar bridging his left eye.

He wore only trousers and a white shirt with the top three buttons undone, exposing his dark olive skin, massive sculpted pectoral muscles, and a dusting of reddish-brown hair. The left half of his chest had a partially visible tattoo laced into it. Theo hitched a breath. No waistcoat, no tailcoat, no semblance of *human* decency. Humans were so particular about what clothing was appropriate to wear in the presence of daylight or a lady.

Unbuttoned shirts were hardly de rigueur.

Theo had to tilt up her chin to meet his arresting gaze. His mahogany eyes sparked with amusement and a tinge of magic. There was something about him that, while human, surged with energy, passion, and ancient spells.

He was unspeakable and unknowable.

It was so utterly foreign to her that she couldn't pinpoint what it was.

Her eyes dipped to his chest again, and heat prickled her cheeks. Her eyes flicked lower down . . . she sucked in a deep breath. A mistake. Flicking her gaze back up to his, she made her third mistake. He cocked his head, a glint sparkling in his amber irises. There was nowhere safe for Theo to look.

A flood of heat and unspeakable emotions washed over her body, and something happened to Theodra; a vile sensation stirred in her stomach—like the fluttering of a set of butterfly wings.

She jolted back, physically reacting to the changes in her body—to the poison flooding through her veins. She clutched the railing, feeling the cold metal against her fingers and trying to gain a semblance of control.

Fortifying the scaffolding surrounding her heart, Theo swallowed before saying, "If you are in charge, then I command you to turn this ship around and take me to Theoden."

The edge of his mouth ticked up, and he squared his shoulders, his muscles flexing with the movement. "You command?" He stepped closer, removing the distance between them, and her traitorous heart surged like a tidal wave.

"Yes, I do."

"No." His voice was low and husky, and his response short, simple, and utterly maddening.

A firestorm swelled in her chest. If she still had her immortality, her ravens would've emerged to stalk this man and send fear into the deepest depths of his heart.

A vein in her neck bulged. "Do you know who I am, boy?" she whispered, dark and deadly.

"Boy . . ." he said as if chewing on the word. "No. I don't know *who* you are, but even if you were the Queen of Simak, I wouldn't appease you."

Theo reached for a weapon, patting the skirts of her priestess dress, only feeling the lovespoon. Of course, Theo didn't have weapons; her mother wouldn't dare give her something to strike out with. But her eyes landed on the boy's waist. He had a knife sheath strapped to his belt. It would do.

Theo pounced and kicked out his legs as she pulled the knife from his belt. His back thudded to the deck, and it only took mere seconds for her to straddle his waist and hold the knife to his throat.

"You think yourself so high and mighty, but you're only a weak and decaying mortal." Her pitch dropped and was more frightening than the keening song of a banshee. Yet the boy wasn't scared. His lips drew into a brilliant smile. A smile that could rival the sun goddess. So remarkable in its beauty that even the great Adonis couldn't hold a candle to this young man when he flashed his teeth. He was amused—lying vulnerable on the deck with her knife to his throat *amused* him. She didn't know what to think of that.

His eyebrows pinched together. "You are also a decaying mortal." He raised his head closer, and his neck scraped against the metal, his breath dancing on her throat. "While I do not know who you are, you're no god."

She shivered at the insult, but her legs squeezed his torso tighter, and she pressed the knife down, pricking his skin. A drop of blood emerged, proving that she was serious. "Can you be so certain?"

He chuckled, and with barely any effort at all, he lifted her by the waist and flipped their positions, slamming her back into the wood. In her shock, he wrenched the knife from her weak human fingers and slid it against her throat.

"Yes. I'm certain." The words flicked off his tongue. "I've met a god, and you don't even come close to their radiance."

His audacity was astounding. The gall. He was like all the other cruel men she punished. After all, men were all the same. Vile, rotten creatures. When she got her divinity back, she would make him pay for this.

Theo's chest rose with furious breaths, the knife moving against her skin. Theo stared into his soul, whispering a promise of vengeance. When she was done with this creature, he would be in the depths of the underworld.

War was a villain, and she would be the villain of this foolish boy's story.

"Now, if you would please get off my ship," he said, egotism dripping from his lips. "We have far more important matters to attend to."

Without another word, he pulled the knife away and bounced to his feet and stepped over her, calling orders to the ship's crew.

Picking herself up, Theo seethed. No one talked to her like that. She had flayed men's flesh for lesser offenses. He actually ignored her. *Ignored* her like she wasn't important enough to acknowledge. It nettled more than anything else could. Men cowered, pissed their pants, or ran for their lives.

But they did not ignore her.

Theo glowered, and he glared right back before he nodded, and three massive, uniformed men charged. One tried to grab her arm, but she wriggled out of his reach, uppercutting him in the jaw.

He staggered back, shocked. The other two men shifted their stances and prepared for a fight.

Theo shook her hand, a sharp pain rippling from the blow she landed. But within seconds, the two warriors were on her. She twirled away, but one caught her in the cheek.

Theo cursed, sharp agony spreading through her face.

She sucked in a pained breath and slammed her elbow into the nose of the attacker while simultaneously kicking the third, who'd charged again. He teetered and crashed into the wooden deck. Only one remained standing, but she feigned a punch before she let him get his bearings.

He dodged, positioning himself in the path of her knee. Clutching his jewels, he crumpled to the ground.

All three warriors were successfully felled.

Unfortunately for Theo, seven more noticed the brawl and joined the first three as they slowly got to their feet. Theo was outmatched and oh-so-frustratingly weak.

A metallic taste filled her mouth, and she realized she'd bit down hard on her tongue during the fight.

Blood dripped from both a split lip and her mouth.

Momentarily distracted by her mortality, one warrior struck her core, causing air to rush out of her lungs, and a second man landed a blow to her shoulder.

She clutched her knees, embers of pain ripping through her.

Theodra was one girl—one mortal girl—against ten of the best-trained Theoden warriors. She was the greatest fighter of all time, but without a weapon, with human pain, trapped in a loose dress, and without knowing her body—its strengths, weaknesses—Theo wasn't a match for these men. She was inferior. Pathetic.

The hairs on her arms rose as Dahlia, the raven tattoo, croaked a warning slightly before an eerie light split the dawn. Everyone froze.

A cruel cackle boomed through the docks, magnified by magic.

Theo pinched her eyes, an anchor of dread dropping in her stomach. Her burning breaths grew stilted. There was no need to turn around and see the devil hovering behind her. Her soul recognized her sister merely by proximity.

"Ah, thank you for finding her for me. Gentlemen, I will take it from here." Death's voice was a promise of unrelenting torture.

SEVEN
THEODRA

~~*Goddess of War*~~
~~*Human of War?*~~
Extremely Enraged Ex-god

PORT OF NEFELI, CITY OF THE GODS

An eerie fog drifted around Havyn dancing pirouettes like in the finale of a grand ballet. It cast her in ominous shadows and clung around her like a bride's virginity veil. A *corpse bride's* virginity veil—perfect for Death.

Theo rolled her eyes. Havyn was a preening peacock. The overstated, overindulgent, grandiose narcissist required her every appearance in front of a crowd to be a show.

For all death was a show.

Shadows flaked and rained down her body like rotten tears. She wore an A-line skirt formed from liquid moonstone, and her hair flowed down her back like cascading spilled ink. She was beauty and terror laced into one tapestry.

Theo rolled her shoulders back and held her head high. "Death."

"Priestess." An insidious smile curled on Havyn's lips.

All the muscles in Theo's back tightened. Havyn knew. Which meant the rest of the gods would surely know, too. It was horrible.

Theo's shame was written for all the gods to see. Possibly all the world to see.

It was bad enough being bested by her mother. It was even worse for everyone to know about it.

Theo's honor was threatened, her place among the gods, her power and strength at stake.

"Aye, Death, punish her." A woman called from the docks; her mortal eyes unable to perceive the twins' likeness—even as she stared right at them.

The goddess's eyes flicked to the crowd, noticing their audience. The woman's voice mixed with other spectators, eager to see bloodshed. In the City of the Gods, people were used to seeing gods and even yelling at them. Everything about the Isle of the Gods was different from the Nine Great Counties, including the technology. The city lived in the ancient times, so all the Gilded-Age inventions like steam engines, telephones, and even guns were not permitted. Gods preferred simpler times. Only the steamships were allowed to dock at the ports, and electricity was allowed in the houses.

"Aye, Death, are you going to flay her flesh?"

Theo grunted. A mob loved gruesome executions. It was why they came from all over the world to watch the Sacrifice—for the carnage. Human nature was vile.

Death let out a chuckle. "No, that's more War's style." Her eyes flicked to Theo. "Isn't it, *Priestess?*"

"Something you might want to remember for later."

"Oh, you are entertaining." Havyn's lilac eyes glittered. "Priestess, accompany me on a walk away from these . . . lovely humans."

Theo pondered rejecting the request out of pure spite, but it was in her best interest to settle their issues out of the view of prying eyes.

"As you wish." Theo smiled through her teeth, Dahlia screeching on her wrist in a warning. The bird didn't want to go anywhere with this devil. She was right to be afraid, but there wasn't a better option.

"No one follows us," Havyn commanded the crowd and the Theoden warriors.

Not a single soul dared defy her. Instead, they let the goddesses push through the crowd, the mortals' faces curious but cowering —their eyes focused on the ground as they passed. The goddesses walked silently through a sea of impertinent humans. It wasn't until they were alone in an alley that Theo finally spoke.

"I see you're enjoying this." Every word was toxic, like a petal from a nightshade bloom.

"Immensely." Havyn chuckled. "I love seeing you squirm. It's wonderfully entertaining."

"Sod off."

"Tsk, tsk, tsk, that's not very sporting, especially not considering the trouble you've gotten yourself into." Havyn clicked her tongue. "Human and bruising."

"Have you come simply to gloat?" Theo's jaw ticked, and her back muscles spasmed from the strain.

"Would it shock you if I didn't come to gloat at all?"

A mocking laugh slid from Theo's lips. "Of course, it would."

"You're so disappointing." Havyn clicked her heels and sat back onto a shadow throne in the middle of the alleyway.

"Why have you come?"

"Can't I spend time with my sad little sister?" Havyn asked as the darkness played with her inky curls. "Always so glum. You know, you could use some levity in your miserable existence."

A wisp of shadow patted Theo on the cheek, and she shook it off. "There was a time when you were the sad one."

"True, alas, love ruins our torturous ways." A smile danced on Havyn's cheeks. "Besides, even then, I had a sense of humor." What Death meant to say was that even depressed, she was always an obnoxious peacock that never shut up.

"Why are you here, Havyn? You don't meddle. It's the one thing I like about you."

"I resent that," Havyn's lips twitched, "I meddle sometimes, and believe it or not, I'm here to help."

Theo's brows drew together. "How?"

"By bringing you to where you need to go."

"Why?"

"Do I need a reason? You're my sister, and I love you." Havyn drew her long nails against her shadow chair, almost as if she were sharpening them.

"You're a god. We always need a reason. We do nothing out of charity."

"Hmm," Havyn trilled, her shadows slithering across the bruise forming on Theo's face. "Then you shall pretend I'm here for nefarious reasons. But alas, someone has to clean you up and heal you. You're human, after all."

Theo's eyes narrowed. The one truth she knew to the core of her being: *Never trust Death.*

"Time to get going," Havyn said as her shadows snaked around Theo's throat. They clasped on like a noose and ripped Theo from the alley, pulling her through time and space to a prison cell formed from volcanic rock.

Havyn had refracted them, causing Theo to bend over, and clutch her knees for support, nausea pooling in her stomach. The refracting experience was foul as a human. Her body twitched, and her limbs coursed with foreign energy.

It felt like termites had carved tunnels through her skin.

When she got enough energy to look up, Theo noticed she was in a cell with no windows or doors. The only way in or out was through magic.

Magic which she didn't have.

Theo was trapped.

Reaching into her toga, she clutched the wooden lovespoon for support, running her fingers along its edges. Everything was different and ruined.

"Welcome to the Sacrifice, Priestess from Theoden," Havyn said. "It's going to be immensely fun watching you try not to die as a human."

Eight

Kellyn

Prince of Theoden

VOLCANIC PALACE, CITY OF THE GODS

The day whispered arias of rotting dreams.

Most people entering the City of Gods vibrated with wonder and amazement because the city was alive and glittering with enchantment. For most, it was the opportunity of a lifetime—to meet the gods.

The audience of the Sacrifice gambled, drank in excess, and explored the magic of the holy city. But for the eighteen souls in the Sacrifice, the Day of Arrival only represented dread and the possibility of death. For Kellyn though, it was a certainty. No one —not even himself—believed he would live through the five challenges of the Sacrificial Week. His only hope and goal were to die honorably and help Cecile survive.

If he could take back Decision Day, he would. He didn't want to die, but if he didn't go through with the games, Theoden would be riddled with plague and cursed by the gods. That was the deal. Him or his country. And he would always choose his country.

Kellyn walked through the city with his head held high and the Sacrifice guards at his heels. He wouldn't be dragged to his death. Like the other eight champions, he walked with honor, paraded from the docks to the Volcanic Palace, and guided to the center of the grand ballroom, where he was forced to kneel. A torc was laced around each champion's neck. In Kellyn's case, a raven was carved into the end—the symbol of the Theoden Champion. The magical necklace kept the champions within the palace walls and stuck in the games. If Kellyn tried to escape while wearing it, it would kill him.

Not a fun way to die—nor an honorable one.

Kellyn swallowed past the lump in his throat, and his heart slammed in his chest.

Anticipation plagued the air, and it felt terrible. Not knowing what would happen next was worse than knowing he'd die. The soft murmurs of the crowd stroked the room as he knelt, waiting, the skin of his knees resting on the cold marble floor.

The Sacrifice was unpredictable. No two events were ever alike, and it was impossible to guess how or when the gods would appear to start the games.

They liked keeping everyone on their toes.

Kellyn's eyes nervously flicked to the champions beside him. The Nefesian girl, on his right, was petite with soft features and a powder blue crinoline dress hugging her body. She seemed timid but brilliant. Both features the Queen of the Gods revered in a champion. The goddess preferred intelligent, regal, and reserved people to represent her country.

The Simark lad on Kellyn's left had the expression of a hydra and nasty scars littering his pale face. He seemed fierce and brutal, just like the God of Fire.

Kellyn thanked the stars that the Champions didn't have to fight each other. They were neither his competitors nor allies. Each played their own game against the gods at their own pace. It was entirely possible for the champions never to meet during the games—save for in the common areas.

Kellyn sucked in a breath, sweat dripping from his temple. He pulled his chisel out of his pocket and started carving a lovespoon. Building, carving . . . doing anything with his hands settled him.

The guards searched him before the opening ceremonies for weapons, but it was just for show because no matter what Kellyn did or had, a human couldn't kill an immortal—especially not with a tiny knife. So, he was allowed to bring his carving tools.

As Kellyn carved, his gaze drifted through the grand ballroom, which glowed and crackled from the decor. Waterfalls of lava carved intricate patterns in the walls, forming the shapes of the nine pantheon gods out of glowing fire. It was warm but spelled to not roast human flesh. The floor was constructed from dried lava and mixed with white marble, creating a dichotomy of light and dark—just like Nefeli's half-moon-white, half-raven-black hair.

The atmosphere should've felt calming, like fire on a cold winter's day, but it rankled instead.

Bells struck, ringing throughout the city, and a rainbow of color coursed through the room, creating a twilight mist. The bells mingled with the sound of his anxious intake of breath. His chest burned as if working far too hard, and he swallowed around the knot forming in his throat.

From the mist and twilight, eight gods sprang fully formed, decorated in finery and immortal cruelty. An aura of magic and unmatchable power vibrated around them like leeches clinging to their skin. Kellyn wanted to look away from their glory, but his gaze wouldn't budge. With silent grace, the gods' eyes tracked the mortals as they glided—not walked—to the nine thrones at the head of the room. In even the simplest of movements, it was clear they weren't human.

The throne on Nefeli's right glittered and mocked Kellyn with its emptiness—another year, the Goddess of War refused to join, another year leaving the Theoden champion without a protector. But it was okay. Kellyn knew she had a reason for being gone.

Kellyn swallowed hard; his mouth as dry as the Viridian Desert.

Tension radiated and hovered in the room. No mortal dared to offend the gods inside their palace, so no one knew how to behave.

As Nefeli rose, her tiara sparkled like a diamond in the midnight sky. No, it didn't sparkle. It moved. Upon closer inspection, the tiara was formed from golden bees and animated peacock feathers.

All the gods' garments lived, pulsing with their particular style of unknowable magic. Shadows clung to Havyn's skin like a dress. It was unclear if she wore any garments or if her attire was spun from darkness. Andromache, Goddess of Light's dress, was woven from starlight and would be almost impossible to look upon were it not for an enchantment. As if she wanted to cause pain, but still be seen.

"Greetings, dearest champions. Welcome to the Sacrifice—our deadly game of tricks, magic, and deception." As Nefeli talked, her gaze stopped and rested on each of the nine mortals.

When her eyes hit Kellyn's, a full-body shudder stroked through him. It felt like having his soul excised from his body. Sinew by sinew, bone by bone, the goddess's gaze raked over him—a physical force like he'd been shot by a cannon.

Kellyn played with his tartan cuffs, internally begging for the violet eyes to pass him.

"Please rise and greet your gods with the respect we deserve," Nefeli commanded.

Kellyn shot to his feet, wary of offending the gods. He bowed deeply to each one before standing straight and awaiting his fate like a strong, obedient soldier.

"A Sacrifice cannot occur without a priest to preside over it," Nefeli continued. "As is our time-honored tradition, all nine champions will receive a priest, priestex, or a priestess to aid them through their seven-day journey here. So without further ado, it's time that we introduce you to them."

Nefeli's violet eyes cleaved a path through the room, exposing pools of lava in the floor where nine people emerged—one of which was Emmett.

Kellyn's heart surged at the sight. It turned out that Emmett didn't have to choose between his two friends because Andromache had hand-picked a priest for Cecile. One that would perfectly match and aid her.

So, Emmett could fulfill his vow to Kellyn. They had promised to aid each other and have each other's backs. And if Kellyn would die in the Sacrifice, he felt better knowing that his friend would be by his side. Emmett was still livid about the champion mix-up, and he hadn't spoken one word on the ship over, but *he'd still come.* He'd shown up and vowed to help.

That was true friendship, being there even when it hurt.

"Please, join your champion." Nefeli motioned to the priests.

Kellyn sucked in a breath and held his head high, towering over all the other competitors. He'd never met a mortal taller than him, and probably never would.

His eyes scanned the priests and latched onto Emmett, whose russet skin glowed under the lava light. Kellyn flashed a soft smile at his friend. But the other boy refused to look back and bypassed him completely.

What?

An anchor dropped in Kellyn's heart, and his smile dropped to a flat line as Emmett took place beside Cecile.

Had Andromache chosen Emmett to be Cecile's priest? Or had Emmett asked to be?

Kellyn's fingers trembled, and he squeezed his lovespoon and knife tightly, accidentally nicking his palm. But that didn't hurt compared to the guttural pain swirling in his stomach. He tried not to show it outwardly, but his eyes stung.

He was all alone.

Entirely and utterly abandoned in this.

Kellyn knew Emmett was mad, he knew he had wounded his pride and honor, but Kellyn never expected it would rock their friendship this much.

He gritted his teeth to hold in the pain. *Never show weakness.* But Kellyn wasn't enough. He'd never be enough for his parents, country, for the Sacrifice, and he wasn't even enough for his best mate.

As his priestess approached, his heart sank completely.

It was the arrogant girl from the port. An arrogance far exceeding his own.

As she stepped next to him, Kellyn felt her presence like a physical force. Crooked and toxic. Everything from how she moved to the poison etched into her face said *she didn't want to be here* like she radiated a haunting unease. Nothing about her was normal, both far too stunning and far too broken to be real. But the most disconcerting thing was her expression. It was like battle spirits clung to her skin and murmured curses in her ears, her torment etched into the lines of her pouty lips.

Her hair was twisted into delicate raven curls that tapered around her neck, and the scarlet Theodic styled dress clung to her womanly curves, the sequins and rose petals dripping down her skirt like a river of bloody tears.

The girl was the embodiment of wrath, temptation, and bloodshed.

A true War Priestess.

She glared at the gods, her defiance a visceral, breathing thing. The fiercest aspects of her ire were directed at Nefeli.

A shiver ran along Kellyn's skin, leaving gooseflesh in its wake.

Nefeli clapped her hands to gather attention back to her. "Thank you for generously joining us for our seven-day journey." At the word generous, the priestess snorted and whispered *bullshit* under her breath. "A journey so intoxicating that even the gods can't predict the outcome. At the stroke of midnight, the Sacrifice begins. You will have seven days to complete five challenges. Make it through alive, and you will be given a God-Blessed life. Fail, and you die."

The priestess huffed beside him and whispered dark muffled words. It was hard to pay attention to her and Nefeli simultaneously. But Kellyn had to focus.

"Once you're in the Champions' Quarters, you will find the Room of Mirrors. Each mirror represents one of the nine gods and a possible challenge."

Nefeli snapped her fingers, and an inching, burning sensation coursed through Kellyn's arm. Black spilled over his wrist, and a long riddle etched into his flesh. His eyes fixed on his arm, and he tried to translate the words, but he only got as far as, *Welcome Kellyn to your fate*, before Nefeli began speaking again, and his focus shattered.

"Use this riddle to find your first mirror. But be wary: step into a mirror out of turn, and you will die—forever trapped in its embrace." Nefeli's lips lifted in a devilish smile. "Between each challenge, you must face the Tribunal of Gods, where you will be scored on your performance and given your next clues."

Kellyn's stomach broiled, and his palms clammed up. The Tribunals were used in the past and were no joke. A mortal could live or die on how well they faced the panel of gods.

"Be warned, dear mortals, every moment is a test." Nefeli's voice was a commanding echo. "And trust is deadly at its best."

Nine

KELLYN

Prince of Theoden

CHAMPION'S QUARTERS, CITY OF THE GODS

After the ceremony, Kellyn and the seventeen other souls cursed to be this year's Sacrifice were escorted to the Champions' Quarters and locked inside.

Now, the only means of escape rested in completing the five challenges in seven days, which sounded easy, but some challenges required days to complete. Or some required days to recuperate from.

Kellyn's throat bobbed, and he clutched his carving tools tightly. His eyes scaled the two-story Common Room, fixing on the most striking aspect. The nine floor-to-ceiling hourglasses were carved into the walls like pillars—five on the right side of the room and four on the left. Each color represented a champion—Kellyn's spilled blood-red sand. The hourglasses, one grain at a time, counted every second of the games. When the sand ran out, so would the corresponding champion's life.

Kellyn tensed and ran a thumb over the coarse wood of his unfinished lovespoon. He needed to finish it so he could sacrifice it to the Goddess of War and ask for help in the games. Kellyn was a devoted follower, praying at his altar every morning and offering a lovespoon to her weekly. He didn't want to court War. He wasn't so arrogant to think that he could, but he thought she needed a sign of love. It was instinct, and he'd been doing it since he was sixteen years old. He hoped his devotion would pay off and she would show up for him.

But first, he needed to find Cecile and get to work solving their riddles so that they could find their first mirror and challenge.

He searched the room, his eyes catching first on the passageway to the Hall of Mirrors and then on his priestess. She stood seething on one of the four spiral staircases leading to the nine Champions' private suites.

She marked every statue lining the walls with her gaze like she wanted to devour them. Swallowing and clutching his carving tighter, he diverted his focus because she seemed to be bad news incarnate.

He spotted Cecile, walking across the room. "Cecile," he called and waved her down, moving to intersect her path, but instead of acknowledging him, Cecile marched up to *his* priestess, pulled the raven-haired beauty into a champion's suite, and closed the door behind them.

What in all the pantheon was that?

There was no way Cecile could know the priestess. It didn't make sense.

He rubbed his finger along his carving again before sliding it into his pocket and walking over to Emmett, who sat on a comfortable lounge with four others beside the cozy fireplace.

Before Kellyn could open his mouth, a tall blond with a face of scars said, "These seats are taken." The Simark Champion.

Kellyn's brow furrowed. "Emmett, I was wondering if we could speak about—"

"—No," Emmett said.

The competitors flanking Emmett wore expressions ranging from shock to utter elation. The latter belonged solely to the Simark boy.

Emmett was hurt. His pride and honor meant everything to him, but Kellyn never imagined it might lead to this—lead to total abandonment.

Kellyn's heart beat in his throat, and his lungs tensed. Betrayal and sorrow churned between the two boys, and he didn't know how to fix it.

"You should probably move on and infect someone else with your presence." The Simark boy smiled, immensely pleased with his cruelty.

Kellyn's shoulder blades drew together.

"I don't understand. What is going on," breathed a curvy redhead hailing from Rougeland, her eyes glancing between Kellyn, Emmett, and the Simark lad.

A boy with russet-brown skin and clever eyes leaned over to her and whispered loud enough for the entire room to hear, "He's the Theoden Champion. They are cursed, and whoever aids them in the games will die alongside them."

"So they're all bad luck?" the redhead asked.

Emmett's eyes twitched at this, his lips drawing into a flat line. "Bad luck and a bad friend."

A sharp pain surged through Kellyn's chest, the words hitting like a physical blow. "I shall take my leave." Kellyn bowed respectfully, trying to hold onto his honor and dignity, all the while screaming on the inside. He walked away, posture regal as he headed up the stairs to the Theoden Suite.

He entered a modest chamber. A four-poster bed was draped in blood-red curtains with embroidered ravens, and over the bed hung a sign that read, *Courtesy of the Goddess of Love*. The only other piece of furniture in the room was a wardrobe with raven heads as handles. A mirror hung on the wall, and in the corner was a hearth. Three sculptures stood at attention, their eyes striking and animated—almost as if they were watching. A shiver coursed through Kellyn's legs as he inspected them. The statues slowly moved. One—a peacock—shone blue with the jubilance of the moon. The second, a cat, had midnight black hair which rippled like skipping stones on a lily pond. And the third ruffled its raven wings.

A keen part of Kellyn understood these statues meant something.

They were important.

He didn't know why, but he didn't have the time to unravel that riddle. First, he must focus on the puzzle etched into his arm.

First, he needed to read.

Indeed, a nightmarish task.

After what felt like an eternity of squinting his eyes, clumping letters together, and trying to decipher them, Kellyn finally made out the whole thing ... mostly accurate. It wasn't that he was incapable of reading. Rather it was incredibly hard, and given enough time and less heightened emotions, he could eventually read the words.

Welcome, Kellyn, to your fate
A lesson to learn, and you're the bait
Temptation strikes at apathy's curse
Soon to discover what it's worth.
For this is your first riddle:
I consume shadows
And never speak a word
But you cannot miss my presence, dear lord
I die at night but resurrect in the morning.
What am I?

Well fuck. Kellyn was screwed. He had no help, minimal reading skills, and no idea how to solve the riddle.

TEN
THEODRA
Goddess of War

ROUGELAND SUITE, CITY OF THE GODS

"What are you doing here?" Cecile asked, releasing Theo's arm after pulling her into the Love Champion's rooms.

Cecile showed no fear in the presence of Theo. She was forged from steel, bowing to no one, and taking no prisoners. Theo had spent the last eleven years shaping her Godmarked into the representation of War, and the girl was more than perfect. Smart, strong, and willing to fight for what she wanted. Gone was the timid little girl, and in her place was a true warrior.

Theo greatly respected her. She respected any human who could hold their ground against her—any human with a backbone.

"What are you doing here?" Theo raised a raven-haired brow, the corner of her lips pulling up into a smirk. "Oh right, you're here because my sister has a sick sense of humor." Theo didn't know if Andromache had forced Cecile into the games because she was Theo's servant or for other nefarious purposes. But Andromache always had a reason.

The response flustered Cecile a bit. She stepped back but didn't have time to formulate a response because the bird tattoo on Theo's wrist squawked and wagged its tail feathers—a sign of happiness. Theo's gaze momentarily landed on the creature until a second distinctive squawk came from Cecile's wrist—her War Mark.

The tattoos were talking to each other.

They trusted each other.

It was both surprising and inevitable. Godbonds forced a connection between the marked and the god. It stood to reason that the same would be true for tattoos. The bond was why Cecile *saw* Theo for what she truly was instead of a human who slightly resembled Havyn. The human mind shouldn't have figured it out, but Cecile could.

"You haven't shown up to the Sacrifice in over 500 years. Why are you here now?" Cecile bit her lip. "Is it for me?"

Theo gulped. She hadn't even thought of that as an option, and she didn't know if she would've come if Cecile was in trouble in the games. She probably would have sent Destruction—her second in command of the War Court—because Theo boycotted the games for a reason. She didn't like taking innocent lives, and nine times out of ten, the champions were innocent. Theo preferred killing vile men who deserved it.

"No . . ." Theo started. She didn't want to lie to her Marked, but she also didn't want to hurt her feelings. "It's complicated."

Cecile's raven tattoo squawked, and the girl eyed it before lifting her gaze to Theo. She cocked her head and examined the Goddess-turned-human intensely. "Something is off about you. I feel it, and so does my raven."

"It is."

Cecile squinted. "You're human," she breathed, clutching her mouth in shock, knowing she was correct.

Theo stepped back as if slapped. How did she know? So quickly? The girl had inhuman insight; something that far outreached the gifts of a Marked. "Are you an oracle?"

"No." Cecile blinked. "I just have a feeling. The bond is different, and you look . . . human."

"It's because I am human," Theo said bluntly before telling her Marked everything. Theo didn't trust many people, but once she did, she trusted them with everything. The War Court and Cecile were bound together. They couldn't betray each other, even if they wanted to.

So while the story made her look weak and wounded her pride, Theo knew it was better to put all her cards on the table and trust because if she were going to get out of this situation and get her divinity back, she needed help. To best Nefeli, Theo needed allies.

"So . . . you're fully human?" Cecile asked. "Not just in the games?"

"Yes." Theo's mouth drew into a flat line.

Cecile scrunched her nose in apparent disbelief. "Fully, entirely, completely, absolutely, totally, wholly, unreservedly—"

"Are you just going to name synonyms?"

" . . . human." Cecile finished almost as if she didn't hear Theo's question. "Meaning, if you die in the Sacrifice, you die for good?"

"Yes."

"Oh, holy pookas, this is bad." Cecile bit her lip and sank against the volcanic wall.

Holy pookas? Theo snorted.

"What are you going to do?"

Theo rolled her shoulders back and forced ice into her veins. "I'm going to defy my mother and find a way to get my divinity back, and then I'm going to show her the wrath of War."

"How are you going to do that?"

"I need to get a message to Destruction," Theo said. Destruction had access to all of Theo's spelled objects and books.

Cecile rubbed her skirt, thinking. "Well, you'll have to make it through the first challenge and get to the Tribunal since we're stuck in the Champion's Quarters until then."

"Right." Theo scrunched her face, annoyed. The girl was right, which meant Theo had to participate in the first challenge despite her utter reluctance. But she didn't have to help her champion. If her mother wanted her to play the Sacrifice and respect it, Theo would do precisely the opposite, and since Nefeli wanted Theo to help her champion, she would outright refuse. There was nothing in the rules saying a priestess had to help.

Cecile ran a finger along a wrinkle in her dress, her face trapped between two emotions—emotions too hard to decipher. "I need you to help Kellyn."

The girl had to be talking about her friend—the Theoden Champion. The rude boy from the pier. The odious—far too attractive—boy bursting with arrogance and pride. Just like every other man in existence.

"Who?" Theo asked cavalierly.

Cecile stifled a gasp before trying to compose herself. "Your champion. You need to help him."

"I *need* to?" Theo hissed.

"Yes, *you need to.*" Fire stirred in Cecile's voice, and a smile widened on Theo's face. She liked it when people stood up for themselves. Cecile visibly swallowed and continued in a slightly softer tone, "He'll die if you don't help him."

Theo shrugged. "Vile men deserve to die."

"He's not vile. He's a good man, Theo. One of the best I've ever known."

"There are no good men."

Cecile's forehead wrinkled, and her eyes darkened—literally darkened. "What man hurt you so much to make you think that?"

"How dare you, girl," Theo snapped, her blood turning to ash, a fire consuming her insides. Cecile had no right to say something like that. No right.

"I'm sorry, I shouldn't have said it." Cecile softened. "But please help him. Do it because I care about him." She sucked in a twisted breath. "If you care at all for me or this bond," she held up her wrist with the tattoo, "please, I beg you, keep him alive."

"I cannot."

"What of your divine mercy?" Cecile switched tactics, appealing to Theo's honor.

"My mercy doesn't extend to men."

Cecile shook her head, her eyes clouding with held-back tears. "I trust you with my life, and I respect you." Cecile's voice cracked. "I know how much you've done for me. You've saved my life on multiple occasions, so I'm begging you now, please save my friend."

"He means that much to you?"

"He means everything to me."

Theo angled her head like a raven. The girl truly cared about the boy. Deeply. Enough to beg. Was it love? It meant something, and maybe under any other circumstance, Theo would've complied with her Marked's wishes, but she couldn't. Not now. Not when her honor depended on defiance.

"I cannot aid your friend."

"Why?"

"Because it's what my mother wants."

"You would let someone die to spite your mother?"

"Yes," Theo said, and from Cecile's horrified reaction, she added, "Gods are rarely prone to forgiveness."

Red blossomed on Cecile's face, painting it with deep frustration, and in a voice so low, Theo almost didn't hear it, "Then maybe you deserve this punishment."

The words were a knife wound; if any other human had said it, Theo would've retaliated harshly. But the bond between them forced her to practice patience. Theo understood her servant's frustrations, so she let the harsh words slide off her skin.

"This relationship . . ." Theo said harshly but softened her tone and took Cecile's arm. "The Godmark is reciprocal. You serve me, but I also serve you. I cannot do what you ask of me, but I will do all in my power to help and protect you, and if there comes a moment when you must choose between helping me or saving yourself . . ." Theo lingered on the last word and rubbed the girl's tattoo with her thumb. "Choose yours—"

Theo was distracted as Bella appeared from shadow and jumped onto her lap, purring and snuggling in. Theo's familiars were banned from being with her for the tournament—another wicked gift from her mother, so Bella had to be here for Cecile. "I see she is still with you."

"Yes, ever since the boat." Cecile swallowed, trying to keep the emotion out of her voice.

"Keep her close in your challenges, she will help—"

The sound of cracking lava cut off the word and the wall split in two and flowed orange with volcanic light. Andromache stepped out, forming a dress of lava around her, clinging to her curves.

She was the third triplet and by far the most grandiose. She shared the same face structure as her twins but altered her features so much with light that she looked merely related instead of identical. Her skin was arctic-fox white, as were her eyelashes, eyebrows, and hair. She looked like a La Dame Blanche witch.

Andromache shook out of her hair, embers falling from the snowdrop strands. "Cecile, darling, we must strategize for tomorrow and discuss your first riddle."

"Wait, not so fast," Theo cut in, "we need to talk." The glare she threw at her sister could melt an artic fox.

"I don't see what about." Andromache's lips curved up at the sides.

"You helped mother curse me."

"Oh, that, yes, I did." Unapologetic and cold.

"Why?"

"I will curse anyone and do anything to get him back. You know that."

"Cursing me will not bring Devereaux back."

"Perhaps not, but sometimes it feels good to be a villain." Andromache smiled. "You would know, I learned from you." She turned her back on her sister, stepping in front of her to only talk to Cecile. "Now, I came for a reason. Your riddle, please."

Cecile was startled by the goddess's presence and the sisters' exchange so much, so it seemed like she didn't know where to place her hands. "Yes, of course," she finally responded with not nearly as much confidence as she'd shown towards Theo.

"What is it?" Andromache asked. She wouldn't already know it because it was forbidden for a god to design the games for their own country. Each champion had a different god create their games, and that god developed all the clues leading to the challenges.

Besides playing games against the champions in the Sacrifice, the gods also played against each other. They took pride in their champion being the best and outwitting, outsmarting, and outlasting the rest. Gods placed bets and bargains on how well their champions did. They also tried to trick other champions into deadly mistakes and bargains which would hinder their games.

It was the game within the games.

Cecile sucked in a breath and read from the new tattoo inked into her arm. "*Welcome, Cecile, three knots connected to your life be bound. A Vow, a Conductor, and a Crown. To survive and find divinity's blessing, seek the truth so gravely pressing.*"

Andromache's eyes twitched ever oh so slightly at the words. Her telltale sign she was rattled.

Interesting.

Theo stroked through the riddle in her head. *A Vow, a Conductor, and a Crown.* It pointed to three people. But who?

"For your first challenge," Cecile continued reading. "Find the mirror that coils and proclaims the scales of justice. Formed from any color of the rainbow, it rattles with deadly delight. But don't be mistaken, for Poison bites, and Death will soon follow."

Andromache raised her brows, knowing the answer, but she couldn't directly say it, for it was against the rules for a god to solve the riddles. However, they could point their champion in the correct direction.

Theo had no such restrictions, so she said, "A snake."

Cecile ran a finger over her tattoo. "Yes, it must be a snake, but which mirror is that? It could be any of you." She waved at Theo and then Light.

"And, of course, Death," Theo said. The triplets all had snakes as their symbols, and the three of them together were symbolized by three interlocking serpents.

"War, your presence isn't needed," Andromache said, "I will take it from here." Which was code for she wanted to say something she didn't want her sister to hear.

"No, you're not needed here, Light," The Goddess of Love said, twisting out of the pink curtains surrounding the heart-shaped bed. "These are my champion's rooms, and I would very much like to talk with Theodra alone."

She snapped her fingers, and pink ribbons formed from god magic hauled both Andromache and her champion from the room. Bella disappeared from Theo's lap in a puff of smoke as if she weren't allowed to stay without Cecile around.

"She's going to get back at you for that," Theo said, rubbing her face and not looking forward to this conversation.

Love and War were old friends, but Love would enjoy seeing Theo this vulnerable far too much.

"I count on it." Love's dark olive skin glistened with mirth. Theo didn't understand. "So you're human."

"So it would seem."

"How delightful!" Love said, "I have so many fun things in store for you this week."

"I'm sure you do, Rougoine." Theo sighed, her eyes flicking to the door, already over this exchange.

"Isn't your champion quite handsome? Almost the perfect man for you. Tall, silent, and serious." Love wiggled her eyebrows. "And I'm sure he would be quite fun in the—"

"Please do not finish that sentence." Theo held up a hand. "What will it take for you to leave me alone?"

"What are you willing to give?"

"I would do quite a lot," Theo said flippantly.

"I would be *bound* to leave under the right circumstances," Love said, "would that suffice?"

"Yes, just do what you came for," Theo said, "say what you need to and leave me in peace."

Love's olive face lit up with a brilliant smile. The type of smile that would launch a thousand ships into battle. "Tsk, tsk, you shouldn't have said that. You're human now and can easily be bound to bargains." Love wiggled her nose and clasped a hand around Theo's wrist. "Oh, this is going to be wondrously fun."

Theo's skin burned at the touch, and a phantom sensation wrapped its talon around her wrist, clutching it and not letting go. A magic chain appeared.

Love had tricked her . . . and it was far too easy. Theo knew better. She knew the gods were tricksters, yet she easily fell into Love's trap. Theo's heart pounded like a bat caught in a cage. "What did you do?"

"I've bound you until you've completed my spell's purpose." With those horrifying words, Love disappeared into a puff of glitter-filled smoke.

"Bound me to what?" Theo yelled after her.

She soon found out because the magic chain tugged her out of the room, forcing her feet to a destination, not of her choosing. It felt like an invisible cord, pulling her like a dog on a leash, going where its owner wanted. And that was to the Theoden Suite.

The magic wanted her near the Theoden Champion.

Well fuck.

Eleven

Kellyn

Prince of Theoden

THEODEN SUITE, CITY OF THE GODS

"Great Goddess, I ask you to lend me strength and fortitude for all the challenges ahead." Kellyn knelt at the hearth in prayer, his fingers whittling away at his lovespoon. He didn't have an altar for worship, so instead he used the flames.

A thud sounded from behind him, ripping him from prayer. Kellyn whipped his head around to see who or what was causing the disturbance.

It was his priestess, and she let out a long and impressive string of curses aimed at the Goddess of Love. "Why?" She glared, and he had no idea if the question was for him or Love. So he sewed his lips shut.

A thick, stilted silence pulsed through the room, clinging to his body like burning tar. Kellyn didn't know what to do or say, so he watched, wordless, with his hands curling into his carving. The wood bit into his palms and helped ground him during the awkward moment.

The priestess rubbed her wrist and glowered. She embodied a bewitching battle, and he hoped her ire wouldn't be directed his way. For battle, even if beautiful, was still a battle.

She stalked to the bed and sat down fiercely—as if she wanted to murder either the bed or Kellyn. Then her glower turned on him.

Perfect.

"You're praying?" she asked.

"I was."

"What's the wood?"

"A lovespoon tribute to the Goddess of War."

Her eyes widened a fraction and traced the spoon like the chalk outline of a dead body at a crime scene. "Hmm . . ." She tapped her pocket and repeated, "Hmm."

Kellyn waited for her to add more, but she never did. "I don't think we've been properly introduced. I'm Kellyn Ellis."

She flipped a midnight curl and pretended not to hear him. But from the slight twitch of her lips, she clearly had. The girl didn't need to speak because she screamed her opinion with her body language, every muscle taut, and her head held high like a god sitting on a throne. A deep, dark disdain swam in her irises, simmering with annoyance—like Kellyn was a gnat that needed to be squashed. He was a peasant not worthy of her attention.

The room smelled of incense and firewood, which should have felt calming, but in her presence, they were signals for alarm.

Kellyn grunted and placed the carving in his pocket, rocking back on his heels, not knowing what else to do. He was a man of few words, and he had even fewer for this situation.

An awkward tension licked the space between them.

The priestess's gaze caught on the peacock statue, and her already frigid features crumbled to dark sooty ash. Without warning, she sprang up from the bed, charged at the peacock, and kicked it hard onto its side, toppling it to the ground.

Shock spiked in his blood as the crash sound reverberated like a thunderclap. Shards of marble clinked against the redwood floor, a dust cloud exploding outward, coating the room with sharp edges.

"What are you doing?" Kellyn asked, standing up quickly and putting distance between them. The girl was an unoiled hinge. No, she was unhinged.

"Spies." Her voice was a dark promise, but she didn't glance in his direction.

Kellyn let out a long-suffering sigh. Utterly confused and exhausted with everything. This would be a torturous week—for however long he survived.

The priestess bent down and picked up the fractured head of the peacock. She rotated it between her fingers. "You're going to have to try harder than that." A wicked smile painted on her ruby lips, and a vicious glint lit her eyes as she threw the fragmented head against the floor, fully destroying it.

Kellyn itched his scalp; this girl was visceral—living anger. His heart drummed in his ears, and he sat on the bed.

She angled her head like a snake, examining its prey at the other two statues—the raven and the cat. "You're loyal to the House of War?"

Kellyn rubbed his face, utterly confused and a bit horrified.

The cat statue inclined its head, rocks popping with its movement, and the raven statue said, "Yes, we are loyal to War." Its voice was a hollow, guttural croak that sent shivers down Kellyn's spine. Gods magic. He shouldn't have been surprised because he was in their city, and it lived and breathed their power. Yet he still was because it was so utterly different from Theoden.

"Will you promise not to report or record anything unless I command it?" She narrowed her eyes as if she were looking into the cat's soul and judging if it was worthy. The stone crackled with its movement as it bowed its head again. The girl nodded as if appeased, her stare cutting through the raven like a sharpened blade. "And you?"

The raven statue ruffled its wings. "I'm always loyal to War."

"Excellent." She carefully stepped over the shattered pieces and went to the bedside table. Methodically, she removed the pins in her hair one by one, and black curls fell down her back like waves of spun midnight.

Kellyn gulped, fixated. In Theoden, it wasn't proper for a lady to wear her hair down. It must always be properly pinned in place. This would be scandalous under most circumstances. Kellyn wasn't proper per se, he had bedded more than his fair share of ladies, but he wasn't used to watching a woman undo her hair so slowly and so seductively—usually, he loosed it for them in the heat of passion right before he fucked them. He hadn't known how much not touching someone could be so . . . enticing. The sight was utter torture because he couldn't do anything about it. Several improper sensations passed through his body and shifted uncomfortably, his mind latching onto a forbidden—and foolish—desire. He wanted to run his fingers through her silky strands and kiss along her dainty neck. What would her flesh feel like against his coarse, calloused hands?

He wanted to silence her rage with a good fuck, but that was foolishness. Fucking his priestess could only lead to terrible consequences—not to mention he was pretty sure she would devour him as a praying mantis did to its lovers. She was the deadly one here.

Kellyn cleared his throat and shook out his hands. He needed to get a hold of himself.

Remembering his place as a gentleman, Kellyn coughed, stood up, averted his gaze, and shifted his legs again. He stared at the mess on the floor, trying to get his thoughts off the priestess, who was far too alluring for her good.

Her eyes flicked to him, and she said, "They're spies. They report back to the gods; some even act as two-way mirrors, allowing the gods to see into private moments and rooms. They also record the games and display them worldwide on magical mirrors like that one there." She pointed to the mirror on the wall.

He knew about the mirrors, having watched the games in Theoden as a boy, but he never knew how the gods received the images.

"If you would turn around, I would like to change."

Kellyn pivoted, facing the wall, trying not to think about what she was doing. He added equations in his head and pulled his chisel and wood from his pocket. With the blade's tip, he formed Theodic knots into the lovespoon. The design formed a shield knot with endless loops representing eternal love, loyalty, and protection from battle. It was one of the Goddess of War's symbols and one of the major symbols in Theoden.

Kellyn was drawn to forming Theodic knots because the image embodied an unbreakable bond, and there was nothing more important to him than loyalty. Once his loyalty was solidified, he'd do everything to protect the bond—it would never break . . . never shatter.

Which was why the fracture in his friendship with Emmett was so painful.

"You can turn around now," the woman said. She wore a light pink—nearly sheer—cotton nightgown. Lace hemmed the sleeves and the train. Her face was framed with loose, bouncing raven curls, and she looked almost sweet, but cruelty still lingered in her bones. There was a hardness in the lines of her cheeks and the set of her jaw.

"What's your name?" Kellyn asked softly, not wanting to scare her off. He needed something to call her by. She couldn't just be a priestess.

She cocked her head, and a storm of thoughts crossed her sapphire eyes—like a silent picture show. But none of the emotions were distinguishable to him. After a long while, she finally said, "Morrigan."

"Morrigan," he repeated, playing with the sound on his tongue. "Nice to officially meet you."

She nodded, eying him as she pulled the covers and slid into the bed. She rolled over on her side, her back to him.

Kellyn gawked at the bed for a moment, unsure what to do. "Shouldn't we try to solve the riddle and start the first task? Most of the others will have already started."

She rolled over and tugged the covers even higher. "It is foolish to face the gods unrested."

Kellyn simply stood, watching. He had no answers. He ran a finger over his riddle again, hoping that doing so would help him with it.

It was useless, and Morrigan was right. Rest would do him good.

But he couldn't join her in the bed. It just wasn't done. It was a terrible idea, especially considering the lust he felt coursing through his veins when he looked at her.

Kellyn grunted.

Morrigan huffed. "Join me already. I promise not to bite."

Kellyn froze. He absolutely couldn't. It was indecent. Ungentlemanly. His heart raged in his chest like a hummingbird in a cage.

"Then sleep on the floor," she said with a hiss. "I don't care."

He swallowed.

He'd sleep in the common room. Except as he opened the door and tried to walk through, his wrist burned, and an invisible chain shimmered in the air—solidifying momentarily. He tracked its length and saw the other end circled Morrigan's wrist.

God magic.

An invisible chain bound them together.

This was new. He'd never seen it happen in any Sacrifice before.

Which meant leaving was not an option. If he wanted to rest, he'd have to join her in the bed because she ruined the floor. Kellyn took three tentative steps and removed his House Ellis tartan vest before placing it on a bedside table.

He rolled up his cuffs, memorizing the layout of the room and the hazardous floor. Slowly, he extinguished the sconces and covered the room in pitch black. Making his way to the bed, he froze again.

I consume shadows.

Kellyn carefully made his way back to the sconces.

I die at night but resurrect in the morning.

He sucked in a breath and flicked the electrical switch.

Light.

Light consumed shadows and died at night.

"Light."

"Yes, that's how electricity works," Morrigan mumbled, throwing a pillow over her head.

He'd solved it. All on his own. Perhaps Theodra *was* watching after him because his prayer had come true!

With excitement running through his veins, Kellyn switched the light off again and went to bed, sliding under the covers and curling up on his side. The excitement soon faded as he realized his predicament. Morrigan was the type of girl he might end up with beneath the sheets in a different scenario. Strong, feisty, and curvy. But he had to remember that love and lust were off the table.

He was a dead man walking.

Kellyn stared into the darkness, listening for Morrigan's even breaths. But they didn't come.

She was awake, too.

They both were examining shadows and their anxiety.

Tension coated the space between them and filled his thoughts with agony. Kellyn inhaled sharply and held his breath, his heart racing and knocking into his ribcage.

The girl was unpredictable, untenable, and utterly tempting.

It was the last bit that would kill him.

Twelve

Kellyn

Prince of Theoden

THEODEN SUITE, CITY OF THE GODS

In Kellyn's dream, his fingers stroked down the spine of a beautiful woman who'd fallen asleep on his chest. Lazily, he ran his fingers up her neck and into her hair. The woman groaned, and the dream rotted.

It wasn't a moan of pleasure. It was the sound caused by the trauma of waking up in the morning.

Kellyn stilled, and he held his breath. Silently cursing, he pinched his eyes shut. All his muscles tensed, and his heart pounded in his ears.

His dream *was* his priestess. She'd rolled over during the night and curled into his side. The feeling was at once comforting and anxiety-inducing. It felt right and horribly wrong all at once.

He squinted slightly and considered his options. He had no idea how to move without waking her up. But thankfully, he didn't have to solve the problem because she woke up, flinched, and jumped out of the bed as if bitten by a spider.

She glowered, and he grunted. It was becoming their pattern—the way they communicated with each other.

And at this moment, there was nothing to say.

Quickly, they dressed in silence, neither willing to mention the cuddling incident.

"Are you ready?" he asked, pulling up a boot.

Her sapphire eyes flicked to him. "For what?"

"The first challenge," he said, "it's Light's." He held up his arm, gesturing to the riddle.

Morrigan crossed her arms and leaned against the wall, her eyes swirling like a deadly ocean storm. Indecipherable thoughts flickered across her face, and a twinkle of purple swirled in that storm. It seemed as if she were deciding something, and she settled on, "Yes, let's go to the first challenge," but she said it through her teeth.

"Great." He cleared his throat. "But first, I need to check in with Cecile."

Without waiting for a response, he walked toward Cecile's room—he vowed he would help her—but his eyes caught on the massive magic mirrors on the upper floor of the Common Room. They were playing live broadcasts and replays of the challenges, and Cecile was already playing her first one.

She'd left him.

They played their own games and had different challenges and schedules—although they could face the same challenges at the same time . . . technically—but it still hurt that Cecile hadn't even tried to strategize with him at all. Kellyn's stomach twisted, and his heart leaped into his throat. Emmett's attitude and betrayal were one thing, but Cecile . . .

. . . this broke him.

"You look like you swallowed a jellyfish," Morrigan said as she marched up to him, rubbing her wrist and cursing.

"Are you hurt?" he asked, ignoring the comment.

"It's the chain." She lifted her wrist, showing him the raw skin beneath a flickering chain. One moment it was invisible, the next it appeared solid, connecting the two.

"It likes to play with how much leash it gives us," she growled. "Shall we head to the mirror then?" Morrigan nodded to the broadcast depicting Cecile's task. She was in a shadow maze, being confronted by memories. "Clearly, she's busy."

Kellyn grunted but led the way down the stairs to the Hallway of Mirrors.

The gods certainly liked to use mirrors as a conduit for their magic. Broadcasts, portals, communication devices. Anything they wanted really.

The Hallway of Mirrors was formed from a dome and colonnades with nine massive floor-to-ceiling mirrors held against the flowing lava. That alone would've made the room impressive, but the looking glasses themselves stopped hearts and claimed souls. Silver light coated the room, emanating from each of the nine massive portals, and the floor vibrated like the body of a strummed guitar. The place sang. Songs of sorcery and heartache. Songs of mystery and trickery. Songs of death and promise.

Each mirror had a unique appearance from the frame to the image depicted in it. One was a wheat field with braided ivy forming the frame—belonging to the God of Harvest. Another frame was constructed from wine goblets and grapes, depicting revelry. Havyn's mirror was formed from snakes circling skulls and pomegranate fruits.

Morrigan winced as her eyes caught on War's mirror. Blood dripped down its frame. Depicted on its swirling silver surface was a pile of decaying bodies—a mass grave from a battle.

Andromache's mirror was framed with braided starlight and planetary rings. Its surface didn't show an image. Instead, it rippled with glowing gold light.

Kellyn gulped. It was the one he needed to enter.

He sucked in a breath. The statues lining the room filmed him and played it back for the world to see. He needed to look brave. He needed to die with honor. So he reached out a hand to graze the mirror.

It felt so cold it burned, and he slowly pulled his hand away, holding a breath and stifling his pain and emotions. Sweat dripped down his back, his body not responding to his cues. Fear gripped tightly to his throat and burned.

Closing his eyes, he whispered a prayer to Theodra and plunged into the glass. Holding his breath, the texture cascaded over him—a mixture of heat and silk. It burned, but once his whole body was consumed, it felt like a warm hug instead of guttural pain. It felt like a fetus in the womb. Kellyn couldn't figure out if it calmed his nerves or made the experience more terrifying.

Perhaps it was prophetic that it felt like a womb since Andromache was the light of life—she was the goddess of birth, among other things. All the sisters were both life and death gods. Balances to each other. Andromache was the light of life, Theodra the strife of life and Havyn the end of life.

Stepping out of the barrier, Kellyn fell to his knees in a magical field of silver grass, Morrigan stumbling beside him, and the portal disappeared—trapping them.

Towering at the other end of the field was a building made from river stones, fairy dust, and lizard skins. A wall of sparkling blue and cadmium green rose, dancing against the sky, and glowing yellow orbs drifted in and out of the rocks like fireflies twirling in a cancan dance. Cut into the stones were words, touched by twisting shadows—whisking letters in an unknown language.

They lingered, haunting yet alluring, whispering sinister invitations, and humming shattered love songs.

"What is it?" Kellyn asked, not thinking Morrigan would have an answer.

A muscle ticked in her jaw. "It's the Droma Labyrinth." She gulped. "The Great Lost Library."

"Oh, *shit* . . ." he said, a knot forming in his stomach. "That's not good."

The Droma Labyrinth was a legendary Athenaeum of stolen spirits. A deadly labyrinth of secrets, forbidden magic, and books spelled and protected by monsters and Andromache herself. It was said the place devoured souls.

Kellyn grunted. He had no words, not when anxiety stroked his throat, the vein in his forehead pulsing. A library filled with books and traps perfectly designed to thwart him.

The gods had to know his greatest weakness. Otherwise, why force him into a library?

Kellyn inhaled sharply. He didn't know what the objective of this challenge was, but he knew deep in his bones the only way through was to enter the library.

Death before dishonor. His mantra. "Shall we go?"

"If we must."

"Any advice?" he asked, marching ahead.

Morrigan loosed a sigh. "The three rules of the Athenaeum: eat nothing, never make a deal with an immortal, and never under any circumstance trust a nymph."

Kellyn cleared his throat and let out a low grunt, which sounded like more of a growl. He twisted the doorknob formed from minotaur horns and stepped into the keep. It hummed with electric energy; the walls alive with enchantments. The place was ready to swallow him whole.

But he was ready to fight.

The inside smelled like a forest after morning rain: wet soil, tree oils, and fresh flowers.

The library opened to a grand entrance hall with trees smacking against walls and bookshelves. A grand staircase made from tree bark spiraled and led up to several open floors, the trees growing with it. Hedges grew along the halls and forest animals lurked amongst the tomes.

Shadows twisted through the bookshelves and latched onto anything moving, including Kellyn. As he purposefully placed his footfalls, they clung to his boots like gum. The hedges twisted and followed him as if the leaves had eyes. The place took his measure, finding him wanting.

Having no way to ground himself, he stood, unsure of what to do. It was a library with thousands, possibly millions of books.

He shuddered.

It was his worst nightmare.

Books. His nemesis.

Kellyn rubbed his left pectoral muscle for comfort where his house sigil tattoo was etched into his tawny skin. Maybe he could take strength from his ancestors.

"What do we do?" he asked, his skin draining of color.

Morrigan's eyes were now amethyst voids—switching between blue and purple . . . it was strange but not unheard of for a person to have color-shifting eyes. There were so many magical creatures in the world that some humans were bound to come from magic bloodlines. But Morrigan's color-shifting eyes were devoid of any readable emotion. Hollow and haunted. But her eyebrow arched as her gaze caught words cut by liquid darkness. Signs.

Signs written in a language so beautiful it was unknowable.

"This way," she said, pulling him by the invisible chain between them.

She'd *read* the words. It seemed impossible. "What language is that?" he asked.

"Gods."

"You read the language of the gods?" His voice spiked with surprise.

Morrigan shrugged and pulled him by the chain once more. "Yes," she said as if it were the most insignificant information in the world. Was she magic? If so, why would she be here? Witches, vampires, and other long-lived mortals weren't forced into the Sacrifice.

Kellyn's fingernails bit his palms as he followed his priestess up a flight of stairs and down a hallway littered with autumn leaves and rust-orange books.

Morrigan slammed to a halt, and Kellyn stumbled out of his thoughts.

Straight ahead of them, were three pathways coated in books and greenery. But this time, there was no sign to tell the way.

Instead, there were monsters.

"Hello, kind stranger—" a slithering yet lilting voice whispered on the wind but was cut off by a harsh and grinding tone that added, "And Agony in human flesh."

From the midnight blue yew tracing, the bookshelves clawed a beautiful woman formed from moss and trees, trailed by a hunched-back man chiseled from stone. He looked as if he had the weight of a mountain on his back, rocks clinging to his body.

Nymphs.

Earth Nymphs.

They smelled of fresh soil, wet rocks, and pinecones laced with decaying mushrooms.

"The path to your salvation is on your left," said the pretty nymph with a chirp and a singsong voice.

"Or is it on the right?" the rock man asked, his pebble eyebrow lifting with ghoulish delight.

A wind nymph burst to life beside Kellyn's ear and whispered, "Straight forward is the object you seek."

All three creatures blocked the path, chaos dripping from their tongues.

"I suggest you tell me the way!" Morrigan seethed.

The wind nymph shook her moth wings, spraying water on them. "Tsk, tsk, naughty little human. That isn't how you obtain the correct answer."

"Isn't it?" Murder lurked in Morrigan's eyes, and a vicious smile painted her lips. "What if I curled my fingers around your neck? It wouldn't get me the correct answer, but it would feel satisfying."

Kellyn's heart skittered. He believed her threat. He wouldn't put it past her to murder him, given the proper opportunity.

"Tell me where the book is," Morrigan said through her teeth.

Book?

Did she know the challenge?

There weren't any other options that made sense. Had Theodra strategized with her as all the other gods did with their champions? She was her priestess, after all.

When the nymphs refused to answer, Morrigan took matters into her own hands. With one fluid motion, she reached her hands up, placed one hand on either side of the lady earth nymph's head, and snapped her neck, the movement jerking Kellyn forward because of the chain connecting them.

His mouth dropped with shock, but he said nothing—words swallowed by his nerves and horror. Wind sprites refracted into the air beside him and licked up his emotions.

The girl killed an immortal. She was a devil. Cruel and wicked.

I'm going to die . . . quickly.

Kellyn drew a step back, and his heart hammered in his ears.

The gall of this priestess to openly defy these beings.

Kellyn wanted to shrink back into a bookshelf and disappear. Humans had gotten their entire families slaughtered for less.

Every muscle in his body tensed, and he prepared for an attack.

Which didn't come.

Instead, the nymph formed from rocks pointed down the left hallway and backed up in fear, rolling like a boulder back into the piles of tomes.

An irritated and fearful silence descended between Kellyn and Morrigan. It carried the sensation of lice clinging to his hair.

"Don't look so horrified," Morrigan said, crossing her arms. "Monsters resurrect in the games. It's the deal they made with the gods."

Kellyn gulped. That didn't make it better.

As they traversed the hallway, a mixture of emotions settled in his core.

His stomach flipped. Morrigan knew so much about the games. She knew exactly where she was going and what she was doing, marching through the labyrinthian library easily knowing her way like she'd been there many times. And maybe she had, because she was the War Priestess with a Godmark etched into her skin. A mark giving her access to monsters, inhuman senses, magic, and the gods.

It was disconcerting yet also relieving.

Perhaps with her help, Kellyn might stand a fighting chance in the games.

Maybe he wasn't on his own.

Unfortunately, his newfound hope was short-lived. Turning a corner, Kellyn was struck with the force of a thousand hisses.

Snakes.

Instinctively, his eyes found the source of the sound.

A deadly mistake.

"No, don't—" Morrigan's call was sucked out of the air as she realized the futility of her warning.

Because Kellyn's eyes were already locked onto Medusa's.

Well, seventy thousand fucks.

Stone climbed up his legs. The cracking and popping sound crushed his eardrums with the weight of his fear. His heart strummed like a screeching violin—playing off-key and out of sync —and his muscles tightened.

The stone clawed up his chest, climbing the rungs of his ribs and encasing him in fractured nightmares.

Kellyn gasped a final breath as the stone slid over his neck, chin, cheeks, and eyes, swallowing him whole.

His last and horrible thought was *this is not an honorable death.*

Thirteen
Theodra
Goddess of War

LIGHT'S MIRROR

"Medusa." The word slipped from her tongue like a witch's curse.

This wasn't how Theo planned on sabotaging her champion—it wasn't sabotage if she didn't help him at all. Was it? It was apathy. Theo didn't want the boy to die necessarily; she simply refused to aid him. Simply refused to fall into her mother's machinations.

Theo sighed, making sure not to look into Medusa's eyes. Instead, she scrutinized her champion's limestone form. She didn't bother to remember his name, instead referring to him only as "champion", "foolish mortal", or "boy"—despite knowing he was very much a young man.

But the boy was a beautiful statue. His towering stature and defined muscles made him look like a god or an ancient hero. Even his scarred face shimmered, frozen under the rock.

Theo smiled. Rock was the perfect form for men. They couldn't talk back or commit egregious acts.

Reaching up, she ran a finger along the scar on his brow.

How did you get this?

Without her powers, there was no way of knowing. There was

a beauty in the unknowing, though. If she wanted the answer, she'd have to discover it for herself.

She'd have to work for it.

Theo let her fingers slide down the mortal's face. A pool of emotion stirred in her stomach. She almost felt sorry for the boy. But alas, this was what happened when fools encountered gods and monsters.

A sharp pain radiated through Theo's wrist, and she looked down. The invisible chain glowed before solidifying as it tightened.

Wicked Love, Theo swore.

She had tasted freedom and revenge on her tongue just seconds before. Theo was in the Lost Library of Droma, a place filled with every book imaginable, including witch's spell books. She'd been moments from finding the Room of Witchcraft and the book that would restore her pride, honor, and divinity.

The reckless champion ruined it all. The foolish mortal *had* to look upon Medusa's face.

And now, as Theo examined the stone boy, a battle raged inside between her desire for revenge on her mother and the urge to join him. Theo longed to destroy her endless echo—to find peace. To die.

It was her nature to waffle between depression and action. Sometimes she was overcome by the need to die, her thoughts becoming parasites in her mind, latching on and not letting go, even when she desperately wanted to make them stop.

How did one stop thoughts, save replacing them with new ones?

How did one ever have hope in a life of emptiness?

Theo was too exhausted.

She wanted peace and *could* get it by catching Medusa's gaze. She could find freedom at last.

Spending forever as a stone might be a better fate than repeating a hollow life over and over and over again.

What did she have to live for, anyway?

She had no joy, love, or hope. She'd lived 10,000 years without connection or happiness. The only time she'd let herself love, let herself be vulnerable, she was betrayed.

She was already stone inside. Why not finish it?

With a sharp inhale, she lifted her eyes, and they clasped onto the gorgon. Theo braced for the impact of flesh molding into stone, but it never came. She counted to ten, but it still never came. Glancing down at her feet, she shifted and willed them to stone, but nothing happened.

Utterly disappointing.

Theo slowly let out an irritated sigh.

She longed for the sweet embrace of oblivion. To be cast in stone and never resurrected. It would've been a soft and sweet sorrow—a cruel yet gentle end. But that wouldn't go her way, like all the other unfortunate occurrences lately.

She shouldn't be surprised. Theodra never got what she wanted. Especially death.

Of course, Medusa's curse didn't work.

"*Dirty gods,*" Theo swore under her breath.

"Theodra," Medusa hissed, her snake hair rattling.

The monster and the immortal-made human stared at each other as if across a vast cavernous pit.

Examining and measuring.

But Medusa didn't have only two eyes, she had dozens—each snake fixed onto Theo with hunger vibrating through them. They wanted to devour her . . . and so did their mistress.

Except . . . she didn't.

The Queen of Snakes merely glowered, yet what lurked beneath her gaze sent shivers down Theo's spine.

A universe of despair.

Misery hummed on the scales of the snakes and in the eyes of their mistress. Medusa was a 9,000-year-old ghost ready to be freed—released to the afterlife—but instead was cursed to walk an eternity among humans, never to live with them. Always on the sidelines of life, desperately seeking a connection she'd never find.

It was like looking into a mirror—a mirror of sorrow. All of Theo's brokenness was reflected through the hisses of despair.

Theo's heart shuddered as a realization hit. She might have made another mistake.

Mistakes.

That was all she did lately. First, the girls on the boat, then the accidental deal with Love, and now this . . .

Hot coals burned in her throat, and she tried to bury the guilt deep down within her chest. But it wouldn't budge.

Theo had spelled Medusa to save her—to help her. The God of the Sea had violated her, and Theo gave her snakes and power as protection. So that no man could ever touch her again. Instead, she would turn all men who looked upon her to stone. It was sweet revenge.

Perfection.

But what if it wasn't . . . What if Medusa didn't see it that way? What if the spell was actually a curse? Was this where Medusa's despair stemmed from?

"I cannot affect you," Medusa said, and it was unclear if the words were a malediction or a boon. It was unclear how the gorgon felt at all. "Even in your mortal form."

"Wonderful," Theo said under her breath, taking a moment to view her surroundings.

She was in a grand room with a giant cypress tree at the base of the far wall. Books were strewn over tables, snakes coiling in and around them. Snakes were everywhere, clinging to the walls, hanging from chandeliers, and slithering along shelves and the floor.

Directly across from Theo stood a massive stone structure with a seven-by-six grid of circles cut into it.

Interesting.

A game of stones.

But Theo had no time to worry about the challenge or Medusa. Right now, she needed the book.

Aware of the chain cutting into her wrist, she slowly walked away from the stone boy. The chain had given her a long leash before; maybe it would now. She made it six feet before it pulled tautly. "Perfect."

Medusa laughed, her eyes lighting up at the predicament.

Theo growled and pulled at the links, trying to break them. The stone should've weakened the metal. But no, of course, it didn't. This was Love's magic.

Theo glared at the foolish boy. He had to look. Curiosity was a curse. It ruined lives and toppled nations. This mortal had it in abundance. With one more useless pull, Theo exhaled sharply and considered toppling the statue as she did in her palace rooms.

Considered destroying the boy.

She was a villain, but she had a code. Destroying the statue would forever kill him. While that would free her, it wasn't an option she'd take.

The rotten human deserved his fate, but he hadn't hurt anyone. So she wouldn't kill him.

Circling her arms around his stone torso, Theo tried to haul his statue down the hall and get him into the spell room.

Medusa chortled. "This is wonderfully entertaining."

"I'm glad you're enjoying it," Theo grunted, tugging the stone champion, and gritting her teeth.

It was an impossible task. She only made it three steps before sweat dripped down her face and her muscles gave out. With a huff, Theo slid to the ground and used the stone as her backrest. She was stuck and absolutely wasn't going to save the boy. Yet she had to get the spell book and make it out of the first challenge.

Perhaps, she could bargain.

"You want something," Medusa said before Theo could formulate a plan.

"Of course I do."

"So?"

"So . . ." Theo said, extending the word out.

"What is it you would have me do?" Medusa asked.

Theo countered, "What is it you want?" Deals were always better made with more information and more leverage.

"Tsk, tsk." Medusa clicked her tongue, and all the snakes in the room rose to attention. "You're not in control here."

"Clearly." Theo rested her head against her champion's stone knees. "I'm not in control of much lately."

"Am I supposed to feel sorry for you?" Medusa raised an eyebrow, and a chorus of hisses sounded.

No. "Are you unhappy?" Theo didn't know what possessed her to ask the question, but she immediately closed her lips and pinched them tightly. Half afraid to hear the answer.

Theo hated owning her own mistakes.

"It depends on the day."

Theo's brow creased. "Are you unhappy with your gifts?"

"Gifts?" Medusa scoffed. "You mean my snakes?"

"Yes."

"That would also depend on the day."

Theo sighed and rubbed her face.

"So, what is it you want?" Medusa asked.

Theo's gaze caught Medusa's brilliant golden irises, and she measured how much she could offer. She settled on quite a lot. "Get a copy of Hecate's Grimoire, and I will owe you a favor." The corner of Theo's lips rose. It was a fantastic deal for Medusa. Holding a God's Favor was *power,* and something rarely bestowed.

Medusa mulled it over, chewing on her cheek and petting one of the snakes. "Alas, I'm sorry, Theodra, I cannot."

Medusa seemed to genuinely feel bad about it. Which meant the gods had decreed this. She'd receive no aid during the challenges.

Irritating gnats.

Still refusing to do what was required to free the boy from his spell and death, Theo reached out and grasped the first book she could find. A historical romance. Flipping the book open, Theo sighed and started reading. She had a lot of time to kill.

So, Theo read in silence, long enough for her to finish her book —granted, she was a fast reader. She picked up another historical romance, *Bringing Down the Duke,* and opened it to the first page. Hours slipped away, and Theo was transfixed. A massive squawk sounded from Theo's arm when the book was at its climax.

Squawk, squawk, squawk. The raven wanted her to save the boy. But that was a deed Theo wouldn't ponder. Saving him would fall right into Nefeli's plans, which wouldn't do.

Squawk. Squawk. Squawk. Now, the raven was calling her *a selfish coward*.

Theo glared at it.

"Your raven is right. You'll never leave this library if you don't help him." Medusa stretched out on a table, lying down like a sphinx.

"I know." Theo rubbed her eyes drowsily before glancing down the hallway coated by books and springtime.

Pride.

Honor.

Revenge.

Pride.

Honor.

Revenge.

Theo repeated the words in her head until she got up the nerve to stand up. Facing the champion, she sucked in a shaking breath. Theo's plans required her to rescue the mortal.

"I hate you," she whispered to the statue. The only way to break a gorgon curse was with the most disgusting of acts. Theo would've chosen any other tithe for the magic—pain, torture, sorrow, even laughter. She'd even welcome a slight maiming, but a slight maiming wasn't in the cards.

No. Only unadulterated passion broke the gorgon's curse.

Theo sighed. He was far too tall. Godly even. She huffed and gathered three long, thick tombs and stacked them in front of him. She'd never be able to reach him without them. Then she climbed them carefully and clutched the champion's stone cheeks between her hands and tightly closed her eyes, bracing for a bitter taste.

Tentatively, standing on her tiptoes and trying to balance—geez, the foolish mortal was tall—she placed her lips on his. Theo sucked in a breath, and all her muscles went rigid. Counting to ten, she longed for this horrid moment to be over. When she hit the number seven, rock gave way to flesh, and her mouth lurched away, the books rocking beneath her. It wouldn't be enough to free him but turning the kiss into the level of passion needed to break the spell without his permission felt horribly wrong.

Theo scrunched her face and sent a silent plea to the heavens for forgiveness, her gaze touching the black shadows of the library ceiling.

The champion sputtered, and his eyes widened.

Before making the moment even more awkward or wasting

time, Theo asked, "May I kiss you passionately?" She croaked out the last word. It tasted like molasses on her tongue. Sticky and far too sweet.

The towering champion—whose face was the only portion of him freed from stone—stared at her like she spoke the language of the gods. Still, Theo was sure she'd spoken the common tongue . . . although she couldn't be sure of anything anymore, especially with humans. Theo was rotten at talking to them. It was perhaps her greatest weakness. Humans were far too complicated and full of unwanted feelings.

"Wha—what?" He stuttered, confusion and an emotion Theo didn't understand lighting up his features.

"It's the only way to break the spell. Pure passion." Theo crossed her arms protectively over her chest. She didn't want to do this either. "Medusa turned you into a statue, and kissing is the only way to break the curse."

"What?" He repeated.

Theo loosed a growl. "We don't have time for this."

As if conjured by her words, stone clawed back up his neck.

"Oh, gods," he breathed. "Yes, do what you have to." He croaked the last bit out as limestone clung to his lips, fastening them shut again.

Standing nearly on pointe, Theo tried to reach the correct angle of attack. Perhaps it'd work better if she imagined it as a war —a battle with tactics and strategy.

After all, she *was* War.

Gently, as if coaxing a trapped beast, Theo placed her lips back on his. Her fingers slid over his hair, and she stroked the nape of his neck the way she'd stroke her sword.

Battle . . . she could do battle.

The stone disintegrated from his mouth much faster this time, leaving their flesh mingling. But their lips merely hovered over each other's, neither wanting to move or deepen the kiss. But if they were to break the curse, then they needed passion.

Unfiltered, untamed, animal passion.

Theo swallowed and closed her eyes, digging her fingers into his scalp as she opened her mouth and began to move. She moderated her pressure and tried to get him to join her, to fall into her, but he stood stiff and frozen like a tundra.

Rotten ambrosia, Theo cursed, her eyes opening and staring at the shelves behind the gentleman.

The cast over his body only cracked to the top of his pectoral muscles and refused to move any lower. It *was not* working.

Not like this.

"You have to kiss me back," she breathed into his lips. "I know it's unpleasant. Trust me, I don't want to do this either, but we have to."

To illustrate her point, Theo ran her tongue along his lower lip and tempted him to open to her.

Waking from his daze, the champion moved his mouth. At first, he was hesitant and shy, but when she dipped her tongue into his mouth, a hunger awoke. He had to get inventive with his arms still locked to his sides. His mouth and teeth telling his story. He bit her lip, and tension pulled like a tightrope between them.

Theo laughed into his mouth, the war goddess in her coming alive under his fervent assaults. It awoke her passion. War was a haunting dance, and kissing could be, too.

The pounding of her heart was like the rhythm of battle, the clashing of shields, the firing of guns, the battle cry of an ancient warrior.

And he was a warrior, too.

His body was built by training and battle. He smelled like a mixture of musk, leather, and sandalwood, with a hint of sensual ardor. But what called to Theo was the way he tasted. He tasted like salt, cherries, and ambrosia—like the nectar of divinity.

When his hands were finally released, the warrior proved how skilled he could be. Theo shouldn't have been surprised because she'd seen his skills with a carving knife—his agile fingers—but this mortal was *talented*.

He laced said fingers into her hair and pulled her closer, devouring her with sin and electric energy.

The champion's legs unfroze, but their tempest didn't stop. Instead, he lifted her, the books beneath her feet toppling—exerting almost no effort and his hands slid along her upper thighs as he pinned her against the bookshelves. The movement knocked over a bust.

The passion, the tension, the pure need between them could light the library on fire—could light the world on fire.

It'd been a thousand years—at least—since Theo'd taken a lover—since she'd even thought about carnal desire. The feeling was new and enchanting.

And it was magic.

It was in the humanness of her body—its frail nature, erratic heart, and a chance for death at any minute—that awoke an unfamiliar, untamable desire. A hunger. A potent need. And it was unlike anything she'd ever experienced.

Theo had lovers before, but nothing compared to the feeling of being mortal. The life that surged through *this* body. Pain was heightened tenfold as a human, but so was her pleasure.

Theo stiffened.

She *had* to stop this . . . *now.*

Pulling her lips away, she panted as two humans entered the room, their eyes latching onto Medusa, stone crawling up their forms.

Fourteen
Theodra
Goddess of War

LIGHT'S MIRROR

Theo panted, her chest rising in a frantic rhythm. The champion still held her up, his fingers clutching her thighs.

He glanced toward the two new statues. The champion and priestess from Tierland. Their deaths were unfortunate, but not Theo's problem. They were victims of the Sacrifice, and the Sacrifice was designed to cause death. Theo wouldn't steal this victory from her sister—Andromache. So, she raised her hand and blocked her champion's view of the Gorgon. She couldn't risk saving him again. Whatever feeling stirred in her body when they kissed needed to be eradicated.

Forever.

Theo cleared her throat. "We need to get moving." Her eyes landed on his hands, still holding her thighs.

The champion touched his forehead to hers and grunted his typical big brutish grunt. Then he sighed and slowly lowered her to the ground. Theo's feet touched gently, exemplifying the young man's strength and control.

He still stood close, his eyes swimming with desire. Theo's breath caught, and that foreign feeling burst through her again.

"That meant nothing." She bit her swollen lower lip. "It was only to free you." Her heart surged, and she cursed herself for letting their passion extend that far.

He grunted again and nodded. "Just to free me." He rolled back his shoulders and shook out his arms, and an unknowable expression danced on his cheeks until he schooled it. "Thank you for saving me."

"I wouldn't have, but . . ." she lifted her chained wrist.

He grunted again—most likely an affirmation. Did he only know how to grunt? It was like his primary language was grunts, Theodic his second, and the common tongue his third.

Without telling him what she was doing or where she was going, Theo marched toward the exit back to the hallway. "Make sure you don't look," she said as she pulled at her chain and forced him to follow.

"Doesn't the challenge lie with Medusa?"

Theo didn't bother responding. Instead, she turned fully to her task.

God-made calligraphy looped and etched itself into wooden signs, showing the sections and manner of the tomes. Quickly she found the Room of Witchcraft and started pulling books off the shelf at random, searching for the grimoire. When a book didn't meet her qualifications, she threw it over her shoulder, heedless of its condition.

"Do you need help?" The boy asked in a tone riddled with confusion.

Theo's first response was to curse him, but she contained herself. It wasn't often—if ever—anyone offered to help her. So slowly, as if not knowing how to pronounce the word, Theo said, "Yes." She inhaled sharply. "I'm looking for a book titled *Hecate's Grimoire*."

He nodded and started tearing through the shelves—although much more timidly than she was—and treating the books like royalty—respect dripping from his every touch.

The way she wished he'd touch her again.

No. Stop it, Theo. Control your thoughts.

Ivy and branches were laced into the shelves, and Theo pulled them aside and searched and searched and searched. It felt like hours later, and still nothing. Searching through all the books at least twice left them nowhere . . .

Theo was forced to admit defeat.

The gods were thwarting her at every turn, knowing what she'd do before she did it. Maneuvering, posturing, manipulating, it was the gods' way—their currency.

And she was so easily falling into their traps.

The gods loved playing with humans—dangling them from their puppet strings. They loved exerting power over lesser creatures, tricking and out-scheming them. Theo wasn't immune to this.

She should've been playing these games better, but she was outmaneuvered at every turn since being turned into a human, now forced into helping her champion—at least a little because she needed to get to the Tribunal. She needed to find Destruction, her second, and get aid.

It was *infuriating*.

"We need to return to Medusa, but this time for the love of all the gods, don't look into her eyes," Theo said, forcing him to follow and tugging at the chain which flickered in and out of visibility, today deciding to be formed from pink-metallic glitter.

"Actually," she stopped abruptly and ripped off one of her sleeves, "wear this." And without waiting for a response, Theo tied the blindfold around his eyes, her fingers softly sliding down his face as she did it.

She shivered and touched her lips. *Rotten memories.*

Theo should just fuck him to nullify this wicked attraction, but she promised herself she wouldn't lie with another male and she'd kept to that promise for the last 1,000 years.

With some care—although still very little—Theo guided her champion back to Medusa.

"Ah, you haven't found what you're looking for." A smug expression danced on the monster's lips. "And you've come back to challenge me."

"Yes, yes," Theo spat out, her voice coated with derision, "tell us what we need to do to defeat the first challenge."

"Let's play a game, little mortal." A thousand hisses rang

through the room, and the champion tensed. The sound crawled over Theo's pale skin. "Whichever of us places four of our stones in a row first wins." Medusa motioned to the grid cut to the wall. "Win, and you can leave having completed your first challenge."

"And if I lose?" Theo smiled, but the guise didn't light her eyes. False niceties. It was always better to know all outcomes ahead of time.

"Death."

Every snake tracked Theo and her champion's movements as if waiting to strike—their chance to fulfill that promise.

The task was both physical and mental. The champion had to carry a stone up the wall and place it into the correct slot while keeping the patterns and strategy in mind. But it was worse than that because he'd have to do it blindfolded. It was too risky not to —life and death were on the line.

"Snakes or heads?" Medusa asked.

The mortal rubbed his chin, clearly thinking. "Snakes."

It was a wise choice, because if he had to feel where she placed her stones by touch, the face stone would be far more distinguishable than the snakes.

"You can have the first move," Medusa said.

The champion wasted no time. He walked to his designated pile, heaved up a stone and barely broke a sweat, although his biceps twitched in the most tempting of ways. The chain grew taut as the champion reached the wall. He grunted and tried to pull it while still holding the boulder. It was a rather amusing sight.

"You're being dead weight," he said, looking over her shoulder, unable to correctly navigate where she stood with his blindfold on. "This is *our* challenge."

"It's not my challenge." She crossed her arms, defiantly. Theo didn't like being told what to do. Not by her mother and not by this needlessly attractive young man. "I am not here to help you."

"Clearly," he growled and balanced the weight of the boulder on his side. "Why are you here if you're going to be completely . . . unhelpful?"

He edited himself to say the nicer version and Theo smiled. She respected his restraint. It was a quality she almost completely lacked. She admired it so much she chose to share a version close to the truth with him. "I angered the wrong god."

"So you're being forced?"

"Yes."

"Right." He sighed, exasperated. Pausing for a long moment in thought, he placed the stone on the ground, before rolling the chain between his fingers, and following it back to reach her. When his hand reached hers, she shivered from the contact, despite expecting it. His hand glided up her arm and left gooseflesh in its wake.

She sucked in a breath.

"I understand that might want to make you rebel and refuse to engage," he said, "but it's not just your life on the line here, and I would really prefer making it out of these games alive." He was both soft and stern. A mixture that sent warmth into her stomach. "Can you at the very least stop working against me?"

Theo's brow furrowed. She didn't want to give Nefeli what she wanted, but this champion wasn't so bad. She swallowed and gave in, after all, she needed him to beat this challenge so she could find Destruction. She sighed. "I will stop actively working against you."

"Thank you."

Theo clutched his sculpted arm, so she could lead him back to the wall. The muscle jerked under her touch, and she gulped. It was unnatural to be this handsome. Truly. After all of this was over, she would find the god responsible for this and have a word with them.

The champion lifted his rock again and Theo was forced to climb up the wall a bit to help him land the stones. Luckily, Love gave them a bit more leash. Instead of six feet, they got roughly ten. This still made the challenge irritating because the grid was roughly eighteen feet high.

The champion climbed the rungs of the grid, carrying a stone as big as a tire. Feeling his way, he placed his first one into the direct center.

A brilliant first move.

It gave the most advantages. A player needed to hold the center. If they could, they'd most likely win.

With a snap of Medusa's fingers, she placed her first move on top of his. She had to be borrowing Andromache's magic for this game because, normally, Medusa didn't have god magic.

The boy heard where the rock landed but ran his hands over it to make sure before he picked up his second stone, climbed the grid, and placed it on top of Medusa's. She responded by putting her subsequent move to the right of his original piece.

Back and forth, they took turns, and Theo remained silent, watching.

The boy—man, was a genius.

The mortal was creating a trap. Understanding the big picture, he thought five steps ahead, perfectly placing every stone.

This wasn't an easy feat. He had to memorize the board in his head while physically exhausting himself. Theo hated to admit it, but she was impressed. She could've helped him. She could've been his eyes, calling out the positions, telling him where Medusa was placing her stones. She could've even played the game for him. Theo always won strategy games against Medusa, for she was War, Wit, and Strategy itself.

Theo could've helped the boy.

But she didn't . . . for so many reasons. It didn't matter, though, because he didn't need her help.

Her champion was gifted in all the ways Theo adored. Strong, tall, handsome, *skilled*, and intelligent.

And that was a problem.

A *big* problem.

She couldn't admire the mortal. It would ruin all her plans . . . and possibly more than just plans.

Creating the shape of a seven on the board with his pieces, the champion successfully set up the game so that he'd achieve victory in the next four moves.

Medusa could've played defensively and extended the game longer, but she knew she'd lost. So she placed her following three stones, giving him victory. But as Medusa made her last move, gooseflesh rose on Theo's arms, and Dahlia squawked.

Something was off . . . but she sensed it too late.

Turning around, she saw Cecile and her russet-skinned priest entering the room with a panther-sized Bella at their side. “Nooooo,” Theo called out, but it was in vain.

Cecile pushed her priest down, successfully blocking his view of the gorgon, but Cecile’s eyes locked directly onto the monster’s. Theo sucked in a breath, and her heart tripped. Every muscle in her body grew taut as she waited for the stone to climb Cecile’s form. When Cecile turned, there was nothing Theo could do to help.

But Cecile didn’t turn. Nothing happened, yet her eyes remained fixed on Medusa.

“What are you?” Theo whispered so quietly only the immortal in the room could hear, but Cecile’s eyes flickered to the Goddess of War in human flesh, raising her eyebrows as if asking *What do you mean?*

Super senses and immunity to curses weren’t gifts given to Godmarked, which meant the Goddess of Destruction had been right; there was something off about Cecile. Something almost inhuman.

“How?” Cecile breathed; her ocean-blue eyes locked on the gorgon.

Medusa smiled like an asp. “I do not affect you, child.”

The Andromedan priest started to stir on the ground. “You need to blindfold him,” Theo called before turning on her champion, “And you need to place your last stone and win.”

“But—” his voice shook.

“Your friends are fine.” Theo climbed a rung and placed a hand on his bicep. “They’re fine, I promise.”

His arm tensed against her fingers, but he did as told, ending the game.

“Wonderful work!” Medusa clapped her hands once. “You have successfully lived and completed the first challenge. Stay or go. It’s your choice.”

At these words, a mirror portal twisted and formed from the branches clinging to the walls and the snakes lining the floor. The exit.

Theo made to move, but her honor kept her rooted. She

vowed to watch after Cecile. She couldn't abandon her Marked here.

Cecile must have finished her first challenge quickly and moved on to her second way ahead of schedule. There were only five challenges to do in seven days but some of the challenges could take days to complete or recover from.

"It is time for you, Cecile Declare, to face the wall." Medusa stroked the viper curling around her arm. "Place four stones in a row and win this challenge."

Cecile and Emmett showed perfect teamwork. Blindfolded, Emmett hauled the stones, and placed them while Cecile called out the board. She wasn't nearly as talented or quick as the Theoden boy, but she managed to win easily. Meanwhile, Bella sat at Theo's feet and received long luxurious pets. Theo was wretched, but she loved animals.

When it was all said and done, together, the four exited the mirror and entered an even more dangerous game—the Tribunal, facing the gods and their festivities.

FIFTEEN
KELLYN
Prince of Theoden

VOLCANIC PALACE, CITY OF THE GODS

"Kellyn Ellis, champion of Theoden, you have survived your first challenge." Nefeli's words wreathed through the air like coils of smoke. "And now you will face the panel of gods."

Anxiety clawed through the grand ballroom, and earth sprites emerged, feeding on it.

Kellyn faced nine thrones—one mockingly empty—and Morrigan stood at his right like a general commanding a battle. Emmett and Cecile were to the side awaiting their tribunal. They finished second so they'd go second—even though they'd made it through two challenges.

The gods glittered with grandeur as they sat in their thrones. Everything from their hair to their clothing pulsated with magic. It was fearsome to behold, and Kellyn's fingers tensed. He had no carving tools, so he couldn't keep his hands busy. His veins throbbed, anticipation dancing through his blood as he prepared to face judgment. His performance in the first challenge was mixed at best. He'd nearly died—he would've if it weren't for Morrigan.

A dishonorable death, too.

"The boy is nearly useless like all the Theoden champions

who've come before him," the God of Fire said, ash flaking from his flesh, and his dim gray hair dancing on a phantom wind. A song of joy sculpting his features. A joy that churned Kellyn's stomach, tying unbreakable knots into the lining. "Medusa easily felled him, and the girl," he waved at Morrigan dismissively, "was forced to save him with a vile kiss. I vote that we give him a nearly impossible riddle."

"You're simply jealous, Silas," Love said, her hair flowing like pink diamonds down her chest, striking against her deep olive skin. "We all know your history with the girl."

History?

From the corner of his eye, Kellyn glanced at Morrigan for a reaction. Venom swirled in her irises, and fury poured from her bones, her entire body stiff and ready for war. Like she wanted to purge Love from the world for mentioning a past with Fire.

Had they been lovers?

That wasn't a normal reaction.

The god was no better; he looked like he wanted to strangle Love, using her hair as the garrote.

Definitely a history.

"I enjoyed the show," Love continued. "It started disastrously, but oh my hellfire, it turned steamy. I wonder, boy, did you feel any sensations?" Love winked and glanced at his jewels.

Entirely inappropriate.

A chorus of eyes landed on Kellyn. Awaiting his answer. He didn't know if he had to answer . . . and if he didn't, would it affect how Love scored him?

A truly impossible situation.

"Oh, I'm dying to know the answer to this one, too," Light said, sitting slightly forward.

A flood of heat hit Kellyn's chest. His eyes flickered to the crowd where his friends stood with expressions of confusion lighting their faces.

Kellyn stifled a curse when he saw his parents three rows behind them.

Tribunals were public torture. Anyone could come and stand in the audience. After all, watching the Sacrifice was a sport. People gathered in pubs and bet on which champions would live and which would die.

"So, boy, did you feel anything." This time it was Nefeli, and it felt like a trap.

Rose petals bloomed on his tawny cheeks.

It was humiliating enough admitting to feeling anything in front of the gods, but even more so in front of his friends and family.

"I—" he started, his blush deepening and his heart in his throat. "I—yes, I felt sensations." He cleared his throat, his eyes landing on Morrigan. "I'm a man after all, and she is quite . . ." he cracked his neck, begging for absolution.

"Quite . . ." Love encouraged.

Womanly, luscious, tempting. His gaze raked over Morrigan's curves, and he swallowed and eventually landed on the word, "Beautiful."

"I think that's enough," Havyn drawled. "We should return to the point. I, for one, will dock points for the stone incident, but I admired how the mortal played the game."

The gods took turns critiquing his performance. Some were stuck on his failures, and others focused on the game.

As they talked, he allowed his mind to wander, but a loud pop jolted his attention back to the tribunal as a burst of color lit the room, formed from enchanted fireworks that floated above the ballroom floor.

As nine bells tolled, numbers appeared, dancing like marionettes on strings and hanging from his name.

Morrigan snorted beside him. "The gods and their puppet metaphors," she whispered. Although every god heard her, their heads cocking toward her like birds of prey, she didn't seem to care as she continued. "Too predictable."

Reckless, she was so reckless.

The scores were color-coded to each of the gods' signature colors. Light: purple with a score of five. Nefeli: royal blue with a score of five. War: blood red with a score of zero—because she never showed up, everyone always received a zero from her. Death: black with a score of nine. Love: rustic pink with a score of nine.

Festival: mint green with a score of five. Poison: pale yellow with a score of five. Harvest: leaf green with a score of five. Fire: bronze with a score of zero.

They weren't horrible scores, but they also weren't great.

"Kellyn Ellis, you have received an average score; therefore, the riddle to your next mirror will be of average difficulty." Nefeli snapped her fingers, and ink pooled on his skin before curling into a second riddle. The words were in pure cursive and looked to be complete scribbles.

Acid crawled up his throat.

Reading was going to get him murdered.

"You may leave." Nefeli waved him off as if he were an irritating fly. "Cecile Declare, you have successfully completed . . ." Nefeli continued, calling Cecile to the floor, and quickly starting her tribunal.

The gods hated wasting time or distracting from their revelry. Because while the champions played their five challenges, the gods watched and partied with lucky—hand chosen—mortals, drinking spiked nectar, and eating delicacies from the Nine Great Countries. Meanwhile, after every challenge, each champion was forced into fancy clothing and fake smiles as they withstood judgment at their tribunals, expected to mingle with the gods for at least a couple of hours before returning to their games, during which they were required to watch the other champions' challenges on the mirror monitors stationed throughout the palace.

It was all just an elaborate mind game.

Fortunately for Cecile, the gods seemed to like how she was playing the games, and her tribunal lasted only five minutes, with all eight gods giving her top scores and telling her the answer to her next mirror.

Poison.

It paid to play the games well, and Cecile was playing perfectly. She made it through two of her five challenges in two days.

Passing platters of elaborate food, Kellyn walked up to his friends. Reluctantly, his priestess followed him, snorting as she saw a platter of deer meat. She grabbed a piece as Kellyn asked Cecile, "Two challenges already?"

Cecile blushed. "Oh, yes," Cecile shrugged, "I'm sorry for not finding you before the first. Andromache insisted I start the Death challenge when I did."

Kellyn forced a smile. "It's okay." *But it wasn't.* He felt alone. Betrayed. Although he was incapable of asking for help—the family motto: *Ellises never needed help*—he never imagined Cecile wouldn't be there when he needed her.

"It's not." Cecile's lips twitched. "I was going to return and find you as soon as possible, but you'd already left."

"I didn't mind leaving you," Emmett said, turning his glower on his former friend. He said the words to wound. It was the boy's way. When he was upset, his behavior got brattier and brattier.

"Emmett," Cecile reprimanded.

He ignored the remark, facing Kellyn directly. "The only reason I'm tolerating your presence is for Cecile." His speech slurred slightly. Drunk. Already.

Kellyn swallowed. He hated the situation, and he hated that he might be able to clear it all up if he were honest with his friend, but he couldn't. The secret was too shameful to share. Emmett would leave him no matter what. He wouldn't want a stupid friend.

"Emmett, I'm sorry. I truly didn't mea—"

"Isn't it enough that you're a prince? That you were going to one day rule a kingdom?" Emmett spat out. "No, you'll never be satisfied because you care about nothing and have to have everything." The last words dripped with acid. "You had to steal my glory, too."

Emmett raised the glass as if to throw the liquid on Kellyn, but he realized too late that there was nothing in it, so instead, he cursed and stumbled away.

He was *very* drunk.

"You need to tell him about your—" Cecile crossed her arms, watching their friend leave.

Kellyn flashed a grimace that said *not in front of Morrigan.*

The priestess narrowed her eyes but leaned against a pillar, chewing on a piece of deer meat she'd taken from a footman and pretending not to care.

"I have to go after him," Cecile said, "but I promise I will help you solve your riddle."

She hurried off after the drunk boy, and Kellyn was left alone with Morrigan, who raised her apple-red wrist, indicating the invisible chain binding them together. "I'd run from you, too, but we seem to be on a tight leash today."

Kellyn ignored the gibe. Instead, he took a step closer and examined her injury. "You need jewelweed." He gently grasped her hand and ran a finger over the rash from her chain. "I have some in our room."

"You have jewelweed in our room?"

"I have a lot of herbs in our room."

"Are you an herbalist?" She wiggled her brows, and he couldn't tell if she was mocking him.

Before he could answer, Gallagher Healy, his nemesis from school, sauntered over. Her presence felt like a rash. Irritated and agonizing.

"Are you here to see the fruits of your labor?" Kellyn asked.

"Oh, absolutely," Gallagher said in a soft sprite-like voice, her silver-blonde hair bouncing with her words. "I always enjoy your suffering."

Kellyn simply grunted. He wasn't nearly as good at handling her presence as Cecile was. He never knew what to say.

"And who is this?" Gallagher turned her gentle yet vicious expression to Kellyn's priestess.

"Morrigan," his priestess smiled through her teeth. "Nice to meet you."

If Gallagher was a thorn, Morrigan was an entire briar patch. The girl did not like social interactions. He wasn't sure who would devour the other . . . if it came down to it.

"Oh, it is a pleasure to *meet* you, too." Gallagher smiled back, an eyebrow raising.

But their interaction was cut off by Death's arrival. She strolled over as if floating on shadows. "Miss Morrigan, can I have a word?"

"I—" Morrigan's eyes tracked to Gallagher. "I need—" but Death grasped her wrist, cutting off the words.

The goddess and two girls stood next to each other, looking like a funhouse mirror's reflection of a single smile, distorting more and more with each new mirror. Morrigan's was false and dangerous. Gallagher's was laced with naughty intentions, and Death's was dripping with wicked delight.

"Shall we?" Death asked the priestess.

Morrigan held up her chained wrist to the god in response.

"Ah, no worries, you can have a longer leash for our conversation." Death snapped her fingers, and the chain vibrated before loosening a bit. "We have so much to discuss."

Dark tendrils coiled around Morrigan, crawling up her body and consuming her whole. In a blink, both her and Death were gone.

"Don't worry about Morrigan," Gallagher said. "She'll be fine. Worry about yourself and your new riddle." She laughed like a deranged fairy and skipped away.

Kellyn glared down at his arm, his eyebrows crunched together, and his brow furrowed. The letters danced and blurred together. Oh, how he hated written scripts. Always impossible to decipher.

"A Theoden prince in the Sacrifice," the Goddess of Poison said, slinking up beside him and causing Kellyn to flinch both from the words and the surprise.

Kellyn felt like he was in a revolving door of torture. One person after the other. It could only get worse if his *parents* visited next. But the goddess's words were bad enough. "It seems reading is hard for you." Her umber skin glistened under the soft ballroom light as her eyes touched the riddle etched into his arm, her smile mocking him.

Kellyn stiffened and held his breath. *She knew*. She had to. There was no other reason for her to say such a thing. After all, she was a god with every resource in the world. Since the gods were motivated to kill as many champions as possible, it stood to reason that they would thoroughly research their prey.

They would discover every champion's weakness.

They would know.

This was bad. The world couldn't find out about his affliction. Even the peasant class of Theoden knew how to read. It would ruin him forever if people found out. Destroy his life, but more importantly, it'd ruin his honor and glory.

No one could know.

No one.

Kellyn's heart jumped into his throat, and his mouth grew dry, but Poison wasn't finished playing with her prey before she devoured it. "It would be such a pity if more challenges involved reading, wouldn't it?"

Her lips curled into a cruel promise, and she turned on her heel, walking away. Apparently, she had no interest in sticking around now that her threat was sufficiently delivered.

Poison would torture him with a reading challenge at some point during the games. The only question was when. The worst part about it was that knowing changed nothing. He couldn't defend against a reading attack. No amount of effort could prepare him for words he didn't know and penmanship he couldn't translate.

Sixteen
Theodra
Goddess of War

VOLCANIC BALLROOM, CITY OF THE GODS

"Did you have to do that?" Theo spat at her sister.

Theo hated refracting as a human. It churned her stomach and made it hard to breathe. She gagged, holding onto the deer meat in one hand and pulling at her priestess torc with the other, trying to get more airflow to her lungs.

Havyn chuckled. "Of course I did."

"We barely traveled . . . maybe fifteen feet," Theo grumbled, slouching over, and clutching her knees for support. It felt like centipedes were eating the lining of her intestines.

Mortality was vile.

"Refracting wasn't necessary."

Theo was in a secluded alcove carved into the Grand Ballroom. If Theo leaned out, she could throw a stone at her champion—she was still that close.

Walking would have been less effort.

Theo gagged. The place smelled of cherry blossoms, but it tasted like arsenic, making Theo's unruly stomach all the worse.

"Stop being so dramatic," Havyn said, "you're starting to act like Fire."

Theo snapped up and glared at her sister.

Havyn held up her hands in fake surrender. "Come on, little

sis, enjoy the revelry with me." She grabbed a champagne flute from a footman and handed it to her sister.

Theo eyed the drink like it was a rotten body covered with maggots.

"I didn't poison it," Havyn said. "Just have fun, for once."

Fun. Theo scoffed. She hated the nighttime festivities of the Sacrifice. The fake smiles and the rose-red lips dripping with trickery and disdain, with the air of narcissism and greed permeating every surface of the party.

Acrobats, jesters, fairy ballerinas, pooka illusions, and magicians performed on scattered platforms across the grand lava ballroom. Trickery couldn't decide on one form of entertainment, so he chose all forms.

Exorbitant, lurid, and nauseating.

Three adjectives perfectly encompassed the God of Trickery.

"I don't do fun." Theo crossed her arms.

"Fine, then sit with me and watch the challenges." Havyn sat down on a smooth lava bench and patted the seat beside her. Her eyes locked on a magic mirror that draped on the wall, replaying the champions' first challenges. The footage was recorded from the eyes of statues throughout the games and palace.

The images intermingled with Trickery's revelry, creating a tapestry of beautiful colors and sounds.

"Why have you brought me here?" Theo chewed on deer meat, standing in the shadows like a menacing guard. Mostly doing it just to spite Andromache. Deer were sacred to her, and Andromadens were forbidden from eating the meat. But Theodenites had no such qualms. And War was angry with both of her meddling sisters.

First, Andromache with the Medusa stunt, and now Havyn with whatever this was about.

The sister in question merely pointed to the mirror with her foot.

It depicted Cecile swimming in a sea of shadows, visions bombarding her from all sides, flickering through them like a silent film reel.

The Death Challenge.

"What is it?" The words slipped out of Theo's mouth, and she found herself joining her sister on the bench.

"Her challenge was to face the darkness."

Inner darkness?

It had to be because Cecile was consumed with horrible images after another. Some were her greatest fears made manifest, but others still were memories in the flesh. Memories like being kidnapped and trafficked as a kid. Memories of Andromache visiting her childhood home.

Happy memories, sad memories, and memories yet to be made. Of her defeating the Sacrifice and living a god-blessed life of riches and glory no one human should possess. Another image was simply of her Strings of Life braided to another—to a god. Even more strangely, another depicted her marrying that same god.

An impossibility.

Falling in love with a god was illegal.

"I have plans for your little servant," the words trilled off Death's tongue. "I designed her games, after all."

"If you kill her, I will destroy yo—"

"Look at you caring for a mere human."

"Havyn," Theo growled. "Don't—"

"What are you going to do? You're mortal." Havyn squeezed her sister's blistered arm. "And fragile."

Theo sucked in a pained breath and pinched her eyes shut. It hurt. It hurt so fucking much to be human. It hurt so fucking much to be so damn fragile. She slowly pulled in air; her lungs tight and burning. Then she opened her eyes and devoured Havyn with her gaze.

"Oh, calm down. I don't plan on killing her . . . or even harming her."

"Then what are you doing?"

Havyn raised an ink-colored brow, her lips twisting into a sneer. "Perhaps I'm showing her the truth. Or maybe I already did."

Havyn pointed again at the mirror with one of her long slender feet. A scene played out as Cecile watched.

A deep horrible sound sang from the surface. The sound of

regret. The sound of death—a death that was forever carved into Theo's heart.

A woman wailed, and chains clicked against slick marble, the sound haunting and foreboding.

A sound that had been burned into Theo's soul.

"No, please, please, I beg you, don't do this," Andromache pleaded, her voice imbued with a river of devastation. "Please."

A ghost version of Nefeli towered in front of a limp, blood-coated body strapped and dangling from the ceiling by magic ropes.

Poison and Harvest stood nearby, forcing a chained Andromache to watch as her mother tortured Devereaux—her mortal lover.

"Theo, please, do something," Andromache screamed, her eyes anchored to a ghost Theodra's hollow face.

A face that was empty of all emotions. A hollow echo. An endless emptiness that would never be filled—especially not at this moment. "I can't do anything." Theodra blinked, her eyes fastened to the tortured boy. "It's the law."

The law. A god shall never fall in love with a mortal—long-lived or human.

"Please, end it," Andromache begged.

Theodra cocked her head like a raven examining roadkill. She'd never looked more like a bird. Liquid darkness leaked from her eyes. Eyes that shifted between her sister and her sister's lover, a decision stirring in them.

The exact moment of the decision was accompanied by Theo conjuring a sword. A sword forged from shadow.

Without hesitation, she took the broad sword in two hands and swung, swiftly and nearly painlessly decapitating Devereaux, his head falling off and rolling to Andromache.

Andromache keened and clanged the chains against the floor, picking up the head and clinging it to her breast. The scene went on for what seemed like forever, and all the other gods left Andromache there—all save Theodra and Havyn.

In a rare and almost touching moment, all three triplets were aligned with one aim. They formed a tableau of grief and twisting rage.

None of them spoke, and only continual wails cut through the night.

Theodra didn't understand her sister's pain. Romance had only caused unspeakable evils in her own life. Theodra felt justified in her actions because Nefeli would have tortured the boy for a hundred years, bringing him to the edge of death and then healing him so she could do it again. All the while forcing Andromache to watch.

It was sickening, and Theodra could end it. It was the kinder thing to do.

Real Theo's eyes grew heavy with unshed tears. It was the worst moment of her life—even worse than her own pain, for when she had fallen in love, she loved with all of her being.

And she loved Andromache.

The vision morphed into a new one.

Andromache was chained atop a mountain, where every day for one hundred years, an eagle came and devoured her liver. Over and over again. But every day, Theodra appeared and poured healing magic into her sister's limp form, stealing the pain.

The scene played out on repeat, neither sister speaking, spending days, years, even decades in silence until one day, Andromache broke it and said, "I need to ask you for a favor."

"Anything." Theodra's voice was coated in a winter so cold it could cause an ice age.

"You haven't heard what I would ask of you," Andromache said, strangled by pain.

"What is it you need?" Theodra asked without hesitation. She'd do anything for her sister—especially after killing the one person she loved.

"Can you cast a privacy shield?" Andromache said, her eyes thick with worry, shifting them to the sky as if she were nervous it might overhear.

Theo snapped her fingers, and a clear bubble formed around them—protecting them from outside ears.

"I need you to shield my daughter and all her future descendants from the eyes of the Pantheon." Andromache paused and spoke all the details in a long-dead language that even Theodra had a hard

time remembering. "I need you to shield her from yourself, too, Thee."

"It shall be done." Theodra disappeared.

The vision shifted again, but the real Theo spoke over it, "Why show Cecile this?"

"Why indeed." A self-satisfied smirk twitched on Death's lips. "Perhaps I want her to hate you. Or perhaps something else entirely."

"Havyn, if you—"

"*Help,*" Theo was cut off by Cecile's Death Challenge playing out on the mirror. Havyn was forcing the twenty-four-year-old Cecile to face a vision of herself at sixteen during her Agoge schooling.

Cecile tried to scream, but it was muffled by the hand of an attacker.

"Oh, now it's getting interesting," Death said, staring at the mirror.

Cecile's attacker pinned her to the ground with his knees, his hands curling around her neck, strangling her. Purple colored her face, and the vein in her forehead bulged. She frantically clawed at his hands, to no avail. She was dying. Murder in the Agoge was frowned upon, but it wasn't against the rules. As long as a person wasn't caught in the act, it was mostly overlooked.

Cecile curled her fingers into the dirt beside her, the vessels in her eyes red and straining for life. With her last ounce of energy, she threw the dirt into her attacker's eyes.

He released his hands for a moment. Cecile kneed him and tried to get his weight off her. But the boy was nearly the size of Kellyn and far heavier. Even with her extra-human strength, she was no match for the lock-hold he had her in.

Angry, the attacker slammed her head into the ground.

Blood blossomed from a wound, and her eyes glazed over. Defeated, Cecile's hands fell limp. Her gaze drifted to the side, her fate sealed in the rough calluses encircling her throat and cutting off her air supply.

Hovering in a bush—a mere foot away—perched Gallagher.

Their eyes met. Gallagher's swirled with a storm of thoughts. Yet she didn't make any move to intervene.

"Help!" The strangling noise escaped Cecile's throat.

Gallagher tilted her head like a cobra but still made no move to help. She was just sitting and watching. Bathing in the ruination of it.

Cecile's lips formed the word please, and her eyes said she knew Gallagher wouldn't help . . . they were nemeses, after all . . . it was possible she'd orchestrated the entire event.

An eternity ticked by.

Nothing.

Then Gallagher took out a dagger. She rubbed the point against her lips tauntingly. Playing with Cecile, like she always did. Gallagher lived for small tortures. After a moment, she stopped and stared at Cecile like prey.

With a mischievous wink, Gallagher slid the dagger into Cecile's outstretched fingers, and without hesitation, Cecile plunged it into the throat of her attacker. A waterfall of blood poured onto her, and the attacker fell dead over her chest. The energy left Cecile, and she let go of her fight, her eyes pinching closed for a moment. She was still in dire straits, and she needed medical attention soon. She might lose too much blood from her head wound and fall unconscious, never to wake again.

With a groan, she glanced over to Gallagher and cracked, "Help," but the girl was gone. Almost as if she were never there to begin with.

Conjuring a surge of stamina, Cecile pushed the boy off her, but it stole all her energy, and she collapsed back on the forest floor.

A single raven flew down from the heavens and landed on Cecile's shoulder. A blue healing light flowed from its talons and blanketed the girl with enchantment.

"When she finds out about your part in that, she is going to hate you," Havyn's voice was a guillotine.

"Yes, she will." Theo sighed. "Did you bring me here to gloat?"

"Well . . . it wasn't the only reason." Havyn rested her hands in her lap, her shadow dress curling around them like gloves. "Your servant did well, far better than most who enter my mirror."

Havyn changed the subject with a new vision.

It was years earlier, and a little four or five-year-old Cecile was playing marbles with a woodland nymph at the side of a secluded cabin.

"Cecile, your father doesn't want you to play so far away from the house," said the Goddess of Night, her flowing golden hair shimmering in the rays of the setting sun. She stood next to the Goddess of Light, who had a yellow aura glowing around her, casting her divinity on full display.

"Ah, fine." Cecile pouted.

"How is the girl?" Andromache asked.

"She's getting inhumanly quick, which, of course, makes it hard for her father to keep up with, and she absolutely adores the nymphs and vampires, which will eventually become problematic for her father; you know how he is."

"Indeed."

Why were Night and Light watching a little Cecile? Did it have something to do with her inhuman nature?

The scene faded, and Havyn waved, magic spilling from her fingers as she cut off the replay.

"Please get to your point, Havyn. I tire of your antics," Theo drawled.

"I want you to answer something honestly for me," Havyn said, "and I wanted to torture you with my presence. I can't help myself. I hardly ever see my little sister."

"Do I get a choice?" Theo growled. "It seems like you're going to do whatever you please."

"Aren't you in a testy mood?" Havyn tsked in response. "I'm trying to be helpful."

As helpful as a tick. *Blood-sucking parasites.*

"I heard that." Havyn laughed. "And I consider it an honor to be compared to a blood-sucking parasite."

"Are you going to ask your question?"

Havyn loosed a belabored sigh. "You're so difficult. Love is right; you're no fun."

"Ask your question, Havyn, or let me go."

"Do you truly want to die?"

Theo's brows drew together, the question catching her off guard. Her heart surged, anxiety crawling up the rungs of her ribcage one by one.

"What?" she breathed.

"You stared straight into Medusa's eyes as if you were asking her to turn you into stone." Havyn's lips fell into a flat line. "So, do you truly want to die?"

Theo didn't know. There were moments when it was all that she wanted, but then sometimes she wanted to fight—wanted to live. At the core of her, Theo didn't know what she wanted. Perhaps to feel something.

Anything.

"What is there to live for?" Theo said lazily.

Havyn cocked her head, sadness swimming in her lilac eyes. "So much, Thee. So, so much."

"Like what?" Theo's voice broke.

"Love." The answer was simple and horrible.

Love was betrayal. Devastation. A dance with decay. Love was the worst of all punishments and the ruination of one's soul. Love began with hope. A hope that would eventually shatter into endless chaos. Love was the deepest form of pain, and Theo vowed never to feel it again.

Love was ruination.

It was the biggest mistake she'd made in her 10,000-year life.

"Love," she repeated mockingly, cyanide pouring from her lips.

"Yes, love, little sister," Havyn said. "Life is beautiful and meaningful, not because of the power we possess or the wealth we hold, or the successes we achieve. It is meaningful when it is shared."

"Shared," Theo breathed.

Havyn pinched her lips together as if she were speaking to an annoying child. "When you're vulnerable enough to allow yourself to be fully seen and fully accepted by another." Havyn squeezed her sister's arm. "When you allow yourself to care about someone else and to be cared for in return, that is when life has meaning."

"It sounds tedious." A*nd horrifying.*

Havyn's words were sappy and pathetic, not something Theo could ever consider. Because Theo had no heart. She was unlovable.

Unredeemable.

Who could ever love War? Who could ever care for her?

No one.

No one *had* ever cared for her.

"You're responsible for your own happiness, Theo." Havyn's face turned soft and sympathetic. "As long as you run from connection, as long as you ruminate on the pain, you will stay there."

"What else would you have me do?" Theo asked. Havyn made it all sound so easy. But connection and happiness weren't easy.

"Change." Havyn shrugged. "Start with the Sacrifice. You saved Cecile's life. She is your servant; get to know her . . . truly. Or the handsome priest, or even the big, alluring brute. Just try, Thee."

"Try." Theo chewed on the word.

"And stop trying to kill yourself." Havyn shook her head disapprovingly. "Also, stop trying to defy Mother. I know what you're doing, and it's not going to work."

Oh, but it would.

Theo would get the spell, and she would get her divinity back.

"This is brilliant," the Goddess of Destruction said, poking her head into the alcove. It was as if she were summoned by Theo's thoughts.

Destruction was Theo's second in command and direct subordinate in the War Court.

Destruction had the voice of a fairy and the demeanor of a candy-dripped demon. In her god form, she had deep azure hair laced with a crown of decaying roses that fell like tears from her hair. The goddess's tawny skin often was sprinkled with periwinkle sugar glitter, and her eyes were cotton-candy pink. They shined like rose quartz glittering in the moonlight.

She was a petite thing, and she seemed entirely harmless, but her bite was that of a black widow.

Today, she wore a bubblegum-pink Theodic bustled dress with an azure blue pendant of a dog.

"What did you do to anger your mother so?" A sugarplum smile floated on Destruction's face.

"Murder," Havyn said with a debonair grin.

"Some call it murder; some call it justice," Theo retorted. "It's all perspective, really."

"A little mayhem never hurt anyone," Destruction agreed with her boss, her blue hair flickering between silver blonde and azure blue. She said it with such a twinkle in her eyes, which made Theo's skin crawl.

"I hope you haven't been causing mayhem with—"

"If you were going to say Cecile, don't worry, Great Goddess, I've only slightly been antagonizing her."

"Don't call me that," Theo cut in, "and what does slightly mean?"

"Oh, a little discord here and there." Destruction's blue waves bounced with her glee.

Havyn chortled and shared a knowing look with Destruction.

"Oh, hydras, tell me you two haven't been conspiring again." Theo crossed her arms. There was no world in which Destruction would ever actively go against War. The goddess didn't want power. She'd hate the responsibility of it all. Besides, Destruction's loyalty was like diamonds; once formed, it was unbreakable.

"You asked me not to lie to you." She flashed a jungle-cat grin. "So I won't say anything at all."

"Don't worry. Our meddling is all for the greater good," Havyn said.

"That is not comforting at all."

"Fantastic. Now if you would go away, Havyn, your sister, and I have important matters to discuss," Destruction said. "Shoo, shoo, little Deathy." The blue-haired goddess waved her hands as if trying to get a puppy away from her food.

Havyn simply chuckled and disappeared into shadow, leaving them alone.

"Before you ask or say anything more, you know I'd only work with Death to aid you." Destruction's blue hair bounced as she dropped down in a huff at Theo's side on the bench. "And it was only after your mother had already spelled you. Which, by the way, is so unfair. You barely murder anyone, and all the men you do kill deserve it."

Theo's lips twitched up at her friend's defense of her.

"Besides, if I had your position and authority, I'd have done far worse by now." Destruction talked at a mile a minute when alone with War. It was where she felt safest to let out all her stored energy.

"You would have probably burned the world down."

"Oh, absolutely."

Theo rubbed her temples. Half of her job as leader of the War Court was keeping her subordinates from destroying the world.

"So what is it you need from me?" Destruction asked. "I saw your signal in the ballroom."

"I need you to get Hecate's Grimoire from Theoden and bring it to me."

"Oh, that's easy." Destruction snapped her fingers, and the azure blue dog pendant on her dress transformed into the spell book. "Havyn told me you might be wanting this."

Theo's stomach dropped. Havyn did nothing without seventeen reasons for it. She did no favors that wouldn't come back to bite the recipient tenfold in return. If Havyn knew Theo wanted the book, then that meant there had to be something wrong with War's plan.

Theo took the magical, sentient book from Destruction's hands. It sparkled with stardust and blood diamonds, a Hecate spiral etched onto the cover, but its moods were coated in venom and sprinkled with bile. A truly *lovely* book.

Opening the first page, Theo understood her horrible problem. The book could only be read by a member of the House of Azraelle or by Pantheonan sight—meaning only one of the nine gods of the Pantheon could read it. And Theo was no longer divine.

Not a single member of the pantheon would be willing to transcribe it without a hearty price.

Worse, Theo hadn't kept a good record of the House of Azraelle. She had no idea if there were any descendants still alive.

Not to mention, she wouldn't have access to them. Destruction couldn't read it either because she wasn't a major—Pantheon god.

Theo loosed a string of cuss words.

"What?"

"I can't read it."

"Oh, that is a problem." Destruction's features lit up with mirth. She was loyal, but she also reveled in chaos. "Well, I must be going. So much discord to sow. Do let me know if you need anything else."

Her form started to disintegrate into silver bubbles.

"Wait—" Theo grasped the goddess's wrist. "If you can, watch after Cecile. Help her get through this alive."

"I always watch after her." Destruction's voice was soft and bright as she completely disappeared, leaving soap bubbles in her wake.

Theo had one second of respite before the magic around her wrist—Love's chain—tightened and pulled her like a magnetic force closer to her champion, forcing her legs to move.

But he wasn't alone.

Two middle-aged humans boxed the boy in. One lady and one gentleman. Grey streaks laced their pristinely decorated hair, their clothing decadent and expensive. A human wouldn't dare wear a crown in the City of the Gods, but it was clear from their posture, attire, and general demeanor these two were royalty.

His parents?

The Andromaden Priest had called him a prince.

"Everybody saw your disgrace," the male said. "And it wasn't even—" The last three words were hushed and indistinguishable to Theo's ears, but the boy heard it and physically drew in like a turtle retreating into its shell. "You're so pathetic."

"Iwan," the woman said, "not here. People can hear you—"

"At the very least, try to die with honor." The Theoden king scoffed. "Can you do something that simple?"

The champion grunted, but he was cowering. Afraid.

The tall, disgustingly handsome, strong warrior *cowered* in the presence of his parents.

It wasn't right.

Theo really shouldn't intervene. She *should've* walked away. She didn't owe this boy anything . . . but she hated seeing people mistreated—especially by their parents.

Grinding her teeth and scrunching her hands into fists, Theo marched over to them like a Lieutenant Commander on a battlefield. "Oh, there you are, Champ—" She cleared her throat. "Kellyn," his name tasted like sour apples on her tongue, "I've been looking all over for you. We truly must be returning to our quarters . . . to strategize."

Her words were stilted and utterly rang false, but it didn't matter.

"Oh, look, it's your equally useless priestess," Kellyn's father said.

She glowered at his parents with her fiercest Goddess of War glare. "I don't like you." Her words spewed like acid. "And most people I don't like end up dead."

Those felt like good words to let settle with the prince's wretched parents, so she hauled said prince away toward the Champion's Quarters.

"Thank you for that," Kellyn said, his confidence slowly returning.

"I have a shitty parent, too," Theo said. "Honestly, my sisters can be quite horrible as well."

He laughed. "I understand that. I have a spoiled younger brother." He grunted and shifted on his feet as if he were unsure what to say next, settling on, "Are you okay?"

Theo flinched. She wasn't expecting that question. "Why?"

"Death . . ."

"Oh, yes, that," Theo said, not knowing what to say. "She wanted to taunt me. Nothing new." The last bit was said under her breath.

The champion grunted, clearly not knowing how to respond, and fell back into an uncomfortable silence.

They walked into the Champion's Common Room. The hourglasses representing the champions' lives were slowly releasing pebbles of sand, except the forest green hourglass—the Tierland hourglass. It was frozen like concrete—frozen to stone like the champion and priestess.

Theo passed the infirmary and paused at its entrance. Gods were healing their champions and talking strategy with them. In fact, almost every god was now in the Quarters, aiding their patron champion. Cecile and Emmett sat in the corner of the common room, with Andromache doing just that.

Most champions had successfully beaten their first challenge and were recuperating—all save the Tierland pair. So far, they were the only casualties. Others had been gravely injured, yet most were easily healed by their patron god.

An unfamiliar—and horrifying—feeling stirred in Theo's blood. She didn't quite know how to categorize it, but it certainly felt eerily like guilt or responsibility.

Theo shuddered.

She hated feeling anything—let alone something about humans.

Seventeen

Kellyn

Prince of Theoden

THEODEN'S QUARTERS, CITY OF THE GODS

Kellyn stared—glared—down at his second riddle. The key to his next challenge. Pressure did not help his affliction. It only made everything worse. The words weren't the hardest to read . . . he thought the first word was Ivy and the fourth bane . . . but the handwritten script with twirls and loops made translating the shapes to words rough. It made making out the letters, and especially the phonemes, nearly impossible.

Morrigan sat on their bed with her knees against her chest, watching him out of the corner of her eye.

Watching, but not helping.

He tried not to look over at her, with her raven curls spilling down her chest and her indecent nightgown clingy to her every curve—and she was wonderfully curvy. The sight caused unmitigated lust to burn in his veins.

It also caused him and his body to remember their kiss and how she felt in his arms. Soft and pliant. The way she smelled like smokey vanilla, olive trees, and majestic dreams. The way she tasted like blood orange seduction. The way she—

Kellyn cleared his throat and grunted.

He needed to stop thinking about her and focus on his task.

Only danger lurked there. But he'd never felt so attracted to someone in his life.

Morrigan huffed. "Fine, show it to me. I'm sick of watching you struggle." She was still an untamable wildfire, her demeanor monstrous . . . but she'd softened a bit. A tiny bit. Ever since seeing his parents. Seeing his shame.

Kellyn gulped. "What?"

"Your riddle."

Grunting, he held out his wrist for her to examine. As her silk fingers touched his skin, Kellyn sucked in a breath and held it. Her touch was lightning. Electric energy that felt like a mortal sin. A deadly mistake.

She stroked a thumb up his forearm, and a shiver ran through him. "It's a haiku." She smiled and read it to him.

"*Ivy, snake, foxglove, bane*
Harbinger of sickness reigns
Tormented are we"

"Poisons."

"Yes."

"Relatively easy riddle, don't you think?"

If it weren't written in script. Sure.

Her blueish-purple eyes captured Kellyn's, and his heart stumbled in his chest. "The gods were impressed with the way you played the game."

His lips twitched up, but he was too captured by her presence to speak. Her touch rattled him.

"It was impressive." She visibly swallowed and licked her lips before touching them with her fingers. "How fast you won the game."

"Oh," he breathed. A man of few words. "Thanks."

He took in her uniqueness. Her beauty, power, knowledge of magic, and the gods. He'd seen the replay of their challenge on the mirrors earlier. She'd looked Medusa directly in the eyes and lived. But not only that, she had an entire conversation with the monster in the god tongue. *The god tongue.* There was something special about Morrigan—like Cecile. Morrigan was God Marked, but there was something more.

She *was* special.

Kellyn focused on her like a gentle caress. Transfixed by her beauty and strength. There was a deep vulnerability lingering behind her pure power. A softness hidden deep underneath her buried secrets. Kellyn wanted to know what those secrets were and see what brought fury to her lips and unending darkness to her eyes. She was terrifying and arrogant, but there was far more to her than that. More than he had ever imagined, and he wanted to know it all.

Not just because he was deeply drawn to her physically, but because he was drawn to all of her, even if the darkness was terrifying. But he'd liked to flirt with fire—play with danger.

Morrigan licked her lips again, and his gaze traced her tongue. Emotions and hunger stirred in his stomach. He wanted this girl too much. Lust was a powerful emotion, but Kellyn was a dead man walking—what harm was a little passion?

He leaned in and tentatively grazed her neck with his thumb. She sloped into the touch, her eyes purple fire. He ran his fingers through her hair and tipped her chin to meet him. Morrigan sucked in a breath.

They were magnets. They wanted connection. Closeness. Kellyn's heart pounded, anticipation warming his stomach. His lips hovered over hers, barely touching, asking for permission—

The raven tattoo on Morrigan's arm squeaked. A warning. Kellyn pulled away quickly, putting space between him and his priestess. His heart was percussion in his ears like a war drum before a deadly battle.

The chamber door clicked open fiercely, and Cecile stormed in. "Apologies, I've been so distant . . . Andromache is . . . *specific*." Cecile said the word like she truly meant *demanding*. She entered the room and sat on the bed beside Kellyn, clearly not noticing the tension igniting the room. Emmett trailed behind and stood against the wall with his arms crossed. "Have you solved your newest riddle?"

Kellyn swallowed, his mouth dry and his tongue unable to move, but Morrigan cut in and saved him. *Again*. "Yes, we have the Poison challenge next."

"Us, too," Cecile said, "Andromache thinks we need to do the challenge on a full night's rest because Poison loves mind games."

"It's good advice." Morrigan cracked her neck and pulled the covers up her chest. "Poison likes to play with human expectations and take what is meant for comfort and crumble it into unimaginable tortures." Morrigan bit her lip, her eyes fixed on Kellyn for a long moment before quickly glancing away. "She also loves playing with your greatest weaknesses." Morrigan was suddenly more talkative and helpful with Cecile in the room. Perhaps it was to distract from what they'd almost done. "Have you any weaknesses?"

Kellyn's intestines hardened. He had many weaknesses, and Poison had already promised to exploit his reading skills. But Kellyn couldn't say that.

Cecile and Kellyn shared a knowing look. They both had their afflictions. Cecile had difficulty distinguishing between colors, particularly reds and greens. The Agoge's botany class was challenging because she struggled to see berries on plants and distinguish between slight color variations.

Kellyn decided to change the subject instead of answering it. "Has anyone done the Poison challenge yet?"

"Not that I saw," Cecile said.

"Why would it matter? Most of the challenges are changed between champions." Emmett leaned against the wall with his arms crossed. He refused to look at Kellyn, directing his response to the girls.

"Light's was the same," Cecile said.

"Poison's will be different. It's her way." Morrigan glanced between the three friends, her mind ticking like the gears of a clock, and Kellyn desperately wished he knew what she was thinking.

They discussed plans for the Poison challenge into the late reaches of the night. Ultimately, they decided that they would try to play the game together so that they could help each other.

The morning was steeped in plague and wrapped in a blanket of spider silk.

The mood seduced by peril.

The second challenge awaited, and Kellyn had a crick in his neck from trying not to touch Morrigan in his sleep. Which was a useless endeavor, for once again, he woke up to her on his bare chest. He must have gotten hot and undressed in his sleep.

The thought caused heat to rise in his cheeks.

But he woke up before her and quickly dressed.

Kellyn ran a hand down his face, staring at the poison mirror. It dripped green liquid from its surface, and its frame was made of skulls, crossbones, poison ivy, and multi-colored frogs. But it was stepping inside that was truly unsettling.

Kellyn, his priestess, and his friends entered a white void that felt like it went on for eternity.

Carved into the void were a marble table and a chair forged from strangler fig trees—the wood twisting together like the nightmares found in a witch's dungeon. It was the only thing in the room save the statues watching in the whiteness.

"Welcome humans, welcome to our date. It's the challenge of Poison, so let's test fate." Poison appeared in the room, her ivy-green hair pulled into an updo by vines, and her lips the purple of belladonna flowers. Poison's umber skin glowed under the stream of light spilling from the white void. She was glorious, stunningly beautiful, but like all gods, she was terrifying. "Today, your knowledge of poisons will be tested."

She snapped her fingers, and Morrigan was ripped through space and dropped in a heap onto the strangler fig chair, the branches twisting around her arms and legs. A second snap of the goddess's fingers had branches and thorns curling up and cocooning Kellyn in place before growing over his mouth like a gag.

He couldn't speak or risk severe injury to his face.

"You'll play in threes. Cecile, you shall go first, and Kellyn, dearest boy, if you try to help your friends, I will take payment from your flesh." The goddess's smile glinted, amusement pouring from every inch of her body.

With a third snap, fourteen clear jars filled with poisons appeared before Cecile. No words were written on the jars. Instead, a visual inspection was the only way to tell what plants rested inside.

From the color.

Kellyn sucked in a breath and cursed internally.

"At the end of the task, you will feed dearest Morrigan one of your jars." Poison's belladonna lips rose with a vicious smile. She clapped her hands together excitedly. "Wonderful, you have three minutes to select seven jars." The goddess's voice hung like a black widow searching out its next victim.

"Shit," Emmett said, staring at the jars before flicking a mournful gaze at Kellyn—he was the plant expert of the group. "Now is a time I ardently wish I'd paid more attention during our botany lectures."

Cecile eyed the jars wearily. "Seven thousand fucks." She tried to return her attention to the task, picking up a pot and examining it. "Are these berries?" She pointed to a plant with purple flowers and blueberries.

Nightshade.

"Yes," Emmett said.

"What color are they?" Cecile asked.

"Blue." Emmett ran a hand through his dark midnight locks. "I wish I'd been paying more attention in class instead of flirting with Lily."

"You mean flirting with everyone," Cecile said, moving a jar, her focus shifting back to the nightshade. "What are you?" She whispered to it.

"Nightshade," Morrigan answered from the chair, and Kellyn's eyes flickered to her with hope.

She knew her plants. Well, she seemed to everything.

"Tsk, tsk," Poison clicked her tongue. "Naughty, naughty. You shall remain silent, too." As the words left the goddess's mouth, strangler fig branches grew across Morrigan's lips.

"Which pile do we put it in?" Cecile asked.

"Ugh," Emmett mumbled. "She said to pick seven, but she

didn't specify what would happen to those seven. They might be the discard pile, or they might be the keep pile."

"Fuck." Cecile ran her fingers across the lid of the pot closest to her. "We need to strategize."

"These four are extremely poisonous, I think." Emmett visibly swallowed and sorted through the containers, placing them into three nearly even piles. When he finished, he took three steps back, checking his work. He pointed to the left pile. "These four are the least deadly . . ." he hedged, pointing at the right pile.

"I have no idea. I can't distinguish any of them." Sweat dripped down Cecile's temple, and she pinched her lips tightly. Her eyes were frantic and scared. The gods took her greatest weakness and turned it into a bullet aimed directly at Morrigan.

"One minute left." Poison's voice rippled through the room like a soft steam of water, deceptively calming.

"Oh, *dirty pookas*." Cecile's composure completely decayed, and she started moving the middle jars at what seemed to be random into the good and bad piles.

Anxiety's claws gripped Kellyn's back tightly. Cecile was falling apart and making hasty and terrible choices. She needed to get a hold of herself because she would feed one of those poisons to his priestess.

Earth sprites crawled out of white marble and swam around Cecile's head. She was so frazzled she didn't even notice.

Morrigan let out a mumbled curse from beneath her gag.

"We need to create the final two piles." Emmett ran a hand through his hair, a nervous tic.

"If I'm eventually going to feed one of them to her, then it needs to be survivable," Cecile said. "So we must split up the most dangerous ones and disperse them."

"Right." Emmett grabbed one jar from the bad pile and one from the good pile and started a new pile. One by one, he alternated mixing the most and least toxic into two evenly distributed piles, leaving the three unknown pots in the middle of the table.

Cecile picked up one and scrutinized it. "This is the least offensive . . . I think . . . but which pile do I place it in? In the chosen seven? Or the remaining seven?"

Emmett bit his lip. "I guess we assume that the ones we choose will stay?"

"Ten seconds."

Emmett randomly moved the remaining three from the middle into place, but Cecile stood frozen, with the only non-toxic pot resting between her fingertips.

"I don't know." Her voice cracked from the stress of it.

"It's impossible to know. You have to choose one."

With a small squeak, Cecile chose the pile on the right of the seven she was supposed to select.

"Time's up."

The words gnawed at Kellyn's insides, and a haze of stillness churned through the room. A stroke of energy crooned and set an uneasy tenor. It felt like the moments before a rat was lured into a trap.

It felt like a harbinger of bad news.

With a pop, a hiss, and a rattle, the seven jars in the chosen pile burst into liquid hellfire and vaporized into nothingness.

"Holy nymphs," Emmett hissed, jumping back.

The only non-toxic plant was off the table. Disintegrated.

Kellyn's heart quivered.

The remaining jars glimmered in the fluorescent light like shiny sharp shark teeth preparing to devour her.

"Choose three," Poison's voice mushroomed, sliding along their skin like pestering fleas. "You have one minute."

Cecile and Emmett didn't move. They were frozen like a jackal caught in an eagle's gaze. They stood fixated, not knowing what to do.

With a mixture of a moan and a groan, Morrigan told them *to get back to work*. At the noise, their eyes flicked to her, and they snapped out of their daze, rearranging the jars once more.

"The last pile we chose was discarded," Cecile said. "Do we continue that pattern? Or change it?"

Watching and being able to contribute nothing nettled Kellyn. He hated not being able to help. It felt horrible. Being helpful was who he was.

"What do you want to do?" Emmett asked. They held a jar each as they stared at their arrangement on the table.

Cecile bit her lip nervously. "I think we have to stick with the pattern."

"Ten seconds."

They placed their jars down in opposite piles. Emmett put the second-best option in the unselected pile—on the left.

"Time's up."

This time, the left pile exploded into a kaleidoscope of color and sound. Poison floating down in a cloud, spelled to miss the mortals. As the particles touched the floor, they dyed it with various shades of green and the colors of vibrant toxic flowers.

Shit. The challenge wasn't fair. It was a game of chance in the end. Chance with strategy.

"Choose one. You have fifteen seconds."

Without hesitation, Cecile grabbed the water hemlock jar, a plant that would definitely kill. "This has to be the one, right?" She darted a frantic glance around the room.

Fuck. She must've mixed it up with celery or parsnip. An easy mistake. Dread tied a knot in Kellyn's stomach. She was going to kill Morrigan. And he couldn't let it happen. Kellyn screamed past the thorns coating his lips. "No."

The pain was instant. It cut into his cheek and sliced some flesh, but he didn't care. He already had scars coating his face.

"Naughty boy," the goddess hissed.

Cecile hesitated before switching jars. "It has to be this pile, right?" She placed a plant that looked like Wisteria down and made it her final choice.

"Time's up."

This time—for the first time during the challenge—Cecile was right, and the remaining two jars disappeared off the table as if they were wrapped in a comfortable cloak of invisibility.

"Feed your final jar to Miss Morrigan." Her lips curved into a sinister smile. "Fail to do so, and you will be given the worst of all my little toys."

Cecile visibly gulped, scooped up the jar, and walked over to Morrigan as if she were a reluctant bride at an arranged wedding ceremony.

She pulled down her gag with a small whimper. "Apologies, I'm so, so sorry." Heartbreak carved tracks down her porcelain cheeks. Thick, guilty tears.

Morrigan squared her shoulders. "It's okay."

Cecile fed the plant to Morrigan. It would cause her severe food poisoning, but she'd survive. Morrigan ate each bite while staring down the goddess with murder in her eyes. Morrigan chewed on each seed as if savoring it. The vein in her neck ticked, and her eyes burned with sinister promises—all directed at Poison.

Once she was finished, the goddess cackled. "Let's speed this up. Shall we?"

Poison snapped her fingers again. The gesture released Morrigan from the chair. She fell to the ground and clutched her stomach, liquid hate bleeding from her irises as her expression soured and turned a pallid green. Poison had sped up the process, releasing the toxin into Morrigan's system and making her immediately sick instead of taking roughly an hour.

Kellyn banged on his cage, trying to escape to reach her and aid her in the sickness. But he was trapped.

Morrigan swallowed and held onto her composure for as long as possible. Still, eventually, she gave in and began moaning in pain, writhing on the floor, beginning to empty the contents of her stomach. There was nothing that Kellyn could do.

"Kellyn Ellis, Prince of Theoden, it is time for your test to start," Poison said, releasing him from his cage. Kellyn instantly ran toward Morrigan but was stopped as Poison continued, "If you touch your priestess before you're finished, I'll instantly kill you and your friend." He slid to a stop, inches from Morrigan. He desperately wanted to help her, but he couldn't. He turned his head toward the evil goddess. "Wonderful. Let's start."

Poison waved her hand, Emmett was refracted to the strangler fig chair, his hands bound, and Cecile refracted to Kellyn's wooden cage.

It was Kellyn's turn, and he had to feed Emmett his toxin. But Poison was cruel, and Kellyn's jars were solid white—instead of glass—and the only way to tell them apart was by the handwritten scientific lettering. *Cursive.*

It always had to be cursive.

The gods truly knew his weaknesses.

Kellyn faltered.

He tried his best to arrange his first piles, but he could only decode two of the fourteen jars during the first round, leaving him utterly unaware of what he was doing. Morrigan was useless, lying violently sick in the middle of the room, and Emmett and Cecile were tied up and gagged.

Kellyn was completely alone.

Sweat trickled down his brow, and his hands shook. He squinted, trying to break the last seven words into smaller parts—sounding them out.

Cicuta maculata

Atropa belladonna

Ficus carica

Ricinus communis

Batrachotoxin

Vaccinium

Nicotiana tabacum

All scientific names. All incredibly difficult to sound out. Kellyn knew the scientific names. He'd memorized them during class, but he just couldn't read them. His legs went numb, and his heart thrummed wildly in his veins. He'd never been a good reader and wouldn't start now.

It was impossible.

Sweat dripped down his back, and his vision blurred with anxiety. His parents were right. Kellyn was stupid and useless, and he couldn't even die correctly. Except it wasn't his death on the line. It was his best friend's. His best friend hated him because he couldn't even tell the truth.

Kellyn hid everything from Emmett.

That wasn't friendship.

Emmett stared, confused, his eyes screaming and lighting up with fear. His eyes said, *but you're the herbalist, the botanist. This should be easy.*

Kellyn sucked in a breath.

His lies filled the gap between the boys, cutting through the air like a physical thing. Kellyn wanted to tell the truth. He wanted to confess his affliction to his best mate, break down and say everything.

But he couldn't.

The games were public.

And he was too much of a coward to tell the world about his affliction.

Emmett was going to die, and he'd never know why. Never understand what killed him—why Kellyn was so useless.

It was awful.

All of it.

He couldn't give up. Kellyn tried to tackle one word. Tried to sound it out: Cic-ut-a . . . Ci-cut-a? Ci-vic-a . . . the letters were jumbled and mixed, and it was hard to determine if the letters were C's, V's, U's, or S's.

Even if he managed to read the word, he still had to remember the meaning, which felt like a human flying—impossible.

Kellyn bit the inside of his cheek. His veins throbbing. His breath stilling.

He was an idiot, and his best friend would die because of it.

Eighteen
Theodra
Goddess of War

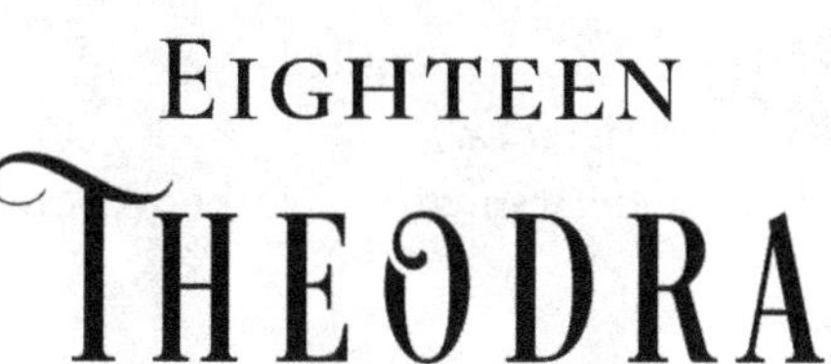

POISON'S MIRROR

Death might have been preferable.

Theo's mouth burned, and her stomach roiled. Flames licked her esophagus, hotter than an untamed wildfire. Hotter than Fire's magical blue-ember whip. It felt like fire ants crawling and clawing from her mouth down the entire digestive tract.

It was far, far, far worse than being stabbed in the chest. At least that had adrenaline and shock to soften the blow. But this was liquid agony.

And agony was spewing out from both ends.

The velvety seed pods went down smoothly like a kiss of magic, but they came out like demons swimming in the Orcus River. Clawing, cruel, and consuming.

Theo was currently rolled in a ball with her arms wrapped around her stomach, her head on the floor of the white void. She had no idea what was happening. She heard muffled noises and felt bile rising in her throat. She couldn't process anything but the agony churning her stomach and splitting her insides apart.

Dahlia, the tattooed raven on her wrist, puffed out her feathers and urgently knocked at Theo's skin with her beak.

When she wouldn't stop, Theo scratched at her skin and

moaned, "What?" Getting the word out of her lips seemed nearly impossible.

Dahlia squawked and nudged more. Typically, Theo could easily translate, but her mind was foggy, and the bile caressing her throat wasn't helping. She was far too sick to make sense of anything.

"What?" Theo groaned and vomited.

Squawk, croak, caw, squawk.

The bird desperately wanted her to know something or do something.

Squawk.

Theo moaned and pinched her head, a headache forming.

Caw. Caw. Caw.

"Shhh," she whimpered.

Caw, caw, squawk.

She held her hands over her ears, the noise causing a brutal piercing sensation at the front of her skull.

Caw, squawk, tap, tap, tap, squawk.

The bird's crescendo peaked, its tapping causing red marks to form on her wrist.

"What?" She groaned again and, this time, squinted her eyes and tried to focus.

*Caw, caw, caw, w*hich roughly translated to *Kellyn, Kellyn, Kellyn.*

"What about him?" Her words tasted like they were coated with poison—because they were. Death was preferable. Not that she knew what a human death would entail. Maybe it was fire and brimstone and lakes of acidic demise.

Caw, croak, squawk, squawk, squawk.

Which might have translated something like *Kellyn, champion, poison, bad reading.* Even if Theo was in her normal physical state, she still wouldn't have understood.

"Kellyn, poison, bad reading?" She repeated through a pained breath as she tried to keep the contents of her stomach *inside* of her stomach.

The raven repeated it but added, *must get up now, life and death.*

"Help Kellyn in the challenge?" Theo clutched her stomach and tried to sit up straight. And failed.

Dahlia flapped her wings and cawed twice. *Yes, yes*.

Theo moaned and rested her forehead on the ground, wishing for a sweet demise.

Doing anything—never mind following her raven tattoo's instructions—felt impossible. Besides, she'd promised not to help. She wouldn't do what her mother wanted. Defiance was her sword and shield. Nefeli wanted Theo to support the champion, and therefore she would not. It was that simple.

Squawk!

But the bird was insistent.

"Yes, yes," Theo grumbled.

Somehow, she lugged herself off the floor. With weak arms, Theo lifted her head and saw the boy standing in front of the marble table, and this time Emmett was strapped to the chair.

Crawling on her hands and knees, Theo tried to reach the toxins. A fog floated over her vision, and her ability to think was quite impaired, but even in her current state, she could see Kellyn floundering.

Grasping the edge of the table, she clawed herself up, and through a dance of blinking eyelashes and overwhelming blurriness, she saw only four jars remaining—and they were all terrible.

But the challenge was slightly altered from Cecile's. Instead of clear jars, they were opaque with writing on them. And the ones left read: *Atropa belladonna*—also known as deadly nightshade—*Cicuta maculata*—water hemlock, *Ricinus communis*—castor bean and batrachotoxin—frog venom. The latter three were exceptionally fatal and incurable.

His only option for survival was nightshade. It had an antidote.

"I don't understand," Theo forced out, her breathing heavy, "you're supposed to be a plant expert."

"I am but—" he hesitated, shame coating his eyes. He opened his mouth to say something—to explain—but he must have thought better of it because he stopped and adopted a mask of indifference.

Confusion kissed the lining of Theo's intestines. Or perhaps it was nausea because she turned away a moment later and heaved again.

"Thirty seconds," Poison said, her voice swinging through the room like an acrobat about to perform their final stunt.

"How can I help you?" Theo asked, wiping her face.

"Can you read them to me?" Kellyn's face glowed red with embarrassment.

Theo read two of the jars before she was interrupted.

"Time's up."

Theo clutched her knees, bent over with sickness as one of the jars shattered into a hundred pieces and shifted into falling red rose petals. They rained down like blood against the white void.

A prelude to what was to come.

Three of the worst poisons remained. Nightshade, ricin, and batrachotoxin. All would cause harm, but only one of them was recoverable.

"Choose one. You have ten seconds to pick a toxin to feed your friend."

In a wave of unmanageable sickness, Theo fell to her knees and dry heaved, her stomach empty of any substance. She rested her head on the floor momentarily before lifting it to see Kellyn holding the wrong jar, his eyes determined yet storming with anxiety.

In his fingers, as he walked closer and closer to Emmett, perched ricin, a deadly poison extracted from castor beans.

"No," Theo tried to yell, but it came out as an indistinctive croak. "No," she said, softer, almost defeated.

Kellyn didn't stop. He would feed his friend a poison with no known antidote if Theo didn't get herself to stand up and intervene.

She lifted herself with the tips of her fingers and stumbled up, walking like a newborn fawn. Getting her footing slightly, she rushed to Kellyn and knocked the jar from his hands.

It fell as if in slow motion, and Theo went with it, both hitting the ground with a thud.

"What have you done?" Kellyn grunted, horror intertwining his words.

Theo was too sick to speak. She rolled in on herself and into the fetal position, but she pointed at the deadly nightshade and wheezed, "Only one. That one."

With fire burning in his face causing his veins to protrude and his cheeks to turn deep red, Kellyn tread angrily to the nightshade and picked it up as his final choice.

"Time's up. Feed the poison to your best friend, or you and your priestess will die."

The champion did just that. Pain and fury etched into his sculpted face.

Theo curled into a ball, watching as Emmett was overcome with convulsions and sickness, his pupils dilated. Poison sped up the process for him, too. He mumbled hallucinations, the toxin deep in his bloodstream.

It was vile.

The challenge ended, and a black portal opened far out in the distance of the white void.

"Time to go," Cecile said.

Kellyn grunted. "Yes." He glanced—glowered—at Theo, hatred glittering in his eyes like a razor-sharp diamond, his anger coursing from his posture as he gritted his teeth.

He blamed Theo for his friend's fate.

Without another word, he turned, refusing to look at her. He lifted his friend, Cecile, at his side, and they heaved Emmett away toward the exit, leaving Theo shaking with sickness on the cold white floor.

She opened her mouth to call out to them, but nothing came save a small inaudible croak. Theo couldn't walk on her own. She tried to crawl but only got a couple of feet when her limbs grew too weary, and she collapsed in a heap.

Kellyn *left* her.

Cecile left her.

Left her to rot and die from the sickness.

Theo shouldn't have been surprised. Kellyn was like all men. A wretched disappointment. The part that rankled and she didn't want to admit—especially not aloud—was that she thought he might be different.

But men were all the same.

Vile, untrustworthy creatures.

Theo rested her head against the cold white stone, her eyelids too heavy to hold up. Blackness consumed her as she passed out, left all alone.

Precisely what she deserved.

Nineteen

Kellyn
Prince of Theoden

POISON'S MIRROR

Kellyn unfastened the jar's lid—the belladonna—and held out the berries, a whispered apology on his tongue.

Kellyn would've taken Emmett's place in a heartbeat. He would die for his friend, but couldn't condemn Morrigan to the same fate, even though she deserved it.

She'd caused it.

Always working against him like a devil sent from the depths of the underworld to destroy him. He wondered in the first challenge if she'd been sabotaging him, but now he knew for sure. He couldn't understand why, but then gods could make deals with anyone. And deals could be quite valuable. Brothers were known to go to war over a god's favor.

He couldn't blame her that much. It was the gods. They were manipulative, cruel creatures who bathed in pain and sorrow. It was why they created the games.

"It's okay, Kel," Emmett murmured, "I understand. You have to do it. I promise I'll be fine."

"It's going to kill you." Kellyn glanced down at the berries and moved them closer to his mouth.

"Don't you dare," Emmett snapped. "This is my burden to bear." He eyed the berries, dripping with black juice. "Don't steal this from me, too. It's my honor, Kel. Please, at least let me have this."

A plea Kellyn couldn't refuse. He'd stolen his best friend's honor by entering the games. And honor was currency in Theoden, only second to strategy and wit. *Death before dishonor.* He couldn't do it again. So he sucked down a breath and poured the berries into Emmett's mouth. "When you survive this, I will tell you everything."

Emmett's eyes flickered.

"I won't lie any longer," Kellyn said, "I promise I'll find a way to save you."

"If anyone can save me, it would be you," Emmett breathed before biting down on the berries. It was the nicest thing he'd said to Kellyn since Decision Day. "Kel, I'm—"

The effect of the poison was instantaneous. Emmett's head lulled to the side, and he passed out. The goddess sped up the process once again.

The branch manacles snapped in half, releasing Emmett, and he fell to the ground, convulsing. Dying. Kellyn knelt and supported his friend's body, fury burning in his bones. He tried to calm himself down, but he couldn't.

Kellyn's death was forgivable. He could accept that, but one of his friends dying was not, and for the first time in all the games, Kellyn let his composure slide and let his anger consume him instead of fear or apathy.

The games had changed. Now they were personal.

The gods were forged from the rivers of destruction. They drank in the death of mortals; after all, a god received power from two sources: worship and sacrifice. The games were designed to trigger both, and the gods reveled in the cruelty of it. They liked pushing mortals until they cracked.

In a game between divinity and mortality, divinity always came out on top.

Always.

The gods wanted Kellyn to bend, break, and die to make them stronger. But Kellyn wouldn't.

He'd had enough.

Holding his best friend's limp body, he vowed he wouldn't break. The vow coursed through him, hardening into resolve. Kellyn hated the gods for this, and he would do all in his power not only to live but to best the gods—seek vengeance. He'd do all within his power to save Emmett and Cecile, and all three would walk out of the Sacrifice alive. Not because Kellyn believed he was good enough to live.

He knew he wasn't.

He was pathetic and always would be, but he was angry, and anger was a brilliant motivator.

The gods tried to kill the wrong person today. And it would backfire on them. Kellyn wouldn't allow them to hurt the two people he loved most—his *true family*.

Poison hurt Emmett. She might even steal his life.

But Kellyn was fury personified.

The gods would learn a lesson today. They would learn never to provoke Kellyn's protective nature—for that nature would burn mountains to the ground. It would consume continents. It would kill.

They would pay for this, and the only way to hurt the gods—the only way to get vengeance for what Poison did to Emmett—was to *survive*. Steal the one thing the gods wanted most.

Power.

Kellyn was done being a pawn.

He was done letting the games play him. He would play the games, and he would win.

In the distance, the portal opened in the void. Not wasting any time—if Emmett was going to live, he needed the intervention of Andromache immediately—Kellyn easily lifted his friend and walked to the exit, Cecile at his side.

She stepped through first, and Kellyn gently placed Emmett's feet on the floor and awkwardly handed him to Cecile. He thought she might struggle, but she was surprisingly—inhumanly—strong.

Putting weight back on the foot inside the mirror, Kellyn considered leaving without returning for his priestess. She'd sabotaged him. She deserved to rot in here. He wanted to lash out because he hated her just as much as the gods for this, but his honor dictated his actions.

Morrigan needed help, and he couldn't find it in his soul to condemn her, even if she deserved it. And there was no doubt that she deserved it. She'd destroyed the only nontoxic plant in the game and forced him to pick deadly nightshade. The only other option was unimaginable. Batrachotoxin had no antidote. It caused paralysis and death within ten minutes.

Belladonna was a better gamble.

Kellyn let his weight shift, and he fell back into the mirror.

Morrigan had her knees pulled into her chest and her head resting on the marble. Miserable moans echoed off the white plane, and the smell of bile permeated everything. It was caked in her hair, clothing, and next to her head, but she was so ill that she didn't notice.

He knelt beside her and tucked an errant lock behind her ear. Dark circles laced her eyes, and her skin was pallid and warm. She looked terrible and probably felt worse. Kellyn was furious, his heart thrumming in his veins, but he couldn't turn off his concern. He scooped her into his arms and hiked through the portal and back to the infirmary. He gently placed her into a bed before turning all his attention to his friend.

Emmett was unconscious, still convulsing, but no one was with him. On the mirrors stationed throughout the room, Kellyn saw that Cecile was forced into her Tribunal.

As if summoned by his thoughts, two gruff nymphs appeared at the bedside. One was an earth nymph, and the other of the sea. The earth nymph resembled the one from the library. It very well could be the same creature. The other was formed from beauty itself. Her eyelashes were carved from black seashells, her eyes were the color of coral, hair the color of seaweed.

"Time to go." The earth nymph grabbed his arm fiercely.

"You're required at your Tribunal," the sea nymph said, her voice dark like the ocean's depths.

Kellyn allowed himself to be steered away. He needed to buy time and plan if he was going to best the gods. Which meant he had to go along with the games.

For now.

The Tribunal passed in a haze. Kellyn couldn't focus. His mind longed only to return to Emmett and see how he was doing. His focus was stoked with a myriad of thoughts on how to beat the gods. He needed to band together with the other champions. They needed to keep each other alive.

Together they were all stronger, but he had no idea how to convince all of them of that. Especially since, to them, he was a plague.

Kellyn couldn't remember what the gods did or said during his Tribunal. He had a new tattoo riddle, but he didn't care. He'd figure it out later.

After it ended, his feet automatically led him to Emmett and the infirmary. But he wasn't alone this time. Two of the creepy triplet goddesses were by his side, along with Cecile. Andromache was administering what looked like medicine.

Kellyn tensed. Havyn was by Emmett's side, a satisfied look on her face.

When Cecile caught his eyes, she said, "It's the antidote." Gliding over to Kellyn, she pulled him into a sweet embrace. It was nice. Just what he needed—the comfort of a friend. Of family. Cecile pulled away but didn't remove her hand from his arm. "The gods aren't allowed to heal after the Poison challenge, but they can administer an antidote."

"Your friend should be fine," Andromache said, running a hand along Emmett's head, taking his temperature.

"He should be dead." Havyn placed her legs up on a shadow table, lounging. "Poison sped up the death process, and now he rests in a coma." The tips of her lips curved up with mirth.

The god didn't have to look so happy about it.

Cecile squeezed his arm. "It's okay, Kel. It's not your fault."

He stiffened. "It is." It was his fault, and the gods . . . and Morrigan's.

"I've got it from here, boy," Andromache said, conjuring a wet compress out of the air. "She might need your help more than he does." Light bobbed her head at Morrigan, who was retching into a bucket on her infirmary cot. War hadn't come to the games, so Morrigan wouldn't receive any godly help.

Havyn chuckled, and the sisters shared a knowing look.

Cecile winced, paled at the sight, and took a step closer to the Theoden priestess, but she hated vomit. The mere presence of it had her gagging.

"It's alright, Cecile. I'll handle it."

Cecile nodded. "Be good to her."

"I will."

Kellyn walked over and scooped the priestess into his arms once again.

She needed a bath, so he walked her to the thermal caves—the bathing chambers for the champions.

Moss grew on the cave walls, ivy interlacing with it. Lava flowed in streams of liquid fire and snaked through the moss, releasing heat but not burning or destroying it. The brilliant—near white—glow was the only internal light in the cave, save the luminescent butterflies. Magical butterflies glimmered in all different colors. Periwinkle blue, cotton candy pink, blood rose red, ghost tree purple, mysterious green, kitten whisker grey, and unicorn gold. All sparkling and graceful, flitting through the cave with no worries and endless energy. The room smelled of spring mornings and twilight dances—flowers, musk, and magic. The rivers of liquid fire poured into the waters and hissed. The sound caressed Kellyn's senses.

It would've been romantic if Morrigan wasn't in such a horrible state.

Taking pains to be gentle, Kellyn washed out her hair, strand by strand, his fingers accidentally grazing her skin.

Each contact sent a shiver down his spine. He hated how much he simultaneously wanted this girl and despised her.

Morrigan groaned, gagging, and resting her hands on the rocks at the side of the pool. She croaked out words in a foreign language that sounded like the language of the gods . . . again. The words were delirious, and her eyes were vacant when they were open.

"Big, care, human . . . I don't," she whispered, her words primarily nonsensical.

She pinched her eyes tight and swayed. Kellyn caught her and held her upright, her body weak from the sickness and exhaustion. There was nothing remotely attractive about her at the moment. She was a jumble of muck and misery, yet his body still reacted to her like she was a drug. Still wanted her like she was air.

Toxic, burning air, but air, nonetheless.

Silently, she let him attend to her without a complaint. Her body was limp, her eyes fogged and glittering, dripping with an emotion he couldn't decipher.

In an awkward display of trying to maintain propriety, he cleaned first the bodice of her Nefesian-inspired dress and then the big hoop skirt.

A Theoden priestess dressing in Nefesian fashion was strange. Each country had distinctive fashion based on its patron god. Nefesians dressed in elaborate crinoline hoop skirts, and Andromadens wore impractical panniers, the styles reflecting the gods' personalities. Nefeli and Andromache preferred dramatic, over-the-top silhouettes that displayed extravagance and riches. But War was practical, so Theodenites favored tartans, the soft-bustles, and A-line skirts that were easier to manipulate. Functionality was essential in Theoden culture, its currency, sports, and activity.

But the gods decided the champion's and priests' outfits. So clearly, Nefeli was clothing Morrigan. But why? Especially when it was clear that Morrigan was an important human in the War Court's servant ranks.

Everything about this girl was odd.

Kellyn's ministrations moved to her skin.

Nothing was spared from the violent sickness, and Morrigan's forehead was damp and dripping with sweat, her body coursing with shivers.

The girl would live, but her battle to rid herself of the poison was beginning, and it would become much worse.

Twenty
Theodra
Goddess of War

INFIRMARY, CITY OF THE GODS

Shivers danced through Theo's bones, and everything ached. Her head lolled to the side, and her breaths were stilted—painful and wheezing.

Her mouth burned like she'd eaten the world's hottest pepper. Fire clawed at her eye sockets, and a regimental drum filled her skull. Chills coursed through her veins, her body shaking with cold and death's stalking presence.

A fever killed far more people than any weapons of war. Infection from a cut. Sickness. A too-high fever was a death knell.

"So cold," Theo croaked. She was freezing. Her limbs convulsed from it. She needed to warm up. "More, I need more." Theo clawed at the blankets covering her body. She was far too cold.

Strong hands caught her and pinned her arms in place. "Shhh, you're okay."

"So cold." But the big muscular body beside her made her feel slightly warmer.

"You're burning up, Morrigan."

"No. Not Mor . . ." Theo trailed off. There was something important she wanted to say, but she couldn't quite find it.

The world twirled on pointe like a sweet ballerina dancing her final show. The artistry of it haunting and coated with delirium. Theo knew she was delirious. She felt her consciousness going in and out. She felt strong hands at her back and a velvet whisky-like voice whispering comforting words into her ear.

Ice coated her forehead, and she tried to bat it away.

"Why did I think you would be more biddable while sick?" The velvety voice was amused.

"You're a pretty human man." Her speech was slurred, delirium sinking its teeth in and not letting go. "I think I like you . . . I don't like human men. But you're—"

The fever came on fast and unyielding like the off-key strokes of a violin. Theo clung to the sounds. The cadence of his breaths and the sweet harmony of his deep voice tended to her. The feel of his arms around her, rocking her and comforting her through it all. The smell of him was magic. Musk, sandalwood, and a hint of leather.

Masculine and warm.

He told her stories of the time he had a fever as a child and funny tales of his adventures in the Agoge. He did all he could to distract her from the agony clinging to her body.

He was gentle, kind, and patient.

Three things she didn't know men could be. Kellyn held her and cared for her. It was the first time anyone had ever done such a thing. Theo didn't know how to feel, but luckily, she was too incoherent to figure it out.

A problem for another day.

Theo fell into fitful dreams, in and out of consciousness.

When she woke, Kellyn was no longer holding her. But she was utterly clean and tended to.

She shuddered.

Theo didn't know how to handle kindness. She didn't know how to handle being taken care of. All at once, she wanted to clutch onto the feeling while simultaneously running as far away from it as she could.

Tangled, tainted emotions bloomed inside her chest, and she tried to rub them out.

Trying to escape the thoughts and feelings, she looked around the room. Two gods were attending their champions, healing, and aiding them in any way they could. One of which was Andromache, Light. Behind her, the mirror televisions played moments from the games.

As if taunting Theo, they all played the scenes from Cecile's challenge when the darkness showed her Devereaux's death.

"Do you think they're torturing you or me?" Andromache said, wincing as she watched her lover's head drop from his shoulders again and again. "I play that moment in my head on repeat anyway." Her beautiful moon-white features were painted in sorrow.

Theo's throat burned; a dryness so thick not even the Ajaxian Desert could compete. What did one say to their sister after murdering her one true love? "I'm sorry, Andrie." Theo croaked, her throat raw and in agony, the poison burning still eating away.

"You know, that's the first time I've ever heard you apologize for anything."

Theo cracked her neck as emotion stirred in her stomach, and she tried to hold back tears. This human body changed everything. It let in a flood that she couldn't endure. "I don't know what to do to make it better."

"You can't."

"Why haven't you punished me?"

"Besides allowing you to be turned into a human?" A soft yet wicked smile climbed Andromache's lips. "I don't have to. All I have to do is wait. You're destined to fall in love with a mortal, too. It's our curse. That will be punishment enough."

The prophecy of the three Death god triplets and their disastrous human love stories. The prediction foretold that all three goddesses would fall in love with a human, leading to death.

But the prophecies were rubbish. At least, the one for Theo was. She'd always loathed human males. It couldn't change, could it?

Theo sighed and rubbed at her temples. Everything in her life had been uprooted and shifted. And she *had* feelings—

Theo sucked in a breath and shifted her focus. She had a plan to fulfill. Despite the sickness twisting her stomach, she hadn't forgotten her goal. She needed to find a way to read the spell book and break her curse. But for that, she needed help, but there was no way she'd ask Havyn . . . but maybe Andromache.

"Do you know how to find the heirs of House Azraelle?" Theo asked, holding her breath. Andromache could easily force a deal for the information, but they had a strong bond and love for each other.

"Heirs of the House of Azraelle have their sigil tattooed into their skin," Andromache said, "and if I had to guess, you will find one soon." Andromache placed a hand on Theo's heart before tipping her chin up. "Not even you can run away from your fate."

Fate.

Theo fought the urge to roll her eyes. She didn't believe in prophecies.

The priest from Andromeda groaned, his eyes still latched shut in a coma. Bella was curled into a ball at his feet, even trying to comfort the unconscious man.

"Will he be okay?" Theo asked.

"Not without my aid." Andromache cocked her head. "Feeling guilty?" her sister asked, once again sliding the back of her hand across her priest's forehead.

"Why would I?"

"Because you've forsaken your champions for the last 500 years. Precisely why you've received no medicine to aid with your poison."

Forsaken? Theo didn't ask it aloud. Her throat ached from too much vomiting and disuse.

Theo laid back down on her pillow and stared at the ceiling pondering. She hated the Sacrifice because she hated the way it toyed with human lives and emotions. She thought that staying away from the Sacrifice was the humane thing to do, the right thing to do. But what if she were wrong?

What if staying away was the reason all her champions died?

Guilt steeped in her stomach. Theo never wanted to harm her champions. She stayed away out of principle. Her throat grew dry again, and bitterness seeped into her mouth as exhaustion claimed her body.

When Theo woke up the next time, Cecile was holding vigil by her bed, her brow creasing her pretty porcelain features.

"How are you feeling?" Cecile asked, sitting in the chair next to the cot.

"Much better," Theo said, throat raw.

That sentiment was primarily true, her body felt much better, but her mind crawled with torment. Theo couldn't get over what Andromache said. She even dreamed of Theoden's champions dying over and over again in the Sacrifice.

Her mind was plagued by it.

"Cecile, do you think the Theoden champions have died for the last 500 years because I haven't shown up?"

Theo expected the girl to pull her punches, at least a bit, but she didn't. Not at all. "Yes, I think that's exactly why they died."

Theo gulped. "You must think of me as a villain." Theo didn't realize that, through her apathy, she'd condemned every Theoden champion . . . every single one.

Cecile didn't say anything. Instead, she watched Theo's expressions like a hawk.

"Are the games unwinnable without a god's help?"

"Yes," Cecile said again. "Kellyn, the champion you so aptly refused to help, nursed you back to health." The tone was biting but not bitter. Cecile was proving a point. "He could have, and maybe should have, left you to your sickness after you sabotaged him."

Theo didn't necessarily qualify refusing to help as sabotage, but she understood the girl's point and fused her lips, absorbing the wrath.

One of the things War admired about her Godmarked was the fire and lack of fear to speak her mind—even to a god. It was a trait that would get Cecile in trouble in the future, but not with the War Goddess.

"I'm sorry about poisoning you." Cecile sucked in a breath and bit her lip, her fingers straightening out the wrinkles in the sheets. The girl hated the mess and had compulsions to clean it up. Almost as if she thought if she could keep the things surrounding her tidy, she could also control her life—keep it tidy, too.

Theo shrugged. "It's the Sacrifice. These things are bound to happen."

"I don't understand. You're the Goddess of War; shouldn't you be angry? Isn't wrath your driving emotion?"

"No." *Not wrath, sorrow,* but Theo didn't want to say that. "I cannot fault you for your actions in a game designed to make you betray the things you hold most dear." Theo rolled her sheet between her fingers. "Though I'd prefer it if you didn't poison me again."

Cecile laughed.

"It wasn't a pleasant experience."

"Oh no?" Cecile raised a taunting brow, a smirk painting her soft face. She opened her mouth to add something else but got distracted by the mirrors replaying a moment from her Death Challenge.

Cecile, twelve years of age, was in chains and being handled by a giant bruiser of a man. Little Cecile fought and kicked, trying to escape, but it was useless. Despite being strong for her age, the man was triple her height and weight.

"Let me go." Cecile kicked him in the shin. "I want to go home to my parents."

With a fierce crack, the man backhanded her, sending her flying like a rag doll. "Your parents are the ones who sold you, girl." The man spat at her feet.

"That's not true," Cecile said, her voice coated with the sadness of a banshee's tears. "It can't be."

"It is."

The low, sinister voice echoed all around the real Cecile and Theo, the man's face appearing in every mirror, mocking with its cruelty.

"Oh, Cecile," Theo breathed, sitting up in the cot and pulling the girl into a hug. It was utterly out of character for the goddess to hug anyone, but she sensed Cecile needed to be held. And if there was any human Theo could stomach trying to care about, it was her human servant. "I'm so sorry."

The mirror shifted to a scene of the Simark priest fighting a hydra.

Cecile's eyes were red and puffy as she held back tears. She brushed off the embrace and backed away. A deep hurt was etched into her features. There was no way that Theo believed the pirate who trafficked in human flesh. It was a tactic to control, make Cecile unstable and question her beliefs.

"It doesn't matter. It was a long time ago." Cecile swiped her tears away with the back of her hand.

"It does matter." Theo's eyes held the girl's, and she tried to create a space of warmth and safety with her expression and demeanor. She tried to be comforting for perhaps the first time in her entire life. She tried to change as Havyn suggested. "Because you matter, Cecile."

"It's fine." Cecile visibly swallowed. "Let's drop it."

They sat in silence for a while until Theo slipped back into sleep. The fever's talons gripped her and pulled her under once more. Sleep was coated in nightmares. She was consumed by visions of Theoden champions repeatedly dying. It was like a god was feeding the dreams to her. But which one?

It wouldn't necessarily have been Andromache. Havyn could dream walk. Maybe it was her. Death was always cooking up plans in the background. She enjoyed playing with humans and the gods like chess pieces, moving them on a playing field. But Havyn had never meddled with Theo before, so why start now?

Theo awoke to her teeth chattering. The fever was back. But *he* was there pressing a cold compress to her forehead.

Their eyes touched.

His were a beautiful chestnut with concern painting the edges.

Her heart jumped into her throat, and she held her breath. Theo liked his concern. She liked his hands on her. Kellyn was like no one she'd ever met. She wanted to run from the feelings stirring in her stomach. It was like butterflies breaching their cocoons.

"You're awake."

"Yes," she said, her voice like sandpaper. "Thank you for helping."

He grunted, his eyes flashing to his friend, almost like he wished it was him awake instead.

"You love him."

"Of course."

"He's horrible to you."

"He's hurtful, not horrible," Kellyn said, his gaze attached to his friend. "It's impossible to go through life without hurting the ones you love. Hurt is inevitable. Harming isn't. True friendship is accepting that we will be hurt and extending grace and forgiveness when it occurs. I'm not perfect. I have done many things to deserve his ire."

"Grace . . ." Theo thought about grace and her lack of it in her punishments. She gave no mercy to the men she haunted and flayed. She didn't believe in mercy for men, and she didn't think men were capable of anything but horror. But that stood in direct opposition to the honorable man standing in front of her. The man selflessly aided her when he didn't have to. "You're very wise, Kellyn Ellis."

Theo's gaze rested on the Goddess of Love aiding her champion after a challenge. "I was wrong."

"Wrong about?"

"So many things . . ." Theo gulped and grasped the hand of her champion. "Thank you. I'm not very good at showing my gratitude."

He tensed at her touch, his Adam's apple bobbing. "You're welcome." His voice was gruff, and he ran a hand across his well-manicured facial hair.

Theo sucked in a breath. The sight was too tempting. She needed a distraction. The friend would do nicely. "I think he'll live."

"No thanks to you," Kellyn said, pulling his hand from hers, his countenance covered by a thunderstorm. "You would have killed him." Without another word, he marched out of the infirmary, leaving her alone.

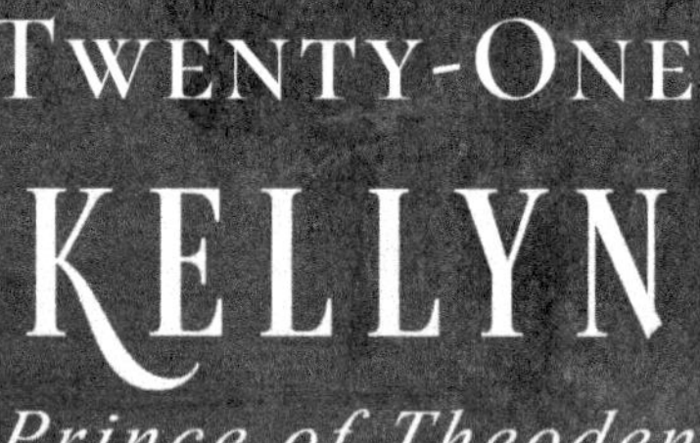

Twenty-One
Kellyn
Prince of Theoden

CHAMPION'S QUARTERS, CITY OF THE GODS

The day was written in cursed spells.

Fury and pain felt like leeches on the skin. Sucking and draining. Kellyn had nearly killed his best friend, and the guilt of it stewed in his stomach.

The entire week was rotten. One terrible thing after the next.

Kellyn needed space. He felt useless once again. Always useless. Emmett was in a coma, Morrigan was nearly recovered but still utterly maddening, and Cecile was forced to halt her progress through the games.

None of it boded well for survival. Because to survive the games, they needed to get moving. Kellyn had three challenges left, and Cecile two, and they were more determined than ever to win—to live. But they couldn't continue without Emmett.

Kellyn didn't care if Morrigan played. It would be better if she didn't because she'd sabotaged him. Multiple times. She destroyed the statues in his room, tried to find a book instead of participating in the first challenge, and switched out the poisons.

"Are you okay?" Cecile asked, hovering at the doorframe of Kellyn's bedroom. "I saw your interaction with The—Morrigan."

Kellyn grunted.

"Yeah, she has that effect on people."

Kellyn chuckled. "How do you know her?"

Cecile bit her lip like she measured what to say. "Through Theodra . . . and the Godmark." She hedged around the truth, or at least not the whole truth. "She's part of the War Court."

"A human member of the War Court?" Kellyn raised an eyebrow. "Then why is she here?"

"As punishment."

"From Theodra?"

"No." Cecile sucked on her lip more, clearly uncomfortable with the line of questioning. "She wouldn't want me to say anymore. Perhaps you should ask her."

Kellyn grunted. He'd rather fight a rabid dog than talk to Morrigan now.

Cecile sighed. "Morrigan is better." She changed the subject. "You should complete your third challenge."

"I'm not going without you." Firelight flickered on his face as he rubbed it. He kneeled at his makeshift altar and fiddled with his nearly finished lovespoon carving. "Especially not when we both have Nefeli's challenge next."

They'd solved their next riddles together. Cecile's answer was a diamond, and Kellyn's riddle read:

I have hundreds of eyes
and preening is my past-time
my train is so glorious that
Maidens do plunder
For hats, coiffures, and drapes, they sunder
I'm metallic blue and diamond bright
my piercing calls do drown the night

Kellyn managed to solve it quickly. He was good with riddles once he managed to read them. The answer was a peacock.

Peacocks and diamonds were both symbols of Nefeli.

"Kel, you need to look out for yourself. Time isn't on your side. It's day four." Cecile's tone dripped with unbridled anxiety, and her posture sang of it, too.

"I could say the same thing to you."

"But I've completed three challenges."

"True . . ." Kellyn took a poker and played with the fire.

"But *we all live.*" His new motto. "We all make it through these games, and I think we have the best chance of doing that as teams."

"Then we will try to play as teams," Cecile said, "but we will never get the other champions on board."

Getting the champions to work with him was a nearly impossible task.

Kellyn placed his poker on the floor and glanced at the lovespoon between his fingers. It reminded him of his fury and his stupid belief that Theodra could be there for him. He'd had unwavering loyalty, but what did he have to show for it? The Goddess of War never showed up for her people. She'd forsaken them—forsaken him.

All the gods were vile creatures who gloried in torment.

Kellyn had watched all the mirror feeds of the other champion's challenges, and in every single one, the gods played with the mortals' minds like puppets on strings.

That's all humans were to them. Puppets.

Entertainment.

Sources of power.

Kellyn was over it. He no longer believed there was any goodness in them. How could a being thousands of years old—who'd spent most of that time smiting humans—have any integrity left in them? He'd been so foolish. So unthinkingly loyal.

No longer.

Kellyn snapped the lovespoon.

"I want them all to suffer like they make us suffer," he said. "I want to rob them of their power."

"Make who suffer?" Morrigan asked, walking through the doorway, her eyes fixated on her wrist. She rubbed it as if in pain, and the invisible chain connecting them rippled in and out of existence.

Kellyn's brow furrowed. Why did the chain seem to affect her more than him and at the most random times? He'd nearly forgotten about it. It was like she was bound to him in the games but not the other way around.

"Was I interrupting?" Morrigan asked, gazing between them,

her ink-black hair shining damply and twisted into warrior braids atop her head. She'd bathed and changed, her skin tone slightly less pallid. She wore a Theodic styled dress with warrior leathers acting as a corset.

She looked like a midnight symphony—part magic enchantress, part inevitable impossibilities.

Although her beauty only managed to anger him more. She was healing, and Emmett wasn't getting better—despite the antidote. Kellyn balled his fists around each half of the broken lovespoon and let out what might have been a growl.

The girls shared a look, standing in the doorway. Morrigan swayed, stepping slightly closer to the exit, responding to Cecile's silent warning. "I wanted to speak with him alone."

"Maybe you should come back later."

"No, let her in; I'd *love* to talk to her." Kellyn lingered on the word love like it was a delicious toxin. He looked like a trapped beast ready to pounce on the person who had ensnared him. Kellyn rarely lost his restrained demeanor, but he was all masculine energy when he did. Seething and wanting release.

"I don't think that's a good idea," Cecile said, glancing between them like they were dangerous predators.

Morrigan's azure eyes landed on him, and she cocked her head, narrowing her eyebrows like a bird of prey. "I can handle him."

Cecile threw up her arms. "Alright, try not to rip each other apart too much." She turned and exited the room, closing the door behind her.

Morrigan held her head high and walked over to him at the fireplace. He sat on his ankles; the broken spoon cradled in his hands. She stood over him, her shadow covering his face. He looked like a warrior about to be felled by an evil demon king in a battle.

Morrigan could easily be a demon.

One thing was for sure: she wasn't normal.

"Giving up on your god?" she asked. Her ability to perceive the truth was uncanny. She'd figured it out merely from seeing the spoon split in half between his fingers.

"Yes," he seethed.

"Probably for the best." The corner of her lips twitched up. "Theo is pretty rotten—especially to men."

He growled his agreement. "As are you."

"Oh, that's a given." Her lips turned into a full smile, dark amusement twisting into them. "You're angry with me, so have it out." She tensed, awaiting an explosion, and she rolled her shoulders back, readying for a fight.

"You want to provoke me."

"Yes," she breathed.

Then he would give it to her. He let go, allowing the simmering fire inside his bones to spill out. Kellyn stood up to his full height, easily towering over her. The cords of his neck tightened, and his fingers dug into the wood still between his fingers. "What the hell is wrong with you? First, you try to kill Emmett, and now you want to provoke me?"

Her brow furrowed, and she took a protective step back at the sound of his deep rumbling bass. "I killed him?"

"You killed Emmett."

"Last I checked, he was alive." She glowered. It eviscerated, leaving only carnage in its wake. It rattled his chest and broke a piece of his resolve, but her next words shattered it. "I saved him. *You* almost killed—"

"—*You forced me* to give him deadly nightshade." Kellyn's words were like a waterfall of mercury. Beautiful yet deadly. He took a step closer to her, and she took a step back like an intense tango, their footfalls jolting with magnetic energy.

"Nightshade has an antidote and won't kill Emmett." Her words rankled, twisting into sharp icicles she might stab him with at any moment. Given her temperament he wouldn't be surprised if she could scour his flesh from his bones.

But he wouldn't be intimidated by her.

"It's *deadly* nightshade." He took another step forward, and she moved back, hitting the jagged wall. "They call it deadly for a reason, Morrigan."

"Andromache administered the antidote." She clutched the wall with her hand, using it to steady herself, her legs still shaken and weak.

"That doesn't matter," Kellyn growled, "you could have killed him."

She arched an onyx brow like it was a shield. "You *would have*. You wanted to give him ricin."

Kellyn jerked back as if hit. His heart startled and skipped a beat. "No, I was going to give him *Ficus carica*." What was she talking about? Ficus was clearly written on his final jar. It was a type of benign fig tree. Kellyn kept it in the game until the end because it was the most nontoxic on the table. He was certain, wasn't he?

His palms began sweating as he thought back on the challenge. It was hard. Impossible. His biggest weakness. He'd floundered, unable to make sense of anything in the first round, all the poisons written out with their scientific names in cursive script. His brain had been waterlogged, and he had guessed on most of the jars. But by the second, he had a better grasp of the words.

Right?

"No," Morrigan said, pausing, her face lighting up with a realization that nettled underneath his skin. It was like she saw his deepest, darkest secrets. "Do you have an issue with your eyesight?"

"No." Kellyn gulped defensively. "My eyes are perfect."

This conversation was getting uncomfortably close to his truth. If she delved any deeper, she might see his great shame. She might discover his stupidity.

Discover, he was a *big dumb brute*, after all.

The valves in his heart clenched. Anxiety cut through his stomach, and he sucked in a deep breath. She couldn't figure it out. His life outside the Sacrifice depended on hiding his affliction from the world.

Morrigan cocked her head like a bird, her eyes cutting through him. Into him. Seeing everything. Exposing his organs and insecurities to her penetrating gaze. "It's okay. You don't have to be perfect."

"My eyesight is fine," he snapped, not wanting her to get any closer. His anger twisted into defensiveness, and his jaw locked, the vein pulsing with the erratic beats of his heart.

"It's the letters, isn't it?"

Kellyn sucked in a sharp breath. The words felt like a guttural punch or a garrote strangling him slowly and viciously.

She knew.

His lungs clenched and hardened into thick, unbreakable stone.

She knew.

He couldn't breathe.

She knew.

Sweat dripped down his back.

He was caught. She knew he was an idiot. An idiot who couldn't read. An unlovable, undesirable imbecile. A big dumb brute whose only value was to guard a king, not become one.

His heart jolted, and fire licked his insides.

She knew.

How? And how so quickly? He'd been able to hide his affliction so well before, with no one figuring it out once he entered the Agoge—no one, including Emmett. He had ensured no one knew he couldn't read—tricking teachers and stealing tests. Sometimes he'd even forced Cecile to read to him.

Kellyn cracked his back to relieve the pressure, and his eyes fixed on her, trying to figure her out. Morrigan was unnatural. She knew far too much—was far too skilled.

"Words look the same and sound the same sometimes, don't they?" she asked. "Or letters swim, or you can't understand them. Or you can't process them properly."

Kellyn's face paled, and he wanted to run away.

His heart drummed in his ears, and the world faded away, his mouth growing dry and hurting from the strain of holding in his shame.

Morrigan inched closer and placed a hand on either side of his face. Her skin soft and comforting. "It's okay," she breathed. "It's called dyslexia, and that's not something you need to feel ashamed about."

His muscles tightened at the words. He didn't understand. That word meant nothing to him.

"It's an inherited condition that affects reading and the language center of your brain," Morrigan said. "It makes it hard to distinguish the parts of the words and the sounds those words make."

Kellyn flinched, unable to process. Everything she said made sense. Kellyn saw the letters in words and often made out their shapes, but they never fit right. And no matter how hard he tried, the meaning wouldn't translate.

Morrigan gave words to the shame he'd carried with him all these years. That shame was like an anchor on his back—an anchor that pulled him down into the ocean deep.

It was like she'd seen and validated all his struggles. She was the first person to say it was okay. The first person to provide answers. Even if he didn't understand those answers in the slightest.

He wanted to ask what that word—dyslexic—meant, and if he was an idiot. But his tongue locked up, and he couldn't answer the question.

"It doesn't affect intelligence," she answered his unspoken query, "but it's why Ricin looks like Ficus—especially in cursive. They look nearly the same to you, don't they?"

Kellyn stumbled and caught himself on the wall, the action pinning her between his arms. Blood rushed from his face. "I nearly killed him, and you."

He stumbled again, and she caught him, her arms around his waist, trying to steady him. At her attempt, he caught himself against the wall.

His shoulders drooped, and a thick layer of ice coated his veins like crystals forming on a window on a winter's day. "Ricin has no cure." His eyes burned. "No antidote."

His head fell in shame.

"No, it doesn't," Morrigan said, her hands fixed on his torso. She moved one to his heart as if to steady him. Her touch was an iron on his dark olive skin, both burning and consoling.

"I would have killed him."

She gently patted him and whispered something indistinguishable. Morrigan would never win an award for warmth or a comforting nature—she was all liquid fire and brimstone—but at least she tried.

He lowered his head to meet her violet gaze. "You saved him."

Kellyn didn't know what to do with her. She brought out parts of him he didn't know he had. Everything in him wanted to pull her close and show his appreciation with a kiss. His body begged for it. But would she want it?

He didn't know, and it was too risky to try without knowing.

Morrigan was the only person who knew his secret and didn't make him feel ashamed.

She accepted him as he was.

"I owe you a debt," he whispered into her hair. "You saved him."

The hair on her neck rose like a bird's feathers puffing out. She shifted her shoulders as if trying to brush off his comments before changing the subject. "You shouldn't feel bad. The gods set you up to fail. They know about dyslexia, and they also know that you're a poison expert." She wiggled her fingers on his chest as if she didn't know what to do with them. She gulped down an emotion he couldn't read, painting her irises midnight purple. "They set you up."

He'd already figured out all of this, but it felt good hearing his suspicions confirmed. "They set the game up to make sure you wouldn't have help from your priestess." She continued, "Not that I would have helped . . ."

Morrigan trailed off, her eyes storming with the sorrow he felt churning his stomach.

"So you are sabotaging me?" It was both a question and an acknowledgment of what they already knew.

"I am not trying to sabotage," she whispered, her breath caressing his cheek. "I never meant for your friend to get hurt. I just didn't want to help you."

"Because of the gods?"

"Because of my mother." Morrigan's eyes flared, and a storm of thoughts and feelings that he couldn't read flashed across them. "And because I'm not good."

She wasn't, but she also wasn't as bad as the torment behind her eyes. Kellyn wanted to ask her about her mother, but instinctively he knew she would burrow back into her shell if he did.

Morrigan was an enigma.

Her throat bobbed, and her fingers curled into his chest, almost as if she wanted to pull him closer. "You're so kind to me."

Kellyn's face scrunched in confusion. He'd just yelled at her.

"Why?" The hand on his heart balled, and she said the word with dripping anguish.

"How have I been kind?"

"You're patient."

"I just yelled at you for saving my friend's life."

"Yes," she shook her head, confounded. "But you didn't hit me. You didn't hurt me."

Kellyn swallowed, his teeth clenching. What type of relationships has this girl had?

"You're ruining everything I've ever known," her voice cracked, "All my understanding."

Kellyn ran a thumb along her jaw. "I would never hurt you."

Her eyes glistened from holding back tears. "Even in this conversation, you're still being fair. I would have probably—" She inhaled sharply, desperately trying not to cry. The girl hated showing weakness. "I've been terrible to you, and yet you helped me. You thought I killed your friend, yet you still nursed me back to health."

"Yes." His brow furrowed. He didn't understand why this was so confounding to her.

"And you're in these games without divine help. Theodra has forsaken you just like all the rest. Why does this fact gut me?" Her fingers curled around his side, pulling him in as if asking for help. Then her eyes went vacant—haunted. "What are these horrible human emotions?"

The real question was, what was she? Cecile said she was a member of the War Court, and Kellyn was starting to believe Morrigan wasn't human. Could she be a banshee, vampire, or fury? Long-lived mortals were devoted to the War Court, which made the most sense.

"I didn't ask for this." Her voice shook. "I didn't want this." Her eyes snapped back to him. Morrigan was like a melted candle wick. Empty and burned up. "I won't let them kill you."

The tattoo on her arm squeaked as if it agreed with her, and he noticed just how close they were standing. Too close because she was *his* type of dangerous.

"Yes, Dahlia," she answered it.

Kellyn expected anything else but what she did next.

Morrigan tilted her chin up, her expression ravenous, and then she touched her lips to his neck like a vampire readying to devour his blood.

He slightly flinched, but he couldn't deny that even if she were a vampire, he would let her. Sucking him dry.

Kellyn's attraction defied all expectations, all sense. She was a magnet, and he couldn't keep himself from craving her . . . even though she'd be the end of him.

Lacing his fingers into her hair, he tilted her chin, tension eating at his core. He wanted her mouth on his again. "You're so beautiful." Kellyn's eyes rested on her lips, and her fingers curled deeper into him, pulling him closer.

His lips moved toward her, hovering too close. Morrigan's breath hitched. "I want you, Kel."

She tugged him down, and his lips grazed hers. Soft and gentle, light and tender. Exploring. This would be different from the first time. It would be—

"You called me here for this?" The voice of a villain wrenched them apart.

Gallagher Healy.

Twenty-Two
Theodra
Goddess of War

THEODEN'S QUARTERS, CITY OF THE GODS

All sense left Theo. She wanted to consume her champion, wanted to taste his seductive lips again—wanted way too much from him.

He was so different from what she ever imagined a male could be. A fact that rocked her entire foundation. If he was a good person, so too might other males be, but that was a thought she couldn't contemplate.

Not now.

So she gave entirely into lust.

Theo pulled him by his white collared shirt into her, losing a couple of buttons in the process. Fire crackled in her stomach, her veins bubbling with delight.

She shivered, her body awakening from ages of sleep. This human was trouble—

"You called me here for this?" Destruction's amused tone ripped Theo from her wicked passions.

Slowly, Theo inched away from Kellyn, a growl on her tongue. Her breath hitched, and her fingers dug into his shirt, exposing his decorated pectoral muscles to the world. Her eyes fixed on the tattoo, and with the pads of her fingers, she shifted the fabric more to the side.

"The House of Azraelle," Theo whispered. *And if I had to guess, you'll be finding one soon.* Andromache's words pounded in Theo's skull.

Kellyn was the key to everything.

"Oh, gods, what is this horrible decor?" Gallagher, Goddess of Destruction, asked, her azure hair forming into a miniature ballerina that twirled on pointe through her long locks. "It's hideous. Let me help."

"No—" Theo opened her mouth to protest, but Gallagher had already snapped her fingers.

Porcelain climbed over the fireplace and carved crimson gingerbread trim into the frame, giving the effect of teeth crying tears of blood. A line of human skulls appeared mounted across the top mantle. Ivy, mushrooms, and mold grew from the eye-sockets and twisted along the walls. On another wall, Gallagher created wallpaper formed from a mixture of skin pelts and hides; the surface was wrinkled and stained red. She turned the light fixtures into taxidermized elk heads.

She turned the place into a shrine of blood and death—a shrine of War.

"Much better." Destruction gleamed, her tawny skin glowing with excitement.

"A thousand fucks, a god?" Kellyn breathed and ran a hand through his hair. "What the—"

"Of course, I'm a god, foolish boy," Gallagher said. "Theodra sent me to the Agoge to watch over Cecile."

"Watch over?" Kellyn's disbelief sounded like that was the very last thing the god did. It sounded like she reveled in antagonism, which, given it was Gallagher, couldn't be far from the truth. Her aid often felt like an attack. "You're a goddess?"

Kellyn's face looked like a broken gear. He was baffled and struggling to comprehend.

"Gallagher, what in all hells are you doing?" Theo asked, interrupting.

"You called."

"I did not."

"Then why did a conspiracy of ravens attack me?"

Theo's eyebrows drew together. She hadn't sent her ravens to Destruction. Theo didn't have that power at the moment.

Squawk, squawk, squawk. Dahlia puffed out her feathers.

"You did this?" Theo asked her tattoo.

The raven gave a motion like a shrug. *Squawk, squawk*.

"Well then," Theo said, "the tattoo sent for you." Theo switched to the gods' language so Kellyn wouldn't understand. "But I'm glad you've come."

"Because you want me to be a voyeur?" A sugarplum smile floated on Gallagher's face. "Dirty, dirty goddess turned human."

"Gallagher, focus, please." Theo stifled a huff. Destruction was always impossible, but Theo didn't have the time or energy for it now.

Gallagher didn't focus. "So, have you been copulating with the mortal for very long?" she said with a sly lift of her eyebrow.

"I haven't been copulating with anyone—"

"Sure, sure." Gallagher winked, jumping onto the bed, and posing like a cat.

Theo sighed and changed tactics. If the irritating goddess didn't focus on her own, Theo would wave a shiny object in front of her face. "Are you still seeking mayhem?" Theo asked, knowing that Gallagher's style of mayhem might be precisely what she needed.

"You know I always am."

"Then I have a job for you."

With this task, Theo trusted Gallagher the most. The girl was manipulative, chaotic, and altogether unstable, but her desire was consistent. She wanted fun, tumult, and excitement. She wanted to dance on the moon and fly too close to the sun. She wanted to skate on rivers of ice and jump from mountains of fire.

She was adrenaline in humanoid form.

"Is it going to be fun?" Gallagher kicked out her feet and sat up straight, like a puppy awaiting a treat. "Do I get to destroy things?"

"Depends on how you look at it," Theo said, praying she was doing the right thing. Gallagher was consistent, but she was also nearly impossible to reign in.

Although she did follow direct orders.

"Color me intrigued." Gallagher wiggled her nose, and a sinister glint danced in her rose quartz eyes.

Theo rubbed her hands together, her stomach grumbling and still upset from the second challenge. "I want you to take my rightful place in the Sacrifice. I want you to act as the War Judge."

"Can I be the antagonist?" Gallagher asked with predatory grace.

Theo rolled her eyes. Gallagher enjoyed watching the world burn. She liked her place in the ranks as a villain amongst the gods. She bathed in heartache and tears. And all she ever wanted to do was bring chaos.

In the past, Gallagher repeatedly asked to cause havoc on the world stage—to be what she was meant to be. Destruction.

But Theo almost always said no.

The two gods had the same conversation when Cecile entered the Agoge, and Theo sent Gallagher to watch over the girl.

But this time it would go slightly different because destruction was what Theo wanted.

Destruction of the gods' plans.

"Whose antagonist?" Theo steepled her fingers under her chin.

"Everyone's."

"No," Theo said sharply.

Gallagher let out a huff. "Always with your nos."

"Do try to be more specific." The side of Theo's mouth twitched with mischievous intent.

Gallagher tapped her fingers on her knees in thought. "The champions?"

"No."

"No, be more specific. Or no, *no*?"

"You're exasperating."

"And you're maddeningly unclear," Gallagher grunted. "Can I at least be Cecile's antagonist?" Gallagher's voice was sweet, like frosting, but tinged with venom. "I won't kill her because you've been frustratingly clear about her being *left alive*." She said the last part in a mocking tone.

"What is your obsession with the girl?" Theo narrowed her eyes and ran a finger along her torc.

"Obsession." Gallagher scoffed. "You told me to watch after her. So what is your obsession with her?"

"You know she has a War mark, Gallagher."

"Your unwavering loyalty is so very irritating."

"You don't find it irritating when directed at you," Theo said.

Gallagher scoffed again but as a show. The girl was ninety percent show and ten percent bite.

"So, you want me to be the War Judge, even though you've forbidden it for 536 years?" Gallagher played with her nails, picking at the dirt like she had no cares in the world.

"You've been counting?"

"Humph, you know how much fun I could get into at the games?"

"Yes." Which was precisely why Theo outlawed it. "As to who you can be an antagonist for, I have some ideas."

Gallagher lit up and sat like a feline waiting to be fed cream.

"The gods."

Gallagher smiled, and although it dripped with sugar and ill intent, Theo was warmed by it.

"I want you to thwart them at every turn," Theo added.

Gallagher bowed respectfully, and her body flaked away like ash on a battlefield.

"Wait," Theo called in Theodic at Destruction's disappearing form.

Piece by piece, Gallagher reformed herself.

"I need you to go to the gods and figure out the pattern of the games this time," Theo said. "What the constraints are."

Every Sacrifice had a different set of rules and objectives for the gods. Each game, they tried to kill as many humans as possible, but some years they made it interesting by adding additional rules to the mix, like trying to kill all the champions in the last round or trying to kill them all in round one. Some years the gods aided multiple champions, and in others, they withheld aid altogether. The gods got bored, so for every Sacrifice, they switched the way they behaved. Therefore, it was always good practice never to trust a god even when they seemed to be offering help.

Beyond simply knowing the gods' ground rules, it would also be good to understand what Kellyn needed.

Theo wasn't nice. She wasn't kind. She had no positive attributes . . . but wanted to repay him. She wanted to be nice to the one who dared take care of her.

Her resolve firmed into granite. She would aid him and start by asking him what he needed. Theo wasn't used to working with a partner, but this was Kellyn's life on the line. It was his game.

Theo turned to him and sucked in a breath. The boy was posed like an ancient statue leaning against the wall. He had a hand on his chin, and his eyebrows knitted together. Confounded yet gorgeous.

"What do you need?"

He didn't answer the question. As if waking from a daze, he asked, "What is going on?" Kellyn's face was a tapestry of horrified confusion. "Gallagher—a goddess—answers to you?" He said it as if mystified.

"Oh, *Morrigan* is a *major* part of the War Court." Gallagher played with the name on her tongue, having far too much fun with it. "It's almost like she bosses us all around."

"Almost." Theo gritted her teeth. She was going to kill Gallagher for this later.

"What are you, Morrigan?" Kellyn asked his tone a mixture of phantom fear and cat-like intrigue. "You're not human."

"Yes, Morrigan, enlighten us. What are you?" Gallagher trilled, laying on her stomach and clicking her heels together on the bed, her head in her hands.

Theo flashed her a *I'm going to flay you alive*, look, which only caused the goddess's smile to widen.

"I'm complicated." Theo needed to change the subject. The boy needed to stop delving into her past. "Kellyn, in these games, what do you want? How can we help?"

He swallowed, still clearly not understanding.

"Gallagher will help us win these games, but we must know what you need."

Kellyn rubbed his face and flashed an untrusting glance at Gallagher. "I want all the champions to live." He sucked in a breath and stared at the blue-haired goddess measuring the level of trust. When he refused to say more, it became clear that he didn't trust her.

"Gallagher will help us," Theo tried to reassure him. "You can tell us whatever is on your mind."

Kellyn arched a redwood brow. Unconvinced.

"The one thing she loves more than anything else is destroying things. That can be focused on destroying what we want her to, like the gods' machinations."

"True." Gallagher's feline smile was dripping with mirth.

"Gallagher, promise that what we say in this room stays between the three of us," Theo said. A god's promise was binding. If Gallagher agreed, she couldn't tell, even if she wanted to.

"I promise that what we speak about in this room will stay between us," Gallagher said and gave a soldier's salute. "I won't tell another soul without permission."

Kellyn shifted his stance, loosening his muscles, but he was still on edge. "I want to best the gods," he said with a gravely seductive voice that sent shivers through Theo. "For what they did to Emmett, for how they use all our weaknesses. I want all of the champions to live so that the gods don't get their power."

Theo's chest warmed, and her mouth curved with . . . pride. The boy spoke directly from her heart. Beating the gods at their own game perfectly solved their problems.

Theo had refused to play the games because it was what her mother wanted. But this plan was better. Play the games to defeat the gods' greatest wishes. It was perfect! A way to get vengeance on the Queen of the Gods.

"A worthy goal," Theo said while Gallagher purred, "Sounds like fun!"

"The one problem is that the other champions will never help us, because they believe the Theoden champion is cursed due to the Goddess's absence."

Theo winced. Another reminder of her apathy causing her people pain. She couldn't make up for the past but could help her champion now. "Gallagher, you have to go to them and find a way to get them to work with us."

"Oh, I'm going to enjoy this so much," Gallagher said as her form slowly, piece by piece, fell to ashes as she refracted away. "You're going to love how I'm going to get them to come." She wiggled her nose and disappeared into a cloud of ash.

Theo groaned. That didn't bode well.

Twenty-Three

Kellyn

Prince of Theoden

THEODEN'S QUARTERS, CITY OF THE GODS

Kellyn leaned in silence against the wall, now covered in animal hide.

A silence that took on a ghostlike shape. A silence with fangs and steel-carved claws and hung between them like a hangman's noose.

Kellyn was a lad of few words, but he didn't know any terms that would suffice in such a situation.

Too much had happened in a few short minutes: finding out his affliction had a name and wasn't something he should be ashamed of, confirming that his priestess was indeed sabotaging him and that she wasn't wholly human, but more impossibly discovering that Gallagher was a goddess—and not any goddess, but the Goddess of Destruction, War's second in command and one of the greatest villains amongst the gods.

It was more than too much.

Kellyn's stomach churned, and his blood snaked through his veins thickly, too many emotions burning, but betrayal rose to the top.

The wood from his fractured lovespoon cut into his palms. He clutched the pieces so tightly his blood mingled with the cypress wood.

Morrigan quietly moved to him and ran her fingers along his, prying the spoon out of his hands. She examined it before placing both halves into a pocket in her dress. Then without any words, she gently placed her hand in his and coaxed him to the bed.

She didn't whisper false platitudes or force him to devise words for his feelings. She didn't waste time on comfort or meaningless phrases; instead, she cut directly at the heart of what he needed—to the crux of what he was feeling.

"Have you forsaken Theodra then?" she asked, sitting beside him.

"She's forsaken me."

Morrigan nodded, stood up, walked to the bedside table, and opened the drawer. Pulling out a silk bundle, she unwrapped an ancient, magical book and a single—*familiar*—lovespoon. Morrigan's gaze caught on his, and a tornado of thoughts crossed her blue eyes. She wanted something. Something from him, but she didn't want to say it. Instead, she took out the fractured lovespoon and lovingly wrapped it with the book and other carving before placing them all back into the drawer.

It was almost as if she were showing him her secrets and weaknesses without saying a single word. That book, those spoons, they meant something.

Something big.

And she was letting him see it.

"You feel she's betrayed you because of this revelation about Gallagher." Morrigan simply stated precisely what he was feeling and sat beside him again. "Gallagher is a villain in your story?"

"Yes."

It was more than just Gallagher being a villain in the Agoge, she'd forced him into the Sacrifice. Gallagher was the sole reason his speech was switched out, the reason he, not Emmett, played these games. And since she was Destruction, it meant that Theodra also wanted this. War had betrayed him. Betrayed Kellyn's long, unwavering loyalty with tricks, deception, and almost certain death.

Kellyn thought War was different than the rest. But she wasn't, and his worship meant nothing. His devotion meant nothing. If

Theodra and Gallagher were involved, did it mean her entire court was, too? Did it mean Morrigan was? Was this all one big rotten game where he was the puppet for their sick enjoyment?

"Did you know about the speech?" Kellyn said between his teeth.

Morrigan flinched as if slapped and tilted her head, a thin raven eyebrow rising. "What speech?"

"What speech?" he shot back. "The one you all switched out to make sure I'd falter, to make sure I'd be here."

"You all?"

"Don't act like you know nothing about it, Morrigan." He stood, his anger rising with him. "You admitted you were trying to sabotage me. You simply left out that your sabotage started before the games."

"Before the games?" Morrigan stood, meeting his ire with confidence. "I promise I had nothing to do with any switched speeches or any before the games. All I ever did was barely help in the first two challenges. I didn't even know who you were before seeing you at the docks."

Her tone rang true. It sounded like a warm summer wind and a fresh picnic display. It sounded like home. And her eyes sparked with hope, the purple flecks almost begging him to believe her.

He sighed. Morrigan lied, sabotaged, and her personality dripped with elegant seething and disgruntled disdain—he didn't even know what kind of creature she was—but at the moment, he believed her.

"Is that how a Prince of Theoden joined the Sacrifice?" Morrigan asked, tilting her chin, and catching his gaze before placing her hands on his biceps for comfort. "Someone switched out the Decision Day speech?"

Kellyn gulped, but his muscles melted into her touch. Morrigan knew about his affliction—his dyslexia. Could he risk her knowing the whole truth? Knowing just how stupid he was?

"A truth for a truth," Morrigan whispered. "I'm sure you have many questions for me."

She smiled, and it was dazzling in its rareness. A smile like a butterfly's dance. Beautiful, graceful, and mesmerizing.

There was something about receiving that smile—something he knew was so rare—that undid his resolve. Kellyn nodded and told her the whole story, except for some reason, he chose to withhold that it was Gallagher who switched the speeches.

"Instead of sending someone innocent to their death, you named yourself?"

"I'm an idiot." His shoulders fell. "An idiot who can't read."

"No, you aren't, Kel." She reached out and slid a hand along his cheek. "You're brave and honorable. Theodra would be proud to have you as a champion."

"If she ever showed up," Kellyn said in a low growl.

"Right." She sucked in a breath, and her hand fell to his shoulder before she stepped back, placing space between them and gently perching on the bed. "So, what do you want to know?"

So, so many things. What was she; what was the book; how did she belong to the War Court; why did Gallagher answer to her; why did she want to defy her mother; who was Theodra to her; was she also a god . . . But he knew he couldn't push her. She was a trapped bird in a cage and would bolt if given the opportunity. "You choose."

Morrigan's face scrunched like she didn't anticipate that response; frankly, neither did he.

Theo sat on the bed, leaning against the bedpost, and pulled her legs into her chest, her demeanor and overall aura like a hammer on an anvil. Hard and unyielding. An impenetrable shell, but underneath, she showed glimpses of a softer interior.

"I don't know why you make me want to be fair, but you do . . ." She paused and sucked in a breath. "And I hope you appreciate that I never tell anyone my vulnerabilities." Her bluntness was like a cloak—her armor. "But I suspect neither do you."

He didn't. It was the entire reason he was here.

Morrigan swallowed, preparing to tell the truth. "Have you ever lost something so fundamental to who you are that you don't know how to be without it?"

He hadn't. Not in the meaningful way in which she meant it.

"I'm different than I once was. Weaker, more vulnerable, more *emotional*," she said the last bit as if it smelled of sulfur. "And it scares me." She flexed her hands and stared at them. "I'm afraid I've lost things that I used to be good at, things that I'm known for, and if I don't have those skills, if I'm not strong, then what am I? Who am I?"

Morrigan's face looked so fragile and raw that he wanted to slide over and roll her into his arms, but he knew she would hate it.

"What types of things?"

"Strength for one, fighting skills . . . I used to be a fierce warrior. Some might say god-like in my skills." She chuckled to herself. "But now?" She shrugged and waved her hand. "Now, I can't even beat a few crewmen on your ship."

Kellyn didn't know what to say to this. She wasn't human. That much was blatantly clear, but what could speak to enough strength that fighting ten armed men would've been feasible for a woman of her size? He wanted to ask, but he knew she wouldn't answer.

Just as he opened his mouth to respond, their bedroom door swung wide open, and in marched the Nefesian and Lokai champions with their priests. Their arms were crossed, and their countenance screamed they wanted to be anywhere else.

Gallagher worked like magic; within fifteen minutes, all living competitors except Cecile were gathered in the room. Notably missing were the Teirland two who had been turned into stone in the Labyrinth, and the Simark priestess and Maladen duo who had been felled in the Trickery and Death challenges, respectively.

Gallagher pranced over to Morrigan like a cat presenting a dead bird to its owner—unadulterated pride radiating from her shimmering skin.

"Where's Cecile?" Morrigan asked.

"Oh, I didn't invite her." Gallagher winked. "I didn't think she'd be pleased with you if she discovered me."

"Good."

"She's going to find out eventually." Mirth sparked in Gallagher's eyes. "And I cannot wait to be there to witness it."

"Yes, she will, but eventually isn't now."

"Have you ever tried not keeping secrets?" Gallagher asked,

and Kellyn laughed. Morrigan was formed from secrets. Asking her not to keep them was like asking the sun not to shine.

Secrets were at the core of her very nature.

Kellyn understood it and could respect it.

"How did you get them all here?" Kellyn cut in, trying to get the two to focus on the task.

Pure, unfiltered, unaltered joy painted across Gallagher's rosy cheeks. "I told them Theodra would owe them a favor if they survived the games."

Morrigan swallowed hard, sucking in a long, slow breath. "Of course you did. I'm sure she'll love that."

"Oh, absolutely." Gallagher winked.

A favor. It was a huge deal and from a god it was worth a ransom in gold—was worth more than any human possession. A favor from the Goddess of War was priceless. She was known as the pantheon's second most powerful and influential god. It was almost as valuable as getting a favor from Nefeli.

"Can you make that deal for Theodra?" Kellyn asked.

"Yes, Theo will fulfill it," Morrigan gritted her teeth, "in this instance."

"You invited us all here. Do you want to get to the point? Some of us have challenges to complete," the Simark champion said from the side of the room, his countenance hard.

Morrigan strolled to the center of the room as if she were an empress and demanded everyone's attention. Her posture and general demeanor were painted with command and confidence—the type of person everyone wanted to listen to. With as few words as possible, she explained the plan to work together. The goal was to group together for challenges so that champions and priests could watch each other's backs.

Fifteen brains were stronger than one, and together, they could outwit the gods—especially since every champion also had a god aiding them. So, in a way, they would trick the gods into helping all of them too. Since Theoden's Quarters were hidden from the gods' eyes, it was the perfect place to strategize without all the others seeing.

The plan was solid, but the other champions weren't as convinced.

"There are certain things we cannot anticipate, like Medusa, but together we are stronger," Kellyn said. "The gods use our weaknesses against us, but we can cover each other's vulnerabilities and counter the gods' attacks."

"What if they force us into challenges alone?" the Lokai champion said, sitting beside the fireplace, his onyx hair glimmering against the flames.

"Then we aid each other in other ways," Kellyn responded. "For example, Morrigan knows how to break Medusa's curse . . . we can save each other with knowledge like that. The next people to play Andromache's challenge can go in there and save the Tierland delegates."

The Lokai champion crossed his arms. "That's only if the challenge stays in the library. The gods switch up their games to mess with us."

"The point is we can try."

"Why does the War Court suddenly want to help us all?" the Ertomesian champion asked.

"Frankly, because Nefeli enraged Theodra," Gallagher wrinkled her nose with delight, "and War sent me here to enact revenge."

"What do we get in exchange?" asked the Nefesia champion. "We're risking the Theoden curse by even being in this room."

"The Theoden curse doesn't exist." Morrigan's tone matched her eye roll. "That's a ridiculous rumor the gods made to make the games harder. They don't want countries working together."

"Still doesn't answer what we get out of this."

The Nefesian champion was grating on Morrigan's nerves because she clenched her fists, slid her mask of disinterest over her features, and spoke in a rich, lazy tone. "Besides a favor from War and a better chance at survival?" Morrigan paused for effect. "Gallagher will also give you all top scores in your tribunals."

"If you don't, I'll give you all terrible scores." Gallagher's words were like venom dipped in candy cherry syrup. "And I'll get my friends to join me. Trickery and Poison love chaos as much as I do!"

At this, the champions capitulated. Threats were better motivators than mutual boons. Kellyn didn't care either way. It was his end goal that mattered.

Save as many champions as possible.

They spent the next two hours sharing their clues and following challenges, and devised a strategy to have two teams go into each game together when possible. Then, after each Tribunal, they would check in with each other to strategize again. The Ertomesian and Maleden champions were going into Andromache's challenge next, and they would free the Tierland delegates if they could.

Kellyn's next challenge was with Cecile, which worked out perfectly . . . if only Emmett would wake up.

Once the champions were gone and they were finally alone again, they prepared for bed, which proved even more awkward than the other nights. Because now, their desire was evident.

They held their breaths, staring at the ceiling, their bodies nearly touching. Kellyn's heart was in his throat.

He tried to distract himself from his physical urges so he asked, "Are you a god?"

It didn't solve the awkward situation.

A hollow, timid silence settled between them. It was like the soft crashing of waves at twilight.

"No," she whispered into the cadence of their beating hearts.

Kellyn loosed a breath. "Good, I'm growing to hate them."

He heard her intake of breath. "Understandable."

Twenty-Four
Theodra
Goddess of War

INFIRMARY, CITY OF THE GODS

The smell of disinfectant and sickness hung like a noose drifting in the wind.

Theo stood vigil over the unconscious Andromedan priest, Bella still at his feet. Theo wore a fierce Theodic-styled dress with raven feathers forming the skirt and her hair tied up in warrior braids.

The boy, however, was in hospital garb and barely dressed. His skin was sickly pale compared to his normal russet-brown color. He was still uselessly unconscious, which was unfortunate because they couldn't continue the games until he woke up.

It had already been one full day since the meeting with the other champions. Working together, they were making headway. The Teirland duo had been rescued, and the rest faced their challenges together. The teamwork added to their progress, but the games were still incredibly difficult, the gods doing all they could to kill them.

The Rougeland champion got stuck under a boulder and broke over a hundred bones, and if it weren't for the Ertomesian champion she would have died.

Theo's focus snapped back to the boy, who moaned in bed.

She didn't know why she cared or watched over this human. He meant nothing to her. But it was her turn.

That was it. The only possible reason she would be here.

She wasn't softening.

It wasn't happening.

Emmett tossed on the bed; his sleep fitful. Theo sighed and reached her hand out, feeling his forehead. It was warm, not hot like before, but she figured a cold compress wouldn't hurt so she ran a washcloth over his head and across his chest. He was sweating.

A good sign. It meant the fever was breaking.

Theo continued her ministrations, and she noticed his body was full of scars. His arms, chest, torso, legs . . . everywhere.

Brandings, with iron and knives. Some sick fuck did this to him.

Shivers coursed through Theo's bones, and a memory struck the back of her mind. She swallowed it down. Theo wouldn't remember it.

Not now.

The boy moaned, and her eyes flashed to his face. Her washcloth was on the lower part of his stomach, near his slacks.

"What a present," he croaked, "Kellyn's beautiful priestess giving me a sponge bath."

The boy *was awake*. Theo turned to yell for Cecile or Kellyn, but neither was around. So instead, she chose to keep him company. If she had just woken up from a coma, she'd want someone to talk to—to orient her to reality.

But Theo was still herself, so she said in a dark, menacing tone, "You have no idea how fortunate you are, boy."

"Oh, I know." He cracked a smile.

Theo removed her hands from him and sat in the chair next to his bed. "Not that I care, but how are you feeling?"

He chuckled and clutched his side in pain. "You truly are as disagreeable as Cecile said."

"A personality flaw." Her lips lifted. She enjoyed the humorous sparring with him. "Or a personality strength."

"You must stop making me laugh."

"Fine." Theo tapped her chin and turned to a subject that would dissolve the smile from his lips. "So why do you hate my champion so much?"

"And as blunt as Cecile said."

"I try not to disappoint." Theo bowed her head in acknowledgment. "You're avoiding the question."

"Because he stole my honor."

"Can honor be stolen?"

"I was supposed to be the Theoden Champion, and instead of naming me, Kellyn named himself because he didn't believe I could do it." Theo's brow creased. That didn't sound like Kellyn at all. "He has to be the hero and so damn self-sacrificing."

"Does he?" She bit her lip. "That's not the Kellyn I know."

"You don't know him at all," Emmett snapped back.

Theo's lips twitched in amusement. "Clearly, you don't either." She ran a finger along her raven tattoo's head. Conversations with mortals could become quite tedious. They all lied and refused to say what they meant, and then they had all those tiring and useless emotions to contend with. It was all *a lot*. It was clear Kellyn had lied to his best friend to save face. He didn't want him to know about his weakness.

Theo didn't care—she truly didn't—yet she still said, "Are you sure that's how Kellyn became the Champion?"

"It's what he said."

"And no one ever lies." Theo ran a finger down her skirt formed from raven feathers—she missed her ravens. Missed her divinity. "Perhaps you should talk to him about it instead of seething in silence. He's been an emotional wreck over your sickness."

"A sickness that was his fault," Emmett growled.

"You should ask him about that, too."

Theo didn't know why she was meddling in human affairs. They didn't matter to her. She was simply getting revenge on her mother. Of course, Theo didn't want her champion to die. That was abnormal. All gods cared about their champions, and Theo had much to make up for since her apathy had led to many deaths.

That was it.

Talking to this boy and trying to get him to mend fences with her champion was only good for the games. The friction between them wasn't good.

"It is better to forgive than to spend an eternity angry," she said, "trust me, I know something about grudges."

"I'm not sure I know how to forgive him when he took everything from me." He shook his head, his eyes clouded. "I needed this."

Theo leaned back in her chair and studied him. Her instinct told her his anger stemmed less from Kellyn's actions and more from childhood wrongdoings. That level of pain wouldn't easily go away.

She sighed. Why did she care to delve? She never did. It wasn't her way. Yet . . . "I have scars, too." Her lips twitched up momentarily as she tried to share her understanding. "Here."

She ran a finger around her ribcage, following a line that a rope of fire once left on her skin. Only a god could damage another, could cause one pain. A lesson she'd learned long ago. Unfortunately, for 9,000 years Theo made the mistake of loving someone. Of trusting someone who didn't deserve it, and *he* destroyed her.

"I have the deeper scars, too," Theo breathed. "The type of scars that not even time can heal."

"Trauma." Emmett's voice was softer than a whisper.

"Yes."

"Who scarred you?" he asked, subtly curling his arms around himself in a protective gesture, almost like he was trying to fold in on himself.

Theo inhaled sharply and stared at the fingers she wrung together. She didn't find it easy to share herself with anyone, and barely knew Emmett.

"My first love," she finally said. "And yours?" She motioned to his entire body.

"My father."

Theo cursed inwardly. There was nothing worse in her mind than abusive parents. Parents were supposed to protect and cherish their young, not destroy them.

"Why is it always the parents?" She laughed harshly.

"I take it you don't have great ones either?"

"It depends on the century, I guess."

He chortled. "You have to stop with your jokes."

"Ah, yes, my jokes . . ." she bit the inside of her cheek. "Tell me more about your father."

"What is there to tell?" He struggled. "He would beat me when I wasn't enough for him."

"And you were never enough."

"Precisely." Emmett grimaced.

"I understand that."

"Never bringing enough honor to the family, never holding up to his legacy . . . but could he truly expect me to rise to the same levels? He's the top general in all of Theoden."

"I'm sorry," Theo said, the hollow words she would have hated to hear, but what else was there to say?

"The sickest part is that I still wish to prove myself to him," Emmett said. "I know it's foolish, but if I'm the best, he'll love me." He ran a finger down a scar. "Maybe then I'll be enough."

"What if you're already enough?"

"I'm not special," he said softly. "I'm not chosen."

Theo tilted her head, examining. "You don't have to be special to be *special*—you don't have to be chosen or possess magic or be the fairest in the land, or the smartest or the best." He let out a noise like a scoff, but she continued. "I have lived a long time and seen so many things, and I know that what makes someone special isn't what others think of them. What makes someone special are the choices they make with the obstacles they're given."

"Even in that, I'm not special." His nearly perfectly sculpted features sank. "I have done nothing with my life."

"Perhaps what makes you special is that you choose to help your friend, and possibly save his life even after he stole your place in the Sacrifice. Despite stealing your honor." Theo stood up and ran a finger along one of his chest scars. "Forgiveness can be honorable, too."

He grabbed her hand, forcing her to lean slightly more into him. "I wish I could."

"If I could take your pain away, I would," Theo whispered,

"but not even the gods could truly take it from you. Your body would still remember even if they erased your memory and scars."

They stared at each other momentarily, Emmett still holding her hand over his bare chest and pulling her closer. It wasn't romantic. Theo had no feelings for the boy, but she understood.

It was baring their souls.

"Oh," Kellyn gulped, walking up behind Theo and eying her closeness. "Oh, I'm sorry to interrupt."

"You aren't interrupting anything," Theo said, trying to pull away, but Emmett pulled her closer and whispered into her hair. "Let's make him jealous."

TWENTY-FIVE

KELLYN

Prince of Theoden

INFIRMARY, CITY OF THE GODS

The sight was sickening. It felt like maggots in his gut, eating from the inside out. Envy's fangs ripped him apart from the inside out.

Morrigan hovered over Emmett, her lips inches from his. Intimate. The sight was personal, romantic—sinful. A growl climbed into Kellyn's throat. He wanted to pull them apart and punch his friend in the face. He wanted to roar. But what right did he have?

Morrigan wasn't his.

She wasn't anyone's.

"Oh," Kellyn gulped, announcing his presence. And because Kellyn was utterly useless at speaking and saying what he meant, he grunted, "Oh, I'm sorry to interrupt."

Morrigan glanced over her shoulder, but Emmett drew her closer and whispered something into her hair. Kellyn averted his eyes.

"Tempting offer, but you two should talk." Morrigan raked a hand across Emmett's chest and flashed him a mischievous glance that promised so much more as she sauntered away, her hips swinging. A temptress on full display.

Emmett responded with a betrayed look, saying *how dare you leave me with him*.

Kellyn sucked down his jealousy and timidly approached his best mate. After all, Emmett was awake and flirting, meaning his mind and faculties were perfectly intact. All good things. Emmett's health was what mattered, and hopefully, Emmett would feel well enough to get back into the games because they'd lost three days to the sickness. Now, Kellyn had only two full days left to play three games.

A daunting prospect.

"How are you feeling?" Kellyn asked, holding his breath.

"What does it matter to you?" Emmett bit out. "I thought you took my place in the Sacrifice to save my life, and here you are, nearly killing me."

The words felt like a knife to Kellyn's gut. None of this would have happened if he hadn't lied. Their positions would probably be reversed. Emmett, the champion, and Kellyn, the poisoned.

Kellyn's intestines twisted, and his tongue was thick with worry. Apologies and truth—conflict resolution—were some of the scariest words one would ever say. Because what if he got them wrong? What if he buried their friendship even more?

He sucked in a breath, the vein in his neck pulsing with the ragged beats of his heart. "I'm sorry—"

"Sorry for what?" Emmett snapped back. "Intentionally trying to kill me? What a useless word, Kellyn."

"You're right. It is useless because I should have told you my secrets long ago." Kellyn fell like a heap into the chair beside Emmett. The chair rocked slightly from Kellyn's sheer size, but he steadied it. "The truth is that I didn't mean to name myself as champion—"

"Didn't mean? What utter bullshit." Emmett shook his head. "If I had enough energy to leave, I would. I don't want to listen to more lies, Kellyn."

"I'm a liar—"

"Yes, you are." Emmett's brow furrowed. He didn't expect Kellyn to admit to it.

Kellyn rubbed the beginnings of a beard, his shoulders slumping slightly. "Would you hear me out? If you don't like what you hear, I promise I'll give you space and not ask again."

Emmett gritted his teeth and balled his fists. He didn't want to listen to anything. Probably livid from the loss of his honor and the poisoning. Kellyn couldn't fault him. He was supposed to be an expert in herbs, yet he failed spectacularly at the second challenge. It wouldn't make sense out of context. "I'll listen if you promise me that if we both live through these games, I never have to see you again."

Kellyn's heart crumbled. The words were squeezing it to death. "I promise to do my best to avoid you after the games if it's still what you want."

"It will be."

Kellyn nodded. "I can't read." He rubbed his temples. "I see the words on the page, and I have a hard time making sense of them. Understanding anything written takes me at least ten times longer than everyone else, and even then, my comprehension isn't good."

"You can't read," Emmett scoffed. "Then how did you get through the Agoge?"

"I cheated." Kellyn blew out a breath. "I stole the assignments and tests beforehand, wrote codes on my arms to remember things, refused to do things, and acted like a privileged dick. I did everything I could to avoid reading aloud."

Emmett glowered, but he seemed to be at least taking in some of it.

"My parents almost didn't let me attend the Agoge," Kellyn continued. "They've threatened to disown me if anyone found out about my affliction. That's what they called it because since I was young, I've struggled to learn. Nothing helped. My parents tried withholding privileges, beating me, and even beating others when I failed, but nothing helped because I couldn't learn like that."

Kellyn's palms sweated, and he couldn't look his friend in the eyes. His shame was out in the open. Emmett would know just how stupid he was. But this was an apology, so he needed to finish it. "Gallagher switched out my speech with one handwritten in cursive, and I got flustered. It's harder to read handwriting because none of the letters look the same. I couldn't read any of it and didn't want to name the wrong person, so I named myself."

Kellyn's mouth was dry, and he swallowed. "When I found out it was your name, I got anxious and lied."

Kellyn sank into silence. Shame swirling around and painting a tableau in his heart. The shame of his affliction, but also the shame of not telling his best mate. If he could reverse time, Kellyn would've told his friend everything years ago, but he was too afraid of losing their friendship. Now, because of his lies, it was already lost.

"You can't read . . ." Emmett repeated slowly.

"I didn't tell you because I would lose everything if my parents learned anyone knew. It was better to die than have people know my shame." Kellyn shook his head and rubbed his temples. "No, that's not completely true either. I didn't tell you because I was ashamed. Intelligence is the most important thing to you, and I felt like you would hate me if you knew."

"I wouldn't have hated you," Emmett said. "Not for that."

Raising his head, he finally met his friend's eyes. "But you would've thought less of me."

Emmett nodded. "Yes."

"You think less of me now."

"Yes." Emmett's lips fell into a flat line, and his eyes hardened. "I need space to recoup and prepare for the next challenge."

Kellyn felt the *yes* like a punch to the chest, and he didn't know if Emmett thought less of him because of his confession or because he thought he was a big dumb brute like everyone always assumed.

Both options gutted him, but he couldn't ask for clarification because Emmett didn't want to continue the conversation.

Twenty-Six

KELLYN

Prince of Theoden

THE HALL OF MIRRORS, CITY OF THE GODS

Emmett was better in the sense that he could stand and walk on his own, but his complexion was pallid, his eyes sunken, and sweat dripped from his brow with barely any movement.

A walking, talking weakness.

All Kellyn's fault. He didn't like their chances in the challenge. They needed all the gods' favor if they were to make it through alive. But they needed to continue. Kellyn couldn't afford any more delays.

It was Queen Nefeli's challenge. Her mirror was framed by twisting oak tree branches with spiral knots. Its silver reflection was intermingled with falling rose petals and yellow diamonds.

"Shall we?" Cecile asked.

Kellyn grunted and stepped into the mirror first. Best to get it over with.

As his hand slipped through, it felt like a calming bubble bath with rose petals floating on the surface. It was like the mirror was greeting him with a comforting hug.

He shivered. Its kindness was just as unsettling as if it had used claws to greet him. It caused his stomach to churn and set his toes on fire. He expected danger around any corner. The gods were evil, and any perceived kindness was a trap. A wolf in sheep's clothing.

Kellyn stepped out onto train tracks leading into a tunnel. Cliff edges surrounded them, and bright pink trees and bushes grew down their sides. Magnolias, crabapples, and cherry trees expanded in every direction, covering the crevices, and shadowing the canopy above. It was a burst of pink; all shades from tea rose to moonstone . . . and even puppy paw pink littered the rocks.

A land of enchantment.

Petals rained down on them, and Morrigan shuddered as she caught a wisteria seed. Her face grew green, and her eyes grew hollow, clearly remembering her sickness.

Sprites danced along the branches, eating her tangled emotions. The little fairies sang songs of joy and unease, sounding like a grand symphony with one of the violinists out of tune. Engrossing, yet slightly off.

"Into the tunnel?" Emmett asked, eying the cave consumed by shadow. Bella stood at Emmett's side in panther form and acted almost as a walking aid.

"So it would seem." Morrigan shooed away a sprite that landed on her shoulder.

Together they walked into the cave, their hands locked so as not to lose each other. But honestly, there was a part of Kellyn that just wanted to hold onto Morrigan for more than traveling through a dark passage.

The darkness whispered to them. Dark secrets and promises of gruesome deaths. Things like *Your flesh will melt from your bones* and *Be suffocated on shadows*, or Kellyn's favorite, *Your insides will drip from your body as hydra acid consumes you.*

"Shadow nymphs," Cecile whispered.

Lovely, little, creepy creatures.

A nymph made from rock and shadow leaned out and whispered in his ear. "The death goddesses' prophecy and curse comes for you, Kellyn." Its voice was crooked and buzzing, causing shivers to dance along Kellyn's spine. "Nefeli's gift to you is only death."

The hair on his nape rose, and all his muscles tightened.

It didn't bode well.

Not at all.

Kellyn swallowed past the lump in his throat. But he couldn't focus on fear; he had to continue. Cracking his neck, he pushed forward into the darkness. He wasn't going to let the gods kill him. Not here and not now.

A light glowed in the distance, marking the next stage in his journey.

Stepping out of the dark, he was greeted by a vast cavern. Etched into the walls were statuettes of the pantheon, their eyes following every movement and sound.

Red sunlight shone down from a break in the rocks, highlighting an island at the center. A grand weeping cherry tree graced its rocks, and small steppingstones led to it. Everything in the cave pointed to the center—to the tree.

"Don't touch the water," Morrigan said, shifting on her feet. "It's safe to say that it's deadly."

The pool was comprised of vibrant blue water, surrounded by a mixture of greens, yellows, and oranges, and resting on a bed of red rock—creating a rainbow illusion. Magic made the pool, but its beauty was borrowed from nature.

Heat licked the air, radiating up, the temperature far exceeding the boiling point.

Lethal yet bewitching.

"Volcanic hot springs," Morrigan whispered. "Your flesh would melt from your bones, indeed. Our lovely little shadow nymphs seemed to be warning of how this cavern will try and kill us."

Emmett snorted. "Wonderful, I've always wanted my flesh to melt off."

"An excruciating death. It would take days for you to die completely. Days in which your nerve endings burn with agony," Morrigan said lightly, "A charming way to go."

"Right," Cecile coughed. "Let's not fall in then."

Kellyn grunted and led the way.

One by one, the group jumped and walked across the stones. Emmett still wasn't steady on his feet, Bella grew to an unnatural size and led him on her back as if she were a horse. Easily, she jumped across the steppingstones and kept him from falling into the boiling waters.

As Kellyn's feet met the island, a curse-forged voice spoke. "Welcome, Kellyn, to your fate. A dance of letters and War is at stake." The voice of Nefeli echoed through the cave, bouncing off the waters and rocks, sinking her chilling tone into his bones. "The challenge is simple: spell the words before the beast eats your pretty little priestess."

Spell?

Kellyn's throat ran dry, and his limbs grew heavy. Spelling was a requiem of nightmares—where all decaying dreams were formed. In the panic, all Kellyn could think about were silent letters.

What was the point of a silent letter?

Appearance? He genuinely wanted to know. Why spell a word with a silent K? Why?

Language was horrifying.

The ground shook, as did Kellyn's bones. From the waters climbed a second island with a sand pit cut into a perfect circle—a gladiator arena. A gust of wind blew like a cyclone and refracted Morrigan into the pit. She clutched her knees, the teleportation stirring her stomach.

"Stop refracting me," she yelled up the ceiling. "You know I hate it."

Nefeli cackled in response. "No helping from the gladiator circle." Her haunting laugh continued, and a silver cross decorated with weapons popped out of the sand. "Choose your weapons, and let the games begin."

Morrigan's face paled. It was the manifestation of the fear she'd shared with him—the fear of not being strong enough, of not trusting her new body to act as she needed it to.

She glanced at him, their eyes locking for a moment. Both recognized the difficulty that lay before them.

Holding her head high, she faced the assortment of weapons that clung to the cross. Swords glinted under the watchful gaze of the cave light. Longswords, broadswords, greatswords, rapiers, and katanas. All waiting for carnage. Yet no guns because modern technology was outlawed in the games.

Morrigan picked up a few and smelled the blades, checking for poisons. Then she lifted the javelins and tested their balance, checking to ensure they'd fly quickly and straight through the wind.

It was fascinating to watch. She was a weapons master.

Knowing precisely how to wield every weapon from the broadsword to the bow to throwing stars.

She treated each with respect and dignity, touching them like newborn babies. Morrigan set three aside before moving on to a more intimate weapon: the sai. They weren't the most practical in a melee—that prize would probably go to the halberd—but from the sparkle in her eye, she seemed to love these the most.

Many weapons killed from afar, but a sai killed up close and personal.

Sliding them into her belt, she nodded and stepped back from the display. As she did, the cross disappeared, sucked under the sand.

"Your first word," the booming voice echoed, and from the sand emerged a massive hydra. Was he spelling the name of the creature?

The beast started with five serpent heads, all snapping and dancing around Morrigan.

She twisted her broadsword in her hand, standing tall before the beast. "Let's do this."

She feinted past one of the heads, sliding beneath its teeth, trying to get a clear shot at the beast's stomach. But she wasn't fast enough, and a second head grazed her shoulder.

"Fuck," she said, ducking around another head, switching her sword arm. The pain must have been intense for her not to want to hold the broadsword with her dominant hand.

"Kel, I don't mean to rush you, but you might want to start spelling," Cecile said, watching the battle unfold, wincing as another snake glided along Morrigan's torso.

She panted, and blood dripped down her corset. But she didn't give up.

Neither would Kellyn.

"Right." Kellyn gulped. "Spelling. H . . ." he hesitated, having no idea how to spell the word. "H . . .I?" He guessed.

"Wrong," the wind whispered, and from the sand sprung a second Hydra.

Morrigan loosed an expressive string of curses as she dodged ten heads.

Shit, shit, shit.

Sweat dripped from Kellyn's forehead, and he glanced at the statues' cameras clustering the sides of the cave. The whole world was watching, seeing his failure on full display.

"You can do this, Kel," Morrigan shouted and rolled out of the way of the hydra's acid, barely stopping before the side of the island. Her hair wasn't so lucky; a loose strand fell into the water and sizzled, melting away. "Take a breath and just think about it."

Kellyn inhaled sharply.

"We can do this," she said, jumping up and tossing the broadsword to the ground underneath the hydra. "Together."

Sliding past its jaws, Morrigan hurled herself between the beast's legs, slicing them with her sais. Being smaller and faster was a definite advantage against a giant. As it fell to the ground, she clutched her broadsword from the sand and cut straight up, disemboweling the beast.

It fell to the ground dead and disappeared into smoke, leaving a black echo of its form as it left.

Turning, Morrigan faced the second monster, but as she stepped, parrying its jabs, two more hydras leaped from the black stain in the sand.

Kill one and two appeared.

That wasn't how hydra attacks were supposed to go. Only the heads were supposed to double if cut off.

"Tsk, tsk," the wind howled. "The objective isn't to kill my little pets. Naughty, naughty *Morrigan*."

"Kel, you need to spell the word," Cecile said, "or every time she kills, another will pop up."

"Yeah, I gathered that."

Kellyn's feet were glued to the floor, and his head buzzed. He needed to spell . . . and correctly. Red wept from Morrigan's wounds, the snakes landing at least four blows now. She'd die if he couldn't do this, which was unacceptable. He couldn't deny it. He cared. He liked her grumpy moods and blunt demeanor. He liked her strange, comforting style and confidence in him.

The cords of his neck tightened, and his heart surged in his chest, beating to the cadence of shame and fear. His weakness was going to kill *his* . . . the girl—

"Kel, you can do this," Morrigan called as she dodged another head. "You're incredibly talented. You solved the stone game in the least number of moves possible. You understand patterns and see the big picture. You can figure this out, too."

Blood rushed to his head, and his nails bit into his palms. Sucking in a slow breath, he thought about it. *The big picture.* What was he missing? Something.

There was something that could help him. He knew it. Morrigan certainly understood it, so what did she figure out before he could?

Kellyn's heart drummed in his ears, and it was the only sound he could hear. So loud. Too loud.

Sweat dripped down his back.

You're a stupid idiot.

He glanced at his friends. The blood had rushed from Cecile's face, and every time a snake got too close, she flinched. Emmett watched with horror and fatigue. He sat on a rock, and he clutched his stomach.

What idiot can't even spell?

Kellyn bit down hard, his jaw aching from the pain.

Morrigan groaned as another hydra got too close. She fell to her knees and stared up at the snakes. But the monsters didn't move in for the killing blow.

They taunted her. Taunted him.

"H . . . Y?" He started, holding his breath, and waiting for the wind to reprimand him, but it didn't come. "D?" He scrunched his nose.

Waiting.

Nothing.

Right again.

"R..."

Kellyn swallowed. He was so close. But was it I, A or E, A or just A. Oh, this language was so stupid.

"I . . . A," he choked out.

"Wrong again," Nefeli's voice laughed. "Oh, how this is fun!"

Another hydra clawed out of the sand, and now Morrigan faced four monsters. Using her sword as a crutch, she stood up. She wouldn't give up.

Kellyn internally kicked himself, and his lungs clenched tight, his chest stinging from the pain of it.

Morrigan should have shown fear, but instead, she faced down the monsters and rolled her shoulders back.

Then she attacked, fighting to maim, not to kill, and Kellyn didn't understand why she'd thought she was weaker. She was brilliant. Watching her fight was like watching a magician's show. Morrigan fought like nothing he'd ever seen, using her body as an instrument. In the same way that a ballerina was all lean muscles, long lines, and formidable grace, Morrigan was all muscle and curves designed to create bloodshed. She moved faster than a human, her body twisting and pulling in unreal ways. Her reflexes were those of the long-extinct demigod. Not human, but not truly divine either.

As Kellyn watched, the answer hit him straight in the chest, like Morrigan's blows with her sai. *No help from the gladiator circle.* Emmett and Cecile weren't in the circle. They could help, and they were both brilliant spellers.

But to receive their help, Kellyn had to ask for it, and the world would see if he did. Everyone would know that the Theoden heir couldn't spell.

If he asked for help, his parents might disown him. They *would* disown him.

Whatever you do, don't ask for help—his father's motto. *Ellises don't need help. Ellises are strongest and toughest alone. Don't be a baby. Suck it up. Toughen up.* All his father's words climbed into his head. The terms screamed at him as a child.

It was blasphemous to ask for aid.

It was dishonoring.

But screw honor and screw his father. If Kellyn didn't ask for help, Morrigan might die. She was mortal, and she would tire. And he wouldn't allow it. Kellyn was done being afraid of what other people thought. He was done being ashamed of his affliction.

He was done being his parents' perfect little pawn.

He was done.

If he had asked for help on Decision Day, Kellyn wouldn't be in this position. Asking for help wasn't weak. It was necessary.

"Cecile, Emmett, I can't do this alone," he said. "I can't spell, and I need your help."

"We can't help, Kel," Cecile breathed, "Nefeli—"

"Nefeli said, no help from the gladiator circle. You're not in the circle."

"Oh . . . oh," Cecile rubbed her face.

But Emmett called out the correct spelling, "H . . . Y . . . D . . . R . . . A, hydra."

"Second word," Nefeli seethed. Not happy with the turn of events. Out of the sand burst four fully armed centaurs.

"Centaur," Emmett said, "C . . . E . . . N . . . T . . . A . . . U . . . R . . . Centaur."

"Incorrect." The wind cackled, and three more centaurs formed from the sand.

"The S, Em, multiple centaurs." Cecile's eyes tracked the half-horse men as they prowled closer toward Morrigan. One threw a spear which she artfully eluded.

"Oh, right, C . . . E . . . N . . . T . . . A . . . U . . . R . . . S."

"Correct, third word."

The game repeated with vampires, giant wolves, harpies, the Dullahan, and pookas. Eventually, Nefeli ended the bout, and Kellyn was freed from the challenge.

Nefeli refracted Morrigan and Emmett switching their places. Emmett threw up from the magic, and Morrigan moaned. "See, it's revolting."

"Cecile Declare," the wind growled. "A color knows no bounds. Find the creature, and freedom will be found." From the pool sprang nine circular steppingstones with murals formed from red and green flowers. "Your task is simple: jump to the correct mural and save your friend from his monsters."

Cecile paled. "I can't see the differences."

A massive wolf surged from the sand, and Emmett was still clutching his knees, unable to hold a sword from his weakened state.

Even if Cecile answered her riddle correctly on the first go, Emmett wouldn't survive.

It was Nefeli's revenge on Kellyn for seeking aid.

TWENTY-SEVEN
THEODRA
Goddess of War

QUEEN'S MIRROR

The foolish, charming human was going to die. He was a man. She should let him.

But she couldn't.

Weird things were happening to her insides. Hideous emotions stirring. It was sickening. Theo scrunched her face. Being mortal was just simply awful. She was slow, bleeding, and full of useless feelings like compassion and fear . . . fear for someone else.

She missed the days of her monstrous heart.

Theo sighed. A belabored and grumpy sigh. She couldn't let the human die. Because she liked him but also because Kellyn loved him.

"Hey, Charming, make sure you catch," Theo yelled across the ravine. Either this would work, or she would die horrifically.

Perfect.

Theo backed up to the end of her island and jumped toward the gladiator arena. Using one of Cecile's new islands as a middle point to land and continue her momentum.

"CATCH," she wailed louder than a banshee, and Emmett turned around, clutching her by her warrior leather corset strings, which was good because her feet barely landed on the sand. Falling backward, he rolled them onto the island between the wolf's feet and gaping jaws. "That shouldn't have worked."

"No, it shouldn't have."

"Can I borrow a knife?"

Emmett handed her one by the hilt, and she swiftly stabbed upward as the wolf tried to clamp down on them, but she'd lodged it between its teeth. Bella appeared from the steam and sat next to them, readying to fight. The cat couldn't aid Theo, but she could aid Emmett.

"So we're clear, I did that for him," Theo said, jumping to her feet and grabbing a loose sword.

On the other side of the cave, Kellyn and Cecile jumped from island to island, finding the one they needed.

As they reached the island, the wolf disappeared, and nine harpies burst from the sand and took to the skies.

"Well, that's fucking perfect," Emmett said, wiping blood off his katana. He'd managed to put a gash in the wolf's leg.

"Yeah." Theo's voice was thick with poison. Her gaze latched on the half-woman half bird, which decided to target Kellyn instead of them.

Nefeli's revenge.

Emmett picked up a bow and quivered.

"Let me," Theo said, holding out her hand. "I don't miss."

Emmett scoffed, unbelieving, but he handed over the quiver anyway. Possibly wanting to see the skill firsthand. "Unleash hell then."

She released a volley of bloodshed. The Goddess of War did not miss; she quickly hit three harpies, aiming to take them down but not kill them—intentionally shooting them over the islands so they would fall on land and not into the boiling waters.

Cooked bird wasn't on the menu. Birds were sacred to Theo and her country, harpies included. They didn't eat birds.

Not to be outdone, Emmett threw a javelin, piercing through the air and finding a harpy by Cecile's head. But the exertion forced him to take a knee. His body was wrecked from his sickness, working at ten percent capacity.

Theo had an awful urge to comfort him, but she didn't have time.

Meanwhile, Bella lounged on the island and yawned as if she couldn't be bothered to help. Truly, what was the point of her being on the island? As if she heard her goddess's thoughts the cat gave a lengthy meow that said, *I think you have it covered.*

Theo shook her head and returned to her work. She loosed three more arrows and took out three more birds. Two hits remained. She loosed another.

Perfection.

Shooting was the one thing this useless human body was equally skilled at. Probably because it only required human strength, and the draw weight on her compound bow was only about thirty pounds.

Nothing.

Theo reached for another arrow, but she was out after taking down six beasts herself.

Fuck.

Dropping her quiver and bow, Theo unsheathed her sais. But she couldn't throw them. Her eyes scanned the gladiator pit, but no far-range weapons remained.

"I suggest finding that island quickly because we're out."

Kellyn's gaze darted to her and then to the bird whose claws were approaching his face. He ducked, giving the creature his back.

The harpy clawed his tunic in two, exposing his chiseled back and chest to the world. Theo would have stopped to take in his physique, but he was losing. Anxiety clawed up her throat, and she shook. Water sprites hopped on the water and consumed her fear.

Theo rubbed her chest. There was a stirring of something happening inside. She was starting to—no, she couldn't even think it.

It didn't matter anyway because if Kellyn knew the truth about her being a *god,* he would hate her. He despised the gods. But she wanted desperately to tell him—all of it—yet if she did, he'd leave.

Not that it mattered because he'd never love her. Theo was unlovable . . . no matter what form she was in. War was a villain, and villains didn't get love stories. They didn't have friends. They had subjects.

None of that mattered if he died. She felt useless. Utterly and completely useless. Theo wanted to burn the world down to protect him but couldn't. She couldn't do *anything*. But it turned out she didn't need to because Kellyn was allowing the bird to get close enough for him to stab his chisel in its eye.

Cecile hopped onto the correct island, and four massive pookas replaced the harpies.

Emmett was still weak, but he managed to flank her as she took the heat of the battle. They worked together perfectly, like four arms being controlled by one body. With his excellent training, she could easily predict where he needed her, and she was getting used to the way her mortal body moved.

It was still far too slow, weak, and vulnerable, but she managed to make it work for her.

Still, she hated it, but there wasn't nearly as much for her to fear as she thought. She was still the most skilled warrior in the world.

A symphony of clangs rained throughout the cave. Blood splattered everywhere and seeped into her mouth, mixing with the taste of sweat, grapefruit, and wax of her lipstick.

But she didn't care. There was beauty in battle, like an aria of gore and glory. It was also a horror-made manifest—the battleground for nightmares to come out to play.

It was majestic and horrible.

All at once, Theo bathed in it and hated herself because of it.

The game continued with four more beasts, but they eventually succeeded. The hardest part was returning to the island because dearest old Nefeli refused to refract them.

Punishment for doing too well in the challenge. Theo and Emmett managed to get to the middle island in between, but he was too weak by far to jump the last section, so Kellyn had to engineer a bridge, literally building it from the willow tree.

Theo smiled. The boy was skilled with his hands, and she wanted to do far more with them than simply build a bridge.

Twenty-Eight
Kellyn
Prince of Theoden

BALLROOM, CITY OF THE GODS

The Tribunal was like swallowing sand. Coarse and utterly uncomfortable.

As soon as they exited the mirror, they were forced to pull on party clothing, directly over their open wounds. Apparently, they needed to be presentable. Another punishment for beating the challenge. Cecile wore a thick corseted dress, and Morrigan was forced into a black silk dress, with a metal snake fastening the plunging back together, while Kellyn and Emmett were put in suits.

Clothing for the Tribunal.

The four-faced down the firing squad together, all eight of the pantheon gods and Gallagher lined up—their magic floating around them—the ballroom light shining down upon them. Gallagher's pink eyes glittered and devoured Cecile, her gaze not letting up for a moment. Her skin was painted with blue sugar dust, and her blue hair moved on a phantom wind, magic surging through it as if proving to all those who gazed upon her, she was indeed divine and meant to be there.

Kellyn's heart sank because he'd unintentionally kept this secret from Cecile. For whatever reason, Morrigan wanted to keep it from her, and Kellyn didn't want to rattle his friend before a difficult challenge.

But had he made a mistake?

The gods spoke to the crowd and the four competitors, decreeing scores and critiquing their performance, but the four couldn't focus, each processing Gallagher's presence differently.

"How the fuck?" Emmett pulled all attention his way. His eyes latched onto Gallagher in all her glory.

Cecile let out a low whimper, caught by a phantom wind and echoed throughout the hall. A god was playing with them. Again.

"Good to see you again, Kellyn," Gallagher said with a debonair grin. The gentle glow of the lava-coating walls reflected in her eyes, causing them to glint mockingly. "Cecile, did you know Kellyn and I have been strategizing about the games? After all, he is the Theoden champion."

Gallagher was intentionally causing strife.

"You knew," Cecile whispered out of the corner of her mouth, her eyes flashing with betrayal.

Kellyn's stomach twisted into knots, and his heart beat to a song of an untuned harp. "Yes." Kellyn hung his head. He should've warned Cecile. He was truly a shitty friend lately. First with Emmett and now with Cecile.

Where was his loyalty?

Cecile's golden-brown curls bounced as she switched her attention to Morrigan, her mouth hanging open and her eyes coated with thick hurt. "Why?"

Morrigan gulped. "I'm sorry."

"Have you missed me, lovely?" Gallagher's voice was fairy bright, but she winked wickedly at Cecile, and in that wink was a pledge of violence or seduction. It was hard to tell with Gallagher.

Cecile jolted forward as if to attack, but Emmett and Kellyn grabbed her arms and held her back.

"You cannot attack a god," Emmett said, biting on the words as if they were a foreign dish he didn't know if he enjoyed. "She is a god, right?" he asked no one in particular.

Morrigan bit the inside of her cheek. "She's Destruction, second in command of the War Court."

"Oh shit, a god hates us." Emmett's eyes widened, and in a comforting gesture, he slid his fingers into the pockets of his ostentatious deep-purple suit.

"I don't know." Morrigan smiled, trying to lighten the mood. "I think she likes you."

"She's tried to kill us at least seven times," Cecile hissed.

Morrigan flinched. "Antagonism is Gallagher's form of affection."

Emmett crossed his arms and glowered. "At least the War Court has finally decided to appear and help their champion for once."

"True, but War herself couldn't even be bothered to show up," Kellyn said, his lips tightening.

"It's probably for the best she didn't show up." Cecile's eyes flicked to Morrigan, and her words were a guillotine. "She'd just disappoint you."

I'm sorry. Morrigan mouthed again.

Nefeli cleared her throat and silenced the crowd, anger flowing from her aura like a physical force. "If you four can't focus on us, leave without your clues." She shooed them away.

"You cannot do that." Morrigan stepped forward and raised her chin in defiance.

"Can't I?" Nefeli raised a brow.

"Per rule twenty-three of the Sacrifice accords, the gods must give clues to the champions based on how they rate their performance in *only the previous event,* not based on personal preference or performance outside of the events." Morrigan quoted the rules precisely and gracefully, almost like she had written them.

Was something wrong with her, to face the gods like that? Or did she genuinely hold that much sway in the War Court? Maybe she was truly untouchable . . . much like Gallagher.

"Oh . . ." Nefeli's lips lifted slowly like she was devouring a delicious cake. "I wasn't aware you paid any attention to the rules."

Morrigan glowered. "If you would do your job, we could go. We have some things to discuss amongst ourselves." Her disrespect rattled the floor, sucking all the air out of the room. No one dared speak. The audience was so silent they could hear each other's heartbeats.

"I should flay you alive for your mouth, girl."

"Then do it." Morrigan put her hands on her hips. "But you can't because of rule fifteen of the Sacrifice accords."

"I'm sure that's the only reason I wouldn't . . ."

"With you, one never knows," Morrigan breathed.

"Has your hatred grown so much?"

Hatred? A muscle in Kellyn's jaw ticked, and a bead of perspiration crawled down his spine.

"What do you think?" Morrigan asked.

"But you're doing so wonderfully." Nefeli blinked her thick white lashes, framing her clever eyes. "The teamwork you displayed was quite brilliant. You've done well, my child."

"Not well enough." Morrigan's voice dropped below a whisper, "Never enough, Mo—" The last words were indistinguishable.

Nefeli clapped her hands. "Alright, the scores." As the words left her mouth, eighteen numbers burst like fireworks into the air above the gods' heads, and ink sank its teeth into Kellyn's wrist.

All roads lead to me.

Without another word, Cecile stomped past the gods and into the heart of the palace, offering one last glare at Morrigan as she went, the lava light framing her beautiful retreating form.

"Fuck," Morrigan groaned. "We should go after her."

Kellyn grunted his approval, and they moved to follow, but barely made it two feet before his parents accosted them.

"How dare you," his father growled in his fiercest bass tones. "You've brought dishonor to our house."

In a quieter voice, his mother added, "Kellyn dear, you know the consequences of the public discovering your secret."

Kellyn opened his mouth to respond, but Morrigan beat him to it. "Because it would be so terrible for your son, for a Theoden heir to be different—to have different strengths."

"Don't speak of things you do not understand, girl." He lifted his hand as if to backhand her but thought better of it at the last minute. "Theodra would be ashamed to have you representing her, Kellyn."

"Don't *ever* speak on what Theodra would or wouldn't approve of." Morrigan's composure slipped, her voice dropped to depths deeper than the underworld, and rivulets of fury leaked from her pores. Ravens squawked in the distance, and Kellyn could have sworn the temperature dropped a degree.

Gooseflesh rose on Kellyn's arms, and fear skittered through his stomach.

Morrigan embodied power, and her threats were laced with unbreakable promises.

"You're not worthy of having him as a son, and I speak for Theodra when I say it is you, not him, who should be ashamed of your actions."

Foolishly, his father didn't back down. "You will not speak to me like this, you gutter—"

"You will not finish that sentence, father." Kellyn cut in, his stance towering and mighty. "Call me all the names you want, but you will not besmirch Morrigan." Confidence burrowed into Kellyn's heart. "As for the throne of Theoden, I don't want it if you're not going to accept me as I am."

His mother gasped. "Then what are you going to do?"

"I'll figure it out," Kellyn said, grasping Morrigan's hand and striding away with his head held high.

"That was brilliant, Kel." Morrigan squeezed his hand and peered at him with bright eyes.

"Thank you for your support. It means more than you know."

"Anytime," she grinned. "But never mention it to anyone. It would ruin my reputation as a shrew, and I've worked hard to develop that."

Twenty-Nine

Kellyn

Prince of Theoden

LOVE CAVES, CITY OF THE GODS

The lava-tube corridors of the place smelled earthy, like the woods after a light rain, but they tasted like tender tension. Kellyn and Morrigan walked silently, their hands swinging like pendulums, barely missing each other. But he felt the near misses like a poisoned Love arrow striking his heart—poisoned with desire. It was no longer easy to escape his growing feelings for her.

She was grumpy, arrogant, and impossible, but she was also supportive and understanding in a way he'd never experienced.

"Do you think Cecile might be in the Champion's quarters?" Morrigan asked.

They were searching for Cecile in the underground caves of the palace. They'd scoured all the upper floors and couldn't find her anywhere.

"No. When she gets upset, she hides in small dark places, burrowing deep within herself and her pain," he said, "I think she has to be down here."

"Alright, you know her better than I do." Morrigan stumbled and caught herself with a hand against the jagged rocks.

Instinctively, his hands circled her waist to catch her, but she flinched at the contact and blood-soaked onto his fingertips. "You're hurt."

"It's nothing," she said, sucking in a breath. "Just a flesh wound." She clutched her side, pain coating her face.

"You're not okay." He swept her into his arms and hunted for a place to attend to her wounds.

Gallagher hadn't come to aid them. It became more apparent each day that Theodra had truly forsaken him completely. The only reason Gallagher helped them before was that Morrigan asked her to. It had nothing to do with goodwill or kindness, and nothing to do with War herself.

Clutching Morrigan close to his chest, he found a cavern with a rose garden designed for romance and midnight assignations. But it wasn't the seductive mood of the cave that made it the perfect refuge. The grass grew along the rock beds, making it the ideal place to rest and check her wounds.

But the cave was designed for something far more scandalous. Glowworms and luminescent butterflies glittered throughout, creating a soft, seductive light. Cicadas and owls hummed sweet arias into the shadows, and dangling from the ceiling were two wooden swings, the ropes formed from rose vines. Farther in, a pool sparkled like a sea of diamonds, its surface tranquil but littered with unclaimed desires. It beckoned couples into its depths to complete their lustful acts. Rivulets of liquid fire poured into the waters and hissed, the sound mixing with the insects' song and rejuvenating Kellyn's hope.

The place was designed for love affairs but would have to do for a sick bed.

He gently rested Morrigan on the grass and slid open her dress —the deep plunging back making it easy—to find a deep, festering wound with teeth marks coiling down her side. More stretched across her shoulders and back.

Kellyn's heart jolted. It was so much worse than he had guessed. How had she even managed to stand? To walk?

Kellyn ripped off a clean section of his tunic and dipped it into the water. He needed to clean her wounds.

Morrigan gritted her teeth and pinched her eyes closed. "I don't need you to take care of me."

"I want to, Morrigan."

Her eyes flashed open and sparked with surprise.

Unable to handle the growing tension, Kellyn placed his makeshift cloth on her gaping flesh, and she hissed in pain but didn't take her eyes off him.

"What if I wanted to take care of you?" she whispered. "Would you let me?"

"Of course."

She rested her head against the grass and stared at the cave ceiling. "I will get a chance to care for you one day."

"I'm sure you will." He ran a finger along the skin surrounding her wound, checking the severity and depth. "But it's not a competition."

She laughed and sucked in a pained breath. "I didn't think it was."

A flash of glittering blue light burst through the darkness and solidified into a ball beside Morrigan's head. They both flinched as the magic settled between them before it dissolved, and in its place rested an ancient book with a leather-bound cover. It glittered with enchantment, and fire diamonds clawed at its spine, lacing the book in glory. Tucked into the pages was a folded letter. Kellyn carefully removed it and handed it over for Morrigan to read.

The book was clearly for her. It looked like the one she kept in her nightstand.

Morrigan unfolded the note and read, "*You're going to need this. —Gallagher.*"

Kellyn's chest warmed. He appreciated that he didn't have to ask her to read it. She did it of her own volition because she knew it was helpful.

"What is it?"

"It's a book of spells." She breathed through a clenched jaw.

He gulped. That was a new development. A spell book. Was she a long-lived witch like Hecate or Circi?

"You have a book of spells." It was a terrible question. He was so clumsy. Clumsy like his hands which were still poorly cleaning her wounds.

"Yes . . ."

"It has spells in it." That was *not* better.

"Yes."

"Can you use magic?" That was worse. He was and always would be a big dumb brute so unused to holding a conversation that he blurted out things like that. He grunted. "Healing magic?"

"I can."

"Good, because you're broken. You need—" The muscle in her jaw ticked. *Oh, Havyn, take him*. Broken was the first word that came to his mind. He was getting so much worse. She made him nervous. Her beauty, the power of her presence, it all confounded him.

"I mean . . ." *What did you mean, fool? Think of something quick*. Morrigan would incinerate him if he didn't say something . . . anything . . . "Who are you, Morrigan?"

Nope. Not that.

He was digging his grave thirty-seven feet deep at this point.

She laughed and trailed her fingers against his face. "There is a spell in there to heal us." She ignored his question, instead pointing at his back with her chin. "Except I can't read the book."

"Oh."

"But you can."

His brows shot straight up.

"Only a descendant of House Azraelle can read Hecate's Grimoire," she said, "but don't worry, you don't have to read it, you just have to tell me the letters."

"Oh . . ." He was so illiterate and dim. He couldn't speak at all around her. Not at this moment.

She handed over the book. "Ask it for a healing spell. It will respond to you."

"Just ask?"

"Yes."

With the soft, old leather caressing his fingers, he asked, "Show me a healing spell?"

The book flipped open of its own accord, stopping on a blank, aged page that slowly filled with blood-like ink. The top of the page was in the common tongue, and he read it out to Morrigan, "*Mix dirt and water and rub into the wound as you read the incantation three times.*"

Reading wasn't so daunting when he knew he wasn't being judged. When it came to reading, Morrigan settled him, giving him confidence. She made him calmer, sturdier . . . better. At least until he met her azure eyes, and his heart started nervously ticking again.

Kellyn's nose wrinkled as he looked at the incantation. "It's in a different language."

Morrigan leaned over but shook her head. "I can't see anything, but why don't you simply read me the letters."

So he did.

Hoc dicto sana quod laesum est, carnem renova

"Scoop up dirt, wet it, and pack it into my wounds," she said.

"Truly?"

"The earth heals."

He followed her orders, packing the earth into her jagged skin. His every touch on her skin was gunfire, piercing and inescapable, consuming him in ways that weren't appropriate for the moment.

When he was finished, she spoke the incantation. As the words left her lips, a silver light emanated from the dirt, enchantment dancing through it and stitching her wounds together. It was like watching a master painter work, mesmerizing and unreal. Morrigan smiled, and the sight was astonishing, almost more so than the magic. Her smile was radiant like stained glass in a stream of silver moonlight.

The magic worked quickly, and within moments she could move again with minimal discomfort.

Scooping up the dirt, she glanced at him. "May I?"

He grunted his approval, but her eyes fixed on his chest, and she made no movements to help him. "It might be easier if you were over there." She pointed to the swing, "Easier to access the wounds."

He followed her command again. He liked following her orders. She was like a grand general of the fiercest army in the world, and he trusted her.

Morrigan followed him to the swing, and she slowly lifted his shirt and removed it. Her touch was pure bottled tension, causing desire to burst inside him. Gently, she packed his wound, her fingers dancing over his skin.

"You were brilliant in the challenge." Her breath caressed his neck.

"Thank you."

The incantation left her rose lips, the sound like molten magic, and the sensation of the spell was like heaven. A waterfall of warmth cascaded through his body, stitching muscles, and leaving pristine flesh in its wake. His blood sizzled, but instead of pain, it was life-giving, like drinking from the fountain of youth. The feeling was intoxicating and electrifying. It was a drug, and he wanted to feel it over and over again. He wanted to bathe in it. To let it consume him. It was the pure, unfiltered energy of life.

The strings of life.

It felt like divine threads were merging with his mortal ones—like an extra one was braided into his mortal three, giving him vitality and power. When the sensation ended, Morrigan didn't remove her fingers. They hovered on his skin, and her lips hovered behind his ear.

Kellyn gulped, trying to reel in the passion stirring at his core. He needed a distraction. "What are you, Morrigan?"

"I don't understand your meaning, *Your Highness*." Her lips touched his ear, and he shuddered.

Oh, she was going to kill him, but he decided to double down. "You're so much more than you say you are."

"Am I?" she asked, stepping around the swing to hover in front of him.

"Your knowledge of the gods is unmatched, and your beauty rivals Love herself."

"Don't let her catch you saying that; she might start a war over it." Another step closer. He couldn't tell if it was an intimidation tactic or something else, but her legs nearly touched his knees, and she looked down on him.

He inhaled sharply, her nearness pulling apart his control. Not because he was afraid of her—which she may want—but because he wanted her.

"That's precisely what I mean. You know the gods almost as if you were one of them."

"One of them," she said the words as if they tasted foul.

"Yes—"

She placed a finger over his lips. "You should stop." The jolt of her flesh against his sent flames of desire through him and held his breath, the rosemary and vanilla scent of her too intoxicating.

His lips remembered the taste of her. The softness. The fire. The war. The pure pleasure. Kellyn sucked in an unsteady breath. Her amethyst eyes held his, staring down from above like a goddess on her high throne.

He wanted to be that throne.

No. *Absolutely not.* His errant thoughts needed to stop.

Her hand fell to his chest, and she stepped closer, her legs straddling his knees. "You really should stop." Morrigan's voice was husky and breathless.

The glowing cave light stroked across her face, Kellyn's heart thrummed wildly in his chest, anticipation coiling in his stomach.

Oh, he wanted her.

Although she tried to intimidate him out of asking questions, her face was soft and pliant, her eyes dripping with the same lust he felt coursing through his bones.

"Who are you?" His voice was rough and thick with need. The need to know the answer and the need to *know* her. Intimately.

Morrigan's breath hitched.

"I told you to stop," she said, "and now I'll have to make you."

She leaned down, and like quicksand, her lips were on his.

The kiss unrelenting in its ferocity.

He stiffened from the shock, but when his brain caught up, he pulled her to him, his fingers curling around the metal snakes holding the remainder of her bodice at her back.

A crash was the only sign she'd dropped the spell book to the ground, freeing her fingers to stroke down his chest.

Running her tongue along his lower lip, she forced him to open to her, and he was happy to oblige.

Oh, gods, she was talented.

He was the woodworker of the pair, but her talent with her hands far outmatched his. She was all power and desire and battle.

Kissing her was like waging war. It was all tongues and teeth and nibbling and hands roaming all over his body. It was the culmination of all his dreams and intimate cravings.

He forgot all his questions because all he wanted was to feast on her and be devoured by her.

He'd spent five days wanting her like this. Five days trying to convince himself he didn't.

But, oh, how he did.

She was unquenched thirst and steeped moon fire—like lightning trapped in a bottle desperately trying to escape. Morrigan was all curves and gunfire—war in human flesh—and she was also home, like fresh-made cookies and mornings next to the hearth.

She was *his* home.

But he couldn't admit it because she would never have him, and he would never be worthy of her.

Never good enough.

Never smart enough.

But he could have *this* moment.

Kellyn raked his fingers through her hair, ruining her coiffure and pulling her closer. But neither of them cared. Her hair was meant to tumble around her shoulders like dark midnight magic, like spilled ink.

Lust rose in his chest, his heart banging like a bat in a cage, begging for an escape.

Their first kiss had been untamed passion, but this one was more. It was eternal because now they knew each other, hated each other, liked each other, and wanted each other.

This time, it was more because there was intimacy.

There was *feeling*.

A low growl escaped his throat, and her nails clawed into his back.

He needed to be closer to her. To be one with her.

Drawing her on top of his lap, her legs straddled his thighs and her core pressed against him in the best way. Her skirt slid up with the movement, exposing all that wonderful flesh.

His desire grew thick and hard, and he ran his fingers along her back, cupping her ass and squeezing.

Not to be outdone, she claimed his body with her fingers, her hands traveling down his torso, playing along the V-shape of his abs.

Taunting him.

Teasing him as she bit his lower lip and laughed.

A laugh like music.

And magic.

So rare in its beauty.

He sucked in a ragged breath, running his fingertips along her silky and wicked curves. His mouth moved along her jaw and down to the column of her neck to the cresting mountains of her breasts.

Letting out a whimper, she rocked into him. "More." Her voice was all rattled need.

Kellyn moaned into her, the swing starting to move as he removed his feet from the ground.

"I want you," she sighed into his lips. "I want all of you."

His hand trailed up her thigh, and he moved his lips to her ear, first nibbling and then sucking it into his mouth. "Then have all of me."

Unbuttoning his pants, she growled with pleasure and excitement.

Tension surged in his blood, bubbling, the anticipation of what was to come a physical and hungry thing.

Morrigan tried to relieve him of his trousers, but the swing tilted with the movement, toppling them onto the ground with a thud and laughter.

A swing was probably not the best venue for what they intended.

Kellyn was splayed out on the ground, Morrigan still straddling him, her fingers curled under the edge of his pants.

Their breaths were frantic and love hazed, their chests pulsing up and down with exertion.

But as they tried to catch their breaths, the world came crashing around them, and they realized what they'd just done.

What they shouldn't be doing. He was a champion in the Sacrifice, and she was his priestess. "We should probably stop."

"Yes." The word nearly soundless.

She rolled off him and lay beside him, still panting. From the effort, and probably the unfulfilled desire.

They both needed a moment.

He tried to think of gross or gruesome things to undo the energy still coursing through his body.

It didn't work.

After a while, he sat up and took in the scene.

Morrigan lay on the ground, her eyes fixed on the ceiling. Her face was all storms, and he wasn't sure it was because of the kiss. Something was eating away at her soul. Something that lingered from before their frantic hands and cresting fervor.

Morrigan didn't like talking about herself. That was clear. But curiosity was his curse, and he wanted to know what caused her eyes to darken and her face to dance with emotions. He wanted to learn more.

Wanted to *know her*.

Especially if he was kissing her . . . like that.

But she didn't let him ask anything. "Kel, whatever you do, you can't fall in love with me."

It might already be too late. "Why?"

"Because I'm a villain." The words left her ruby lips with an agonizingly tortured tone. "Loving me is a death sentence."

Thirty
Theodra
Goddess of War

LOVE CAVES, CITY OF THE GODS

Kellyn had burrowed far too deep into her heart like a parasite. It was too dangerous, deadly even. Nothing good came of falling in love. Not for her.

That's how the Immortal Law got broken.

Theo needed to get far away from Kellyn. She needed to escape the Sacrifice and never see him again. It was time to get her revenge on her mother. "Will you retrieve another spell for me?"

"Yes, of course," he coughed, still trying to tamp his arousal.

"Place your fingers on the edge of the book," Theo said, and he followed the instructions. Switching to the language of the gods, she said, "Show me the spell to restore divinity."

The book hesitated momentarily, and Kellyn instinctively stroked it as he would to a scared puppy trying to calm it. He seemed to sense the book's needs. It responded to his concern and flashed open, turning to—hopefully—the page she needed. She wouldn't know for sure until he read it to her.

Kellyn slowly scoured over the page—taking an eternity. "It says that you need to mix the ichor of a god with your blood and read the incantation." Then like last time, he read each letter to her one by one until she had the complete spell.

Hoc dicto, redde quod ablatum est, deum fias, divinum esto.

It was in her grasp. The spell and her freedom. While most gods wouldn't dare part with their ichor, Theo had a couple of cards to play. Andromache might give it to her freely—after all, Andromache's betrayal led Theo here. Or Havyn might bargain for it. Or Theo could provoke Fire into a fight and take his blood forcefully.

Theo had options. Multiple ways to get her divinity back.

"What is this spell?" Kellyn's face was a cloud of confusion and fear, and his body was rigid. "Why do you need a god's ichor? That could be dangerous."

Theo's stomach dropped. She didn't want to lie to him again. She wanted to trust him with everything, but the last time she truly trusted, she was betrayed.

"What is the spell, Morrigan?" His countenance was bleeding concern.

Theo sucked in a breath. Dare she trust again? Dare she lay it all on the line? Her heart lurched, fireflies warming its chambers, telling her to be vulnerable. Telling her to let go and let the truth soar. "Not Morrigan."

"What—"

Before she could answer, they were disturbed by a torrent of anger. Anger in the form of Cecile's voice. "Stay away from me. I want nothing to do with you. Ever." It was more of a growl than words.

Cecile burst into the cave, followed closely by two people and a cat—no, not people, gods. Gallagher and Night—Andromache's second in the Light Court—stepped into the cavern. Gallagher reverted to her human form, her blonde hair floating down her back as she strolled in like she had no concerns. She lived for chaos. On the other hand, Night wore an expression of hesitation and a dress formed from dying stars.

Her presence was unsettling because Night never attended the Sacrifice.

"I want nothing to do with any gods ever again. Especially not you," Cecile spat out, glaring at Night before her eyes caught on Theo. "Perfect, you're here, too. Rotten gods."

Under his breath, Kellyn said, "Agreed."

Theo's eyes darted to him, hurt stirring in her stomach. He hated *what* she was, and that was probably for the best. It was perhaps best she hadn't just revealed everything to him. Theo opened her mouth to intervene and stop Cecile from unleashing her secrets, but the mortal reacted too quickly and doomed Theo.

"You." Cecile pointed at Theo with accusation. "You're just as bad as them. You sent Gallagher into the Agoge to torture me and asked her to come here for what? To torture me some more?"

"I didn't send—" Theo started, realizing it was a defensive and unhelpful response. It didn't matter that Theo sent the goddess to protect the girl or even that she tried to reel in Gallagher's dramatic tendencies. What mattered was Cecile had been hurt by it.

Theo *hurt* her.

"Did you know about her, too?" Cecile pointed a furious finger at the Goddess of Night.

"Night?" Theo's brow furrowed. "What about Night?"

"That she's my—" Cecile's voice cracked, and Bella rubbed against her leg, "You know what, never mind about that." Fury sparked in her eyes. "Get out, Night. I only want to deal with one god at a time, and I choose to focus on Theo."

"Theo . . . god?" Kellyn whispered, his shoulders rising as he glanced between all three gods and Cecile. Confusion lit up his face. "What?"

Shit. This was going to end very poorly. Theo stepped toward him, wanting to comfort him, tell him the truth, something—

"I hate you. Get out." Cecile reacted in a highly triggered fashion, almost as if it were the broken little girl inside her responding—yelling. She disrespectfully turned her back on the Goddess of Night, deciding to ignore her existence entirely.

Theo needed to step in and do something. She hated seeing Cecile so hurt; strangely, it was Night, not Gallagher or Theo, who represented that hurt. "You should leave, Marguerite," Theo said to Night, who shifted on her feet, the dim cavern light painting her face a mural of sadness.

Night nodded and walked out; her head held high in grace as her feet nearly floated above the ground. Sometimes Night reminded Theo of Light in the weirdest of ways. In their bearing, their sadness, their regal acceptance of fate. At the cave entrance, she said one last phrase, "We can continue this later."

"Never," Cecile hissed before turning her ire fully on Theo. "Now, you."

Gallagher stepped up to Cecile. The blonde-haired nightmare from the War Court took the girl's hand and whispered soft indistinguishable words into her ear as a comforting gesture. The palpable tension between them caused the hairs on Theo's arms to rise. She couldn't decipher if it was good tension—*I want to seduce you*—or bad tension—*I want to kill you*. Or a mixture of both. With Gallagher, the latter was the most likely scenario.

Cecile's sharp features focused on Destruction, but her words were gentle. "You should leave, too."

"But I wanted to watch you rip our Great Goddess apart." Gallagher's nose wiggled with anticipation, and Kellyn's face palled at the words *Great Goddess.* His eyes widened as seven earth sprites crawled out of the rocks and circled his head, causing havoc. "Fine, Theo, I'll let you steal *my girl*."

"I'm not *your* anything," Cecile snapped back, but before she could argue the point more, Gallagher disappeared into the shadows, a maniacal laugh flicking from her rose-tinted lips.

"Maybe not yet, but you will be."

Cecile glowered at the darkness.

The sand shifted beneath Theo's feet as she clutched the swing and pulled herself up. "I'm sorry, Cecile."

"No, you're not. War is never sorry for anything."

Theo cocked her head. "Now, I'm simply War to you?"

Kellyn flinched, his body reacting to the title like a blow. His normally dark olive face paled, every muscle in his body drew tight like a bowstring, and his features were coated with a sick and twisted understanding. A song of betrayal drifted through the space between them.

"Kel, I can explain—"

"Why would you be anything else but War?" Cecile cut in and shook her head. "You're just like every other god playing sick games with mortals."

"No, I'm not." At least she didn't think she'd been . . . but maybe Cecile was right. Theo had a lot to answer for—all the dead Theoden champions, Medusa, Devereaux, the men she'd punished, and many more.

Theo was a villain and had been for thousands of years.

"You're rig—"

"Oh, but you have been, *Theodra*," the name was said like snake venom, "You've never cared about my feelings, never asked me for my opinion. You do things that hurt people, and then you never even have the decency to apologize." Cecile said it all in one, long slurring breath.

It was all true.

"Gallagher, truly?" A tear rolled down Cecile's face. "You know how much pain she causes me."

Gallagher caused more than just pain, but it wasn't precisely the best moment to point that out, so Theo sewed her lips shut. Destruction's actions were extreme. She'd become Cecile's nemesis in order to stay one step ahead of her other enemies. It worked, but it also worked to make Cecile hate her.

Theo rubbed her face. "I would like to apologize—" *now.* Cecile didn't let her finish her thought.

"And that's not to mention what you've done to Kellyn. You vowed not to help him because you've never cared about any of your champions. Ever."

"I—"

"And he's never deserved your scorn. He's only ever been loyal to you."

"You're right, Cecile." Theo forced it out, stopping the other girl in her tracks. Theo sucked in a breath. Her eyes focused on the glittering cave pool covered with jade lily pads. Shame rained down her body like the barrage of a waterfall. "It's recently come to my attention," Theo paused and scrunched her face, the admission painful, "that my good intentions, coupled with apathy, have led to a lot of pain."

"Good intentions," Cecile scoffed. "How is sending a bloodthirsty god into the Agoge good intentions?" Cecile sat down on one of the rope swings with a huff.

Theo swallowed. She didn't want to sound like she made

excuses, but she also wanted to tell the truth. "I knew the Agoge was deadly and wanted to protect you." Theo smoothed out a wrinkle in her skirt, her heart thundering. "I'm not fond of people and especially not children. I didn't know what to do, so I sent Gallagher to ensure you didn't die."

"Make sure I didn't die," Cecile growled.

"I realize now that I should've done much more to ensure you weren't just physically safe but also emotionally."

Silence snaked between them, its venom cutting into Theo's core and leaving her feeling utterly vulnerable in a way she never had before. She'd never wanted to apologize for anything before and never needed an apology to be accepted. As a god, she did things and expected people to be okay with them; frankly, she didn't care if they were because Theo was apathy personified.

She was cold, calculating, and vicious.

Yet now, she wanted Cecile to forgive her. She wanted to fix things and work through it.

"It fixes nothing," Cecile finally said.

Theo's body drew as tight as a violin string. "I know." Her throat worked. "I don't deserve your forgiveness because I'm devastation in human flesh, but I would ask for it."

Cecile played with the swing for a long moment, and it seemed she wouldn't respond. "And why would I give it? You're selfish, and I don't ever see that changing."

The truth hit like a blade to the heart.

"I might have been able to forgive you for what you did to me, but Kellyn never deserved this. He's going to die here because of you." Cecile's eyes latched onto the spell book in Theo's hands. "Let me guess, that book is a way for you to fix yourself so you can leave us all here to die."

"It's—"

"Tell me it's not." Darkness swirled in Cecile's irises. Literal darkness. Theo's eyebrows drew together. "Tell him it's not, Theo." She pointed at Kellyn.

Theo swallowed and clapped her mouth tightly shut. There was nothing to say. Cecile was right. That was Theo's plan.

"You're just like the rest." Cecile seethed. "I was so stupid to trust you. You're a god. It's your nature to destroy. Your nature to trick and play and wound. It's who you are; nothing matters to you, not even this bond." Cecile's raven tattoo squawked in agreement as she waved her arm.

"I never wanted this bond." It slipped out and was the absolute wrong thing to say. Theo pinched her eyes shut. She was making everything worse.

"You've made that abundantly clear. Repeatedly, you told me you'd never care about me, never love me, and I was just too foolish to believe you . . . well, I believe you now."

Now? Just when it wasn't true. This was a true divine comedy. Payback for a millennium of wrongs.

Theo's insides ached as much as her outsides because she cared, and these words killed her. Yet she didn't know how to show affection. She didn't know how to improve it and let someone feel loved. Wetness grew in the corner of her eyes, and she didn't know what to do with it. *Tears*. But she absolutely wouldn't let them run down her face.

"Cecile I . . ." Theo tried to form words that would matter. "I'm sorry." But those words were so hollow. So meaningless.

Cecile stood, violently rocking her swing. "Stay away from me. I release you from this foolish bond." She stomped away, her face red and painted with tears. The shadow cat followed with a sweet little meow—a meow of empathy.

Theo's gaze fell to the floor, her shoulders slumped, the stinging in her eyes crescendoing, and she could no longer hold back. The tears fell like a somber rain. The feeling was utterly foreign to her skin.

"You can't release me," Theo whispered after her. "Only I can release you."

Theo found no respite because she had to answer Kellyn and beg him not to leave her as Cecile had.

"You're a dirty liar," Kellyn's voice was smooth whisky combined with arsenic.

"Yes."

His face fell, and the vein in his jaw ticked. It was his disappointment—his hurt that gutted her. It felt like termites were slowly eating tracks through the lining of her soul.

"You lied *to me*," he breathed again. "Were you ever going to tell me?"

She wanted to. She was about to tell him everything. Wasn't she? But . . . maybe that was just another lie because Theo wasn't brave enough to risk his wrath. Brave enough to lose him to the truth, but now she'd lost him anyway because he'd never accept War. The irony was that if Theo could have anything, she would have his acceptance. She would have him know all of her. Selfishly, she wanted to be *seen* by him.

She wanted to be *loved* by him.

"Kel, I—" Theo swallowed, and she couldn't get words to pass her tongue, shame turning it to stone.

"Theodra." His bearing was as hard as the volcanic rock surrounding them.

"Theo," she whispered, averting her gaze. She wanted him to use her nickname—the name she chose. She wanted the closeness of it.

Everything about the gentle, kind giant vanished, and fury consumed him. This was a betrayal too far for him. After being so wronged by the gods, so abandoned by her . . . it was all too much for him, and she knew it. It was etched onto the structure of his bones.

"What does the spell do, *Theodra?*" The words hissed like the lava flowing into the water.

She pinched her lips together and shooed away a water sprite soaked in her toxic emotions. "It's a spell to get my divinity back."

"Was the kiss just to get me to translate it?"

She looked up, horrified. "No, of—"

"You've been using me this whole time." Heavy emotion fell from his lips. "Getting close to me. Playing with me. Seducing me." He shook his head. "What games are you playing now? Did you enjoy watching me suffer—watching me poison my best friend?"

"No," her voice cracked.

"Did you force Gallagher to switch out my speech, too? So you could play your little games with a devoted follower?" He seethed. "Well, I'm no longer devoted. I despise you."

"I didn't, Kel, I promise . . ."

"I thought you might be different." Betrayal painted his sculpted face. "Did you use me just to get this spell? It's what you wanted from the beginning, wasn't it?"

"Yes . . . but I—"

"Cecile was right not to trust you. She was right to run away from you." He stood up, shaking. "I'm done, Theodra." He cursed her name and stormed from the cave, leaving her with her spell book and a million regrets.

Thirty-One
Theodra
Goddess of War

LOVE CAVE, CITY OF THE GODS

Cecile was right not to trust you. She was right to run away from you.

Pain radiated behind Theo's eyes and through her chest. Emotions bubbled up like acid in her esophagus, and her nose and cheeks ached from holding tears back—from keeping the emotions from spilling down her face.

The spell book sat open on the floor, mocking her. Mocking her choices and goals, and selfish desires. They were right. Theo was wretched—a god who used people for personal gain. A god who murdered and punished and hated. She was no different than her sisters or mother. No different than the gods reveling in the Sacrifice.

Theo was just as bad.

No, she was worse because she hurt her friends. She hurt Cecile with her callousness and Kellyn with her lies.

And she hated herself for it. A tear rolled down her face, and she batted it away.

Kellyn was different. He was her opium. He was poppy tears and poison. Potent both physically and mentally. He was the drug that awakened her soul, melting the ice in her veins. She couldn't turn back the clock and return to the god she'd been before.

She couldn't un-experience his kindness, patience, and caring. He'd shown her what it was like to need someone, to depend on someone, to have *him* take care of her, to have him there for her even when he didn't want to be.

Kellyn had shown her genuine kindness, and Theo couldn't forget it.

His kindness had changed her. Irrevocably.

He'd broken her hollow echo and replaced it with something far more terrifying. Something she couldn't dare name . . .

Theo had her revenge in the palm of her hand. She had everything she needed to regain her divinity . . . but she couldn't take it back. *Not now.* Because taking it back would mean leaving Kellyn to face the Sacrifice alone. The divine couldn't play the games, and he was doomed if she got what she wanted.

Tears flowed down her cheeks freely.

Theo had spent 10,000 years being a selfish god. Ten thousand years focused on her needs, pain, and hollow unbreakable echo. But no longer. She'd change. For Kellyn, for Cecile, but primarily for herself.

She slammed the book shut, and it hissed at her, but Theo didn't care. She vowed to see these sickening games through.

Vowed to save Kellyn at all costs. Even if he hated her.

Cecile was right. Theo had ruined many lives with her cruelty and apathy. Lives like the former Theoden champions and Medusa. Theo was sick of being the villain, sick of breaking everything. She couldn't do anything about her dead champions, but she could at least fix one mistake.

Theo needed Havyn to do it, and as if summoned, she stepped out of the shadows. "Well, that was rather unfortunate."

"You were watching?"

"Of course, I was. I am darkness, after all."

"Have you come to gloat?"

The corners of Havyn's lips twitched. "Partly, but I also sense you might need me."

Theo's brows drew together. *How?*

Havyn was always seven steps ahead. Almost as if she were a seer, but that was an impossibility. Only humans were seers.

"How did you . . . you know, never mind," Theo panted. "I need you to help me—"

"Yes, you need help with a spell, and you need me to counter Love's magic chain for an hour so you can leave the palace, not to mention make sure your torc doesn't kill you while you do." Havyn's lips curled up in a self-satisfied smile. Theo had completely forgotten about the chain and the torc. Love must have been giving them a long leash.

"I will accept an open-ended favor as payment," Havyn said.

"How did you know I needed you?"

"I will always be seven steps ahead of you, sister."

Theo jolted. Was Havyn reading her mind? Another impossibility.

"How?"

"Erety told me," Havyn said, "Did you know my wife is an oracle?"

No. Theo didn't. But it made sense, she had become the Goddess of Fate after turning. But this was just another example of Theo's self-centered nature. She didn't care to know anything that didn't affect her.

"Now, shall we?" Giving no warning, Havyn refracted them to the edge of Medusa's lair.

The place felt like a whispered secret from old wives' tales.

Theo stumbled, catching her balance on the emerald stone path which led up to Medusa's cozy cottage. It was a relatively small house with a thatched roof made from snake skins and doors formed of rosewood and nightingale hearts.

Daydreams and twisted hopes lingered on the soft manufactured wind surrounding the building, warning intruders away and welcoming guests.

Theo wasn't sure which category she belonged in.

"You know what I was pondering the other day?" Havyn tapped her chin as Theo's hand hovered over the door.

"What?"

"Braids."

"Are you serious?" Theo grumbled, "Is this truly the time?"

"There's always time for discussing braids." Havyn wiggled her nose. "There are so many things you can braid. The obvious objects like hair and cords, but there is also magic like strings of life or even clothing . . . Did you know you can braid food together?"

"I don't care." Havyn was so random sometimes, and Theo had no patience for it. So she ignored her sister.

Knocking on the door, Theo shook out her jaw, it ached from clenching it too tightly, and she squared her shoulders back, trying to swathe herself in confidence like a shield.

The light chatter drifting from the cottage stilled, and Medusa slowly opened the door as if expecting an invasion.

"Great goddesses," she said, glancing back at her two sisters, who sat around a table with a tea tray.

It was a bit late for tea, but who was Theo to judge? Perhaps gorgons lived on different schedules than humans. Theo didn't know because she had never cared enough to find out.

Medusa swallowed uncomfortably, her snakes rearing up and hissing. "Would you two like to come in and join us?"

Theo flinched and braced herself for a long, awkward conversation. She still was utter shit with human emotions. And while the gorgons were monsters, they were once human. "Yes, if you wouldn't mind."

A cheerful mask slid over Medusa's features. "It would be our pleasure."

She guided Theo in, set two places at the table, and poured tea, her hands shaking. "Why have you honored us with a visit?"

Sthenno and Euryale openly glowered at the goddesses, their snakes coiling, hissing, and striking out at the surrounding air. Medusa's sisters were not impressed.

A hundred eyes tracked Theo's every movement, from the ringing of her hands to the breaths she took. Snakes slithered on the ground, hung from plants and furniture, coiled around chair legs, and sat on the chair meant for the mortal goddess—and half of them were highly venomous.

Theo's eyes traced the snake on her chair, a lancehead viper—extremely deadly and incredibly unhappy with her presence.

Medusa followed her gaze and said, "Oh, sorry." She scooped

the snake up and placed it around her neck. "Please sit." She waved at the now empty chair.

"Don't mind me. I'll stand," Havyn said, examining a snake in the corner. "I'm just here as the magic."

Theo nodded, her stomach roiling. Not a fan of snakes—especially not of ones lethal to a human body. Theo placed her hands in her lap, her fingers twitching with unease and anticipating an uncomfortable conversation.

Like ripping off a bandage, Theo came right out with it. "Do you like your powers?"

The only signs of Medusa's surprise were the slight widening of her eyes—which she quickly suppressed with her mask—and the vein in her jaw ticking. A saccharine smile danced on her mouth as she sat in thought. Her snakes were less controlled, and at the words they all coiled in on themselves.

"Playing in the Sacrifice has brought to my attention some facts about myself and my actions that I dislike." Theo lifted her chin and straightened her back, trying to lend herself physical courage. "When I bestowed you with power all those years ago, I thought I was protecting you, giving you a way to defend from vile men, but I never asked if it was the right thing to do. I never gave you a choice, and I think my solution might have been more of a curse than a boon."

Silence hung over the room like a corpse bride's veil. Black, depressing, and devoid of hope. Nervousness licked the air, the gorgons sharing hesitant looks. They had to be thinking it was a trap.

"It's not . . ." Theo raised her hands, and every snake in the room followed the movement, shifting back and forth. "It's not a trap. I know it's hard to believe me because I'm a villain, but I mean what I say, and I would like to make it right. I want to alter the spell."

"Alter the spell," Medusa parroted, her brows creasing together.

"I could restore your humanity, or I could alter the spell to give you the ability to choose who you turn to stone and give you the ability to switch between forms."

"You would do this?" Medusa asked, her voice melodic and wary.

Theo ran her tongue along her teeth, trying to figure out how to convince them. "I've made many mistakes in my long life, and I can't take most of them back, but I can help you." She tried to pour as much sincerity into the words as possible.

The sisters glanced at each other, conversing silently.

Medusa stroked one of her snakes. "Would you offer this to all of us?"

Without hesitation. "Yes."

"Then we shall take it."

Theo pulled out the spell book. It pulsed like a beating heart in the palm of a hand. It cooed, sounded as soft as hummingbird wings, and smelled of fresh daisies.

It seemed to be in a good mood.

Havyn appeared next to Theo and pulled the book from her hands. On its own, the book turned to the spell they needed, and it smiled with rotting teeth at Havyn. Turning to the gorgons, Havyn said, "I need your blood, scales from your snakes, three stones, and sea salt."

The gorgons all leaped into action, gathering the needed ingredients quickly.

Following the instructions, Havyn placed the stones at the center of the now-cleared tea table and poured the salt into a circle around them. Havyn sprinkled the snake scales atop each of the rocks. When she finished the setup, she asked each gorgon to cut her palm and spill its blood.

The drips sounded like raindrops in a light spring shower as they danced along the stones, sprinkling like seeping pomegranate juice.

In an ancient tongue, Havyn spoke the spell, the words at once filled with the lightness of dragonfly wings and the darkness of the sea before a storm.

The spell was physical, coating their skin with moon-ray thistles and chocolate candies. It vibrated and hummed, the magic coiling through the air like all the vipers in the room. Its presence was both overwhelming and comforting. But the spell didn't just show up through touch. It was also all soft glows and moonshine —a silver Aurora Polaris gently swaying in the wind.

As soon as the spell hit, it was gone just as quickly, leaving three gorgons staring at their arms and wondering if it worked.

Instinctively, Medusa pulled her magic inward and shifted forms from monster to legendary beauty. Her sisters followed suit.

"Oh, thank you, thank you." Medusa leaped at Theo and curled her into a massive hug, pulling Havyn in too. Theo stilled, utterly unaccustomed to gratitude.

Thirty-Two
Theodra
Goddess of War

PALACE BALCONY, CITY OF THE GODS

Death and War strolled atop the balconies of the volcanic palace in sullen silence, having returned from their outing. Havyn's ink-like cloak flowed in a phantom wind behind her, and her footfalls felt aimless but were anything but. Havyn had a rhyme and reason for all that she did.

The challenge was to figure out those reasons.

"You owe me a soul." And there it was.

Theo flinched, despite expecting the words to come. It was the deal they'd made for Cecile's life, but the words cut open Theo's sternum and wrenched out her heart.

Because no words ever felt more painful.

The wind howled through the birch trees flanking the banks of the Deus River. Theo's eyes locked on the tree's limbs, climbing out of the ground like a witch's claws with overgrown fingernails that curled in on themselves. Sailboat rigging thumped against masts, and an errant human whistled in the distance, the sound distorted and fraying at its seams and mixing with the wind's cruel aria. A thick fog hung like a rotten net, invading the pristine balcony, and clinging to Theo's pores.

Despite having no god magic, the atmosphere mirrored Theo's emotions like she was twisting them and compelling them to her will. She was all stiff spines, tense muscles, fire, and pure battle. "The deal was for a human soul that I love, and I do not love any humans."

Havyn's blood-red lips curled. "Don't you?"

Theo would not give in. She couldn't. The stakes were too high. "I'm not capable of love." There wasn't a star in the sky or a grain of salt in the sea that could alter that fact. It was an impossibility.

Wasn't it?

Theo's mouth grew dry, and her head ached.

It had to be true. Because if it wasn't . . .

Fuck. A concession meant death to the one person Theo didn't want to live without. Kellyn wasn't just any mortal. He was . . .

Oh, decaying Valysia, she couldn't even think of it. It was too close to being . . .

Theo sucked in a breath. "I don't love any humans."

Havyn laughed, the sound like a wailing harpy. High pitched and horrifying. "Now, that is a pathetic lie."

Fire licked Theo's intestines. "You cannot have Kellyn."

Havyn eyed her sister and slowly picked an invisible speck of lint from her onyx dress as if not talking about matters of great importance. "Interesting you'd suggest him." A wicked smile stretched across her smug face.

Oh, fuck. It was a trap, and Theo so foolishly fell into it.

Her eyes stung, and she held back all the emotions pooling in her belly. If she let them out, it would be an acknowledgment. A death knell. "You can't have his soul."

Havyn shook her head and ran a finger along her lip. "And what are you going to do about it, Theodra?" Her purple eyes curled into a blackness filled with crawling spiders. "A deal is unbreakable."

"But not unbendable."

"Oh . . ." Havyn raised an eyebrow, teaming with shadows. "Have you figured out how to bend it?"

"Take another soul." Theo swallowed. "Any other soul."

Shadows twisted around Havyn's neck and reached out as if wanting to taste War. Theo waved them off like an irritating wind sprite. Havyn cocked her head and searched her sister's features. "Which soul would you have me replace him with?" She paused, her voice soaked in cinnamon spice and mischief. "The original soul?"

"No, that's not an option," Theo snapped back, her voice hollow.

Anger pulsed in Theo's veins like a war drum signaling battle. She was sick of being toyed with. Sick of Havyn playing her like a violin, stroking her strings, and forcing her into traps. All the gods did was tempt and tease, and Theo was sick of it.

"Well, well, look at you, loving two souls," the words thrilled from Havyn's tongue. "What an interesting dilemma you have."

"I don't love either of them." Ice crept over Theo's heart, and she willed it true.

Havyn scoffed. "Right, and I'm a mermaid." She waved her hand dismissively. "See, what you said sounds just as ridiculous."

Theo growled, gritting her teeth, and scrunching her fists tightly, resisting the urge to punch her sister.

Havyn's eyes raked over War's skin, touching first the tension in her muscles, then her stance before landing on her haunted face. The examination left goosebumps in its wake. "You have until the end of the Sacrifice. A little over a day to decide which one you want me to steal."

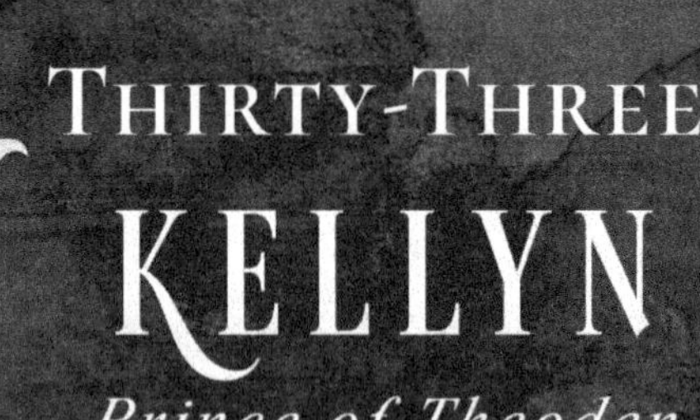

Thirty-Three

Kellyn

Prince of Theoden

THEODEN QUARTERS, CITY OF THE GODS

It was a night forged from fights. First, with Morrigan, no, Theodra—he would never get used to that. Kellyn shuddered. And now a fight with Cecile. She'd lain in wait, accosting Kellyn as he entered his rooms.

"You knew about Gallagher?" Cecile yelled. "You were working with her this whole time?"

"Let's not be mad at each other." Kellyn sighed and fell onto his bed, rubbing his face, emotionally exhausted. He could barely process "Morrigan's" betrayal, let alone anything else today. Kellyn felt bad about Cecile, but it was nothing compared to how used he felt about Theodra.

"Are you truly telling me how to feel?" Cecile was a tornado in human flesh, tearing through the room.

"That's never a smart idea, brother," Emmett said with an amused smirk as he leaned against the wall.

Kellyn laid down and pinched his eyes closed, rubbing at his temples. He wanted to focus on the current argument, but he kept flashing back to the kiss and its disastrous aftermath. It would be his fate to fall for an unobtainable, depraved goddess.

Oh, he was so foolish. Truly a big, dumb brute.

Theo had played him like a fiddle. Using him and disposing of him right as she got what she wanted.

"Kel, are you even paying attention?" Cecile walked over to the bed and hovered over him.

Kellyn inhaled sharply, his veins throbbing from the tension he held all over his body. "No."

"You just don't care about your actions?" Cecile's voice vibrated like an asp readying to strike.

"Aren't you being a bit of a hypocrite?" he said, opening his eyes and catching her gaze.

Cecile opened her mouth to argue but promptly shut it as the realization hit. "Oh, I am. It's the same, isn't it."

"Yes . . ." Kellyn rubbed his temples again, and Cecile floated down to the bed, her face turning from crimson to moon white.

A quick and quaking quiet slid through the room, leaving only the sound of their breathing permeating the air and their hearts rumbling in their chests.

Emmett kicked off the wall and strode over to them. "What is going on?"

"Morrigan is War," Cecile said. "She is Theodra in a mortal form." Cecile shook her head and wrung her hands as she told them the whole story, sparing no details, which only perplexed the entire situation. Kellyn felt—albeit only a little bit—sorry for Theodra. Yet it changed nothing. She was still a deceitful, despicable god. Kellyn might have been able to forgive the fact that Theo was a god if she hadn't lied. It was the lying that truly hurt.

He had asked her point blank if she was a god, and she lied. Not caring one bit for the truth.

"Wait, what?" Emmett stuttered and glanced between Cecile and Kellyn, measuring them. He took in the tense posture of their bodies, to the intense expression coloring their faces. The truth of the words etched into every wrinkle and curve of their flesh.

"Have either of you considered that this might be a good thing?" Emmett asked slowly. "If Morrigan is War, then she's been helping you. You have a chance to survive all of this. I like Morrigan . . . I mean, Theodra."

"I might agree if she hadn't just tricked me into providing the spell to regain her divinity." Kellyn pinched his nose, still lying on his bed and staring at the ceiling. "She's truly abandoned us."

Cecile rubbed her eyes. "I'm sorry, Kel."

"We won't abandon you," Emmett added, and Kellyn sat up to meet his eyes. It was a massive concession, almost an acceptance of the apology. Whatever it was, it was a tectonic shift in their relationship—for the better.

Emmett cleared his throat and changed the subject, his brown skin glowing against the embers popping in the fireplace. "At least the other champions are doing well. Your plan is working. The Nefesian and Ertomesian champions survived their final challenges, and everyone apart from you is facing their next challenges."

Happiness fluttered in Kellyn's core. At least one thing was going well.

"Although, the Simark fellow died," Cecile added. "His bronze hourglass emptied like his life."

"Don't feel bad for him," Emmett cut in, "he betrayed the Ertomesian girl, leaving her to die and deciding to play on his own. Little did he know that Andromache would punish him for it and make his game unwinnable." Emmett pointed at the mirror on the wall, replaying the event.

The death was gruesome and graphic, and Kellyn averted his eyes. "What is your next challenge?"

"I think it's Death . . . again." Cecile's voice quivered slightly.

"How is that possible?" Kellyn asked. "If that's true, then we have the same three challenges back-to-back."

"You have Death next as well?"

"Yeah, it doesn't make sense." Kellyn ran a finger along a throw pillow. "My clue was *All roads lead to me.*"

"There isn't much else that can be," Cecile agreed. "So the gods are fucking with us. Making us feel secure now that we've had success."

Emmett gave them a thin smile. "It has to be."

"It is possible to face the same god twice. It happened to the Nefesian champion twenty-eight years ago." Cecile twitched her lips, thinking through the history. She'd memorized the last seventeen Sacrifices. Studying them over and over again. "My riddle was: *I rest in shadows. I lurk behind corners. I reap all joy and slay all creatures. Some curse me while others embrace me still. But one thing is certain. I'm one strong pill.* It couldn't be anything other than death, but it's strange because nine out of ten times, the final challenge is to face a god, not just their games."

"So what do you want to do about it?" Kellyn asked.

"We go in together and hope for the best." She shrugged, throwing her hands up into the air.

The fire popped and crackled, mirroring his unease.

THIRTY-FOUR
KELLYN
Prince of Theoden

DEATH'S MIRROR

The Death mirror taunted them, its snake frame hissing and coiling, the liquid silver glinting and inviting them into their demise. It was close to midnight, and Kellyn needed to get moving. He had two challenges to complete in just over a day, and some challenges could last the entirety of one. Hopefully, not his last two.

Kellyn stepped up to the mirror and reached out, but Emmett grabbed his elbow.

"Before we go in," Emmett cleared his throat. "I—um," he coughed, shuffling on his feet. "I saw you in the last challenge . . . *your issues*. And while I don't forgive you, I understand."

Kellyn inhaled sharply. His heart was like a caterpillar emerging from its cocoon. Hope burst out with it in the shape of butterfly wings. He dared not say anything to disturb this tenuous peace.

Emmett patted his friend on the back. "We've been through enough. I say we try to move forward."

Kellyn's chest warmed, and his lips rose into a smile. "Thank you."

"Yeah . . ." Emmett slapped Kellyn on the back again. "Let's not mention it again." He changed the topic swiftly. "Shall we?"

Kellyn nodded, and the three of them surged into the Death mirror, their hands clasped.

If someone were ever to take a bath in snakes, this was what it would feel like. He shuddered; every inch of his body covered in scales. It was a mixture of repellent sensations, from smooth to dry to unsettlingly warm to the touch. But the pressure—like someone squeezing around his neck—revolted him.

It had to be snakes.

Gooseflesh crawled down his spine.

As the sensation dissipated, and Kellyn stepped into the challenge, he felt Emmett's hand ripped from his. Whirling around, Kellyn saw it disappear into nothing, and the exit solidified into unbreakable glass.

Havyn had separated the friends. Kellyn was now truly alone.

He was surrounded by thick, reinforced—bullet-resistant—glass. It was a nearly empty chamber. The only objects inside were the statue cameras, recording everything. On the other side of the glass was twisting darkness. There were no clues as to what the game would be. It was simply a trap.

"Wait," a disembodied soprano voice called, and Theo walked out of the disappearing portal. She held a satchel and panted like she'd run an entire marathon. "You can't do this without me."

A commotion coiled in his heart, but he couldn't make out the emotion. It was at once livid, surprised, immensely glad, and heartbroken. It was a lot to feel.

Havyn's pale form appeared amongst the darkness on the other side of the glass. "Wonderful, we're all here—"

"Where are Cecile and Emmett?" Kellyn interrupted.

"Playing their own game with the Mistress of Fate." Havyn's smile was that of a jungle cat. "Tsk, tsk, you should know that all final challenges are faced alone." Havyn clucked her tongue as if disappointed in him. "Now, our game is simple: answer the questions honestly, and you can live."

Havyn cackled, and with a snap of her fingers, a glass barrier climbed between him and Theo, forming shard by shard, crackling with every piece that slid into place. They were in separate chambers now, and Kellyn figured out precisely why, as water started bubbling up from the floor a moment later.

Havyn would drown them unless they spoke the truth to each other. Perfect.

Blood poured down the glass and twisted into a question.

Always reading.

But Theo rescued him and read the question aloud, "*You're fighting. Is there anything you would like to say to each other*?" Theo rolled her eyes and glared at her sister. "What are you, our therapist?"

Havyn's feral smile widened. "Yes, of course I am." Her eyes slid to the water, skating around their feet. "I would get to it; these chambers fill up faster than you would think."

Theo's eyes darted to Kellyn and then to the statues watching the room. "Kel, the statues." One by one, she smashed the four stone gods in her room and turned to Kellyn, expecting him to do the same. "Please."

"I will still hear you," Havyn threatened.

Theo pinched her lips together before saying, "I know." Her voice was fragile. "So be it."

Kellyn tapped his fingers on his legs. He wasn't sure if he should give into Theo's wants, especially since he was still so angry with her . . . but she had shown up. Also, she was right. If he were going to bare his soul, he didn't want the gods or his parents to hear, so he smashed his statues too.

"Thank you," Theo said softly. "Kellyn, I don't know what to say. I'm not good with humans. I never know what to say or do."

Theo rubbed a finger along her bag as if she were deciding something, and then she plunged her hand into the pouch and pulled out a handful of well-crafted lovespoons. She held them out as if she wanted to hand them over, but the glass prevented it. Her eyes were a bit desperate and crazed. "They're yours, all the spoons you carved for me." She dug her hand into the bag full of hundreds of carved spoons. "You matter to me, Kel. You've always mattered to me, even before I knew you."

Kellyn gulped. He didn't know what to say to this—to the fact that she kept every spoon he'd ever carved . . . even the one he broke, the one he didn't offer to her. Theo held out that one now.

"I never believed in fate before, but as I look at all these, I wonder . . ." Her mouth twitched. "I'm sorry, Kel."

"Sorry for what?" His tone was gentle despite the fury still churning his stomach.

"Everything," she blew out a breath, "Everything, but mostly for lying to you." She gulped. "I'm the villain in most stories, but I don't want to be the villain in yours."

"And tricking me into getting the spell for you?"

"Yes." She stepped closer to the glass as if she wanted to reach out and touch him but couldn't. "I know it means nothing, but I didn't do it."

"The spell?"

She dipped her chin. "Yes."

"Why?"

"Because I couldn't stay to help you if I took my divinity back." She touched the glass, splaying out her palm. "I know I'm a monster, but I want to change. I don't want to be so . . ."

He cocked his head, examining her. Her eyes were nearly the violet of her god form, and they were swimming with regret. "Godly?"

"If godliness is synonymous with trickery and cruelty . . . then yes." Her nose flared, and a tear curled down her elegant features. "I'm so sorry, Kellyn. I've been terrible to everyone, but I hate myself for how I treated you."

The water was at her waist, and her skirt flowed weightlessly around her legs. Kellyn wanted to believe her, but her betrayal had its claws deep in his heart, and he didn't know how to let go of it.

"If you didn't take your divinity back, does that mean you can die in this challenge?" He needed to know because the water was slowly crawling up their bodies, and even in his hurt, he didn't want her to die. An asp coiled in his stomach at the thought.

"Yes." Theo bit the inside of her cheek. "I'm mortal."

Havyn clapped from the darkness, drawing their attention back to her. "Wonderful, now for your second question."

Blood poured down every surface of the glass, encasing them into a tomb of red. It clotted together into more words. Theo read, "*Do you forgive your priestess?*" Her eyes were liquid remorse like she was sorry he even had to answer the question.

Kellyn's lungs collapsed as he glanced at his priestess. The water was up to Theo's chest. She had the expression of a wet cat, yet she was still alluring in that way of hers. All ferocity and hidden vulnerability. She was light, the brightest star in the sky. Luminescent yet incinerating if you got too close. And he had gotten too close.

"I don't know," he whispered. "I want to forgive her, but I feel like my entire life was rattled, the ground-breaking out from underneath me, and I don't know how to process it." He swallowed past the lump in his throat. "How does one process that you're a god?" he asked her, his eyes stinging with the emotions the question brought up. "Humans aren't supposed to—"

He couldn't finish the words. They exposed too much.

She stepped closer and placed a second hand on the glass. "I understand." She gulped. "I don't deserve to be forgiven, and I don't expect it either."

Neither spoke. Only the sound of rushing water persisted as their eyes caressed each other. Saying so much without words. Fireflies buzzed in the chambers of his heart. He couldn't stay angry with her. She was a drug he couldn't withdraw from. He'd only known her for six days, yet he felt he had known her for an eternity. Yet, he felt like even if he had 10,000 years to get to know her, he'd never get to her core—never know everything. But he wanted to.

And there was something beautiful about that.

Blood poured down the walls again and formed into the next question. Theo coughed as if choking as she read it. "*Why do you hate men, Theodra?*" The letters shifted again. "*What broke you*?" She let out a low laugh, and under her breath, "Meddling sisters."

Theo rubbed the dark circle under an eye with her knuckle. She was exhausted. "I—" she started slowly. "I hated men because I thought they were all the same. Abusers." She sighed, her eyes sparking with shame. "When I was a young goddess, barely a century old, I fell in love with a beautiful, brilliant god. A god who burned with passion and desire. I was foolish and young and believed that he wanted me, not for my power or the connections to my mother, but for *me*. I was wrong." Theo's voice cracked, and she spoke quickly, like she was ripping off a bandage—like if she took the time to tell it, she wouldn't get it out. "Fire seduced and kidnapped me to help Fumoire—the leader of the Titans—win the Great War of the Gods. They held me as bait and tortured me for years with his fire whip and other horrible contraptions while they waited for my mother to rescue me. But she didn't."

Theo rubbed the scar along her torso, and a thick tear fell down her face. "My mother didn't free me until the war was over, and by then, I was far too broken and was no longer the sweet, naïve goddess anymore. I was vengeance."

The story gutted Kellyn. It was unimaginable to ever betray someone he loved like that or even someone he hated. "Theo," he breathed, "I'm so sorry."

She pinched her lips together, clearly trying to hold back emotions.

It made everything make sense. She was dark and twisted and cold because a man had destroyed her. She'd been destroyed by trusting love. Kellyn wanted to reach through the glass and hold her. He couldn't imagine that level of trauma. He wanted to protect her from it and keep anything like that from happening again. And he wanted to destroy the God of Fire.

"How was he not punished?" The words slipped out of Kellyn's mouth before he could think to hold them in. Because Kellyn wanted Fire punished, he wanted to wrap his fingers around the god's throat and slowly kill him for what he did.

"Fire betrayed Fumoire and helped Nefeli to destroy and imprison the Titans."

Fury boiled in Kellyn's blood. "He can't have been forgiven that easy."

"He wasn't, but that's a much longer story." The muscle in Theo's jaw tensed. "But to answer Death's true question so we can get this terrible game over with, I don't hate men anymore." She released a breath, "At least not all men. I don't hate you."

"Theo, I'm so sorry."

She shrugged and brushed it off as if it were meaningless. "It was a long time ago."

"Good job. Now for my final question," Havyn said, but the

blood didn't appear this time. Instead, she asked it, her voice coated in shadows, "How do you feel about each other? Truly?"

Havyn mocked him, a puppet master, playing with his strings and forcing him into unbearable positions.

Kellyn had to admit the depths of his heart because if he didn't, they would both die. The water was at his neck, and he couldn't kill War. He couldn't hurt her, despite everything.

Kellyn didn't get the choice to keep his love close, nurture it, and let it grow. No, he must burn everything down and let the chips fall as they may. He sucked in a breath and prepared to tell War everything. Kellyn's heart skipped a beat, and every muscle in his body tensed, preparing for battle or heartbreak.

"I think I may fall in love with you." It probably wasn't a great start. He swallowed and tried again. "I'm so mad at you, and I don't know if I'll ever forgive you, yet I want you like air." He swallowed. "I've never been in love before. I don't know what it means." It wasn't getting much better, and Theo wasn't showing him she was listening. She was stiff as a stone across from him; her eyes latched on her hands. He rubbed his temples, and the words poured out like spilled coffee. Hot and glistening. "But what I do know is that the thought of you in pain guts me. I hate you but love seeing your grumpy and unsmiling face."

At this, Theo laughed but still didn't move to meet his eyes.

"I know that the facade you show to the world is only one small piece of who you are," Kellyn said. "I know you make me feel seen and intelligent." He drew in a shaky breath. "I know you make me feel everything."

At this, the water in Kellyn's side of the chamber evaporated into thin air. He'd done it. He'd laid out his heart for her to see.

"I can't." Theo let out a sob, and her eyes finally met his. She looked hollow, like an empty void, with tears streaming down her divine face. "I can't say it."

His stomach sank.

The water climbed up her face, and she took a final breath before being engulfed by the water—swallowed whole.

"Why can't you say it?" Kellyn clutched the glass, begging her to give in and save herself. "Please, Thee . . ."

She was going to die.

Thirty-Five

Theodra

Goddess of War

DEATH'S MIRROR

Theo held her breath, and she felt like screaming. It felt like someone cracked open her chest and tore out her heart, squeezing it and watching the blood falling to the floor like dripping pomegranate juice.

Theo couldn't say it. She was condemned no matter what she said. If she spoke the truth, it would kill him; if she lied, it would also kill him. Either way, Havyn would know. She'd have everything she needed to take her payment.

She'd have everything to take Kellyn's soul. Everything to trigger the Immortal Law.

There were no options. All roads led to losing the only thing she'd ever wanted to hold onto.

Her lungs clenched tight, and the lack of air slowly killed her mortal body. Her blood felt cast in iron, and it weighed her down even more.

Theo couldn't look at Kellyn because doing so would ruin her, so instead she averted her eyes. She'd give up her divinity forever not to love him. She'd give up so much to see him alive and healthy.

Her lungs ached, and she couldn't keep from meeting his eyes.

Devastation crawled up her throat when she saw Kellyn's face pale as their eyes met. Her lack of response was already destroying him.

But she had to destroy him, because he could only live if it was without her. Only in her demise could she save him.

Theo sucked in a breath of water and placed her palm one last time on the glass. He screamed, "No," and banged on the glass as her body went limp and her eyes clouded. Darkness swallowed her consciousness.

Her death would break all deals. All promises. Her death wouldn't trigger the Immortal Law. Her death would save him.

And saving him was all that mattered.

Thirty-Six

Kellyn

Prince of Theoden

DEATH'S MIRROR, CITY OF THE GODS

The glass between them shattered, the water evaporated, and her limp form fell into his arms. He crumpled to his knees, holding her lifeless body. Pain hit him as he cupped her still face, raven hair dripping through his fingers.

"Why did you do that?" He wailed, searching for any signs of life. Nothing. "Why?" His voice cracked. This was destroying him. He placed his forehead to hers. "Theo, why?"

"She did it to save your life." Havyn's soft tones floated on the air between them.

In his agony, he couldn't quite process what the Death God said. He needed to save Theo. He rested her head on the floor and started mouth-to-mouth. Minutes slipped away, melting into nothing, the sand in her hourglass of life running out.

"No, please come back," he croaked, and pounded his fist against her chest, hoping it would start her heart. "Please."

But nothing happened. She was ice-cold and vacant, her lips blue from no circulation. But Kellyn refused to give up. It wasn't in his blood. If he had to, he would march to the underworld and pull her soul back from Death. He would not lose her.

Not now.

So, he slammed his palms into her chest because her heart would start again. It would.

There was no other option.

"It's not going to work," Erety, the Mistress of Fate, said softly, standing above him, her wings on full display.

"You can't bring her back that way." Havyn knelt next to him.

Tears flowed down his face. "How do I save her?" he croaked. "Please tell me."

"I can resurrect her, but my gifts have a cost," Havyn said as strings of darkness coiled out of her eye sockets and wrapped themselves into the strands of her hair.

A tremble writhed down his spine. The goddess was terrifying. "Do it, please. I'll give you anything you want."

"Never promise that, boy," Havyn said darkly. "That's how you end up in situations like this."

"It's sweet," Erety whispered like a lullaby and bent down, placing two fingers on Theo's brow. "Your love for one another. It's sweet."

"Please, bring her back," Kellyn begged Erety, the far more charitable of the two gods.

Havyn smiled at her wife before turning her attention onto Kellyn with the intensity of a lioness readying to strike. "Theodra will not thank you for resurrecting her."

Kellyn swallowed. If that were true, it would be bad. He didn't want to anger Theo, but she'd have to get over it just like Kellyn would get over her lies and godliness.

"If I resurrect her, all of her promises, bargains, and favors will be restored." Havyn patted his cheek with a hand constructed of shadows.

"Fine."

"Even if one of her bargains takes your life?"

"Yes," he breathed, not hesitating for a moment. She was a goddess. The world needed her far more than it needed him, especially if she were truly changed.

Haven nodded. "Here is my deal, foolish mortal. I want you to care for her even when you want to strangle her."

"Why?" His voice was hoarse as confusion's claws stroked his intestines. It didn't make sense. The goddess should want more than that. He'd already freely given that.

"Because I know your heart," Havyn said. "I know, your honor, and she deserves someone who cares. Someone who will fight for her even when they hate her." Havyn picked at her nails. "And I suspect there will be many times when you'll hate her."

Kellyn's brow furrowed. "But I would've already done all of that."

Havyn's phantom shadow fingers wrapped around his wrist. "Are you trying to convince me to ask for more?"

Shit. No.

"I thought so." In a blink, Havyn materialized beside him and held out her hand. "So is it a deal, Prince Kellyn Ellis of Theoden?"

"Yes." Kellyn took the goddess's offered hand, her flesh feeling like a snake coiling around his. With a shake, Havyn stamped the deal into his skin, a black viper tattoo twisting around his wrist. "Now, go to your Tribunal." Havyn shooed him away.

"But I want to see—"

"Trust that I'm a goddess of my word."

The thirty-one minutes of his Tribunal were utter agony. It felt like a thousand ticks were barricading under his skin, and his heart danced in his ears to the rhythm of terror.

Havyn was a god of her word, but even if she weren't, he had the deal stamped into his arm. An unbreakable promise.

Theo would live, but he wouldn't believe it until he saw it.

But the waiting was misery because what if . . . what if so, so many things. What if the promise was a trick? What if she came back but only as a rotting corpse? What if she only lived for a mere moment? What if she came back with no memories of him? What if she didn't love him?

But that was impossible; she'd died for him. What could that be but love?

What if bringing her back killed him?

These torturous thoughts stormed through his mind as he waited for his scores. One thing was sure, though, love was a battlefield, and it was fitting because he was in love with War. The pain, the unknowing, and the immense possibility for deep hurt came from the battlefield of love.

The gods droned on, and his scores' pronouncement couldn't come sooner. When they finally floated into the room above the gods, Kellyn didn't even wait to read them or for the tattoo to become a part of him.

He ran.

He ran for *her*.

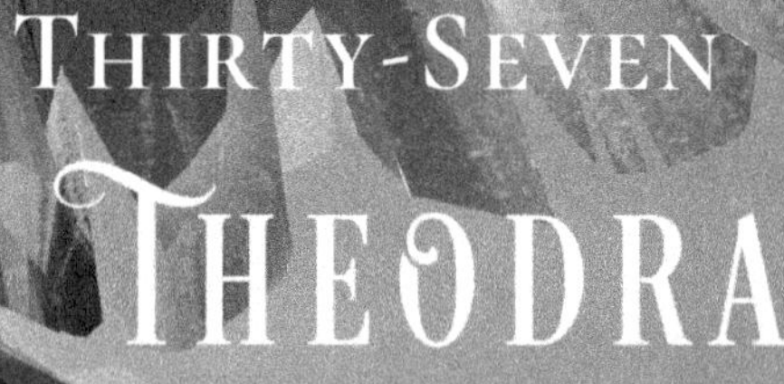

Thirty-Seven

Theodra

Goddess of War

LOVE CAVES, CITY OF THE GODS

Everything was ruined.

Theo hung her head and splashed her feet in a huff. She sat in the cave of wonders, her feet dangling into the warm pool. The rope swings drifted in a manufactured wind, mocking her with the memories of his lips. She touched her fingers to her own, and sorrow dug a hole in her stomach.

He should've left her dead.

Theo needed to hate Kellyn—to save him. She needed to get as far away from him as possible because her walls had crumbled, and she couldn't deny the truth any longer. He had all of her, and she wanted all of him.

She loved—no, she couldn't even think of it.

Because love equaled death. Love was the one thing that would destroy her forever.

Theo hated herself. That foolish deal. It was a deal she'd never pay out. She'd find a way to defy Havyn even if it meant dying again.

A luminescent butterfly landed on her palm, and a tear kissed her cheek. It was beautiful. A symbol of hope and love. She smiled weakly and begged the fates for hope, for a life where she could be happy and with him. But the butterfly jolted off her hand as heavy footfalls entered the cave.

He'd found her.

Theo stood just as he crashed into her, his mouth meeting hers in a frantic frenzy. The pure passion and hunger of the kiss caused her to lose her balance on the pool's edge, and they crashed off the rocks into the water.

They hit with a splash and a laugh. Kellyn surfaced first, a false growl on his lips. He grabbed onto her waist and pulled her back into a kiss.

"Don't do that again," he breathed into her lips. "Don't die for me again, please." It was a plea and command.

But he didn't know what he was asking. Her death was the only way out of their situation. The only way for him to live.

Theo curled her fingers around his cravat and yanked his mouth onto hers again. A distraction. She couldn't answer him.

But Kellyn pulled away to torture her with touch. His eyes locked on hers as he stroked his fingers through her hair, sending shivers down her spine, her body hypersensitive to him. Theo bit the inside of her cheek and breathed deeply through her nose, not wanting him to see how his touch rocked her composure.

But, oh, how it did. With each new caress, her body grew tighter and tighter with need. She was a bowstring, taut and ready for release.

But it couldn't be.

Silence fell between them, and she averted her gaze, staring at the cave walls. She sucked in a deep breath. Spending any time alone with him was dangerous.

Dangerous for him and her heart.

The ice goddess was melting, and she loathed it.

"Why did you do it?" Her voice was all sensual desire and broken hearts.

"What?" he said, playing with one of her raven curls.

"Save me." She shivered. "It will be the death of you."

"So be it." His voice was husky and dripping with the same lust bursting inside her. "I'd die for you." He bounced a curl between his fingers.

"No," her voice cracked. "I can't lose you."

"And I can't lose you, Theo," he said into her hair, stroking her stomach. "I won't."

Tension electrified her blood, sending sparks throughout her whole body.

Wrecking her.

Theo either needed to fuck him or run from him because it was all too much.

With a sigh, she lost her battle with self-control. "You're overdressed," Theo said, water dripping from her cloud of witching-hour hair.

He arched a redwood eyebrow. "Am I?"

Theo gulped, suddenly nervous. What if he didn't want this as much as she did? What if she read the cues wrong? After all, he'd discovered she was a goddess. Some mortals were too insecure about lying with the divine. "I'm sorry, I shouldn't have assumed that . . . you might want . . . me." She drifted away on a surge of water.

He silenced her by lacing his fingers in her hair and pulling her into another kiss. Their lips collided like soldiers on a battlefield. Gunfire and heat. Theo controlled their first two kisses, but Kellyn was the general this time, barking out orders with his silent cues, talented slick tongue, and powerful arms. Arms that coiled around her waist pulled her to the side of the pool and pinned her against the rocks.

Trapping her like prey to feast on, and damned if she didn't want that.

Catching his breath, he whispered, "You're not a villain in my story, Theo." He stroked the side of her face with his thumb. "You could destroy me at any minute—you're a god—I accept that as a fact, but I don't think you will."

Theo never heard more enchanting, glorious words. They were everything. Precisely what she needed; he was what she needed. He was the ceasefire in her War.

"I would never destroy you," she said, panting, her heart a raging monster in her chest.

"I know." His voice was a seductive caress.

An errant lock fell over Kellyn's brow, and she brushed it back behind his ear, her fingertips sliding down the cords of his neck and getting caught in his cravat. She pulled it to her teeth with one finger and untied it with her mouth, her lips lingering on his neck.

When she finished, Kellyn caught her chin with a finger and tipped it up to him, his gaze liquid darkness. Those eyes embraced her with a lustful promise. Naughty and sinful.

Her chest rose with the beats of her heart, and his eyes watched them greedily. The torc around her neck tightened, tension licking at her core and consuming her. Her stomach tumbled with luminescent butterflies.

Oh, she needed this man. Her desire was unending.

A hand traced up her chest, palming a breast, leaving lava in its wake, and increasing her need to unbearable levels. She needed more than his hands on her, *now*.

But he hadn't finished playing with her. And in this, she would let him take charge.

He pressed in, pinning her tighter to the rocks, and her legs wrapped around him. "Now, please." She gasped, her voice shaking with desire.

"Such an impatient goddess." He cracked a smile, wolfish and wicked. In acts of pleasure, Kellyn was no longer a pure gentleman. He turned into temptation and vice.

Sin in human flesh.

He leaned down to meet her, his lips grazing, soft and gentle. Teasing. Toying.

Oh, this man was going to kill her.

Like a lion pouncing on prey, he deepened the kiss, cupping her head as he invaded her senses. Kellyn tasted like sugar hearts and ravenous cherries and smelled like cedar and leather, and pining.

He plunged a hand into the water and ran it along her thigh as he deepened the kiss even further. Navigating his fingers through the opening in her drawers, he plunged a finger into her core. Theo's breath hitched. "Kellyn . . ." she gasped, her fingers running over the buttons on his tailcoat, desperately trying to unclothe him as his finger curled and hit her sensitive and glorious spot. "Kel, oh

—" he moved a second finger to her clitoris, stroking her to the rhythm of untamed pleasure.

She fell apart, shaking in his arms. It had been so long since she felt this. Only a few strokes had her falling over the edge. Theo couldn't breathe. Instead, she keened, unable to think for a long moment, but when she regained her thoughts, she noticed something terrible. "You're still wearing too much clothing." She moved to remedy the situation quickly, unbuttoning his clothes.

"Yes, I am," he responded with a leisurely, randy tenor. His second hand met the first on her other thigh, sliding closer to her ass before cupping it and rocking into her. "But so are you."

She gasped, her fingers wavering from her task. "Naughty."

"For you?" He smiled, his eyes glittering. "Always."

"Let me undress you, sir."

"Yes, ma'am," he said as if he were a soldier following an order.

She ground her hips against him tauntingly, and he growled. She unbuttoned—one by one—his tailcoat, her eyes locked on his, dirty desires lingering in them. A mischievous grin climbed his face as he watched her progress.

When she got to the last button, she slid his arms through the sleeves and tossed the coat onto the floor. Then she pulled his shirt out of his trousers and swiftly relieved him of it, finally exposing his godlike, chiseled body.

The man was perfection.

Kellyn undid her bodice strings and pulled her dress over her head, leaving her in her corset and shift. Slowly, mockingly, he undid her corset while kissing her neck.

He was killing her.

Getting her corset off, he grunted and stole her lips again, starving and demanding to be satiated.

Theo whimpered, and her hands clawed at his back. She needed more. She needed all of him.

His kiss was an enchantment. It was every desire she'd ever had twisted into one, not because he was more masterful than all her other partners—although there was that—but because she'd never felt an emotion like this. It consumed her as much as the kiss, and it was no longer enough to be locked together only by their lips. She needed to be forged with him.

"More, Kel," she moaned into his lips. "I need all of you."

He pulled away, panting, and catching his breath. "You're a goddess."

Confusion knotted her intestines. "Yes?"

"I have a couple of ideas of how to worship you." His hand drew to her core.

"Oh?" She arched a brow, and her breath hitched as he lifted her onto the rock edge out of the water and slipped a finger through the opening in her cotton drawers, teasing her before stroking her inner thigh and up to her stomach, sending a lick of heat in its wake. Curling his fingers into her drawers, he slowly, tauntingly, pulled them down to her ankles.

"Now, here is how one worships a goddess," he said in a low, dark voice dripping with wildfire.

He kissed her inner knee and placed his hands on her pelvis before parting her folds and bringing his mouth to her—kissing her most forbidden parts, licking her clitoris like he was formed for just this task, and proving that he was far more talented with his tongue than his hands. But she knew the depths of her wrongness when he plunged two fingers into her soft opening and stroked that glorious spot. The man was simply talent manifested.

Theo bucked and moaned the building desire nearly unbearable. "Oh, my . . . oh," she whimpered, her fingers tightening in his hair and pressing him harder down on her. "I like this worshi—"

She could no longer speak, trembling, her passion peaked until she lost control and flew apart under his touch, her body shaking with pure pleasure.

She cried out to the night, the stars, and destiny.

Kellyn caught her cries with his mouth and climbed out of the pool himself. He lifted her chemise past her breasts, breaking the kiss only long enough to expose her naked to the world.

"Not alone," she gasped, catching his lips, and tugging his trousers down, finally revealing his beautiful length.

She breathed, stoking a finger down his shaft, which twitched at the touch. He sucked in a sharp breath, and her hand circled him, stroking him in slow, languorous movements as she positioned his tip to her opening.

Kellyn growled in pleasure.

"Good, I need you." Theo sighed and seized his ass. "*Now*."

Then he plunged inside of her, and nothing else existed but him. Now, they were forged together in destiny—in prophecy—linked forever, and their strings of life danced and mingled. Intertwining.

Kellyn kissed her temple as he surged deeper inside her, and she clenched around him, gasping. The pleasure was too intense—too *right*. "Kel," she moaned, digging her heels into his back.

He was her ending and begging and everything that made life enjoyable. He was a piece of healing for her soul; no matter what happened in her lengthy, unending life, her echo was no longer hollow, and she would never forget this and cherish it. Forever.

Love it forever.

One long, thick, slow thrust and her hips rocked up to meet him, seating him to the hilt.

It was ecstasy, every nerve ending in her body lighting up with the indulgence of it all. "You're perfect." She groaned into him, raking her fingernails down his back.

They found a rhythm—a seductive dance, pounding into each other and playing at desire.

Playing at love.

Kellyn palmed her breast; his thrusts fast, wonderful, and aching. His mouth came down to circle her nipple as she cried out. "Yes. Oh gods, you're so—" she gasped again at his truly gifted tongue.

They reveled in each other, in the closeness, the connection, the glorious hard, fast movements until they came utterly undone, falling over the edge together and shattering.

Ruined for anyone but each other.

Thirty-Eight
Theodra
Goddess of War

LOVE CAVES, CITY OF THE GODS

Kellyn held her firmly in his arms, stroking languid fingers down her back, the glowing cave light dancing on his brow. His touch sent fireflies into her stomach, warming her chest, and filling her with an unfamiliar feeling.

Safety.

After coupling a few more times, Love's magical chain broke off with a crack that sounded like a piece of a glacier fracturing. Of course, it was lovemaking that ended the bargain. Theo rolled her eyes.

Afterwards, they'd whispered secrets into the darkness until sleep claimed them.

But now they were awake again, and Kellyn's mouth was on hers. They would never have enough of each other. "I see you enjoy courting danger," she breathed into the kiss.

"No, I enjoy courting War." He tangled his hands in her hair and pulled away to gaze into her eyes. "I love you, Theodra."

"I know," she breathed. *I love you, too.*

Theo flinched when she realized the depths of her thought. The danger in it.

Kellyn's fingers stilled, and he tilted his chin down, his eyes filled with concern and affection etched into the amber irises. "Are you alright—"

"Oh, neither of you are, foolish boy." A dark, hollow, disembodied laugh soaked the room.

"No." Theo shuddered, her entire body shivering, spiders of anxiety crawling all over her skin. She sat up and grabbed her shift into her hands, covering her breasts and awaiting the impact of her mother's magic and wrath. They were in terrible trouble.

The Immortal Law. A mortal couldn't fall in love with a god—at least not true love. True love was forbidden between a god and a human. Gods were forbidden to procreate, and immortals were infertile unless they lay with their true—fated—mortal love. The punishment for breaking the Immortal Law was death for the human and a hundred years of torture for the god. A confession of true love triggered the Immortal Law.

Kellyn's words doomed them because he meant them.

"He didn't mean it." Theo's voice quaked. "Mother, he didn't mean it. He doesn't truly love me."

"Put your clothes on, wretched daughter," Nefeli said, materializing like a nightmare, towering above them. "I thought you would be different. I thought you would resist the sinful temptation of man."

"I have. I just used him for his body." Theo glanced at Kellyn, begging him to understand her lies. Her nostrils flared, and she cracked her neck like a snake preparing to consume its prey whole. To save Kellyn, she would break him. "I mean, can you blame me? Have you seen him? I was having fun playing with him."

Theo's throat ached. It felt like hydra acid devoured it and stole all her words, but she forced the worst of them out, anyway. She said the following words to him. "You don't love me, and I don't love you, and I never will. I'm not capable of loving a human. It's not possible. You were all one big game."

Theo swallowed, wanting to die. His eyes stormed with betrayal and pain. His deep olive skin paled and dripped with broken hopes and tarnished dreams. Seeing the hurt she caused destroyed her, and she hated herself.

War was a villain, and she would forever and always be. Her next sentence proved it. "Thanks for the fuck."

The last words were unforgivably callous, but she needed him and Nefeli to believe them and convince herself of it, too.

"Stop this, Theodra, it is pathetic. Get dressed. The Pantheon has been assembled for your judgment. You've broken the Immortal Law." Nefeli turned on Kellyn. "I would suggest you dress, too, unless you would like to die the way you came into the world."

Theo pulled her shirt over her head and clumsily laced her corset before crawling over to her dress, which was in the pile of his clothing. To put it on, she had to nearly touch him. She took a moment to feel his closeness for maybe the last time, leaning into his protective embrace.

"Kel . . ." Her eyes bled, and her fingertips grazed his jaw. "I'm so sorry. I never meant—" she couldn't say anymore. It would all be used in their trial.

He wrenched her in close, and his lips touched her ear as he whispered, "It will be okay, I promise." It was an empty vow. He was a human and no match for the gods.

A jolt of confusion struck her stomach as they were pulled apart by magic and refracted to the Grand Ballroom in front of the gods and the audience of the Sacrifice. Theo fell hard to the floor, and in a heap, her hair dangled down her shoulders, love-tousled, and her clothing was in a similar state. It was more than clear what they had just been doing. She clutched her chest as if to protect herself.

They were utterly vulnerable and helpless, completely at the gods' will.

Embarrassment mixed with fury coiled in her stomach, hardening into a dark resolve.

She placed a palm against the floor and sat up, raising her head high.

Trying not to make it obvious, Theo checked on Kellyn. She didn't want to cause his death, and the only way he'd make it out of this alive was if he forsook her and declared that he never loved her.

His head was also held high, and he faced the gods with dignity and bravery.

Theo's pinky twitched, slightly reaching out toward him. She wanted to comfort him, and she wanted comfort from him. But she couldn't give it.

That way only held death.

Theo tipped her chin up and met the gods' eyes with a glower. They towered above them on their thrones formed from magic, each throne flowing with its god's tell-tale style. Andromache's twisted from sun rays, Silas—Fire's—was etched from flames, Havyn's from darkness, Harvest's from vines, and so on, and their expressions were as varied as their magic.

Havyn appeared bored; Trickery was jubilant, and Andromache somber. Her chest rose with tense breaths, her purple eyes a sea of devastation. She took a step toward her sister as if to comfort her but thought better of it a moment later.

Theo's eyes flicked to the crowd, finding Cecile and Emmett standing amongst fellow champions. Laurel crowns blessed their heads, signifying that they had beat the Sacrifice successfully, and completed all five of their challenges. Theo's chest warmed at this but was immediately replaced with fissures of fear.

The room smelled of rosemary, cozy winter fireplaces, and nutmeg, but the scent twisted and decayed in Theo's nostrils, leaving only the smell of dead flesh. She didn't know if it was real or simply the manifestation of her emotions.

"Welcome to your judgment." Nefeli's voice was quiet, but its menace carried throughout the whole room.

Magic circled Theo's hands and dragged them back behind her, chains twisting around her wrists before flowing down and fixing themselves into the floor, binding her so she couldn't move. The chains hummed with electricity, and Theo raised a brow. They were God Chains, designed to hold an immortal and tamper their magic.

It didn't make sense. Theo was still human. She couldn't magically break through her chains. Could she?

"Kellyn Ellis, Prince of Theoden, as of this moment, your Sacrifice Games are over. You will not get to finish your final challenge as you have broken the Immortal Law. You're accused of falling in love with a god. You are accused of true love." Nefeli rose slowly, tauntingly from her throne, her magic kissing her skin like glistening rain. "How do you plead?"

"Don't answer that." Theo's eyes whirred to Kellyn, pulling at her chains with the movement.

"You won't speak until *we* request it." A gag crawled over Theo's mouth. It felt like walking face-first into a spider web. Haunting and disgusting. Gooseflesh rolled over her arms, and she shuddered.

"So, prince, how do you plead?"

But before Kellyn could answer, Havyn drawled, "Can he have truly fallen in love with a god when Theo's been mortal the whole time?" At her name, the audience took in a collective breath.

Wait. Was Havyn trying to help? If Kellyn was convicted, he would die, and wasn't that what she wanted? Didn't Havyn wish to fulfill their deal?

"Hmmm," Nefeli made the sound like she was irritated with being corrected. "We shall correct that problem then." Nefeli waved her hand, and a crash of sensation swallowed Theo whole.

It felt like a thousand humming fireflies were flying under her skin, filling the chambers of her heart and swimming through her veins. Every nerve ending in her body sang and electrified. Theo's strings of life knitted together, strengthening, and hardening into immortality. Theo's magic surged but was trapped like a dragonfly in a jar. Trapped by the chains.

The raven torc around her neck fractured in two, drifted to the ground and crumbled like ash. Obsidian feathers circled her neck, morphing and forming a collar. The feathers crawled down her body like warrior paint, creating a shield—an impenetrable barrier—forming a stunning yet terrifying dress. Then just as it returned, the chains around her wrists bound her power.

"Now, he *has* broken the Immortal Law." Nefeli scowled at Havyn.

"I didn't hear him say he loved her. The confession of true love and all that," Havyn drawled, her eyebrows twitching.

Nefeli's purple irises bore into Kellyn. "Boy, do you love her?"

"Don't, Kel," Theo begged. "Don't."

Kellyn sewed his lips together and rolled his shoulders back defiantly.

"Aww, perhaps you need some motivation." Nefeli ran a finger across her blood-red lips. Nefeli snapped her fingers, and a jolt of pure agony slammed into Theo. She crumbled and pulled her knees into her stomach since she couldn't use her arms. "Proclaim your true feelings for our little War, and I'll make her pain stop," Nefeli said. "But every minute you stay silent, her pain will intensify tenfold."

"Don't," the word was a cry as Theo writhed in pain. "Please, don't. I can take this."

Behind her back, Theo tried to reach a hand out to Kellyn, her heart beat a bomb in her ears. He closed the distance and clutched her fragile fingers, his eyes sparking with fury and unshed tears. He hated this. Hating watching her and doing nothing.

And he would break before she did.

Nefeli sauntered across the room, her heels clicking against the marble floors. When she reached Theo, she jerked her up by her chin, breaking the hold with Kellyn. "You've refused to play the game of gods for so long that you've become so easy to trap," she said, leaning down, her violet eyes swirling with fury.

Turning them to Kellyn, Nefeli's smile turned feral. Holding the mortal's gaze, she snapped her fingers, and the pain in Theo's body deepened, becoming unbearable. A blood vessel cracked in her eye, and blood dripped down her face. Her eardrums exploded, crimson mingling with other liquids snaking from her ears, and she howled, whimpering like an abused puppy.

"Theo, I can't."

"Please, Kel, they'll kill you." Her words were a croak. "Please . . ."

Thirty-Nine

Kellyn

Prince of Theoden

VOLCANIC BALLROOM, CITY OF THE GODS

Kellyn couldn't take it anymore. It was horrendous torture. He couldn't let it continue.

It was gruesome.

It was cruel.

But her body sustained it because she was immortal. What would easily kill a human was light maiming for a god.

Kellyn didn't know if Nefeli would kill her daughter, or if it were even possible to kill a god, but he didn't want to find out. Foolishly, he hadn't even known it was possible for a god to feel pain, but it was so clear now that it was. The thought felt silly, but so much about the gods was unknowable. Theo was in agony that his mortal brain could not fathom.

Kellyn knelt beside her and pulled her into his arms, comforting her and whispering settling words into her hair. The gods hadn't chained him. He was a mortal, a tiny bug to be squashed, and no threat to them.

It would be insulting if Kellyn wasn't so gravely concerned for his love.

"Theo, I—" he started. How did he tell her that he couldn't take it anymore? She might have been able to withstand it, but he couldn't.

"I deserve this," she croaked, blood dripping from her lips.

Kellyn shook his head, his fingers grazing her chin. "No one deserves this."

She cried tears of blood. "I can't live in a world where you're not alive."

"Oh, how foolishly sweet," Nefeli said, snapping her fingers again and further deepening the pain.

Theo's eyes fastened on Kellyn. They were pools of obsidian with a dusting of panic. Tortured, she tried to speak, but the agony muffled her words.

"You have the power to relieve her torture," Nefeli's dragonfly crown fluttered and swarmed around her head. "Just say three simple words."

Kellyn looked around for help because he would betray Theo no matter what he chose. Betray her wishes or betray her body.

The seven other pantheon gods stood like their statues, simply looking on and doing absolutely nothing. Andromache's eyes blazed, and her fists were rolled into balls, her bearing and swirling magic pulsing with fury, yet she still did nothing. Havyn seemed resigned—bored even. She picked at her nails, barely paying attention. Trickery glittered and chewed on a green tea cookie as if it were popcorn and he was enjoying a show.

Kellyn rubbed his face in shame because there was only one choice. "I'm sorry, Theo," he whispered, his vision tunneling in on her. He took in the beautiful shine of her ink-black hair, the purple tint of her brooding eyes, the softness of her curves, and the perfection of her soul—for one last time. He would only ever choose her. Never himself.

Any other option was an impossibility.

Kellyn started the Sacrifice thinking he'd signed his death warrant. It turned out, he had. It came true, just not as he imagined. Kellyn joined the games wanting to die honorably. It was his one goal, and now he would fulfill it. There was nothing more honorable than dying for the one he loved.

It wasn't a choice. It was a game of vingt-et-un where there was no other alternative than to catch a twenty-two. There was no winning. Not even a remote possibility. There never had been because he wasn't meant to escape the games alive. He was destined to fall in love with a god and die for it.

Theo had drowned to save him—now he knew why, and he could return the gesture and die for her because there was no other way to move forward. This was his final decision.

"I'm sorry," he said again.

Theo's nostrils flared, and her eyes bled with misery. "No, please."

His bones ached, and his heart beat to the rhythm of calamity. "I love you, Theo. I could no sooner deny that than rip out my soul."

Theo whimpered, a sob escaping her lips. She ran her limp fingers across his cheek, accidentally tracing blood on his cheekbone like warrior paint.

"Wonderful," Nefeli clapped, "we can continue. Kellyn Ellis, as stated from your lips, you are the true love of the Goddess of War—her soulmate—and therefore, you will forfeit your life after a period of torment that befits your crime." *Translation: torture.* "We will convene tomorrow morning to begin your sentence."

Nefeli stepped forward and turned to the crowd. "The Sacrifice has come to an end, and we will celebrate the victories of the six surviving champions with a grand ceremony at which our little prince will be the main entertainment." A smile carved from cruelty rested on her face. "But for now, enjoy the merriment."

FORTY
THEODRA
Goddess of War

VOLCANIC BALLROOM, CITY OF THE GODS

"Wait," Andromache stepped forward from her throne and ended Nefeli's pronouncement for festivities. "I move to abolish the Immortal Law."

A dirty silence exploded through the room, and Nefeli's joyous countenance dimmed.

"As would I," Havyn drawled, not even looking up from picking at her nails.

Butterflies took flight in Theo's stomach, bursting from their cocoons. Her sisters were fighting for her—the way she should have fought for Andromache and Devereaux.

It was beautiful—and surprising.

Theo caught Andromache's gaze, and the goddess nodded. It was a simple gesture, but it spoke volumes. It was true support. An acknowledgment that they would always be on each other's side.

"With a declaration and a seconding, the vote moves forward." Nefeli seethed with the words, dripping with decomposing fury. "All those in favor of abolishing the law say, *Aye*."

Aye, Andromache.

Aye, Havyn.

Aye, Love.

But that was where the voices ended. Only three to the affirmative.

Nefeli dusted off her hands, relieved. Only Havyn's vote was surprising. Love would always vote for the existence of love. "Three is not enough."

"I'm still a member of the Pantheon," Theo croaked, her voice hollow, "I still receive a vote."

"And yet you will still lose."

Theo needed one more god to join them. A simple majority was all it took. But none of the rest even acknowledged the vote. Trickery nibbled on his matcha cookie; a dark eyebrow raised. Harvest averted his gaze altogether, Poison laughed, and Fire burned with vengeance. Theo would find no support from them, but she had to try.

"If one of you supports the vote, I will give you five unbound Favors of War."

The crowd gasped. It was a massive offer. Three kings' randoms.

"Tempting." A chomp on the cookie and a spark in Trickery's eyes let her know she'd get nowhere with him. "But alas, this is far too enjoyable even to take that deal."

"Silas, I'll unbind you," Theo said.

Fire flinched but remained firm, shrugging. "What is power save a way to hang oneself?" She hated it when he talked in riddles that were frequent enough to be immensely irritating.

"Accept that you have lost, daughter, and stop being so pathetic," Nefeli said, and slowly—as if a lion stalking a gazelle—moved toward Kellyn.

A lightning bolt hit the center of the marble, and from it, Night emerged. "I would cast a vote to abolish the law."

"Lesser gods do not receive a vote," Nefeli said, gritting her teeth, clearly over the spectacle. The moment was slowly unraveling from her, and she hated it.

"Perhaps we should," Gallagher said in her typical singsong voice as she held Cecile's hand in a slightly comforting, slightly possessive way.

The veins in Nefeli's face bulged and showed gold through

her skin. "I've had enough of this. Know your place. Andromache, deal with your underling before I'm forced to, and Destruction if you know what's good for you, you will not speak another word."

Gallagher snorted, caring very little for demands.

"Why should you be the arbiter of all things?" Night scoffed, equally as defiant as Gallagher.

Andromache stepped between Night and Nefeli. "Marguerite, please don't."

"No, Mother, someone needs to stand up to her."

Mother? The room collectively inhaled, the statement hitting with the force of a tidal wave. Even Nefeli seemed surprised by the revelation. Everyone vibrated with surprise except Havyn, whose face twisted into a giddy smile.

Mother? Devereaux and Andromache had a child?

Theo sucked in a breath as it all hit her. The spell she cast long ago split in two and a flood of memories poured in. *I need you to shield my daughter and all her future descendants from the eyes of the Pantheon . . . I need you to shield her from yourself, too, Thee.* It was the promise Theo had made Andromache during her punishment for falling in love with Devereaux.

Night was Andromache's daughter which meant . . . oh holy fuck—

"You killed my *mortal* father because of your hatred for their kind," Night said. "It cannot stand."

Andromache stepped in front of her daughter, shielding her from Nefeli's wrath. "Mother, she didn't mean anything by it. Margo's always been hot-tempered and spirited. She's like a dying star."

"Daughter?" Nefeli cracked her neck, a tell-tale sign she was unsettled. The ground cracked, too, and a thick lava-filled gap emerged from the center of the ballroom floor. Oh, Nefeli was furious. At the lies, and that she was discovering it all before the eyes of the world.

"Is my existence truly a crime? Isn't that why you have the law?" Night said, her words coated with disappointment that mingled with fear. "I have done nothing to upset the balance of the gods. I've been a deeply loyal servant to my mother and, therefore, to you my entire life. Why must War's love be punishable by death?"

Night's eyes wandered until she met Cecile's, and they shared an intense but bright moment.

"I've had enough," Nefeli seethed. Her attention shifted to Night and Light, holding hands, a united front. "I'll deal with your insolence later, Night, and with your deceit, Daughter."

The ground rumbled again, and the walls started bleeding molten lava. The palace responded to Nefeli's terrible mood. "The vote has been cast, and the boy will begin his punishment tomorrow."

FORTY-ONE

THEODRA

Goddess of War

VOLCANIC PRISON, CITY OF THE GODS

It was strange how much loving felt like dying.

And how much worse losing love felt than getting stabbed in the gut. Theo much preferred the gut wound. At least that would heal. This never would. She'd only get better at managing it.

Grief was a lifelong journey.

A lifelong punishment.

Kellyn wasn't dead yet, but what hope was there? Unlike Andromache, Theo had support from the other gods, and it still wasn't enough.

Trapped and facing devastation, chained with her powers bound, time whipped and dragged into braids of sand emptying from an hourglass. Theo was lost in it, and she didn't want to be found. Misery coiled around her soul and sank its fangs deep inside of her.

The pain spilled out of her in broken sobs and wrenching screams.

It was unbearable, so she curled into a ball of rage, sorrow, and fear.

The ground was cold against her cheek, and her heart stumbled in her chest as she awaited the most painful day of her life.

The igneous rocks hummed, and lava poured down the sides like angry waterfalls. Theo was stuck in a prison cell with no windows or doors, and no optimism. She wasn't foolish enough to believe she was powerful or special enough to change fate. So she languished. There was nothing else to do, the only way in or out of her cell was through magic, and while Theo had her divinity back, the only magic she possessed were fragments of healing. Only enough to fix the torture Nefeli inflicted on her.

"I've never known you to give up so easily." Havyn solidified beside her sister, her voice softer and kinder than Theo had ever heard. "Shhh, it's going to be okay." Death touched War's back as she sobbed.

"What is there to do?" Theo breathed. "Andromache didn't have a single god standing beside her. I had five, and the outcome was the same. It will never be enough."

"And that's it?" Havyn scrunched her nose, her features dancing with unease. "No bargaining? No fighting? No defying the impossible."

"That's why it's called impossible."

"Nothing is truly impossible, only fairly improbable."

"Havyn, I can't do this right now."

Havyn sighed and leaned back against the wall, watching her sister sob. When bored, she conjured a book and began to read. Her presence was both a boon and an assault, but ultimately Theo appreciated the attempt at comfort.

"You mentioned a bargain. Is there one?" Theo's voice was hoarse.

"No."

Theo scoffed. "So you're unwilling to make a deal with me?"

Havyn bit her lip and glanced up at the volcanic ceiling. "Not unwilling, unable. Mother declared that we couldn't aid you in any way."

"Then what's the point, Havyn?" Theo made a frustrated gesture with her hands. "What's the point of any of it?"

"You have so many options available to you, Thee." Haven wiggled her obsidian eyebrows. "Strings and strings of them."

"Then give me one."

"I cannot." Havyn grinned. "You have a visitor." She waved her hand, and the rock wall shifted, allowing Cecile to walk through it.

Havyn stood and crossed paths with Emmett and Cecile. She placed a loving squeeze on the girl's shoulder. "Don't worry. It will all work out as it is meant to." Havyn's eyes traced the shaking form of her sister. "Before I go, let me just say one thing, War: don't allow him to die without telling him you love him."

The wall closed behind Havyn's retreating form, and Theo finally raised her head. "How is he?" Theo's words were raw from having screamed and cried for hours.

"Better than you." Emmett knelt next to Theo. "How are you?"

"I don't think I'll survive this."

Cecile knelt, too, brushing an errant curl out of Theo's face. "You will."

"Cecile, I'm so sorry for everything. Kellyn, Gallagher, nearly killing you in the fire. Everything."

Emmett leaned back on his heels and let the two have a moment.

Cecile sucked in a breath. "Well, isn't that what family is supposed to do? Almost accidentally kill each other in fires?"

"How long have you known?"

"That I'm a demigod and your great-niece?" Cecile chortled. "Less than a day. Although I've always known I was different." Not simply different. She was a demigod and would become fully immortal at age twenty-five. Cecile had a year left until she was death resistant and divinely powerful. One year until she became a god herself. "It was the riddle to my final challenge. Havyn has a messed up sense of humor."

"She truly does."

Theo should have known the moment she met the girl on the steamship eleven years ago, that she had extra strings of life. It meant she was either a long-lived mortal like a vampire or witch, or she was a demigod. Then she should have known when she discovered Cecile's powers and inhuman strength, but she *truly* should have known when Medusa didn't affect Cecile.

But the spell Theo cast all those years ago obscured her vision and kept the truth at bay, because Theo didn't just hide Night's origins from the world, she also hid her descendants.

"Did you know Andromache chose me to be her champion because she lost a bet with Havyn?" Cecile asked.

"What?" Horror tensed Theo's stomach.

"Yeah . . ." Cecile shrugged.

"That's not all," Emmett cut in. "Havyn was responsible for both Kellyn and me entering the Sacrifice. Havyn also bribed Gallagher to switch out Kellyn's Decision Day speech."

"Oh, fuck, the speech." It finally made sense—Kellyn's anger at Theo about the speech. A god was responsible for it, just not the one he blamed. "Havyn planned the whole thing, didn't she?" It was more a hypothetical question rather than being directed at anyone.

"Yep," Emmett said. "Death's a bitch."

Havyn wanted the truth about Cecile's parentage to come out. She wanted Kellyn in the Sacrifice. She wanted Theo to fall in love with him. It was her all along, pulling the puppet strings.

But why?

What motivation did Havyn have?

Theo needed to find out because the answer might hold the key to saving Kellyn's life.

"Theo, I wanted you to know that no matter what happens, and no matter that I'm still upset about Gallagher, I love you." Cecile clutched Theo's hand, red lava reflecting in her irises and emotions stirring in her heart. "I forgive you and want you to know I don't think you're selfish. I never have. I was just furious and trying to hurt you."

"I know." Theo swallowed. "Cecile, I should release you from our bond." Theo motioned to the raven tattoos on their wrists.

"I don't want to be released," she said adamantly. "I'm proud to be your Godmarked and even more proud to be your niece."

Forty-Two
Theodra
Goddess of War

VOLCANIC BALLROOM, CITY OF THE GODS

"Let's begin." Nefeli clapped her hands and commanded the attention of the entire audience.

Theo and Kellyn were at the center of the volcanic ballroom, facing each other, gagged, and chained with their hands behind their backs. They couldn't speak, but they could communicate with their eyes. His were molten and filled with so much love and promises that it hurt, and her eyes were nearly obsidian colored—so dark purple they were nearly black.

The gods were on their thrones, and the audience was filled with crowned champions and privileged human guests, but Theo had no eyes for them; her entire focus was on the man she loved.

"Wait." Andromache stepped forward again and walked up to Theo, placing a hand on her shoulder. "I move to abolish the torture portion of the boy's punishment. If he must die, fine, but don't torture him."

Like last time, Havyn seconded the motion. The sisters, for the second time in a thousand years, were all in alignment.

The veins in Nefeli's neck bulged and turned black like her daughters' shadow magic. "All in favor of removing the torture portion of the boy's punishment, say, aye."

Andromache, Aye.

Havyn, Aye.

Love, Aye.

Theo, a muffled Aye.

Then silence descended through the room, and this time the lesser gods were noticeably resigned to the sidelines. Nefeli must have threatened them to the degree that they dared not step forward.

Theo's throat worked. She needed one of the other gods to join them. Losing Kellyn would be horrible enough; watching his torture for years was simply unbearable. Her 100-year torture would be watching him brutalized until the edge of death, to be healed, just to repeat it again and again. It was what Andromache was supposed to experience, but Theo had killed Devereaux before it could happen.

"Aye." Theo's eyes snapped up, and she met the gaze of the God of Fire. Silas had voted with them. *Why?*

In the murmured chaos of the crowd, Andromache whispered into Theo's ear, "You're welcome."

Andromache had done it. Light had bribed, bargained, or cashed in a favor for her sister. Warmth welled in Theo's chest from the support and love she'd received from both of her sisters.

"Aye," Poison and then Trickery said in unison. All but Harvest and Nefeli had joined the vote.

What magic had her sisters wrought?

"Fine," Nefeli gritted her teeth. "I'll take matters into my own hands." In a blink, Nefeli refracted to Kellyn and thrust the dagger into his chest, an inch from his heart. She clutched him tightly, her lips dancing over his ear. "You were never going to live, boy." She twisted the knife. "Not when you're her fated love."

A guttural wail escaped Theo's lips.

"It's okay, Theo," Kellyn croaked, "I will fight all the forces of death, and any god to get back to you. I promise."

Kellyn knelt, his eyes fixed on his true love, his life force draining from him, dripping on the ground around him.

"Fight a god?" Nefeli kicked him over with a foot. "You're a pathetic human. You were born to die for her, but be thankful she never said *I love you,* or she would incur a hundred years of punishment. And you wouldn't want that." Nefeli slapped his cheek condescendingly.

"She doesn't need to tell me she loves me, because I already know."

Nefeli twisted the knife, piercing his heart, then she strolled away, devastation in her wake.

"No, noooooooooooo," the scream enveloped the room, consuming it. Theo pulled against her chains, trying to break free and get to him.

In defiance, Havyn waved her hand and magically dissolved the chains so that Theo could scurry forward and cradle Kellyn's dying body between her arms. Theo half crawled, half ran to his side, falling to her knees, and heaved his body—limp and as cold as the deepest parts of space—into her lap, cradling his face.

But she was too late.

Kellyn's eyes stared at the volcanic ceiling, empty and glazed over. There was no light left. No life left.

A scream clawed from her throat, and it wasn't until she felt the rawness—the pain in her throat that she knew it originated from her. It crawled out from the depths of her soul and assailed the shocked crowds.

Blood pooled like a heap of poinsettia blossoms littering the marble and seeped into her clothing like water dripping down a drain.

Kellyn was dead.

His lips were stained plum-red from blood, and his chest was as pale as swan feathers.

Theo had no chance of saving him.

If she didn't already know for sure—if she didn't already feel the ache pouring from her splintered spirit—she knew now.

Theo *loved* him.

The kind of love that she would burn the world to the ground to save.

He was everything she needed and everything she wanted. He had saved her and proved that love didn't always betray. He proved that love was sacrifice.

Kellyn healed her soul by refusing to run and shy away from her darkness. He met it with kindness and light.

He was loyal and steadfast, and he made her better.

Theo couldn't undo his love and kind effects on her soul. They would live forever inside her, rewriting her heart, mind, and actions. She'd never be the same.

But it wasn't only his love.

It was Cecile and Emmett, and her sisters. They taught her about love and sacrifice and kindness and friendship. They spoke into her darkest parts and forced her to be better, forced her to mend fences and undo her apathy. They breathed life into her dead soul. All of them. The community.

One person couldn't be her happiness. One person couldn't save her. Only she could save herself.

Theo's eyes tracked down to the body in her lap. His eyes were still open and empty, a purple glow reflecting on them. She ran her fingertips over his brow, across his scars, until she reached his eyelids and gently and lovingly closed them, a sob wracking through her body. She didn't want to live without him. The idea tasted like poison eating away at her insides.

Tears rolled down her face. Thick and silver and divine.

Theo screamed, her body convulsing with the pain, and the marble all around her—square by square inch— turned black and flaked to ash, incinerated by Theo's magic, leaving the room desolate. It looked like a bomb went off and tore through all of civilization.

Her destruction rattled the ballroom, and humans screamed, the terror licking the air, sprites popping up everywhere to consume it.

A conspiracy of ravens flocked down and landed on the dead floor and nine massive black panthers—Theo's familiars—appeared beside them. War's pain was unbearable, and her magic answered the call of her emotions. She felt sorrow everywhere, from her aching bones to her taut muscles, to her suffocating heart.

Despite the divine form, her constant two-step heart rate didn't return. Instead, it thundered like a storm that birthed tornados.

"Please." Theo clutched Kellyn's face and whispered, "Please, come back." Her voice was cavernous, deep, and cracked. "Please."

Her breaths were ice, jagged and slow.

Everything hurt.

She was a dying star. Rupturing from the inside out. It felt like her rib cage had caved in on itself and exploded in a burst of flames and shrapnel.

She *loved* him.

And love was utter agony because losing it was far more devastating than any battle scar.

Love was devastation. A dance with decay. Love was the worst of all punishments, and the end of one's soul. Love began with hope. A hope that would eventually shatter into endless chaos. It was the deepest form of pain.

Love was ruination.

It was hers.

Theo once thought love was the biggest mistake she'd made in her 10,000 years, but she was wrong.

Love was also her salvation.

It was the greatest and hardest thing she'd ever done and would ever do. And to live past loss was the bravest.

"Thee, my love, your rot is spreading through the palace, and soon you'll infect the city." Havyn pressed three gentle fingers to Theo's shoulder and knelt beside her, her voice as soft as a spring breeze and acting as if she truly cared.

Theo's attention snapped up and out of her tunnel vision, and she saw how the decay, ash, and desolation spread from her fingertips, the gods sheltering as many mortals as possible.

"Oh," she said in a voice lower than sound and pulled back her power—contained it.

"I don't want to rush you, but you must act now. Once a river is crossed, it cannot be undone without intense trials." Havyn spoke in riddles and insinuated that Theo needed to bring Kellyn back from the dead.

But that was impossible.

Theo could pull Kellyn's soul back herself. With the ability to control matter and energy, she could do nearly anything. But gods couldn't interfere in another's domain. It was possible to do almost everything, but certain things weren't done because disrupting the order of things would lead to anarchy. It would lead to desolation and, most likely, the apocalypse—a war of all the gods. It would cause billions of deaths, if not all of humanity's annihilation.

Not even Andromache tried to intervene when Devereux died.

Theo wouldn't do it now.

"Have you ever pondered weaving as a companion in your grief? It can be quite restorative," Havyn said. "An art form, you know."

Theo's eyes glowered at her sister. "Enough with your nonsense." Havyn and her stupid obsession with crafts that entwine things. First it was braids, and now weaving.

"Go away."

"Don't give up," Havyn said gently. "You're the Goddess of War."

Theo wouldn't give up, but she wasn't Death, she didn't know its secrets. She was one of the death triplets, true, but she didn't rule over death, not like Havyn. Yet there had to be a way to defy death because Erety existed. She was once human, and she should have met Devereaux and Kellyn's fate, but she didn't.

There was a way.

But what was it?

Havyn had made a bargain with Erety thousands of years ago. Erety's human lover died, and she traversed the underworld to rescue him. Death gave her a bargain that if she served the goddess in perpetuity Death would give the boy's soul back. That bargain bound them together and gave Erety an immortal life. But the bargain didn't make her a god.

So how?

Gods were born or sprung from nature organically. They weren't made.

Theo couldn't make a deal with Kellyn like Havyn had because he was already dead and even if she did it wouldn't protect him from Nefeli.

He would only be protected if he, too, were a god.

But that was an impossibility because humans only had three

strings of life. Only Demigods grew strings of life, but they started with nine, just not nine fully formed ones.

"How many strings of life does Erety have?" Theo drew her voice so low only Havyn could hear.

"Hmm," she rubbed her chin. "Nine plus three equals?"

"Twelve, how?"

"Now that's a fascinating question."

"How many strings do you have?"

"And that is a better question." Havyn wiggled her brows. "Twelve."

Shit. Holy shit. There was only one way to get twelve. "Oh," Theo breathed. *The answer.*

Havyn nodded, a vicious smile coating her porcelain face.

The hairs rose on Theo's arms, and her stomach hardened. "Braids."

"Yes."

Forty-Three

Kellyn

Prince of Theoden

RIVER ORCUS, UNDERWORLD

Some souls floated in the River Orcus, some sat on its banks, and others picnicked beside it, gossiping and playing at an afterlife. Some souls frolicked in the water like mermaids, but none clawed, begged, or bartered.

No, they were happy and at peace.

It wasn't the river foretold in story books or whispered about in the dead of night.

It wasn't a warning; it was a welcome.

"What?" he asked, awed.

Erety giggled, her white wings folding into her back. An Angel of Death indeed. "It's not as advertised."

"Not at all."

"Death is not a curse, Kellyn," Erety said. "It's a new beginning. A new awakening."

Kellyn felt a jerk on his back. At his tether.

All souls were tethered to their bodies until their funeral. Kellyn felt like a puppy on a leash, waiting for his owner to release him into a field. He couldn't truly enter his new life until that leash was severed. But instead of breaking, it was pulling him back. Confusion riddled him.

He stumbled.

It pulled him back.

He stumbled again; the tether tight. "I don't understand."

"You're not meant to stay here." Erety smiled. "You're meant for much greater things. After all, you won the heart of a death god triplet."

His brow furrowed. "I—what?"

"Let the tether take you back, Kellyn," she said. "Let go."

Kellyn listened because he had made Theo a promise. He'd stop at nothing to get back to her.

Forty-Four

Theodra

Goddess of War

BALLROOM, CITY OF THE GODS

Turning on her God Sight, Theo saw Kellyn's strings of life wrapping around his body. They were frayed and crumbling to ash but weren't yet broken. That wouldn't happen until his soul crossed the River Orcus. She couldn't mend Kellyn's strings. She couldn't restore them to their mortal form because of the rules governing the god's realms of influence, but . . . she didn't have to.

All Theo had to do was braid them into hers.

And she did, softly lifting one of his fraying strings with a single finger. It felt like velvet electricity. Hard to hold due to all the energy, yet delicate and beautiful. With much less care, she folded her strings between her fingers and slowly and methodically laced the glittering silver and lilac strands together. As she moved, she wove all three of his strings into hers.

Theo held her breath the whole time, not wanting to get her hopes up—not wanting to risk it failing.

But she shouldn't have worried.

Because as his strands touched hers, they solidified and remade themselves stronger—taking on the essence of the surrounding strings. Absorbing the energy. Theo wasn't bringing him back to life. She wasn't stealing his soul from Death. She was simply braiding strings and letting them respond. It was a loophole she was willing to exploit.

Love was more important than rules.

As she worked, his skin darkened back to its tawny olive color and warmed, and with one last knot of the strings she was done.

Silence and frozen time mingled together. It felt like Theo was in a stadium filled with 20,000 people who collectively took a breath and held it.

The tension was palpable.

Theo's heart pounded in her ears like a symphony. Every muscle in her body, every bone and every tissue hardened and went rigid.

What if it didn't work?

Forty-Five

Kellyn

Prince of Theoden

BALLROOM, CITY OF THE GODS

Kellyn sucked in a deep breath and jerked up far too quickly, disoriented.

A crack sounded as his forehead met something hard yet soft.

"Ouch," Theo's beautiful soprano whispered, happy tears streaming down her face. She clutched his cheeks and placed a kiss on the offending rock-solid forehead.

Kellyn blinked up at her. "You're bleeding."

"It doesn't matter." She smiled brightly as a summer's day. "You're alive."

"And you're a god." His finger swiped away the silver blood.

Her smile faltered. "Yes." She gulped. "I hope that's okay." But before he could respond, she lightly punched him in the arm. "You're a fool. Why did you have to say you loved me?"

"They were torturing you."

"Let me be tortured then."

"I could never." His tone was severe and laced with an unbreakable love. "Never."

She punched him again, silver tears racing down her face. "If there is ever a choice between my torture or losing your life again, you will let me suffer. If the choice is to kill me, you will do it. You understand?"

"I—"

"If you don't kill me, I will raise you from the dead and kill you myself."

There was nothing he could say to that. He wanted to be a good partner. He wanted to love and respect her, but how could he betray her? Or kill her? Or watch her be tortured.

He couldn't.

It wasn't an option.

So instead of answering, he used her favorite tactic and kissed her to change the subject.

The kiss was soft as floating feathers and bunny fur. It was sweet and filled with a thousand promises of more to come.

"That's cheating." She sucked in a heated breath, her fingers stroking his hair, and because she couldn't bear to remain silent any longer, she said, "I love you, Kellyn Ellis."

"I love you, too, Theodra, Goddess of War."

Her mouth met his again, and they reveled in each other—in their love and their happiness.

A happiness that would span a thousand lifetimes—or even longer.

Except magic wrenched them apart.

The dust settled from Theo's destruction, and she saw her mother wielding her magic against them. "You broke the Law of Realms. You brought a human back from the dead, for this you will be executed, daughter." Nefeli's voice shook.

It appeared Nefeli didn't want her daughters to love, but she also didn't want them dead. Just their partners.

"Actually, Mother." Havyn stepped over falling debris nonchalantly. "He's not human. Theo broke no laws. Before you stands the newest god of our world."

"Sits," Andromache corrected, a bright smile on her face.

"Sorry," Havyn drawled, "sits the newest god of our world."

A chorus of voices rang through the ballroom, but two echoed above the rest. *Cecile and Emmett.* They both ran to Kellyn's side, kneeling beside him.

"God?" Emmett's voice was soft and coated with twisting emotions. "You're both going to be gods, and I am just . . . human."

He was jealous. At his core, Emmett wanted to be special, and Kellyn had stolen his chance at glory in the Sacrifice—and now, had become a god. It would be a lot for him to accept and he would probably be mad about it for a long time, but it was okay.

Because Kellyn now had an eternity to make it up to his friend.

Epilogue
Theodra
Goddess of War

BELLUM CLIFFS, THEODEN

Theo stood on the cliff's edge, her eyes barely focusing on the crimson light far off in the distance. Ravens circled and croaked overhead, scouring the landscape. The aroma of salt permeated the air as the navy waves crashed into the jagged cliff edges—sharp like the granite edges of her heart.

Granite was hard yet beautiful. And with the proper tools, it could be smoothed and transformed into marble, just like Theo's hard edges could be smoothed with the proper people filling up her life.

A lover, a friend, two sisters, and a War Court.

A community of people polishing her rough edges and building her into a better person—a better god.

Shifting her eyes to the seaside below, Theo pondered small miracles. Life was no longer a hollow echo, repeating through time and space, but a vivid watercolor painting full of warmth. After all, marrying the God of Peace had its advantages. It had a calming effect on her War—on all her broken pieces.

Muscular arms curled around her waist and embraced her from behind, pulling her into his strong, warm body, the light of the sunset casting its rays on his deep olive skin. He rested his chin on her head. "Why are we staring at a steamship, my love?"

"Flesh traffickers," Theo said, her voice caught by the autumn wind. Overhead her ravens croaked in unison, their fury piercing the night sky.

Kellyn's fingers increased their pressure against her waist, and he pulled her in tighter. A protective stance. "What do you want to do?" he whispered into her hair.

"What do you think we should do?" Theo twisted and tilted her chin up to meet his eyes. "I'm not always the best at doling out punishments to men."

"Perhaps, we save the girls and let the victims and society decide what to do with them?" His amber eyes sparked, and he ran a gentle finger across her jaw and met her lips with his for a short, gentle kiss. A quick kiss that symbolized a thousand short kisses. A thousand kisses because they had forever.

Kellyn refracted them onto the creaking wood of the ship, and he deepened the kiss. Theo knew he was in no hurry because he wanted to let their presence seep into the men's souls. He wanted them to anticipate their punishment. He wanted fear to lick at their spines. While War and Peace wouldn't kill them today—wouldn't burn the flesh from their bones—these men didn't know that.

Sometimes anticipation was a beautiful tool.

Theo loved everything about her partner. His steady hand, wit and smile, and loving soul, but mostly she loved that he allowed her to be fully who she was, and the truth was that War still bathed in fear of evil men, despite no longer soaking in their blood.

Kellyn knew this and allowed her to terrify the men and helped her in this ambition.

The men screamed and ran across the deck, panicked, and some jumped into the unsteady ocean while others tried to hide in cracks of the wood. It was useless.

Within a few minutes, Theo had the girls out of their coffins—where they had been trapped on their journey across the sea—and returned them to the shores of Theoden. Theo summoned Cecile to aid them with their crisis and recovery.

Despite her best efforts, Theo still struggled to deal with

human children. Meanwhile, Kellyn chained up the men for the Theoden High Council to deal with.

When they were done, they stood together, staring at their bound prey, wicked smiles on their faces.

"Tsk, tsk." A feminine voice clicked her tongue. "Hello, sister . . . and *her consort.*"

Theo's neck prickled at the sound of the Goddess of Death. Havyn appeared out of the shadows, her black cloak billowing in the crisp night wind. Her presence, as always, was haunting.

"This is an improvement over burning ships to the ground with the girls still on board." Havyn tittered. "I hate to pull you from your vital tasks, but you owe me a favor."

An anchor dropped in Theo's stomach. Havyn was here to cash in the favor for spelling Medusa. It was bound to happen eventually, but Theo expected it to be hundreds of years from now, not six months after the Sacrifice.

"Are you going to tell me what this favor entails, or do I get to bask in the unknowing?" Theo sighed, and her ravens circled them menacingly.

Kellyn placed a steadying arm around her waist. "Whatever it is, I'm coming with."

Havyn wrinkled her nose. "I'm going to regret fighting so hard for you two to end up together . . . I cannot take the sweetness of it." She mimed vomiting.

"Havynnn," Theo dragged out the name, "would you like to inform us of your plans this time?"

Havyn shrugged. "Not particularly," At Theo's glare, Havyn continued, "We're going to the underworld because our little sister requires our help to bring her lover back from the dead."

A bright smile was painted on Theo's blood-red lips. "A worthy cause." She turned to Kellyn, his amber eyes sparking in the rays of the setting sun. "I don't want you to come. You have—"

"Let the boy come along. He could be useful." Havyn winked, making Theo even less comfortable with Kellyn coming.

But before Theo could beg him to stay safe, he said, "Nothing will keep me from your side in this."

"I see you enjoy courting danger." The words were a resigned sigh; she wouldn't ever demand anything from him. They were equal partners, and if he wanted to come, he would.

Kellyn tipped her chin up into a sweet kiss, and on a breath, he said, "No, I enjoy courting War."

War, Peace, Death, Light, Destruction, Emmett, and Cecile will return in other Vicious Gods novels

Acknowledgments

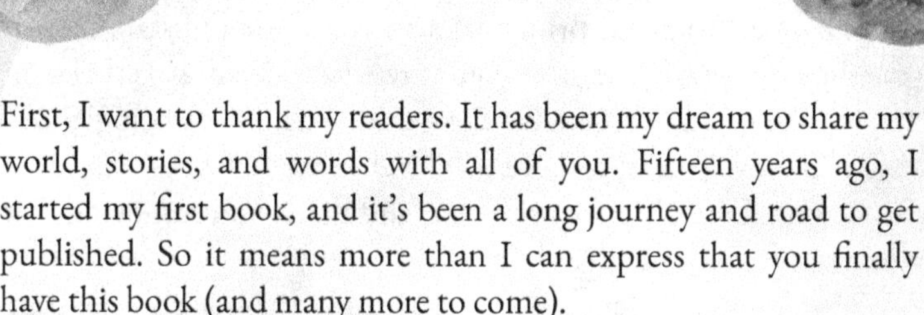

First, I want to thank my readers. It has been my dream to share my world, stories, and words with all of you. Fifteen years ago, I started my first book, and it's been a long journey and road to get published. So it means more than I can express that you finally have this book (and many more to come).

Mom and Dad, thank you for everything. You are the best parents a girl can have. I would not have been able to follow any of my dreams without your continuous support. I cherish every moment I get with you and want a million more. Dad, thank you for being my first reader. On a less sappy note, please tell me you skipped the end of chapter 29 and all of chapter 37! Lie to me if you didn't. I think God made lies for situations like these.

I want to thank my siblings, Jennifer and PJ. I love you so much. Jennifer, I expect that you listened to the whole book despite, as you put it, "the veiny penises" (and no, I didn't describe them that way).

Bacardi, Bella, Loki (and Tigger and Cinder), I promised I would dedicate my first published book to my cats, and so I have. Every day you are slowly killing me (I am allergic), but I keep you. That is love.

Chinelo, this book would not exist without you (seriously, if you like this book, go thank her). I am so thankful and love you so much.

Ellie, I would like to write you an epic poem or a love letter or something so grand it would encompass how much I appreciate you. The number of times you've read my books and the number of times you had to pull me off a ledge makes you a saint. But alas, I am not very good at writing love letters, so this is what you get.

Donna and Rachel, you make me buy too many pretty books.

You are terrible (the best) influences. Thank you for being my BFFs. You mean too much for me for words to describe.

Carrie and Val, I am not sure what to say. Thank you for subbing to me in AMM because although I didn't choose you. I CHOSE YOU. You are my ride-or-die CPs, and I am so grateful for you. Jamye and Sienna, I am lucky to have you in my life. You two are truly good friends who make me a better person, and I love you! Dianna, Amanda, Brittany, I stan you the way I stan Cardan (the highest praise). Truly, you three have been so crucial in helping me get this book into the world. Thanks for being cheerleaders!!! I love you and will be forever thankful!

Angela, I am obsessed with you, and thank you for loving that stone kiss scene as much as I do!

Thank you, Adrienne Young, Kristin Dwyer, and the Writing with the Soul community. Writing communities have changed my life!

Anni, thank you so much for being my first ride-or-die CP. Love you!

Sarah (SK), and Audrey, you were some of my first writer friends and helped me get through some of the hard earlier years, and I love you deeply. Courtney, thank you for all of your mentoring! I appreciate your friendship so much and all of your help! Melissa and London, you are the best mentees, and I cannot wait to see what lies in your future (spoiler alert: big things). Jaime, Stephanie, and Nicole, you were my first agent sisters, and I am so thankful to you three in different ways. I am so excited for you and your future!

Thank you to all of the following people for being amazingly supportive! Skyler, Natalie, Lily, Shelly, Nadine, Michelle, Rosebud (Emily), Eva, and Skyla. I also want to give a special shout-out to everyone from the forge (there are too many to name) but especially Kelly, Michael, Mandy, Ruth, Amber, and Jen. To my Clubhouse friends, Jennifer, Satia, Vanessa, Aubrey, Rachel, Rachel, Bart, Deanna, Michael, K.L., Kanika, Ngozi, Stephanie, and so many more. Thank you for everything. I could not do this without you.

To Rie, Rosanna, Becky, and Victoria, you were my first

writer's group and the reason I've gotten this far. Your encouragement, grace, and love build me up in the hardest moments, and I love you all so deeply—special thanks to Rie for teaching me everything. You were my first mentor.

To all my Instagram followers who constantly watch my procrastination stations, even when there are thirty meandering videos, know that I love you.

Aylin, you are my ride-or-die best friend, and I am so utterly thankful for you in my life.

Hot Worship Leader, Boss, and Worship Mom. I love you and am so thankful God sent you into my life at the perfect timing (one might call it God's timing). I also am so, so, so grateful for you.

Haley, Sarah, Lauri, and Shannon, you are wonderful therapists and people.

Opulent Designs, Leila and Kate, thank you so much for making this book so gorgeous! It is truly stunning inside and out! Thank you, thank you, thank you!

To my fantastic editors, Noah and Jennifer, thank you for helping me strengthen my words and book. To my first agent, I appreciate the time we worked together and all I learned from you!

Christian and Ashley, as a dyslexic person, the audiobook is the most important format to me, so I want to thank you for perfectly portraying Theo and Kellyn (and everyone else)! And Jess and Audiobook Empire, thank you so much.

I couldn't mention everyone here, and I am sorry. I am so blessed because I have so many amazing people in my life (many not mentioned here). Thank you all!

Finally, I want to thank God for being there for me in all things. Thank you for giving me grace and love even when I don't deserve it. I have a beautiful, joyous life, and it's all because of you.

Love, Hazel

About the Author

Hazel St. Lewis is a Northern California-based Fantasy Romance author. Diagnosed with dyslexia at a young age, she struggled to read and write, but fantasy stories inspired her to start storytelling. Unfortunately, now, she is a little too obsessed with Dracula. When she isn't writing, she can be found playing with her hoard of cats (too many to count...it's a problem), singing songs to said cats—like Cinderella—or painting.

Facebook Group: Shadow Daddy Books, TikTok @hazelstlewis, Instagram @hazelstlewis

Stay in Touch!

Newsletter Sign-Up

Sign up using the link below for Hazel's newsletter to be the first to receive exciting news, updates, and bonus content.

https://www.hazelstlewis.com

Follow me:

Facebook Group: Shadow Daddy Books, TikTok @hazelstlewis, Instagram @hazelstlewis

Please Leave a Review!

If you enjoyed this book, please consider leaving a review. One of the best ways to support authors (especially new ones like me) is to leave a review!

Hazel's Book Recommendations

Check out the link below to see Hazel's latest book obsessions and recommendations: https://www.hazelstlewis.com/favorites

Printed in the USA
CPSIA information can be obtained
at www.ICGtesting.com
CBHW021409230124
3684CB00006BA/320